EN

Encounters

edited by
Isaac Asimov
Martin Greenberg and Charles Waugh

HEADLINE

First published in Great Britain in 1988 by HEADLINE BOOK PUBLISHING PLC

ISBN 0 7472 3091 9

Printed and bound in Great Britain by Collins, Glasgow

HEADLINE BOOK PUBLISHING PLC
Headline House, 79 Great Titchfield Street London W1P 7FN

Contents

Encounters

Introduction

by Isaac Asimov

Human beings have never yet made an alien contact. Explorers, particularly Europeans in the great "Age of Exploration" have, to be sure, encountered strange organisms they had never seen or imagined before. In Africa, they discovered giraffes, for instance, and gorillas, and ostriches, and even as late as 1900, okapis. In North America they found bison by the millions, and moose; in South America, llamas and spider monkeys; in Australia, koalas, and kiwis.

None of these represented serious dangers. Human beings could deal with them rather easily. (Mosquitoes, lice, and tsetse flies were disease-spreaders that were much harder to deal with, but even these could be fought.)

By science fiction convention, however, an "alien contact" is one with organisms that are equal or even superior to human beings in *intelligence*.

Such contacts have been made in myth and legend, where human beings have encountered gods, angels, devils, demons, afrits, genii, ogres, giants, and so on almost ad infinitum. Rational people are quite certain, however, that none of these stories represent the literal truth.

At worst, they are the creations of a human imagination intent on telling an interesting story. At best, they are dramatic distortions of something that exists. (Thus, a centaur may have originated when a culture innocent of horses encountered their first mounted raiders; Odysseus' Scylla and Hercules' hydra may have been exaggerations of the octopus, as Medusa may have been; dragons may have been combinations of snakes and crocodiles, and so on.)

Even the Bible tells how Israelites, after wandering for forty years in wilderness, reached Canaan and encountered giants there. Only fundamentalists, however, accept that as literally true. It is quite evident to rational readers that the Israelites were using the term metaphorically to speak of people not of giant size but of giant technologies; people who were capable of building walled cities and making use of chariots.

Nowadays, it has been suggested that human beings had encountered extraterrestrial organisms in the form of intelligent "ancient astronauts" in places such as ancient Egypt and in pre-Columbian South America. It has also been suggested that people are constantly encountering intelligent aliens that arrive on Earth in unidentified flying objects (UFOs). Such suggestions are accepted seriously only by cultists and by unsophisticated people who are also quite ready to believe in Santa Claus and the Easter bunny.

The encounters that come nearest to the science fictional concept of "alien contacts" have been made between human beings and other human beings where each group had no knowledge, or even suspicion, of the existence of the other.

In ancient times, people generally knew in detail only of the people who lived in their own constricted area. Any land beyond their constricted horizons, if it existed at all, might be a lifeless desert or might contain incredible monsters for all they knew. Settled agricultural people rarely ventured far from their farms for obvious reasons.

Nomadic peoples, however, generally carried their possessions with them and, under conditions where overpopulation or bad weather decreased their chances at an adequate food supply, went on far-ranging expeditions looking for new land and more food. In that case, they were liable to stumble upon farming communities. Sometimes the nomads had the advantage of greater mobility and hardihood, and sometimes the farmers had the advantage of greater population and better organization and weapons. In either case one side or the other would suffer badly.

The immobile farmers were usually the more surprised,

however, for the nomads in their wandering life easily gained the impression that the Earth was filled with a wide variety of people with strange customs and cultures. The farmers knew only their own, and invading nomads, especially if their intent was rapine and conquest, were greeted with the utmost horror and were often considered as monsters. The "Uighurs", who settled down to become Hungarians, are still remembered in modern fairy tales as "ogres."

Europeans knew this a number of times in their history. In the 6th Century, the Huns poured in from the East and reached central France before being stopped. In the 9th Century, Vikings poured down from the north and harried all the coasts of Europe. Worst of all, though briefest, there was the Tatar incursion, again from the East, in the 13th Century. This would not have been stopped at all, if the Tatar Khan had not died in 1241 and if the all-conquering horsemen had not been compelled to return to central Asia to elect his successor. The horrified Europeans distorted their name to "Tartars"; that is, creatures from Tartarus, the ancient Greek version of Hell.

It was the Europeans themselves who inflicted such a semi-alien contact upon other people in the worst form. From the 15th Century onward, European vessels, equipped with the mariner's compass and cannon, explored and dominated all the coasts of the world. They enslaved Africans and exploited Asians. The worst of all was when they took over the American continents, utterly destroying the Aztec and Inca civilizations and practicing genocide on a large scale.

One can well imagine that to native Americans and to Australian aborigines, who had been isolated beyond ocean barriers for twenty five thousand years or more, the sudden arrival of pale-skinned strangers with a clearly superior technology must have seemed as horrifyingly strange as an invasion of Martians would to us.

These semi-alien contacts over the four-century span from 1500 to 1900 was one of a long-continued assault of Europeans on non-Europeans, and firmly fixed in the modern mind that violence and merciless cruelty was the only form of interaction possible.

Science fictional accounts of true alien-contacts
(human beings and non-human beings, both intelligent
and both technologically advanced) had always been
pictured as peaceful till the end of the 19th Century. Such
alien-contact stories were written as satires or exploration
stories in which civilized understanding prevailed among
the intelligences. (Consider "Gulliver's Travels".) It was
not till 1898, that H.G. Wells published "The War of the
Worlds" and the modern "alien contact" story was born.

The European nations had just finished carving up
Africa (with Great Britain taking the lion's share) and, in
the process, displaying a total callous disregard for the
"natives". Wells, with bitter irony, pictured the Martians
fleeing their own dying planet to take over the Earth
(Great Britain in particular) with similar callous
disregard for Earth's natives.

And yet *must* this be so? The European view was
poisoned by the fact that they felt themselves to have the
only "true" religion, and the various peoples they met,
with other religions, were therefore considered sub-
human. Surely we know better now and we need no
longer behave like Spanish conquistadores or Puritan
zealots when we meet other intelligences. And perhaps
they need not either.

Have we, and they, I hope, learned that there is room
for variety in the Universe and that we can gain more by
learning from each other than by killing each other.

Perhaps.

In any case, here are a number of excellent alien-
encounter stories, where encounters, and responses,
come in a wide variety of forms. In my own story (written
when our fortunes were at a low point in World War II), I
am ashamed to say the response threatens to be violence.

CONTACT!

by David Drake

Something shrieked over the firebase without dipping below the gray clouds. It was low and fast and sounded so much like an incoming rocket that even the man on Golf Company's portable latrine flattened instantly. Captain Holtz had knocked over the card table when he hit the dirt. He raised his head above the wreckage in time to see a bright blue flash in the far distance. The crash that rattled the jungle moments later sent everyone scrabbling again.

"Sonic boom," Major Hegsley, the fat operations officer, pontificated as he levered himself erect.

"The hell you say," Holtz muttered, poised and listening. "Paider, Bayes," he grunted at the two platoon leaders starting to pick up their bridge hands, "get to your tracks."

Then the klaxon on the tactical operations center blatted and everyone knew Holtz had been right again. The captain kicked aside a lawn chair blocking his way to his command vehicle. The radioman scuttled forward to give his powerful commander room in front of the bank of radios. "Battle six, Battle four-six," the tanker snapped as he keyed the microphone. "Shoot." Thirty seconds of concentrated information spat out of the speaker while Holtz crayoned grid coordinates in on an acetate-covered map. "Roger, we'll get 'em." Turning to the radioman he ordered, "Second platoon stays for security here—get first and third lined up at the gate and tell Speed I'll be with him on five-two." While the enlisted man relayed the orders on the company frequency, Holtz scooped up a holstered .45 and his chicken vest and ran for his tank.

Golf Company was already moving. Most of the

drivers had cranked up as soon as they heard the explosion. Within thirty seconds of the klaxon, the diesels of all nine operable tracks were turning over while the air still slapped with closing breechblocks. Tank 52 jingled as Hauley, its driver, braked the right tread and threw the left in reverse to swing the heavy war machine out of its ready position. Holtz ran up to the left side, snapping his vest closed at the shoulder. He was one of the few men in the squadron who wore a porcelain-armored chicken vest without discomfort, despite its considerably greater weight than the usual nylon flak jacket. In fact, Holtz was built much like one of his tanks. Though he was taller than average, his breadth made him look stocky at a distance and simply gigantic close up. He wore his black hair cropped short, but a thick growth curled down his forearms and up the backs of his hands.

Speed, a weedy, freckled staff sergeant with three years' combat behind him, grasped his captain by the wrist and helped him swing up on five-two's battered fender. As frail as he looked, Speed was probably the best track commander in the company. He was due to rotate home for discharge in three days and would normally have been sent to the rear for stand-down a week before. Holtz liked working with an experienced man and had kept him in the field an extra week, but this was Speed's last day. "You wanna load today, Captain?" he asked with an easy smile. He rocked unconcernedly as Hauley put the tank in gear and sent it into line with a jerk.

Holtz smiled back but shook his head. He always rode in the track commander's position, although in a contact he could depend on Speed to fight five-two from the loader's hatch while he directed the company as a whole. Still smiling, the big officer settled heavily onto the hatch cover behind the low-mounted, fifty-caliber machine gun and slipped on his radio helmet.

"OK, listen up," he said on the company frequency, ignoring commo security as he always did when talking to his unit. He had a serene assurance that his gravelly voice was adequate identification—and that his tanks were a certain answer to any dinks who tried to stop him. His boys were as good and as deadly as any outfit in 'Nam. "Air Force claims they zapped a bird at high altitude and it wasn't one of theirs. We're going to see whose it was and keep Charlie away till C-MEC gets a team out here. Four-four leads, west on the hardball to a trail at Yankee Tango five-seven-two, three-seven-nine; flyboys think the bird went down around seventy-forty, but keep your eyes open all the way—Charlie's going to be looking too."

Holtz's track was second in line with the remaining five tanks of the first and third platoons following in single file. As each one nosed out of the firebase its TC flipped a switch. Electric motors whined to rotate the turrets 30 degrees to one side or the other and lower the muzzles of the 90mm main guns. The big cannon were always loaded, but for safety's sake they were pointed up in the air except when the tanks prowled empty countryside. Otherwise, at a twitch of the red handle beside each track commander a wall or a crowd of people would dissolve in shattered ruin.

"Well, you think we're at war with China now?" Holtz shouted to Speed over the high jangle of the treads. "Hell, I told you you didn't want to go home—what do you bet they nuked Oakland five minutes ago?" Both men laughed.

The path from the firebase to the highway was finely divided muck after three days of use. The tanks, each of them burdened with fifty tons of armor and weaponry, wallowed through it. There was nothing laughable in their awkwardness. Rather, they looked as implacably deadly as tyrannosaurs hunting in a pack. On the asphalt hardball, the seven vehicles accelerated to thirty-five miles an hour, stringing out a little. Four-four had all its left-side torsion bars broken and would not steer a straight line. The tank staggered back and forth across the narrow highway in a series of short zigzags. From the engine gratings on its back deck, a boy with a grenade launcher stared miserably back at the CO's track while the rough ride pounded his guts to jelly.

Holtz ignored him, letting his eyes flick through the vegetation to both sides of the roadway. Here along the hardball the land was in rubber, but according to the map they would have to approach the downed aircraft through broken jungle. Not the best terrain for armor, but they'd make do. Normally the tanks would have backed up an air search, but low clouds had washed the sky gray. Occasionally Holtz could hear a chopper thrumming somewhere, above him but always invisible. No air support in a contact, that was what it meant. Maybe no medevac either.

Ahead, four-four slowed. The rest of the column ground to a chattering halt behind it. Unintelligible noises hissed through Holtz's earphones. He cursed and reached down inside the turret to bring his volume up. Noise crackled louder but all sense was smothered out of it by the increased roar of static. Four-four's TC, Greiler, spoke into the ear of his grenadier. The boy nodded and jumped off the tank, running back to five-two. He was a newbie, only a week or two in the field, and young besides. He clambered up the bow slope of the tank and nervously blurted, "Sir, Chick says he thinks this is the turn-off but he isn't sure."

As far as Holtz could tell from the map, the narrow trail beside four-four should be the one they wanted. It led south, at any rate. Hell, if the MiG was what had gone howling over the firebase earlier the flyboys were just guessing for location anyway. The overcast had already been solid and the bird could have fallen anywhere in III Corps for all anybody knew.

"Yeah, we'll try it," Holtz said into his helmet mike. No reaction from four-four. "God damn it!" the captain roared, stabbing his left arm out imperiously. Four-four obediently did a neutral steer on the hardball, rotating 90 degrees to the left as the treads spun in opposite directions. Clods of asphalt boiled up as the road's surface dissolved under incalculable stresses. "Get on the back, son," Holtz growled at the uncertain newbie. "You're our crew for now. Speed!" he demanded, "What's wrong with our goddam radio? It worked OK at the firebase."

"Isn't the radio," Speed reported immediately, speaking into his own helmet microphone. "See, the intercom works, it's something screwing up off the broadcast freeks. Suppose the dinks are jamming?"

"Crap," Holtz said.

The trail was a half-abandoned jeep route, never intended for anything the width of a tank. They could shred their way through saplings and the creepers that had slunk across the trail, of course, and their massive rubber track blocks spewed a salad of torn greenery over their fenders. But full-sized trees with trunks a foot or more thick made even the tanks turn: grunting, clattering; engines slowing, then roaring loudly for torque to slue the heavy vehicles. Holtz glanced back at the newbie to see that he was all right. The boy's steel pot was too large for him. It had tilted forward over his eyebrows, exposing a fuzz of tiny blond hairs on his neck. The kid had to be eighteen or they wouldn't have let him in the country, Holtz thought, but you sure couldn't tell it by looking at him.

A branch whanged against Holtz's own helmet and he turned around. The vegetation itself was a danger as well as a hiding place for unknown numbers of the enemy. More than one tanker had been dusted off with a twig through his eye. There were a lot of nasty surprises for a man rolling through jungle twelve feet in the air. But if you spent all your time watching for branches, you missed the dink crouched in the undergrowth with a rocket launcher—and he'd kill the hell out of you.

Sudden color in the sky ahead. Speed slapped Holtz on the left shoulder, pointing, but the CO had already seen it. The clouds covered the sky in a dismal ceiling no higher than that of a large auditorium. While both men stared, another flash stained the gray momentarily azure. There was no thunder. Too brightly colored for lightning anyway, Holtz thought. The flashes were really blue, not just white reflected from dark clouds.

"That can't be a klick from here, Chief," Speed's voice rattled. Holtz glanced at him. The sergeant's jungle boots rested on the forward rim of his hatch so that his bony knees poked high in the air. Some people let their feet dangle inside the turret, but Speed had been around too long for that. Armor was great so long as nothing penetrated it. When something did—most often a stream of molten metal blasted by the shaped explosive of a B-41 rocket—it splashed around the inner surface of what had been protection. God help the man inside then. 'Nam offered enough ways to die without looking for easy ones.

The officer squinted forward trying to get a better idea of the brief light's location. Foliage broke the concave mirror of the clouds into a thousand swiftly dancing segments. Five-two was jouncing badly over pot holes and major roots that protruded from the coarse, red soil as well.

"Hey," Speed muttered at a sudden thought. Holtz saw him drop down inside the tank. The earphones crackled as the sergeant switched on the main radio he had disconnected when background noise smothered communications. As he did so, another of the blue flashes lit up the sky. Static smashed through Holtz's phones like the main gun going off beside his head.

"Jesus Christ!" the big officer roared into the intercom. "You shorted the goddam thing!"

White noise disappeared as Speed shut off the set again. "No, man," he protested as he popped his frame, lanky but bulbous in its nylon padding, back through the oval hatch. "That's not me—it's the lightning. All I did was turn the set on."

"That's not lightning," Holtz grunted. He shifted his pistol holster slightly so that the butt was handy for immediate use. "Hauley," he said over the intercom to the driver, "that light's maybe a hair south of the way we're headed. If you catch a trail heading off to the left, hold it up for a minute."

Speed scanned his side of the jungle with a practiced squint. Tendons stood out on his right hand as it gripped the hatch cover against the tank's erratic lurches. "Good thing the intercom's on wires," he remarked. "Otherwise we'd really be up a creek."

Holtz nodded.

On flat concrete, tanks could get up to forty-five miles

an hour, though the ride was spine-shattering if any of the torsion bars were broken. Off-road was another matter. This trail was as straight as what was basically a brush cut could be—did it lead to another section on the plantation that flanked the hardball?—but when it meandered around a heavy tree bole the tanks had to slow to a crawl to follow it. Black exhaust boiled out of the deflector plates serving four-four in place of muffler and tail pipe. The overgrown trail could hide a mine, either an old one long forgotten or a sudden improvisation by a tankkiller team that had heard Golf Company moving toward it. The bursts of light and static were certain to attract the attention of all the NVA in the neighborhood.

That was fine with Holtz. He twitched the double handgrips of his cal-fifty to be sure the gun would rotate smoothly. He wouldn't have been in Armor if he'd minded killing.

The flashes were still intermittent but seemed to come more frequently now: one or two a minute. Range was a matter of guesswork, but appreciably more of the sky lighted up at each pulse. They must be getting closer to the source. The trail was taking them straight to it after all. But how did a MiG make the sky light up that way?

Speed lifted his radio helmet to listen intently. "AK fire," he said. "Not far away either." Holtz scowled and raised his own helmet away from his ears. As he did so, the air shuddered with a dull boom that was not thunder. The deliberate bark of an AK-47 chopped out behind it, little muffled by the trees.

Speed slipped the cap from a flare and set it over the primed end of the foot-long tube. "We can't get the others on the horn," he explained. "They'll know what a red flare means."

"Charlie'll see it too," Holtz argued.

"Hell, whoever heard of a tank company sneaking up on anybody?"

The captain shrugged assent. As always before a contact, the sweat filming the inner surface of his chicken vest had chilled suddenly.

Speed rapped the base of the flare on the turret. The rocket streaked upward with a liquid *whoosh!* that took it above the cloud ceiling. Moments later the charge burst and a fierce red ball drifted down against the flickering background. Holtz keyed the scrambler mike, calling, "Battle six, Battle six; Battle four-six calling." He held one of the separate earphones under his radio helmet. The only response from it was a thunder of static and he shut it off again. Remembering the newbie on the back deck, he turned and shouted over the savage rumble of the engine, "Watch it, kid, we'll be in it up to our necks any time now."

In the tight undergrowth, the tracks had closed up to less than a dozen yards between bow slope and the deflector plates of the next ahead. Four-four cornered around a clump of three large trees left standing to the right of the trail. The tank's bent, rusted fender sawed into the bark of the outer tree, then tore free. Hauley swung five-two wider as he followed.

A rocket spurted from a grove of bamboo forty yards away where the trail jogged again. The fireball of the B-41 seemed to hang in the air just above the ground, but it moved fast enough that before Holtz's thumbs could close on his gun's butterfly trigger the rocket had burst on the bow slope of four-four.

A great splash of orange-red flame enveloped the front of the tank momentarily, looking as if a gasoline bomb had gone off. The flash took only a split second but the roar of the explosion echoed and re-echoed in the crash of heavy gunfire. Four-four shuddered to a halt. Holtz raked the bamboo with the cal-fifty, directing the machine gun with his left hand while his right groped for the turret control to swing the main gun. Beside him, Speed's lighter machine gun chewed up undergrowth to the left of the trail. He had no visible targets, but you almost never saw your enemy in the jungle.

The muzzle brake of the 90mm gun, already as low as it could be aimed, rotated onto the bamboo. A burst of light automatic fire glanced off five-two's turret from an unknown location. Holtz ignored it and tripped the red handle. The air split with a sharp crack and a flash of green. The first round was canister and it shotgunned a deadly cone of steel balls toward the unseen rocketeer, exploding bamboo into the air like a tangle of broom straw. Brass clanged in the turret as the cannon's breech sprang open automatically and flung out the empty case. Speed dropped through the reeking white powder smoke evacuated into the hull.

Holtz hadn't a chance to worry about the newbie behind him until he heard the kid's grenade launcher chunk hollowly. Only an instant later its shell burst on a tree limb not thirty feet from the tank. Wood disintegrated in a puff of black and red; dozens of segments of piano wire spanged off the armor, one of them ripping a line down the captain's blue jowl. "Not so goddam close!" Holtz shouted, just as a slap on his thigh told him Speed had reloaded the main gun.

The second rocket hissed from a thicket to the right of five-two, lighting up black-shrouded tree boles from the moment of ignition. Holtz glimpsed the Vietnamese huddled in the brush with the launching tube on his shoulder but there was no time to turn his machine gun before the B-41 exploded. The world shattered. Even the fifty tons of steel under Holtz's feet staggered as the shaped charge detonated against five-two's turret. A pencil stream of vaporized armor plate jetted through the tank. The baggy sateen of the officer's bloused fatigues burst into flame across his left calf where the metal touched it. Outside the tank the air rang with fragments of the rocket's case. Holtz, deafened by the blast, saw the newbie's mouth open to scream as the boy spun away from the jagged impacts sledging him. Somehow he still gripped his grenade launcher, but its fat aluminum barrel had flowered with torn metal as suddenly as red splotches had appeared on his flak jacket.

Holtz's radio helmet was gone, jerked off his head by the blast. Stupid with shock, the burly captain's eyes followed the wires leading down into the interior of the tank. Pooled on the floorplate was all that remained of Speed. The gaseous metal had struck him while his body was bent. The stream had entered above the collarbone and burned an exit hole through the seventh rib near the spine. The sergeant's torso, raised instantly to a temperature of over a thousand degrees, had exploded. Speed's head had not been touched. His face was turned upward, displaying its slight grin, although spatters of blood made him seem more freckled than usual.

The clouds were thickly alive with a shifting pattern of blue fire and the air hummed to a note unconnected to the rattle of gunfire all along the tank column. The third tank in line, four-six, edged forward, trying to pass Holtz's motionless vehicle on the left. A medic hopped off the deck of four-six and knelt beside the newbie's crumpled body, oblivious to the shots singing off nearby armor.

Hauley jumped out of the driver's hatch and climbed back to his commander. "Sir!" he said, gripping Holtz by the left arm.

Holtz shook himself alert. "Get us moving," he ordered in a thin voice he did not recognize. "Give four-six room to get by."

Hauley ducked forward to obey. Holtz glanced down into the interior of the track. In fury he tried to slam his fist against the hatch coaming and found he no longer had feeling in his right arm. Where the sleeve of his fatigue shirt still clung to him, it was black with blood. Nothing spurting or gushing, though. The main charge of shrapnel that should have ripped through Holtz's upper body had impacted numbingly on his chicken vest. Its porcelain plates had turned the fragments, although the outer casing of nylon was clawed to ruin.

Five-two rumbled as Hauley gunned the engine, then jerked into gear. A long burst of AK fire sounded beyond the bamboo from which the first B-41 had come. A muffled swoosh signaled another rocket from the same location. This time the target, too, was hidden in the jungle. Holtz hosed the tall grass on general principles and blamed his shock-sluggish brain for not understanding what the Vietnamese were doing.

With a howl more like an overloaded dynamo than a jet engine, a metallic cigar shape staggered up out of the jungle less than a hundred yards from five-two's bow. It was fifty feet long, blunt-ended and featureless under a cloaking blue nimbus. Flickering subliminally, the light was less bright than intense. Watching it was similar to laying a bead with an arc welder while wearing a mask of thick blue glass instead of the usual murky yellow.

As the cigar hovered, slightly nose down, another rocket streaked up at it from the launcher hidden in the bamboo. The red flare merged with the nimbus but instead of knifing in against the metal, the missile slowed and hung roaring in the air several seconds until its motor burned out. By then the nimbus had paled almost to non-existence and the ship itself lurched a yard or two downward. Without the blinding glare Holtz could see gashes in the center section of the strange object, the result of a Communist rocket detonating nearby or some bright fly-boy's proximity-fused missile. MiG, for Chrissake! Holtz swore to himself.

A brilliant flash leaped from the bow of the hovering craft. In the thunderclap that followed, the whole clump of bamboo blasted skyward as a ball of green pulp.

To Holtz's left, the cupola machine gun of four-six opened fire on the cigar. Either Roosevelt, the third tank's TC, still thought the hovering vessel was Communist or else he simply reacted to the sudden threat of its power. Brass and stripped links bounded toward Holtz's track as the slender black sent a stream of tracers thundering up at a flat angle.

The blue nimbus splashed and paled. Even as he swore, Holtz's left hand hit the lever to bring the muzzle of his main gun up with a whine. The blue-lit cigar shape swung end on to the tanks, hovering in line with the T-shaped muzzle brake of the cannon. Perhaps a hand inside the opaque hull was reaching for its weapons control, but Holtz's fingers closed on the red switch first. The ninety crashed, bucking back against its recoil stop while flame stabbed forward and sideways through the muzzle brake. Whatever the blue glow did to screen the strange craft, it was inadequate to halt the point-blank impact of a shell delivering over a hundred tons of kinetic energy. The nimbus collapsed like a shattered light bulb. For half a heartbeat the ship rocked in the air, undisturbed except for a four-inch hole in the bare metal of its bow.

The stern third of the craft disintegrated with a stunning

crack and a shower of white firedrops that trailed smoke as they fell. A sphincter valve rotated in the center of the cigar. It was half opened when a second explosion wracked the vessel. Something pitched out of the opening and fell with the blazing fragments shaken from the hull. Magnesium roared blindingly as the remainder of the ship dropped out of the sky. It must have weighed more than Holtz would have guessed from the way the impact shook the jungle and threw blazing splinters up into the clouds.

The tanks were still firing but the answering chug-chug-chug of AK-47's had ceased. Holtz reached for the microphone key, found it gone with the rest of his radio helmet. His scrambler phone had not been damaged by the shaped charge, however, and the static blanket was gone. "Zipper one-three," he called desperately on the medical evacuation frequency, "Battle four-six. Get me out a dust-off bird, I've got men down. We're at Yankee Tango seven-oh, four-oh. That's Yankee Tango seven-oh, four-oh, near there. There's clear area to land a bird, but watch it, some of the trees are through the clouds."

"Stand by, Battle four-six," an impersonal voice replied. A minute later it continued, "Battle four-six? We can't get a chopper to you now, there's pea soup over the whole region. Sorry, you'll have to use what you've got to get your men to a surgeon."

"Look, we need a bird," Holtz pressed, his voice tight. "Some of these guys won't make it without medevac."

"Sorry, soldier, we're getting satellite reports as quick as they come in. The way it looks now, nobody's going to take off for seven or eight hours."

Holtz keyed off furiously. "Hauley!" he said. "C'mere."

The driver was beside him immediately, a dark-haired Pfc, who moved faster than his mild expression indicated. Holtz handed him the phones and mike. "Hold for me, I want to see what's happened."

"Did you tell about the, the..." Hauley started. His gesture finished the thought.

"About the hole in the jungle?" Holtz queried sarcastically. "Hell, you better forget about that right now. Whatever it was, there's not enough of it left to light your pipe." His arms levered him out of the hatch with difficulty.

"Can I—" Hauley began.

"Shut up, I can make it," his CO snapped. His left leg was cramped. It almost buckled under him as he leaped to the ground. Holding himself as erect as possible, Holtz limped over to four-six. Roosevelt hunched questioningly behind his gunshield, then jumped out of his cupola and helped the officer onto the fender.

"Quit shooting," Holtz ordered irritably as the loader sprayed a breeze-shaken sapling. "Charlie's gone home for today. Lemme use your commo," he added to the TC, "mine's gone."

He closed his eyes as he fitted on the radio helmet, hoping his double vision would clear. It didn't. Even behind closed eyelids a yellow-tinged multiple afterimage remained. The ringing in his ears was almost as bad as the static had been, but at least he could speak. "Four-six to Battle four," Holtz rasped. "Cease firing unless you've got a target, a real target."

The jungle coughed into silence. "Now, who's hurt? Four-four?"

"Zack's bad, sir," Greiler crackled back immediately. "That rocket burned right through the bow and nigh took his foot off. We got the ankle tied, but he needs a doc quick."

Half to his surprise, Holtz found that four-four's driver and the newbie blow off the back of his own track were the only serious casualties. He ignored his own arm and leg; they seemed to have stopped bleeding. Charlie had been too occupied with the damaged cigar to set a proper ambush. Vaguely, he wondered what the Vietnamese had thought they were shooting at. Borrowing the helmet from four-six's loader, the officer painfully climbed off the tank. His left leg hurt more every minute. Heavily corded muscle lay bare on the calf where the film of blood had cracked off.

Davie Womble, the medic who usually rode the back deck of four-six, was kneeling beside the newbie. He had

laid his own flak jacket under the boy's head for a
cushion and wrapped his chest in a poncho. "Didn't want
to move him," he explained to Holtz, "but that one piece
went clean through and was sucking air from both sides.
He's really wasted."

The boy's face was a sickly yellow, almost the color of
his fine blond hair. A glitter of steel marked the tip of a
fragment which had zig-zagged shallowly across his
scalp. It was so minor compared to other damage that
Womble had not bothered to remove it with tweezers.
Holtz said nothing. He stepped toward four-four whose
loader and TC clustered around their driver. The loader,
his M-16 tucked under his right arm, faced out into the
jungle and scanned the pulverized portion. "Hey," he
said, raising his rifle. "Hey! We got one!"

"Watch it," the bloodied officer called as he drew his
.45. He had to force his fingers to close around its square
butt. Greiler, the track commander, was back behind his
cal-fifty in seconds, leaping straight onto the high fender
of his tank and scrambling up into the cupola. The loader
continued to edge toward the body he saw huddled on the
ground. Twenty yards from the tank he thrust his weapon
out and used the flash suppressor to prod the still form.

"He's alive," the loader called. "He's—oh my God, oh
my *God!*"

Holtz lumbered forward. Greiler's machinegun was
live and the captain's neck crawled to think of it, hoping
the TC wouldn't bump the trigger. The man on the
ground wore gray coveralls of a slick, rubbery-appearing
material. As he breathed, they trembled irregularly and a
tear above the collarbone oozed dark fluid. His face was
against the ground, hidden in shadow, but there was
enough light to show Holtz that the man's outflung hand
was blue. "Stretcher!" he shouted as he ran back toward
the tracks.

Hauley wore a curious expression as he held out the
scrambler phone. Holtz snatched and keyed it without
explanation. "Battle six, Battle four-six," he called
urgently.

"Battle four-six, this is Black-horse six," the crisp voice
of the regimental commander broke in unexpectedly.

"What in hell is going on?"

"Umm, sir, I've got three men for a dust-off and I can't get any action out of the chopper jockeys. My boys aren't going to make it if they ride out of here on a tank. Can you—"

"Captain," the cool voice from Quan Loi interrupted, "it won't do your men any good to have a medevac bird fly into a tree in these clouds. I know how you feel, but the weather is the problem and there's nothing we can do about that. Now, what happened?"

"Look," Holtz blurted, "there's a huge goddam clearing here. If they cruise at five hundred we can guide them in by—"

"God damn it, man, do you want to tell me what's going on or do you want to be the first captain to spend six months in Long Binh Jail?"

Holtz took a deep breath that squeezed bruised ribs against the tight armored vest. Two troopers were already carrying the blue airman back toward the tanks on a litter made of engineer stakes and a poncho. He turned his attention back to the microphone and, keeping his voice flat, said, "We took a prisoner. He's about four feet tall, light build, with a blue complexion. I guess he was part of the crew of the spaceship the Air Force shot down and we finished off. He's breathing now, but the way he's banged up I don't think he will be long."

Only a hum from the radio. Then, "Four-six, is this some kind of joke?"

"No joke. I'll have the body back at the firebase in four, maybe three hours, and when they get a bird out you can look at him."

"Hold right where you are," the colonel crackled back. "You've got flares?"

"Roger, roger." Holtz's face regained animation and he began daubing at his red cheek with a handkerchief. "Plenty of flares, but the clouds are pretty low. We can set a pattern of trip flares on the ground, though."

"Hold there; I'm going up freek."

It was getting dark very fast. Normally Holtz would have moved his two platoons into the cleared area, but that would have meant shifting the newbie—Christ, he didn't even know the kid's name! If they'd found the captive earlier, a chopper might have already been there. Because of the intelligence value. Christ, how those rear echelon mothers ate up intelligence value.

"Four-six? Blackhorse six."

"Roger, Blackhorse six." The captain's huge hand clamped hard on the sweat-slippery microphone.

"There'll be a bird over you in one-oh, repeat one-oh, mikes. Put some flares up when you hear it."

"Roger. Battle four-six out." On the company frequency, Holtz ordered, "Listen good, dudes, there's a dust-off bird coming by in ten. Any of you at the tail of the line hear it, don't pop a flare but tell me. We want it coming down here, not in the middle of the jungle." He took off the helmet, setting it beside him on the turret. His head still buzzed and, though he stared into the jungle over the grips of the cal-fifty, even the front sight was a blur. Ten minutes was a long time.

"I hear it!" Roosevelt called. Without waiting for Holtz's order, he fired the quadrangle of trip flares he had set. They lit brightly the area cleared by the alien's weapon. While those ground flares sizzled to full life, Greiler sent three star clusters streaking into the overcast together. The dust-off slick, casting like a coonhound, paused invisibly. As a great gray shadow it drifted down the line of tanks. Its rotor kicked the mist into billows flashing dimly.

Gracelessly yet without jerking the wounded boy, Womble and a third-platoon tanker pressed into service as stretcher-bearer rose and started toward the bird. As soon as the slick touched down, its blades set to idle, the crew chief with his Red Cross armband jumped out. Holtz and the stretcher with the newbie reached the helicopter an instant after the two nearer stretchers.

"Where's the prisoner?" the crew chief shouted over the high scream of unloaded turbines.

"Get my men aboard first," Holtz ordered briefly.

"Sorry, Captain," the air medic replied, "with our fuel load we only take two this trip and I've got orders to bring the prisoner back for sure."

"Stuff your orders! My men go out first."

The crew chief wiped sweat from the bridge of his nose; more trickled from under his commo helmet. "Sir, there's two generals and a bird colonel waiting on the pad for me; I leave that—" he shook his head at the makeshift stretcher—"that back here and it's a year in LBJ if I'm lucky. I'll take one of your—"

"They're both dying!"

"I'm sorry but . . ." The medic's voice dried up when he saw what Holtz was doing. "You can't threaten me!" he shrilled.

Holtz jacked a shell into the chamber of the .45. None of his men moved to stop him. The medic took one step forward as the big captain fired. The bullet slammed into the alien's forehead, just under the streaky gray bristles of his hairline. Fluid spattered the medic and the side of the helicopter behind him.

"There's no prisoner!" Holtz screamed over the shuddering thunder inside his skull. "There's nothing at all, do you hear? Now get my men to a hospital!"

Hauley tried to catch him as he fell, but the officer's weight pulled them both to the ground together.

The snarl of a laboring diesel brought him out of it. He was on a cot with a rolled flak jacket pillowed under his head. Someone had removed his chicken vest and bathed away the crusts of dried blood.

"Where are we?" Holtz muttered thickly. His vision had cleared and the chipped rubber of the treads beside him stood out in sharp relief.

Hauley handed his CO a paper cup of coffee laced with something bitter. "Here you go. Lieutenant Paider took over and we're gonna set up here for the night. If it clears, we'll get a chopper for you too."

"But that . . . ?" Holtz gestured at the twilit bulk of a tank twenty feet away. It grunted to a halt after neutral steering a full 360 degrees.

"That? Oh, that was four-four," Hauley said in a careless voice. "Greiler wanted to say thanks—getting both his buddies dusted off, you know. But I told him you didn't want to hear about something that didn't happen. And everybody in the company'll swear it didn't happen, whatever some chopper jockey thinks. So Greiler just moved four-four up to where the bird landed and did a neutral steer . . . on nothing at all.''

"Nothing at all," Holtz repeated before drifting off. He grinned like a she-tiger gorging on her cubs' first kill.

CAPSULE

by Elizabeth Morton

Byron stares into the bathroom mirror and wonders if his nose will ever be the same again. Only two days into the allergy season and he has reached crisis. "You know I don't like to take medicine," he tells the puffy-faced man in the mirror. "I'm a naturalist. Pure mind. Pure body."

"Right," the puffy-faced man says, "but don't blame *me* when they carry you away and hook you up to the tubes like last time, dummy."

"Yeah," Byron says wearily, "yeah." He sighs and opens the medicine chest, takes out the fresh bottle of capsules and struggles with it. No one ever died from hay fever, he thinks. On the other hand that is a qualified blessing.

He struggles with the difficult top, grunts, opens it convulsively. Tiny time-release beads spew from the vial, scamper over the porcelain and a few split open.

Out of one of them a tiny orange creature, perfectly formed, emerges. Byron can see it well; allergy has left him, if nothing else, clarity of vision. The orange creature is a tenth of an inch high with beautiful hands and piercing, expressive eyes.

"Greetings, earth person," the creature says in a thin but clear voice. "We come in peace—"

Byron shakes his head and shudders. Inside the sink another creature, green this time, emerges from a time-release bead. "I *told* you so," it says furiously in a slightly deeper voice, "you orange-headed fool, you wanted an inanimate object, something inconspicuous; I hope you're satisfied: Look at us. We have no dignity. What will the report say?"

"Shut up," the orange creature says, "I'm a *supervisor*, you green zyxul. I'm following procedure."

"That's easy for you to say," the creature says and begins to argue floridly in another language. The orange supervisor argues back. Byron feels faint. He props himself against the sink, dreading its contents. How many aliens are in there?

The thought is horrifying. Byron sneezes convulsively.

Beads rattle and the arguing creatures are blown away as if by an explosion.

Byron takes some tissue and wipes his nose mournfully. Guilt struggles with relief. After a while, relief wins.

"After all," he says, "it *was* my first Contac."

CABIN BOY

by Damon Knight

The cabin boy's name was unspeakable, and even its meaning would be difficult to convey in any human tongue. For convenience, we may as well call him Tommy Loy.

Please bear in mind that all these terms are approximations. Tommy was not exactly a cabin boy, and even the spaceship he served was not exactly a spaceship, nor was the Captain exactly a captain. But if you think of Tommy as a freckled, scowling, red-haired, willful, prank-playing, thoroughly abhorrent brat, and of the Captain as a crusty, ponderous old man, you may be able to understand their relationship.

A word about Tommy will serve to explain why these approximations have to be made, and just how much they mean. Tommy, to a human being, would have looked like a six-foot egg made of greenish gelatin. Suspended in this were certain dark or radiant shapes which were Tommy's nerve centers and digestive organs, and scattered about its surface were star-shaped and oval markings which were his sensory organs and gripping mechanisms—his "hands." At the lesser end was an orifice which expelled a stream of glowing vapor—Tommy's means of propulsion. It should be clear that if instead of saying, "Tommy ate his lunch," or, "Tommy said to the Captain . . ." we reported what really happened, some pretty complicated explanations would have to be made.

Similarly, the term "cabin boy" is used because it is the closest in human meaning. Some vocations, like seafaring, are so demanding and so complex that they simply cannot be taught in classrooms; they have to be lived. A cabin boy is one who is learning such a vocation and paying for his instruction by performing certain menial, degrading, and unimportant tasks.

That describes Tommy, with one more similarity—the cabin boy of the sailing vessel was traditionally occupied after each whipping with preparing the mischief, or the stupidity, that earned him the next one.

Tommy, at the moment, had a whipping coming to him and was fighting a delaying action. He knew he couldn't escape eventual punishment, but he planned to hold it off as long as he could.

Floating alertly in one of the innumerable corridors of the ship, he watched as a dark wave sprang into being upon the glowing corridor wall and sped toward him. Instantly, Tommy was moving away from it, and at the same rate of speed.

The wave rumbled: "Tommy! Tommy Loy! Where *is* that obscenity boy?"

The wave moved on, rumbling wordlessly, and Tommy moved with it. Ahead of him was another wave, and another beyond that, and it was the same throughout all the corridors of the ship. Abruptly the waves reversed their direction. So did Tommy, barely in time. The waves not only carried the Captain's orders but scanned every corridor and compartment of the ten-mile ship. But as long as Tommy kept between the waves, the Captain could not see him.

The trouble was that Tommy could not keep this up forever, and he was being searched for by other lowly members of the crew. It took a long time to traverse all of those winding, interlaced passages, but it was a mathematical certainty that he would be caught eventually.

Tommy shuddered, and at the same time he squirmed with delight. He had interrupted the Old Man's sleep by a stench of a particularly noisome variety, one of which he had only lately found himself capable. The effect had been beautiful. In human terms, since Tommy's race communicated by odors, it was equivalent to setting off a firecracker beside a sleeper's ear.

Judging by the jerkiness of the scanning waves' motion, the Old Man was still unnerved.

"Tommy!" the waves rumbled. "Come out, you little piece of filth, or I'll smash you into a thousand separate stinks! By Spore, when I get hold of you—"

The corridor intersected another at this point, and Tommy seized his chance to duck into the new one. He had been working his way outward ever since his crime, knowing that the search parties would do the same. When he reached the outermost level of the ship, there would be a slight possibility of slipping back past the hunters—not much of a chance, but better than none.

He kept close to the wall. He was the smallest member of the crew—smaller than any of the other cabin boys, and less than half the size of an Ordinary; it was always possible that when he sighted one of the search party, he could get away before the crewman saw him. He was in a short connecting corridor now, but the scanning waves cycled endlessly, always turning back before he could escape into the next corridor. Tommy followed their movement patiently, while he listened to the torrent of abuse that poured from them. He snickered to himself. When the Old Man was angry, everyboy suffered. The ship would be stinking from stem to stern by now.

Eventually the Captain forgot himself and the waves flowed on around the next intersection. Tommy moved on. He was getting close to his goal by now; he could see a faint gleam of starshine up at the end of the corridor.

The next turn took him into it—and what Tommy saw through the semi-transparent skin of the ship nearly made him falter and be caught. Not merely the fiery pin-points of stars shone there, but a great, furious glow which could only mean that they were passing through a star system. It was the first time this had happened in Tommy's life, but of course it was nothing to the Captain, or even to most of the Ordinaries. Trust them, Tommy thought resentfully, to say nothing to him about it!

Now he knew he was glad he'd tossed that surprise at the Captain. If he hadn't, he wouldn't be here, and if he weren't here. . .

A waste capsule was bumping automatically along the corridor, heading for one of the exit pores in the hull. Tommy let it catch up to him, then englobed it, but it stretched him so tight that he could barely hold it. That was all to the good; the Captain wouldn't be likely to notice that anything had happened.

The hull was sealed, not to keep atmosphere inside, for there was none except by accident, but to prevent loss of liquid by evaporation. Metals and other mineral elements were replaceable; liquids and their constituents, in ordinary circumstances, were not.

Tommy rode the capsule to the exit sphincter, squeezed through, and instantly released it. Being polarized away from the ship's core, it shot into space and was lost. Tommy hugged the outer surface of the hull and gazed at the astonishing panorama that surrounded him.

There was the enormous black half-globe of space— Tommy's sky, the only one he had ever known. It was sprinkled with the familiar yet always changing patterns of the stars. By themselves, these were marvels enough for a child whose normal universe was one of ninety-foot corridors and chambers measuring, at most, three times as much. But Tommy hardly noticed them. Down to his right, reflecting brilliantly from the long, gentle curve of the greenish hull, was a blazing yellow-white glory that he could hardly look at. A star, the first one he had ever seen close at hand. Off to the left was a tiny, milky-blue disk that could only be a planet.

Tommy let go a shout, for the sheer pleasure of its thin, hollow smell. He watched the thin mist of particles spread lazily away from his body, faintly luminous against the jet blackness. He shivered a little, thickening his skin as much as he could. He could not stay long, he knew; he was radiating heat faster than he could absorb it from the sun or the ship's hull.

But he didn't want to go back inside, and not only because it meant being caught and punished. He didn't want to leave that great, dazzling jewel in the sky. For an instant he thought vaguely of the future time when he would be grown, the master of his own vessel, and could see the stars whenever he chose; but the picture was too far away to have any reality. Great Spore, that wouldn't happen for twenty thousand years!

Fifty yards away, an enormous dark spot on the hull, one of the ship's vision devices, swelled and darkened.

Tommy looked up with interest. He could see nothing in that direction, but evidently the Captain had spotted something. Tommy watched and waited, growing colder every second, and after a long time he saw a new pinpoint of light spring into being. It grew steadily larger, turned fuzzy at one side, then became two linked dots, one hard and bright, the other misty.

Tommy looked down with sudden understanding, and saw that another wide area of the ship's hull was swollen and protruding. This one showed a pale color under the green and had a dark ring around it: it was a polarizer. The object he had seen must contain metal, and the Captain was bringing it in for fuel. Tommy hoped it was a big one; they had been short of metal ever since he could remember.

When he glanced up again, the object was much larger. He could see now that the bright part was hard and smooth, reflecting the light of the nearby sun. The misty part was a puzzler. It looked like a crewman's voice, seen against space—or the ion trail of a ship in motion. But was it possible for metal to be alive?

II

Leo Roget stared into the rear-view scanner and wiped beads of sweat from his brown, half-bald scalp. Flaming gas from the jets washed up toward him along the hull; he couldn't see much. But the huge dark ovoid they were headed for was still there, and it was getting bigger. He glanced futilely at the control board. The throttle was on full. They were going to crash in a little more than two minutes, and there didn't seem to be a single thing he could do about it.

He looked at Frances McMenamin, strapped into the acceleration harness beside his own. She said, "Try cutting off the jets, why don't you?"

Roget was a short, muscular man with thinning straight black hair and sharp brown eyes. McMenamin was slender and ash-blond, half an inch taller than he was, with one of those pale, exquisitely shaped faces that seem to be distributed equally among the very stupid and

the very bright. Roget had never been perfectly sure
which she was, although they had been companions for
more than three years. That, in a way, was part of the
reason they had taken this wild trip: she had made Roget
uneasy, and he wanted to break away, and at the same
time he didn't. So he had fallen in with her idea of a trip to
Mars—"to get off by ourselves and think"—and here,
Roget thought, they were, not thinking particularly.

He said, "You want us to crash quicker?"

"How do you know we will?" she countered. "It's the
only thing we haven't tried. Anyhow, we'd be able to see
where we're going, and that's more than we can do now."

"All right," said Roget, "all *right*." She was perfectly
capable of giving him six more reasons, each screwier
than the last, and then turning out to be right. He pulled
the throttle back to zero, and the half-heard, half-felt
roar of the jets died.

The ship jerked backward suddenly, yanking them
against the couch straps, and then slowed.

Roget looked into the scanner again. They were
approaching the huge object, whatever it was, at about
the same rate as before. Maybe, he admitted unwillingly,
a little slower. Damn the woman! How could she possibly
have figured that one out in advance?

"And," McMenamin added reasonably, "we'll save
fuel for the takeoff."

Roget scowled at her. "If there is a takeoff," he said.
"Whatever is pulling us down there isn't doing it to show
off. What do we do—tell them that was a very impressive
trick and we enjoyed it, but we've got to be leaving now?"

"We'll find out what's doing it," said McMenamin,
"and stop it if we can. If we can't, the fuel won't do us any
good anyway."

That was, if not Frances' most exasperating trick, at
least high on the list. She had a habit of introducing your
own argument as if it were not only a telling point on her
side, but something you had been to dense to see. Arguing
with her was like swinging at someone who abruptly disappeared and then sandbagged you from behind.

Roget was fuming, but he said nothing. The greenish
surface below was approaching more and more slowly,

and now he felt a slight but definite tightening of the couch straps that could only mean deceleration. They were being maneuvered in for a landing as carefully and efficiently as if they were doing it themselves.

A few seconds later, a green horizon line appeared in the direct-view ports, and they touched. Roget's and McMenamin's couches swung on their gimbals as the ship tilted slowly, bounced and came to rest.

Frances reached inside the wide collar of her pressure suit to smooth a ruffle that had got crumpled between the volcanic swell of her bosom and the front of the transparent suit. Watching her, Roget felt a sudden irrational flow of affection and—as usually happened—a simultaneous notification that his body disagreed with his mind's opinion of her. This trip, it had been tacitly agreed, was to be a kind of final trial period. At the end of it, either they would split up or decide to make it permanent, and up to now, Roget had been silently determined that it was going to be a split. Now he was just as sure that, providing they ever got to Mars or back to Earth, he was going to nail her for good.

He glanced at her face. She knew, all right, just as she'd known when he'd felt the other way. It should have irritated him, but he felt oddly pleased and comforted. He unstrapped himself, fastened down his helmet, and moved toward the airlock.

He stood on a pale-green, almost featureless surface that curved gently away in every direction. Where he stood, it was brilliantly lighted by the sun, and his shadow was sharp and as black as space. About two thirds of the way to the horizon, looking across the short axis of the ship, the sunlight stopped with knife-edge sharpness, and he could make out the rest only as a ghostly reflection of starlight.

Their ship was lying on its side, with the pointed stern apparently sunk a few inches into the green surface of the alien ship. He took a cautious step in that direction, and nearly floated past it before he could catch himself. His boot magnets had failed to grip. The metal of this hull—if it *was* metal—must be something that contained no iron.

The green hull was shot through with other colors here, and it rose in a curious almost rectangular mound. At the center, just at the tip of the earth vessel's jets, there was a pale area; around that was a dark ring which lapped up over the side of the ship. He bent to examine it. It was in shadow, and he used his helmet light.

The light shone through the mottled green substance; he could see the skin of his own ship. It was pitted, corroding. As he watched, another pinpoint of corruption appeared on the shiny surface, and slowly grew.

Roget straightened up with an exclamation. His helmet phones asked, "What is it, Leo?"

He said, "Acid or something eating the hull. Wait a minute." He looked again at the pale and dark mottlings under the green surface. The center area was not attacking the ship's metal; that might be the muzzle of whatever instrument had been used to pull them down out of their orbit and hold them there. But if it was turned off now . . . He had to get the ship away from the dark ring that was destroying it. He couldn't fire the jets otherwise, because they were half buried; he'd blow the tubes if he tried.

He said, "You still strapped in?"

"Yes."

"All right, hold on." He stepped back to the center of the little ship, braced his corrugated boot soles against the hard green surface, and shoved.

The ship rolled. But it rolled like a top, around the axis of its pointed end. The dark area gave way before it, as if it were jelly-soft. The jets still pointed to the middle of the pale area, and the dark ring still lapped over them. Roget moved farther down and tried again, with the same result. The ship would move freely in every direction but the right one. The attracting power, clearly enough, was still on.

He straightened dejectedly and looked around. A few hundred yards away, he saw something he had noticed before, without attaching any significance to it; a six-foot egg, of some lighter, more translucent substance than the one on which it lay. He leaped toward it. It moved sluggishly away, trailing a cloud of luminous gas. A few seconds later he had it between his gloved hands. It squirmed, then ejected a thin spurt of vapor from its forward end. It was alive.

McMenamin's head was silhouetted in one of the forward ports. He said, "See this?"

"Yes! What is it?"

"One of the crew, I think. I'm going to bring it in. You work the airlock—it won't hold both of us at once."

". . . All right."

The huge egg crowded the cabin uncomfortably. It was pressed up against the rear wall, where it had rolled as soon as Frances had pulled it into the ship. The two human beings stood at the other side of the room, against the control panel, and watched it.

"No features," said Roget, "unless you count those markings on the surface. This thing isn't from anywhere in the solar system, Frances—it isn't even any order of evolution we ever heard of."

"I know," she said abstractedly. "Leo, is he wearing any protection against space that you can see?"

"No," said Roget. "That's *him*, not a spacesuit. Look, you can see halfway into him. But—"

Frances turned to look at him. "That's it," she said. "It means this is his natural element—space!"

Roget looked thoughtfully at the egg. "It makes sense," he said. "He's adapted for it, anyhow—ovoid, for a high volume-to-surface ratio. Tough outer shell. Moves by jet propulsion. It's hard to believe, because we've never run into a creature like him before, but I don't see why not. On earth there are organisms, plants, that can live and reproduce in boiling water, and others that can stand near-zero temperatures."

"He's a plant, too, you know," Frances put in.

Roget stared at her, then back at the egg. "That color, you mean? Chlorophyll. It could be."

"Must be," she corrected firmly. "How else would he live in a vacuum?" And then, distressedly, "Oh, what a smell!"

They looked at each other. It *had* been something monumental in the way of smells, though it had only lasted a fraction of a second. There had been a series of separate odors, all unfamiliar and all overpoweringly strong. At least a dozen of them, Roget thought; they had gone past too quickly to count.

"He did it before, outside, and I saw the vapor." He closed his helmet abruptly and motioned McMenamin to do the same. She frowned and shook her head. He opened his helmet again. "It might be poisonous!"

"I don't think so," said McMenamin. "Anyway, we've got to try something." She walked toward the green egg. It rolled away from her, and she went past it into the bedroom.

In a minute she reappeared, carrying an armload of plastic boxes and bottles. She came back to Roget and knelt on the floor, lining up the containers with their nipples toward the egg.

"What's this for?" Roget demanded. "Listen, we've got to figure some way of getting out of here. The ship's being eaten up—"

"Wait," said McMenamin. She reached down and squeezed three of the nipples quickly, one after the other. There was a tiny spray of face powder, then one of cologne (*Nuit Jupitérienne*), followed by a jet of good Scotch.

Then she waited. Roget was about to open his mouth when another blast of unfamiliar odors came from the egg. This time there were only three: two sweet ones and one sharp.

McMenamin smiled. "I'm going to name him Stinky," she said. She pressed the nipples again, in a different order. Scotch, face powder, *Nuit Jupitérienne*. The egg replied: sharp, sweet, sweet.

She gave him the remaining combination, and he echoed it; then she put a record cylinder on the floor and squirted the face powder. She added another cylinder and squeezed the cologne. She went along the line that way, releasing a smell for each cylinder until there were ten. The egg had responded, recognizably in some cases, to each one. Then she took away seven of the cylinders and looked expectantly at the egg.

The egg released a sharp odor.

"If ever we tell anybody," said Roget in an awed tone, "that you taught a six-foot Easter egg to count to ten by selective flatulence—"

"Hush, fool," she said. "This is a tough one."

She lined up three cylinders, waited for the sharp odor, then added six more to make three rows of three. The egg obliged with a penetrating smell which was a good imitation of citron extract, Frances' number nine. He followed it immediately with another of his own rapid, complicated series of smells.

"He gets it," said McMenamin. "I think he just told us that three times three are nine." She stood up. "You go out first, Leo. I'll put him out after you and then follow. There's something more we've got to show him before we let him go."

Roget followed orders. When the egg came out and kept on going, he stepped in its path and held it back. Then he moved away, hoping the thing would get the idea that they weren't trying to force it but wanted it to stay. The egg wobbled indecisively for a moment and then stayed where it was. Frances came out the next minute, carrying one of the plastic boxes with a flashlight.

"My nicest powder," she said regretfully, "but it was the only thing I could find enough of." She clapped her gloved hands together sharply, with the box between them. It burst, and a haze of particles spread around them, glowing faintly in the sunlight.

The egg was still waiting, somehow giving the impression that it was watching them alertly. McMenamin flicked on the flashlight and pointed it at Roget. It made a clear, narrow path in the haze of dispersed particles. Then she turned it on herself, on the ship, and finally upward, toward the tiny blue disk that was Earth. She did it twice more, then stepped back toward the airlock, and Roget followed her.

They stood watching as Tommy scurried off across the hull, squeezed himself into it and disappeared.

"That was impressive," Roget said. "But I wonder just how much good it's going to do us."

"He knows we're alive, intelligent, friendly, and that we come from Earth," said McMenamin thoughtfully. "Or, anyhow, we did our best to tell him. That's all we can do. Maybe he won't want to help us; maybe he can't. But it's up to him now."

III

The mental state of Tommy, as he dived through the hull
of the ship and into the nearest radial corridor, would be
difficult to describe fully to any human being. He was the
equivalent of a very small boy—that approximation still
holds good—and he had the obvious reactions to novelty
and adventure. But there was a good deal more. He had
seen living, intelligent beings of an unfamiliar shape and
substance, who lived in metal and had some connection
with one of those enormous, enigmatic ships called
planets, which no captain of his own race dared
approach.

And yet Tommy *knew*, with all the weight of knowledge accumulated, codified and transmitted over a span
measured in billions of years, that there was no other
intelligent race than his own in the entire universe, that
metal, though life-giving, could not itself be alive, and
that no living creature, having the ill luck to be spawned
aboard a planet, could ever hope to escape so tremendous
a gravitational field.

The final result of all this was that Tommy desperately
wanted to go somewhere by himself and think. But he
couldn't; he had to keep moving, in time with the scanning waves along the corridor, and he had to give all his
mental energy to the problem of slipping past the search
party.

The question was—how long had he been gone? If they
had reached the hull while he was inside the metal thing,
they might have looked for him outside and concluded
that he had somehow slipped past them, back to the
center of the ship. In that case, they would probably be
working their way back, and he had only to follow them
to the axis and hide in a chamber as soon as they left it.
But if they were still working outward, his chances of
escape were almost nil. And now it seemed more
important to escape than it had before.

There was one possibility which Tommy, who, in most
circumstances, would try anything, hated to think about.
Fuel lines—tubes carrying the rushing, radiant ion vapor
that powered the ship—adjoined many of these corridors,

and it was certain that if he dared to enter one, he would be perfectly safe from detection as long as he remained in it. But, for one thing, these lines radiated from the ship's axis and none of them would take him where he wanted to go. For another, they were the most dangerous places aboard ship. Older crew members sometimes entered them to make emergency repairs, but they got out as quickly as they could. Tommy did not know how long he could survive there; he had an unpleasant conviction that it would not be long.

Only a few yards up the corridor was the sealed sphincter which gave entrance to such a tube. Tommy looked at it indecisively as the motion of the scanning waves brought him nearer. He had still not made up his mind when he caught a flicker reflected around the curve of the corridor behind him.

Tommy squeezed himself closer to the wall and watched the other end of the corridor approach with agonizing slowness. If he could only get around that corner . . .

The flicker of motion was repeated, and then he saw a thin rind of green poke into view. There was no more time to consider entering the fuel line, no time to let the scanning waves' movement carry him around the corner. Tommy put on full speed, cutting across the next wave and down the cross-corridor ahead.

Instantly the Captain's voice shouted from the wall, "Ah! Was that him, the dirty scut? After him, lads!"

Tommy glanced behind as he turned another corner, and his heart sank. It was no cabin boy who was behind him, or even an Ordinary, but a Third Mate—so huge that he filled nearly half the width of the corridor, and so powerful that Tommy, in comparison, was like a boy on a bicycle racing an express train.

He turned another corner, realizing in that instant that he was as good as caught: the new corridor ahead of him stretched straight and without a break for three hundred yards. As he flashed down it, the hulk of the Mate appeared around the bend behind.

The Mate was coming up with terrifying speed, and Tommy had time for only one last desperate spurt. Then the other body slammed with stunning force against his, and he was held fast.

As they coasted to a halt, the Captain's voice rumbled from the wall, "*That's* it, Mister. Hold him where I can see him!"

The scanning areas were stationary now. The Mate moved Tommy forward until he was squarely in range of the nearest.

Tommy squirmed futilely. The Captain said, "*There's* our little jokester. It's a pure pleasure to see you again, Tommy. What—no witty remarks? Your humor all dried up?"

Tommy gasped, "Hope you enjoyed your nap, Captain."

"Very good," said the Captain with heavy sarcasm. "Oh, *very* entertaining, Tommy. Now would you have anything more to say, before I put the whips to you?"

Tommy was silent.

The Captain said to the Mate, "Nice work, Mister. You'll get extra rations for this."

The Mate spoke for the first time, and Tommy recognized his high, affected voice. It was George Adkins, who had recently spored and was so proud of the new life inside his body that there was no living with him. George said prissily, "Thank you, sir, I'm sure. Of course, I really shouldn't have exerted myself the way I just did, in my state."

"Well, you'll be compensated for it," the Captain said testily. "Now take the humorist down to Assembly Five. We'll have a little ceremony there."

"Yes, sir," said the Mate distantly. He moved off, shoving Tommy ahead of him, and dived into the first turning that led downward.

They moved along in silence for the better part of a mile, crossing from one lesser passage to another until they reached a main artery that led directly to the center of the ship. The scanning waves were still stationary, and they were moving so swiftly that there was no danger of being overheard. Tommy said politely, "You won't let them be too hard on me, will you, sir?"

The Mate did not reply for a moment. He had been

baited by Tommy's mock courtesy before, and he was as
wary as his limited intelligence allowed. Finally he said,
"You'll get no more than what's coming to you, young
Tom."

"Yes, sir. I know that, sir. I'm sorry I made you exert
yourself, sir, in your condition and all."

"You should be," said the Mate stiffly, but his voice
betrayed his pleasure. It was seldom enough that even a
cabin boy showed a decent interest in the Mate's pros-
pective parenthood. "They're moving about, you
know," he added, unbending a little.

"Are they, sir? Oh, you must be careful of yourself, sir.
How many are there, please, sir?"

"Twenty-eight," said the Mate, as he had on every
possible occasion for the past two weeks. "Strong and
healthy—so far."

"That's remarkable, sir!" cried Tommy. "Twenty-
eight! If I might be so bold, sir, you ought to be careful of
what you eat. Is the Captain going to give you your extra
rations out of that mass he just brought in topside, sir?"

"I'm sure *I* don't know."

"Gosh!" exclaimed Tommy. "I wish I could be
sure..."

He let the pause grow. Finally the Mate said
querulously, "What do you mean? Is there anything
wrong with the metal?"

"I don't really know, sir, but it isn't like any we ever
had before. That is," Tommy added, "since I was spored,
sir."

"Naturally," said the mate. "*I've* eaten all kinds
myself, you know."

"Yes, sir. But doesn't it usually come in ragged shapes,
sir, and darkish?"

"Of course it does. Everybody knows that. Metal is
nonliving, and only living things have regular shapes."

"Yes, sir. But I was topside, sir, while I was trying to
get away, and I saw this metal. It's quite regular, except
for some knobs at one end, sir, and it's as smooth as you
are, sir, and shiny. If you'll forgive me, sir, it didn't look
at all appetizing to me."

"Nonsense," said the Mate uncertainly. "Nonsense,"

he repeated, in a stronger tone. "You must have been mistaken. Metal can't be alive."

"That's just what I thought, sir," said Tommy excitedly. "But there are live things in this metal, sir. I saw them. And the metal wasn't just floating along the way it's supposed to, sir. I saw it when the Captain brought it down, and... But I'm afraid you'll think I'm lying, sir, if I tell you what it was doing."

"Well, what was it doing?"

"I swear I saw it, sir," Tommy went on. "The Captain will tell you the same thing, sir, if you ask him—he must have noticed."

"Sterilize it all, what *was* it doing?"

Tommy lowered his voice. "There was an ion trail shooting from it, sir. It was trying to get away!"

While the Mate was trying to absorb that, they reached the bottom of the corridor and entered the vast globular space of Assembly Five, line with crewmen waiting to witness the punishment of Tommy Loy.

This was not going to be any fun at all, thought Tommy, but at least he had paid back the Third Mate in full measure. The Mate, for the moment, at any rate, was not taking any joy in his promised extra rations.

When it was over, Tommy huddled in a corner of the crew compartment where they had tossed him, bruised and smarting in every nerve, shaken by the beating he had undergone. The pain was still rolling through him in faint, uncontrollable waves, and he winced at each one, in spite of himself, as though it were the original blow.

In the back of his mind, the puzzle of the metal ship was still calling, but the other experience was too fresh, the remembered images too vivid.

The Captain had begun, as always, by reciting the Creed.

In the beginning was the Spore, and the Spore was alone.

*(*And the crew: *Praised be the Spore!)*

Next there was light, and the light was good. Yea, good for the Spore and the Spore's First Children.

(Praised be they!)

But the light grew evil in the days of the Spore's Second Children.

(Woe unto them!)

And the light cast them out. Yea, exiled were they, into the darkness and the Great Deep.

(Pity for the outcasts in the Great Deep!)

Tommy had mumbled his responses with the rest of them, thinking rebellious thoughts. There was nothing evil about light; they lived by it still. What must have happened—the Captain himself admitted as much when he taught history and natural science classes—was that the earliest ancestors of the race, spawned in the flaming heart of the Galaxy, had grown too efficient for their own good.

They had specialized, more and more, in extracting energy from starlight and the random metal and other elements they encountered in space; and at last they absorbed, willy-nilly, more than they could use. So they had moved, gradually and naturally, over many generations, out from that intensely radiating region into the "Great Deep"—the universe of thinly scattered stars. And the process had continued, inevitably; as the level of available energy fell, their absorption of it grew more and more efficient.

Now, not only could they never return to their birthplace, but they could not even approach a single sun as closely as some planets did. Therefore the planets, and the stars themselves, were objects of fear. That was natural and sensible. But why did they have to continue this silly ritual, invented by some half-evolved, superstitious ancestor, of "outcasts" and "evil"?

The Captain finished:

Save us from the Death that lies in the Great Deep...

(The creeping Death that lies in the Great Deep!)

And keep our minds pure...

(As pure as the light in the days of the Spore, blessed be He!)

And our course straight...

(As straight as the light, brothers!)

That we may meet our lost brothers again in the Day of Reuniting.

(Speed that day!)

Then the pause, the silence that grew until it was like the silence of space. At last the Captain spoke again, pronouncing judgment against Tommy, ending, "Let him be whipped!"

Tommy tensed himself, thickening his skin, drawing his body into the smallest possible compass. Two husky Ordinaries seized him and tossed him at a third. As Tommy floated across the room, the crewman pressed himself tightly against the wall, drawing power from it until he could contain no more. And as Tommy neared him, he discharged it in a crackling arc that filled Tommy's body with the pure essence of pain, and sent him hurtling across the chamber to the next shock, and the next, and the next.

Until the Captain had boomed, "Enough!" and they had carried him out and left him here alone.

He heard the voices of crewmen as they drew their rations. One of them was grumbling about the taste, and another, sounding happily bloated, was telling him to shut up and eat, that metal was metal.

That would be the new metal, however much of it had been absorbed by now, mingled with the old in the reservoir. Tommy wondered briefly how much of it there was, and whether the alien ship—if it *was* a ship—could repair even a little damage to itself. But that assumed life in the metal, and in spite of what he had seen, Tommy couldn't believe in it. It seemed beyond question, though, that there were living things inside the metal; and when the metal was gone, how would they live?

Tommy imagined himself set adrift from the ship, alone in space, radiating more heat than his tiny volume could absorb. He shuddered.

He thought again of the problem that had obsessed him ever since he had seen the alien, five-pointed creatures in the metal ship. Intelligent life was supposed to be sacred. That was part of the Creed, and it was stated in a sloppy, poetic way like the rest of it, but it made a certain kind of sense. No crewman or captain had the right to destroy another for his benefit, because the same heredity was in them all. They were all potentially the same, none better than another.

And you ate metal, because metal was nonliving and certainly not intelligent. But if that stopped being true...

Tommy felt he was missing something. Then he had it: in the alien ship, trying to talk to the creatures that lived in metal, he had been scared almost scentless—but underneath the fright and the excitement, he had felt wonderful. It had been, he realized suddenly, like the mystic completion that was supposed to come when all the straight lines met, in the "Day of Reuniting"—when all the far-flung ships, parted for all the billions of years of their flight, came together at last. It was talking to someone different from yourself.

He wanted to talk again to the aliens, teach them to form their uncouth sounds into words, learn from them ... Vague images swirled in his mind. They were products of an utterly different line of evolution. Who knew what they might be able to teach him?

And now the dilemma took shape. If his own ship absorbed the metal of theirs, they would die; therefore he would have to make the Captain let them go. But if he somehow managed to set them free, they would leave and he would never see them again.

A petty officer looked into the cubicle and said, "All right, Loy, out of it. You're on garbage detail. You eat after you work, if there's anything left. Lively, now!"

Tommy moved thoughtfully out into the corridor, his pain almost forgotten. The philosophical problems presented by the alien ship, too, having no apparent solution, were receding from his mind. A new thought was taking their place, one that made him glow inside with the pure rapture of the devoted practical jokester.

The whipping he was certainly going to get—and, so soon after the last offense, it would be a beauty—scarcely entered his mind.

IV

Roget climbed in, opening his helmet, and sat down warily in the acceleration cough. He didn't look at the woman.

McMenamin said quietly, "Bad?"

"Not good. The outer skin's gone all across that area, and it's eating into the lead sheathing. The tubes are holding up pretty well, but they'll be next."

"We've done as much as we can, by rolling the ship around?"

"Just about. I'll keep at it, but I don't see how it can be more than a few hours before the tubes go. Then we're cooked, whatever your fragrant little friend does."

He stood up abruptly and climbed over the slanting wall which was now their floor, to peer out the direct-view port. He swore, slowly and bitterly. "You try the radio again while I was out?" he asked.

"Yes." She did not bother to add that there had been no response. Here, almost halfway between the orbits of earth and Mars, they were hopelessly out of touch. A ship as small as theirs couldn't carry equipment enough to bridge the distance.

Roget turned around, said, "By God—" and then clenched his jaw and strode out of the room. McMenamin heard him walk through the bedroom and clatter around in the storage compartment behind.

In a few moments he was back with a welding torch in his hand. "Should have thought of this before," he said. "I don't know what'll happen if I cut into the hull—damn thing may explode, for all I know—but it's better than sitting doing nothing." He put his helmet down with a bang and his voice came tinnily in her helmet receiver. "Be back in a minute."

"Be careful," McMenamin said again.

Roget closed the outer lock door behind him and looked at the ravaged hull of the ship. The metal had been eaten away in a broad band all around the ship, just above the tail, as if a child had bitten around the small end of a pear. In places the clustered rocket tubes showed through. He felt a renewed surge of anger, with fear deep under it.

A hundred years ago, he reminded himself, the earliest space voyagers had encountered situations as bad as this one, maybe worse. But Roget was a city man, bred for city virtues. He didn't, he decided, know quite how to feel or act. What were you supposed to do when you were about to die, fifteen million miles from home? Try to calm McMenamin—who was dangerously calm already —or show your true nobility by making one of those deathbed speeches you read in the popular histories? What about suggesting a little suicide pact? There was nothing in the ship that would give them a cleaner death than the one ahead of them. About all he could do would be to stab Frances, then himself, with a screwdriver.

Her voice said in the earphones, "You all right?"

He said, "Sure. Just going to try it." He lowered himself to the green surface, careful not to let his knees touch the dark, corrosive area. The torch was a small, easily manageable tool. He pointed the snout at the dark area where it lapped up over the hull, turned the switch on and pressed the button. Flame leaped out, washing over the dark surface. Roget felt the heat through his suit. He turned off the torch to see what effect it had had.

There was a deep, charred pit in the dark stuff, and it seemed to him that it had pulled back a little from the area it was attacking. It was more than he had expected. Encouraged, he tried again.

There was a sudden tremor under him and he leaped nervously to his feet, just in time to avoid the corrosive wave as it rolled under him. For a moment he was only conscious of the thick metal of his boot soles and the thinness of the fabric that covered his knees; then, as he was about to step back out of the way, he realized that it was not only the dark ring that had expanded, that was still expanding.

He moved jerkily—too late—as the pale center area swept toward and under him. Then he felt as if he had been struck by a mighty hammer.

His ears rang, and there was a mist in front of his eyes. He blinked, tried to raise an arm. It seemed to be stuck fast at the wrist and elbow. Panicked, he tried to push himself away, and couldn't. As his vision cleared, he saw that he was spread-eagled on the pale disk that had spread out under him. The metal collars of his wrist and elbow joints, all the metal parts of his suit, were held immovably. The torch lay a few inches away from his right hand.

For a few moments, incredulously, Roget still tried to move. Then he stopped and lay in the prison of his suit, looking at the greenish-cream surface under his helmet.

Frances' voice said abruptly, "Leo, is anything wrong?"

Roget felt an instant relief that left him shaken and weak. His forehead was cold. He said after a moment, "Pulled a damn fool trick, Frances. Come out and help me if you can."

He heard a click as her helmet went down. He added anxiously, "But don't come near the pale part, or you'll get caught too."

After a while she said, "Darling, I can't think of anything to do."

Roget was feeling calmer, somehow not much afraid any more. He wondered how much oxygen was left in his suit. Not more than an hour, he thought. He said, "I know. I can't, either."

Later he called, "Frances?"

"Yes?"

"Roll the ship once in a while, will you? Might get through to the wiring or something, otherwise."

". . . All right."

After that, they didn't talk. There was a great deal to be said, but it was too late to say it.

V

Tommy was on garbage detail with nine other unfortunates. It was a messy, hard, unpleasant business, fit only for a cabin boy—collecting waste from the compartment and corridor receptacles and pressing it into standard capsule shapes, then hauling it to the nearest polarizer. But Tommy, under the suspicious eye of the petty officer in charge, worked with an apparent total absorption until they had cleaned out their section of the six inmost levels and were well into the seventh.

This was the best strategic place for Tommy's departure, since it was about midway from axis to hull, and the field of operations of any pursuit was correspondingly broadened. Also, the volume in which they labored had expanded wedgewise as they climbed, and the petty officer, though still determined to watch Tommy, could no longer keep him constantly in view.

Tommy saw the officer disappear around the curve of the corridor, and kept on working busily. He was still at it, with every appearance of innocence and industry, when the officer abruptly popped into sight again about three seconds later.

The officer stared at him with baffled disapproval and said unreasonably, "Come on, come on, Loy. Don't slack."

"Right," said Tommy, and scurried faster.

A moment later Third Mate Adkins hove majestically into view. The petty officer turned respectfully to face him.

"Keeping young Tom well occupied, I see," said the Mate.

"Yes, sir," said the officer. "Appears to be a reformed character, now, sir. Must have learned a lesson, one way or another."

"Ha!" said the Mate. "Very good. Oh, Loy, you might be interested in this—the Captain himself has told me that the new metal is perfectly all right. Unusually rich, in fact. I've had my first ration already—very good it was, too—and I'm going to get my extras in half an hour or so. Well, good appetite, all." And, while the lesser crewmen clustered against the walls to give him room, he moved haughtily off down the corridor.

Tommy kept on working as fast as he could. He was draining energy he might need later, but it was necessary to quiet the petty officer's suspicions entirely, in order to give himself a decent start. In addition, his artist's soul demanded it. Tommy, in his own way, was a perfectionist.

Third Mate Adkins was due to get his extras in about half an hour, and if Tommy knew the Captain's habits, the Captain would be taking his first meal from the newly replenished reservoir at about the same time. That set the deadline. Before the half hour was up, Tommy would have to cut off the flow of the new metal, so that stomachs which had been gurgling in anticipation would remain desolately void until the next windfall.

The Mate, in spite of his hypochondria, was a glutton. With any luck, this would make him bitter for a month. And the Old Man—but it was better not to dwell on that.

The petty officer hung around irresolutely for another ten minutes, then dashed off down the corridor to attend to the rest of his detail. Without wasting a moment, Tommy dropped the capsule he had just collected and shot away in the other direction.

The rest of the cabin boys, as fearful of Tommy as they were of constituted authority, would not dare to raise an outcry until they spotted the officer coming back. The officer, because of the time he had wasted in watching Tommy, would have to administer a thorough lecture on slackness to the rest of the detail before he returned.

Tommy had calculated his probable margin to a nicety, and it was enough, barring accidents, to get him safely away. Nevertheless, he turned and twisted from one system of corridors to another, carefully confusing his trail, before he set himself to put as much vertical distance behind him as he could.

This part of the game had to be accomplished in a fury of action, for he was free to move in the corridors only until the Captain was informed that he was loose again. After that, he had to play hounds and hares with the moving strips through which the Captain could see him.

When the time he had estimated was three quarters gone, Tommy slowed and came to a halt. He inspected the corridor wall minutely, and found the almost imperceptible trace that showed where the scanning wave nearest him had stopped. He jockeyed his body clear of it, and then waited. He still had a good distance to cover before he dared play his trump, but it was not safe to move now; he had to wait for the Captain's move.

It came soon enough: the scanning waves erupted into simultaneous motion and anger. "Tommy!" they bellowed. "Tommy Loy! Come back, you unmentionable excrescence, or by Spore you'll regret it! Tommy!"

Moving between waves, Tommy waited patiently until their motion carried him from one corridor to another. The Captain's control over the waves was not complete;

in some corridors they moved two steps upward for one down, in others the reverse. When he got into a downward corridor, Tommy scrambled out of it again as soon as he could and started over.

Gradually, with many false starts, he worked his way up to the thirteenth level, one level short of the hull.

Now came the hard part. This time he had to enter the fuel lines, not only for sure escape, but to gather the force he needed. And for the first time in his life, Tommy hesitated before something that he had set himself to do.

Death was a phenomenon that normally touched each member of Tommy's race only once—only captains died, and they died alone. For lesser members of the crew, there was almost no mortal danger; the ship protected them. But Tommy knew what death was, and as the sealed entrance to the fuel line swung into view, he knew that he faced it.

He made himself small, as he had under the lash. He broke the seal. Quickly, before the following wave could catch him, he thrust himself through the sphincter.

The blast of ions gripped him, flung him forward, hurting him like a hundred whips. Desperately he held himself together, thickening his insulating shell against that deadly flux of energy; but still his body absorbed it, till he felt a horrid fullness.

The walls of the tube fled past him, barely perceptible in the rush of glowing haze. Tommy held in that growing tautness with his last strength, meanwhile looking for an exit. He neither knew nor cared whether he had reached his goal; he had to get out or die.

He saw a dim oval on the wall ahead, hurled himself at it, clung, and forced his body through.

He was in a horizontal corridor, just under the hull. He drank the blessed coolness of it for an instant, before moving to the nearest sphincter. Then he was out, under the velvet-black sky and the diamond blaze of stars.

He looked around. The pain was fading now; he felt only an atrocious bloatedness that tightened his skin and made all his movements halting. Forward of him, up the long shallow curve of the hull, he could see the alien ship, and the two five-pointed creatures beside it. Carefully, keeping a few feet between himself and the hull, he headed toward it.

One of the creatures was sprawled flat on the polarizer that had brought its ship down. The other, standing beside it, turned as Tommy came near, and two of its upper three points moved in an insane fashion that made Tommy feel ill. He looked away quickly and moved past them, till he was directly over the center of the polarizer and only a few inches away.

Then, with a sob of relief, he released the energy his body had stored. In one thick, white bolt, it sparked to the polarizer's center.

Shaken and spent, Tommy floated upward and surveyed what he had done. The muzzle of the polarizer was contracting, puckering at the center, the dark corrosive ring following it in. So much energy, applied in one jolt, must have shorted and paralyzed it all the way back to the ship's nerve center. The Captain, Tommy thought wryly, would be jumping now!

And he wasn't done yet. Tommy took one last look at the aliens and their ship. The sprawled one was up now, and the two of them had their upper points twined around each other in a nauseating fashion. Then they parted suddenly, and, facing Tommy, wiggled their free points. Tommy moved purposefully off across the width of the ship, heading for the other two heavy-duty polarizers.

He had to go in again through that hell not once more, but twice. Though his nerves shrank from the necessity, there was no way of avoiding it. For the ship could not alter its course, except by allowing itself to be attracted by a sun or other large body—which was unthinkable—but it could rotate at the Captain's will. The aliens were free now, but the Captain had only to spin ship in order to snare them again.

Four miles away, Tommy found the second polarizer. He backed away a carefully calculated distance before he re-entered the hull. At least he could know in advance how far he had to go—and he knew now, too, that the energy he had stored the first time had been adequate twice over. He rested a few moments; then, like a diver plunging into a torrent, he thrust himself into the fuel line.

He came out again, shuddering with pain, and pushed himself through the exit. He felt as bloated as he had before. The charge of energy was not as great, but Tommy knew that he was weakening. This time, when he discharged over the polarizer and watched it contract into a tiny, puckered mass, he felt as if he could never move again, let alone expose himself once more to that tunnel of flame.

The stars, he realized dully, were moving in slow, ponderous arcs over his head. The Captain was spinning ship. Tommy sank to the hull and lay motionless, watching half attentively for a sight of the alien ship.

There it was, a bright dot haloed by the flame of its exhaust. It swung around slowly, gradually, with the rest of the firmament, growing smaller slowly.

"He'll get them before they're out of range," Tommy thought. He watched as the bright dot climbed overhead, began to fall on the other side.

The Captain had one polarizer left. It would be enough.

Wearily Tommy rose and followed the bright star. It was not a joke any longer. He would willingly have gone inside to the bright, warm, familiar corridors that led downward to safety and deserved punishment. But somehow he could not bear to think of those fascinating creatures—those wonderful playthings—going to fill the Captain's fat belly.

Tommy followed the ship until he could see the pale gleam of the functioning polarizer. Then he crawled through the hull once more, and again he found a sealed entrance to the fuel tube. He did not let himself think about it. His mind was numb already, and he pushed himself through uncaring.

This time it was worse than ever before; he had not dreamed that it could be so bad. His vision dimmed and he could barely see the exit, or feel its pressure, when he dragged himself out. Lurching drunkenly, he passed a scanning wave on his way to the hull sphincter, and heard the Captain's voice explode.

Outside, ragged black patches obscured his vision of the stars. The pressure inside him pressed painfully outward, again and again, and each time he held it back. Then he felt rather than saw that he was over the pale disk, and, as he let go the bolt, he lost consciousness.

When his vision cleared, the alien ship was still above him, alarmingly close. The Captain must have had it almost reeled in again, he thought, when he had let go that last charge.

Flaming, it receded into the Great Deep, and he watched it go until it disappeared.

He felt a great peace and a great weariness. The tiny blue disk that was a planet had moved its apparent position a little nearer its star. The aliens were going back there, to their unimaginable home, and Tommy's ship was forging onward into new depths of darkness— toward the edge of the Galaxy and the greatest Deep.

He moved to the nearest sphincter as the cold bit at him. His spirits lifted suddenly as he thought of those three stabs of energy, equally spaced around the twelve-mile perimeter of the ship. The Captain would be utterly speechless with rage, he thought, like an aged martinet who had had his hands painfully slapped by a small boy.

For, as we warned you, the Captain was not precisely a captain, nor the ship precisely a ship. Ship and captain were one and the same, hive and queen bee, castle and lord.

In effect, Tommy had circumnavigated the skipper.

FIRST LOVE

by Lloyd Biggle, Jr.

Walt Rogers laid aside his brush, pushed back the easel, and switched off the dim light. The storm had faltered momentarily, and now it surged back with a pounding torrent of rain. Walt stepped to the open window and stood there, oblivious of the water that flooded against his eager young face.

Flashes of lightning ripped aside the darkness and laid bare a familiar landscape twisted strangely. Towering trees bowed submissively before the angrily moaning wind. Water veiled the accumulated filth of the barnyard, and cattle huddled pathetically under a shelter. The rain blurred the outlines of the barn and gave it a somber loveliness.

Lightning flashed again, and thunder snapped and rumbled after it, and Walt leaned forward with his elbows on the windowsill and whispered, "Beautiful! Beautiful!"

But how to paint it?

Of course he could paint how it looked. Any darned fool could paint *that*. But how to paint the sound of it, and the feel of it, and the wonderful, glorious fresh-breathing smell of it?

He turned away and kicked disgustedly at the easel, and at that moment the thunder struck. It came with a thickening roar that impaled him in clinging fright against the windowsill. As he stood crouched in numbed astonishment, it swelled to a bloated, consuming agony of sound until he winced in pain and clapped his hands to his ears, and still it grew and crescendoed until, at the instant it seemed no longer bearable, it exploded.

He was lying on the floor under the window, in the full blast of the driving rain. Glass tinkled as he moved, and cascaded from his back as he got to his feet. His first thought was to close the window, and he cut his hand on a sliver of glass that remained attached to the empty frame. His ears rang painfully, and the wild roar of the storm now seemed only a subdued mutter. As he stared into the night, fire glowed in the distance, sent an exploring tongue of flame up into the rain, and suddenly leaped skyward.

He ran from his room and down the hallway. As he reached his parents' room his father opened the door, flashlight in hand.

"The lights are out," his father said. "Did your window break? Ours did." He flashed the light into a spare bedroom. "That one's broken, too."

"Dad," Walt said breathlessly, "something happened over by the quarry. There's a big fire. The flames are shooting way up."

"Damn the flames. What happens at the quarry is Zengler's business, not ours." He was looking into the bathroom. "Every window in the house is broken. In this storm, too. We'll be flooded out. Mother, get some plastic, or oilcloth, or anything you can dig up. Get a hammer and some tacks, Walt. We'll have to work fast."

"Shouldn't we telephone?" Walt asked. "About the fire, I mean."

"I've tried the telephone," Walt's mother called from the bedroom. "It's out of order."

Walt turned obediently to go for a hammer and tacks. His father's sharp exclamation halted him. "Walt, your back is cut. It's covered with cuts. What were you doing? Standing by the window?"

"I—yes—"

"What on Earth for?"

"I was watching the storm."

"Good God! At three in the morning—fix him up, Mother. I better get started on those windows."

There was no more sleep for the three of them that night. They covered windows, and swept up broken glass, and mopped. Walt slipped away once to open a door a crack and peer out into the continuing storm. "The quarry—" he began.

"Damn the quarry!" his father said.

"It's still burning."

By the time they finished their cleaning, the storm had passed and a pink dawn was staining the horizon. Walt went out with his father, and they walked across the yard with the water-soaked grass squishing underfoot. Before they entered the barn to check for damage there, they stood looking toward the quarry.

"Whatever it was," Jim Rogers said, "it's burned out now. I'll go take a look. Maybe Zengler had some gasoline stored over there—though I wouldn't know why. But if he's responsible for this, he's going to pay for these windows or he'll never get another lease."

But it seemed that Zengler was not responsible. The fire had burned out a corner of the north pasture, where Zengler certainly had nothing stored. The quarry, and Zengler's property, were undamaged. Neighboring farmers had heard the explosion as a distant roar, and it had done no damage except to their sleep. No one but the Rogers family had seen the fire.

The net result was a brief item in that week's edition of the Harwell *Gazette*, under "Local Briefs." "A mysterious explosion, which might have been a clap of thunder, broke windows at the James Rogers farm during the storm last Monday night."

On the Saturday following the storm, Walt helped his father with the morning chores, as he usually did, and then he took the cows to the pasture. As they lurched away, he cut diagonally across the pasture toward the quarry. The morning was warm, even for early June. White wisps of cloud drifted serenely across the purest of blue skies.

"Beautiful," Walt whispered and wished he had brought his paints.

The mysterious fire had scarred a circle almost a hundred yards in diameter. At the point nearest the quarry it had ruined the fence, and Walt had come out with his father on Tuesday after school to string new strands of barbed wire. The haste had been unnecessary. The cows, for strange cow reasons comprehensible only to themselves, refused to approach the burned area.

Walt climbed through the fence and walked over to the quarry. Water filled a vast hollow that had been excavated long before Walt's birth. The little lake was said to be fifty feet deep at its deepest point. Beyond it, the hill had been sliced away neatly where Zengler's men were blasting out the rock.

Walt sat down by the water and amused himself with the reflections, imagining how he would put them on canvas. The clouds overhead, the one towering oak tree, the mass of the hill beyond—all were mirrored splendidly in the dark, still water. His own image had an amusing, elongated perspective.

He seized at an inspiration. "I'll come this afternoon," he thought, "and do a self-portrait, using the water instead of a mirror. I wonder if it's ever been done."

He felt gloriously happy. School had ended the day before, and he had the entire summer before him. There would be the farm work, of course, but he'd be able to find plenty of time to paint, and paint, and—

He looked longingly at the water. The morning was warm, but it was too early in the year for swimming. The water would be icy. His mother was waiting breakfast for him.

He was out of his clothes in an instant, carelessly dropping them on the rocky bank, and he turned and stepped off into ten feet of water. The chilling shock spurred him to a frantic churning of arms and legs. He broke water, wiped his eyes, and turned to strike out for the opposite side.

Suddenly he whirled and threshed wildly for the bank. He pulled himself out and turned to stare at the water. He could see nothing but his own reflection, peering back at him quizzically.

But he had seen something, something long and dark, drifting up out of the deepest water and nosing purposely toward him. A fish? But there never had been any fish in that water, and a fish of that size would be a monster.

Then he saw it again, a long, sinister-looking shadow that drifted slowly toward the bank and then hung motionless, too deep for him to see it clearly. He waited breathlessly. It tilted and slowly coasted toward the surface, and he found himself gazing into the face of a girl.

He sucked his breath in sharply, and it was seconds before he realized that she was staring at him, too, and that he was nude. Moving slowly, he got to his knees and stretched out on a flat rock, moving his face close to the water.

She remained well below the surface, but by watching her intently he began to make out her features. Her dark mass of hair swayed gently in the water, stretching back the length of her body. A smooth material, greenish even in the dark water, covered her body, molding the contours of her small breasts so distinctly that he felt himself blushing. The water gave her face a curiously flattened appearance, but he measured its perfect oval with an artist's eye and wondered what mysterious color her eyes might have.

Then he noticed the gills.

One of her hands, with delicately webbed fingers, made a circle and pointed to her open mouth. It circled and pointed again. The third time he understood. She was hungry.

Even as he watched, his alert sixteen-year-old mind was proving the imponderable with relentless logic. She was hungry. Of course she was hungry. The storm had been Monday night, so whatever it was that had brought her had crashed and burned Monday night, and this was Saturday. She must be starved. There was nothing in that water for her to eat.

He had read of flying saucers and possible life on other worlds, and he did not pause to speculate. He *knew*. She could not be of this world, so she must have come from another world. How had she come? The charred edge of the pasture was a mere two hundred yards from the water. Could her people, water people, have mastered the intricacies of space flight? She was here. That was answer enough. She was here, and her ship had consumed itself in that mysterious fire that had tossed flames high but seemed to have produced relatively little heat.

He extended one hand slowly, toward her face. She

darted backward in alarm, approached again as he withdrew his hand, and repeated her signal. Her webbed hand
moved toward her mouth. She was hungry.

Walt leaped to his feet and pulled on his clothing. With
one last glance at the face in the water, he started back
across the pasture, running.

Edna Rogers took in her son's disheveled appearance and
wet mop of curly hair and exclaimed, "What *have* you
been doing?"

"Dad," Walt said breathlessly, "I'd like to go fishing.
Could I take the car?"

"By yourself?"

"Why—yes."

"Well," Jim Rogers said easily, "I guess summer's
officially here. Things are pretty well in hand, and a mess
of fish would taste good. Where are you going?"

"I know some good places," Walt said evasively.

Fishing had never interested him. Nothing had
interested him except painting and drawing, but he
remembered a submerged tree stump in the river south of
town. Once when he was out sketching he had seen a boy
catch several sunfish there. It was as good a place to start
as any.

The girl was hungry. But what could she eat? Raw meat
or fresh? What about fruit and vegetables? She lived in
the water, so he would get her some fish, if he could. And
then he could try some other things.

He left the car parked by the road and cut across the
Malloy farm to the river. No one was about, which
pleased him. Tense with excitement, he baited his hook
and dropped it into the water.

Nothing happened. The bobber drifted idly with the
current and eventually snagged Walt's hook on the
stump. He freed it and tried again, impatiently counting
the minutes. The girl was starving. He told himself that he
should have taken her something else. His mother
wouldn't miss one steak from the deep freezer. He had to
do something quickly, and if the fish weren't going to
co-operate—

He whipped his line from the water and ran back to the

car. Two miles down the road he pulled in at Marshall's Service Station. Old Ed Marshall sat by the door of the weathered frame building, tilted back in a chair, reading and enjoying the sunshine.

"Minnows?" he said. "I can let you have some. But if you'd rather get your own, you know where the net is. Take it any time you want it. And say—Sadie'd like another of those pictures of yours. She wants to put it in the guest room."

"She'll get one," Walt said fervently.

He found the neatly folded net in the shed behind the station. He was on his way back to his car when Old Ed called after him, "Sure you can manage by yourself?"

"I can manage," Walt said.

The net was twenty-five feet long and a rather large-meshed affair for capturing minnows. There were those who thought maybe Old Ed used it on larger prey, and Walt, who had seen him in action one morning, was certain of it. And everyone knew about the way the Marshall family lived on fish during the summer.

Old Ed got to his feet and walked over to the car. "I'll tell you, Walt," he said with a confidential grin. "It's a little late in the morning to start out with that thing. And you have to know where to go. If you want fish, why don't you come with me tomorrow?"

"I'd like to give it a try," Walt said.

"I could let you have a few for today."

"And—tomorrow?"

"I go every morning. You're welcome to come along any time you like."

"Thanks," Walt said.

Minutes later he was driving wildly toward the quarry with three healthy-sized bass splashing in a bucket.

Fortunately Zengler's men did not work on Saturday. The quarry was deserted, the water dark and lifeless. Walt leaned over and splashed frantically with his hand. Then he saw her gliding swiftly toward him. She halted well below the surface.

He caught one of the fish and held it low over the water. She did not move until he lowered it into the water, and then she backed slowly away. Suddenly the fish jerked and slipped from his clutching fingers. He gasped in dismay as it darted away.

But in a flash the girl was after it. She overtook it with dazzling speed, captured it deftly, and with a graceful twist headed downward and disappeared. It all happened in an instant—a blur of movement in the water directly below him, and then he saw only her long, shapely legs receding as she sped away from him.

He waited for a time, and then, when she did not reappear, he released the other fish. It would be humiliating for her, he thought, to be summoned for her food like a trained animal. And if the fish were there, he now had no doubt that she could catch them.

Then, off to one side, he saw the dark form lying motionless in the water. She was watching him. He stretched out on the bank, his face close to the water, and looked at her.

"Beautiful," he murmured.

There was a strange, unearthly loveliness about that water-shrouded face, and in the blurred gracefulness of her slender figure, and in the long, flowing hair. The hair fascinated him. Most of the girls of his acquaintance were wearing their hair in disturbingly short, boyish styles. He considered girls formidable enough when they looked like girls.

He wondered how he appeared to her through the shimmering veil of water. Did he possess an alien ugliness that fascinated her? Suddenly the question became very important. He told himself bitterly that he was only her provider, her meal ticket, and she could not possibly have any interest in him beyond that; but he lingered long that morning, and he was back again after the evening chores, lying on the bank as the sun vanished and the shadow of the scraggly old oak tree that lay quietly on the water sank into invisibility. He stayed on until the dusk deepened and her face was no longer visible.

He remembered a poem he had once seen in an old schoolbook of his mother's when he went through it looking for subjects to draw. It suggested rich colors and strange scenes to him, but he had not understood it. Now he found it again.

Come live with me, and be my love,
And we will some new pleasures prove,
Of golden sands, and crystal brooks,
With silken lines, and silver hooks.

There will the river whispering run
Warm'd by thy eyes, more than the Sun.
And there th'enamour'd fish will stay,
Begging themselves they may betray.

When thou wilt swim in that live bath,
Each fish, which every channel hath,
Will amorously to thee swim,
Gladder to catch thee, than thou him. . . .

He dreamed that night of a sheltered mountain stream, pure, crystal clear, deep, where young lovers could splash and play and love in the tumbling torrent. He awoke in a chill of fright. What would become of her? He could care for her during the summer. With Old Ed's help, he could get plenty of fish. But winter would come, and thick ice would cover the water. Even if she could survive the cold, it would be difficult to get food to her. It might be impossible.

And she might die a lonely death in the cold, stagnating water of the quarry.

The river? He rejected the thought instantly. He knew instinctively that she needed deep water, that she would be helpless and at the mercy of any passerby in the shoals of that small stream. It was thirty miles to the nearest lake, which was small. But in the opposite direction, fifty miles would take him to Lake Michigan. That was where she should be, with the vast, connecting waters of the Great Lakes to conceal and protect her solitary life on this strange planet. But how could he get her there?

He would have to think of something.

He was out before dawn with Old Ed and his net, and they brought in fish by the milk can full. Walt swore him to eternal secrecy and confided that he wanted to try to stock the quarry. Old Ed allowed that he didn't think it would work, that the fish would lack their natural food and the water might be queer for them. But if Walt wanted to try, why, he enjoyed catching fish, and he'd never rightly caught all he wanted to catch because he hated to waste them. Walt saved out enough fish for the Rogers' table and triumphantly dumped the rest into the quarry with the shadowy face watching him silently from the depths.

Walt took advantage of a lull in the dinner-table conversation to say cautiously, "Mother, I'd like one of those aqualung outfits."

Edna Rogers set down the steaming dish of mashed potatoes and stared at him. "Did you ever! What would you do with it?"

"Go in the water," Walt said.

Jim Rogers seemed interested. "Now where around here is there water for a thing like that?"

"There's the river," Walt said evasively, "and the quarry—"

"You couldn't swim long under water in the river without your tail fins sticking out. And the quarry's deep enough, but there's nothing there to see. If there was, you probably couldn't see it in that water. Those lung things are for places where there's lots of water and lots of fish and things to see."

"Mr. Moore has some of that equipment in," Edna Rogers said, giving Walt a worried look. "It wasn't very expensive."

"He just has goggles and the things you wear on your feet," Jim Rogers said. "I told him he'd never sell them. Walt's talking about these outfits where you have a tank of air on your back and you can stay under for hours. No sense in it around here. But if you want the goggles, Walt, go ahead and buy them. You've got your own money, and if you want to waste it—"

"Thanks, Dad."

"Take some more potatoes, Walter," Edna Rogers said. "You're burning up a lot of energy these days. All this fishing and swimming—"

"Does him good," Jim Rogers said.

Walt's mother shook her head. "What about your painting, Walter? You haven't touched it for a week."

Walt said impatiently, "There'll be plenty of time for painting when I can't go fishing or swimming."

"He spends too much time by himself," Edna Rogers said. "Walt, Virginia Harlon asks about you every time I see her, and she felt awfully bad because you wouldn't go to her party when she asked you. She'd teach you to dance, if you'd let her. Then you could go to the Saturday dances."

Jim Rogers chuckled dryly. "He's young. He'll have plenty of time to chase after girls."

"I still think he spends too much time by himself." Edna Rogers shrugged resignedly and changed the subject. "What did Mr. Zengler want?"

Jim Rogers laughed and laid down his fork. "His boy thinks he saw some fish over at the quarry. He tried to catch them and didn't get a nibble, so he wants to dynamite and see what will come up. Zengler wanted to know if I had any objections."

"Dynamite?" Walt blurted. "Dynamite—the quarry?"

"Yeah. I told Zengler there'd never been any fish there and couldn't be any, and if he wanted to waste the dynamite that was all right with me."

"Did you ever!" Edna Rogers said. "Is he going to do it?"

"I don't think so. Zengler's not one to waste anything. What's the matter, Walt?"

"I've finished," Walt said, getting to his feet. "I'm not very hungry."

"You might excuse yourself."

"Excuse me, please," Walt said humbly and fled before they could answer.

The quarry was a blending of dim shadows. In the gathering darkness, the motionless water looked like a smooth extension of the pasture. Walt circled around it and went directly to the shack that served Zengler as office and storehouse. Zengler's four trucks were parked haphazardly nearby, three of them battered hulks and the fourth new, its sleek lines evident even in the dusk.

Walt sat down next to the shack and waited.

He knew Roy Zengler. The kid was a young punk who

did what he pleased, and if his father told him not to use dynamite, he'd be sneaking around the first chance he got to do it. And old man Zengler would think it was a joke, afterward, and laugh it off.

Crickets chirped busily, and a rabbit loped slowly past, hesitated, and scampered away. The ground became insufferably hard, and Walt finally got to his feet and leaned against the shack. He did not know what to do. If Roy didn't come, Walt could see him in the morning and warn him off, but that would make him much more certain to try it.

A light bounced toward him on the quarry road. A bicycle lurched and skidded in the sand, and its rider leaped off and wheeled it forward. He leaned it against the shed and moved toward the door, keys jingling. Walt stepped out and faced him.   "Roy?"

"Oh, it's you, Walt. Jeez, you scared me. Gonna have a little fun—want to join me?"

"Those fish are mine," Walt said. "I put them there. You let them alone."

"Like hell they're yours. Dad leases this place, doesn't he? You got no business—"

Walt swung. His fist spattered against Roy's face and sent him sprawling. Walt was on him in a flash, his hands found the throat and circled it, and he applied pressure. "Try dynamiting those fish," Walt said grimly, "and I'll kill you."

"All right," Roy said weakly.

Walt released him, and Roy got up slowly. "All right," he said again. "I didn't know. Your old man said—you could have been nice about it. Why didn't you tell me?"

"You let them alone."

"All right."

Roy went to his bicycle, wheeled it out to the road, and mounted. "You can't watch this place all the time," he shouted. "I'll be back. You'll see."

Walt fumbled frantically on the ground, found a stone, and threw it.

"Missed!" Roy shouted. "I'll be back! Just you wait!"

He vanished into the darkness, and Walt stood looking after him, white-faced and trembling with rage and fright, knowing he would be back.

"Your mother and I would like to go over to Colevill tomorrow," Jim Rogers said. "She wants to see her sister, and maybe we'll take in a movie. Think you could manage the evening chores all right?"

Walt, lost in thought, said nothing.

"Walt? Did you hear what I said?"

"What? Oh, sure. I can manage. I always have, haven't I?"

Jim Rogers chuckled. "Sure you have. I was just wondering if you were still with us."

"Will you stay overnight?"

"Nope. We won't be back very early, though. Don't wait up for us."

Walt nodded absently, looked up, found his father regarding him with a troubled frown.

"Something bothering you, Walt?"

"No. Why?"

"You've been acting odd. Your mother's worried about you. So—when you went out last night, I followed you. Don't look so guilty," he went on, as Walt started and flushed crimson. "She was afraid you were getting into trouble, the way you've been staying out nights. I reckon maybe she was more afraid you were getting some girl into trouble. Anyway, I don't see much point in sitting over there by the quarry until after midnight, but if you want to do it, I can't see that any harm can come of it. I know you've always enjoyed going off by yourself. It isn't our way, your mother and I, but we try to understand. So I want you to know we're on your side, and if you have something on your mind we'll try to help."

Walt moistened his lips and swallowed. "Thanks, Dad."

"You're sure there isn't something bothering you?"

"No. Nothing."

"Well—you weren't over there to meet someone, were you? A girl, maybe?"

"No!" Walt said defiantly.

"If you have a girl, or when you have one, you don't have to sneak off and meet her. Bring her here, and we'll make her welcome. Otherwise, well, you're young. There are lots of problems in this life, and you'll run smack into them soon enough. There's no point in rushing around trying to tangle with them now. Might as well enjoy yourself. And—are you sure it's all right about the chores?"

"It's all right," Walt said.

Later, when his parents were safely out of hearing, Walt risked a telephone call. Carl Reynolds, a friend Walt's age, accepted his request as a matter of course. "Sure," he said. "Sure—I'll do chores for you Saturday night. I owe you one, you know. I'll have to clear it with the old man, though."

"Carl," Walt said tremulously, "tell him you're going to help me. Don't tell him I won't be here."

There was a moment of silence, and then Carl laughed. "Sure. I'll tell him that. And I wish you luck, old fellow. Do I know her?"

"No," Walt said. "You don't know her."

Late Saturday afternoon, Walt walked slowly over to the deserted quarry. Somewhere in the depths she was—doing what? He knew that he had only to splash, and she would come. But instead he sat down under the oak tree and thoughtfully studied the quiet, dark water. He had come to realize that his was a hopeless love, that there was no middle ground where a creature of the air and one of the water could meet. He had gone swimming in the quarry twice since he had found her. The first time she had fled in seeming panic, and when she did return she kept her distance cautiously.,

He wanted only to touch her, to caress the beautiful, flowing hair. She eluded him easily, and then, when she found how awkward his movements were, she circled around him with dazzling speed. He dove to the depths with her, but in the dim, uncertain light it was only a nimble shadow that cavorted about him. His second effort had been as frustrating as the first, and he had not tried again.

True love, he told himself, must be selfless. The happiness of the loved one was the important thing. He had spent hours trying to think of some place, some way for her to live in comfort and safety, where he could still visit her from time to time, even if only to see her through the blurring water. There was no such place, He would have to get her to Lake Michigan, and once those vast waters closed over her he must accept the fact that he could never see her again.

He glanced at his watch and walked toward Zengler's shack. "Has to be timed just right," he reminded himself. A single blow with a rock snapped open the flimsy padlock. There weren't—never had been—any thieves around Harwell, and that lock had served Zengler for years.

Walt lifted the rings of keys from a nail inside the door and ran an appreciative eye over Zengler's new truck. Gas? He could siphon some out of the other trucks if there wasn't enough. Anything else? A bucket. He found two in the corner and set them aside.

Looking up at the truck's high tailgate, he started apprehensively. How would she get in?

In the shack were tools and nails. Scattered about were lengths and scraps of lumber. Walt nailed frantically, fearful that now he might be too late. He should have thought of it sooner. He could have made something easier for her than this rough ramp with strips nailed across it. But this would have to do. He carried the ramp, and the buckets, down to the water, to the spot he had picked out, and then he ran back to the truck.

He drove slowly at first, getting the feel of the truck, timidly testing its deep-throated power. Dusk was settling on the town when he reached Harwell. Nearly everyone would be uptown, but he took no chances. He followed a circuitous route toward the business section, using alleys as much as he could, driving without lights, crossing side streets cautiously.

He kept glancing at his watch. Mr. Warren always closed up promptly at nine, Saturday night or no Saturday night. He couldn't be late, but he didn't dare be too early.

He turned into the alley paralleling Main Street and carefully backed into position. "A. J. Warren and Sons, Farm Implements," the weathered sign over the rear door said. Walt glanced at his watch again, went to the door, and looked in. There were several farmers up front, casually inspecting a new tractor. One of the Warren boys was sweeping up. Walt dropped back into the shadows and waited nervously.

The farmers left one by one. Not until Mr. Warren followed the last one to the door, and locked it, did Walt step forward. Mr. Warren turned and saw him.

"Evening, Walt," he said. "Just closing. Can I do something for you?"

Walt fought to make his voice sound normal. "Dad's decided to take that big stock tank you were talking to him about."

Mr. Warren beamed. "Glad to hear it. What changed his mind?"

"Ours sprung another leak."

"I told him it wouldn't last much longer. I'll send the new one out Monday morning. That be all right?"

"I'll take it now, if you don't mind," Walt said. "I borrowed a truck. It's out back."

"Why, sure. Tank's out in the shed."

"I know," Walt said. "And—Mr. Warren—"

"Yes?"

"Dad will be in Monday to see you about—about—"

"Sure thing, Walt. Your pa's credit is good as gold. Come on, and we'll get it in the truck."

It was easy—so easy that Walt giggled hilariously when he got the truck out of Harwell and pointed toward the quarry. Then he soberly reminded himself that this was only the beginning, and he stopped laughing.

At the quarry he drove down to the water, set his brakes, and got Zengler's pump going. The ancient gasoline engine made a racket that should have been heard for miles, and Walt felt panicky as he directed the stream of water into the tank. Across the fields he could see the lights in the barn, where Carl Reynolds would be finishing the milking. It was taking him longer than Walt had expected. Supposing he heard the pump when he took the cows to the pasture, and came to investigate?

It couldn't be helped. It would take forever to fill the tank by hand.

When the water reached the brim, he cut off the motor

and slowly backed the truck into position where he had left the ramp and the buckets. It took him some jockeying to place the truck so that the ramp just reached the edge of the water, and he had to be careful about it. A false move, and Zengler might never find out what had happened to his truck.

He set the brakes. He stopped the tailgate and wedged the ramp into position. Then he leaned over and splashed the water.

She did not come.

"The pump must have frightened her," he muttered.

He splashed again and again.

Suddenly he saw her, a dark shadow in the darker water. He waited for her to edge closer, and then he mounted the ramp. Looking down at the water, alarm gripped him. How could he make her understand what he wanted? He could scarcely see her, and he could only hope that she could see him better. But even if she could, if she understood what he wanted, would she trust him?

He gestured. He moved up and down the ramp. He splashed the water in the tank. And all the while her shadowy form hung motionless in the water below him.

"Oh, God," he pleaded, "make her understand!"

It was getting late. He had to drive fifty miles, and drive fifty miles back, and leave Zengler's truck and get home before his parents got there. And somehow he'd have to explain about the tank.

The darkness deepened, and the moon had not yet appeared. Lights went off in the barn as Carl finished up and headed for home. He could hear the cattle on the other side of the pasture. He stumbled frantically up and down the ramp. There must be some way—

He leaped down and ran for Zengler's shed. Maybe a rope—

He stopped before he got there and turned back. How could a rope help? He couldn't drag her out of the water. Was she afraid of the air? But she'd gotten from the place the ship came down over to the water. He turned back toward the truck, turned again. A light—perhaps if he could light the tank she could see what he wanted her to do. Even a match might help. He fumbled wildly about the shed, knocking things down and finding nothing.

A new fear splashed over him coldly. Perhaps there were others there. Perhaps she woudn't want to leave by herself. Suppose there were dozens of them?

He started to run back to the truck, and the sound of—something—brought him to a halt. Something, followed by a splash. He ran again.

A wet trail led up the ramp and into the truck. The truck was flooded with the tank's overflow. "She did it!" he gasped. He leaped up the ramp and looked into the tank. She was there, the closest he had ever seen her, a dark form somehow shimmering and dimly luminescent. He threw the ramp and the buckets into the truck and put up the tailgate. With a wild song of joy throbbing in his throat, he started the motor and got the truck into gear.

He took a route that would carry him around Harwell on back roads. He had studied maps—how he had studied them!—and he wanted to keep to lightly traveled roads most of the way. But he would have to hurry. He had no idea how long the girl could live in that tank without having the water changed.

He had been under way only a few minutes when, topping a hill, his lights picked out a car parked by the roadside. He recognized the long lines of Zengler's new Cadillac, the only one in the township. He caught a glimpse of a pair of heads close together in the front seat and guessed that it would be Roy Zengler, out with some girl too young to know better.

His foot dug hard at the accelerator. As the truck picked up speed he glanced at the side-view mirror. He saw the light flash on in the Cadillac as Roy flung open the door and leaped out. As long as Walt could see him he was standing in the road, staring after the disappearing truck.

Walt thought with reckless abandon, "He'll tell. They'll go to the quarry, just to make sure, and they'll find the truck gone. They'll think some kids took it for a joy ride, and they'll be looking for them around Harwell, so they'll probably catch me on the way back." He felt a twinge of uneasiness, but he told himself boldly that what happened didn't matter—on the way back. The truck roared on smoothly, powerfully.

He was only ten miles from the lake when he had to risk a stretch of main highway. He was worrying about the girl and trying to decide whether to look for fresh water for her or try to get to the lake as quickly as possible. He kept going because that was easiest, but he continued to worry.

Traffic on the highway was light, and Walt was so engrossed in his concern for the girl that he did not notice the car approaching him from the rear. He did not notice it until it pulled alongside and the red light flashed, and he realized that a state trooper was ordering him to stop. His numbed hands and feet obediently made the proper motions. The truck eased off the road and halted. The police car stopped behind him. Then, as the trooper got out and walked forward, he stepped on the accelerator.

For precious seconds the trooper seemed bewildered. He stood outlined in the lights of his car, waving his hands. Then, as Walt glanced again at the mirror, one hand spouted fire. Walt thought wildly, "The tires—if he hits a tire—"

Glass tinkled behind him as the rear window shattered, and the bullet thudded into the roof of the cab. The fire flashed again, and then the truck nosed over a rise and was safe. Walt drove with the accelerator crushed to the floor, peering anxiously beyond the racing beams of his headlights. A dirt road veered off at a sharp angle to the right, and he made the turn with screaming brakes. He found himself on a winding country road. Around a curve and out of sight of the highway, he switched off his lights. A farmhouse beckoned, and he slowed and skidded into the driveway, rolled as far as the barn, and turned sharply to come to a stop between the barn and a corn crib. Seconds later the police car roared past and disappeared.

A yard light came on. A man opened the farmhouse door and stood looking out at him. Walt backed up, turned, and drove back to the highway. He followed the highway for a short distance, took the first turn to the left, and breathed freely once more as the truck bounced along a rough dirt road. At the next crossroad he turned right and headed for the lake.

In the moon's half light the gently tossing water was beautiful. Walt drove past an unoccupied summer cottage, turned at the edge of the beach, and backed toward the water. A few yards short of his goal, his wheels spun in the loose sand and dug themselves in.

Walt leaped out and dropped the tailgate. Water soaked his knees as he hauled himself up. He placed the ramp in position, and then, as he turned, a stream of water brushed his foot. He knelt, fumbled in the darkness, and found the holes. The trooper's last shots had struck the tank.

And the tank was two-thirds empty.

With a moan he seized the buckets and ran for the lake. For the moment he had no thought that the shots might have struck the girl. He thought only of life-giving water. He splashed into the lake, dipped the buckets, and raced back to the truck. Again and again he made the trip, until his breath came in tormented jerks and his aching legs could carry him no faster than a plodding walk. Still he worked on, dumping water into the tank and seeing it gush forth through the holes.

He lost all sense of time. The water level in the tank was rising slowly—too slowly, he feared—and when finally it occurred to him that she might be wounded or dead, he could not bring himself to look and see. Like an automaton, he continued to carry water.

Then, turning once more with full buckets, he saw her. She stumbled down the ramp and staggered toward him—toward the lake. She moved awkwardly, her feet churning in the sand, and as he hurried to meet her she fell at his feet with weird, whistling gasps.

He bent over to help her and fell back with a cry of horror.

Her face was a gruesome, rubbery mask, her eyes large and sunken. She had no nose. Needlelike fangs protruded from her gaping, gasping mouth. Her hair, her lovely, flowing hair, was short tufts of fur that covered her back from the crown of her head to the base of her spine. The glimmering dark green fabric that she wore was her flesh, spongy and slimy to the touch.

As he stared helplessly, she lurched to her feet,

staggered forward, and sprawled at the water's edge with her head submerged. A moment later her webbed feet kicked and tore at the sand, and she slid into the water and disappeared.

Stunned to paralysis, Walt looked after her, unable to move, or think, or do anything but stare bewilderedly at the ruffled sand and the lapping waves. He did not hear the car drive up and stop. He did not notice the lights that pinioned him against the watery horizon. He heard nothing at all until the trooper approached with a sharp command. Then he turned slowly and raised his hands.

The trooper moved forward cautiously, shined a light into his face, and exclaimed, "Why, you're only a kid!"

Walt said nothing.

The trooper searched him deftly, stepped back, and signaled him to drop his hands. "That wasn't very smart. What were you trying to do?"

Walt shook his head. The enormity of what he had done horrified him. The truck, stolen and damaged. The tank, which his father would have to pay for. Running away from the police. And now he'd have to face his parents. What could he tell them? What could he tell anyone?

A few yards out from shore, something broke water with an echoing splash—something big. The trooper whirled. "Good God! What was that?"

Walt shrugged wearily. "Only a fish," he said.

ALL THE WAY BACK

by Michael Shaara

"Great were the Antha, so reads the One Book of history, greater perhaps than any of the Galactic Peoples, and they were brilliant and fair, and their reign was long, and in all things they were great and proud, even in the manner of their dying—"
Preface to Loab: History of The Master Race.

The huge red ball of a sun hung glowing upon the screen.

Jansen adjusted the traversing knob, his face tensed and weary. The sun swung off the screen to the right, was replaced by the live black of space and the million speckled lights of the farther stars. A moment later the sun glided silently back across the screen and went off at the left. Again there was nothing but space and the stars.

"Try it again?" Cohn asked.

Jansen mumbled: "No. No use," and he swore heavily. "Nothing. Always nothing. Never a blessed thing."

Cohn repressed a sigh, began to adjust the controls.

In both of their minds was the single, bitter thought that there would be only one more time, and then they would go home. And it was a long way to come to go home with nothing.

When the controls were set there was nothing left to do. The two men walked slowly aft to the freeze room. Climbing up painfully on to the flat steel of the beds, they lay back and waited for the mechanism to function, for the freeze to begin.

Turned in her course, the spaceship bore off into the open emptiness. Her ports were thrown open, she was gathering speed as she moved away from the huge red star.

The object was sighted upon the last leg of the patrol, as the huge ship of the Galactic Scouts came across the edge of the Great Desert of the Rim, swinging wide in a long slow curve. It was there on the massometer as a faint *blip*, and, of course, the word went directly to Roymer.

"Report," he said briefly, and Lieutenant Goladan—a young and somewhat pompous Higiandrian—gave the Higiandrian equivalent of a cough and then reported.

"Observe," said Lieutenant Goladan, "that it is not a meteor, for the speed of it is much too great."

Roymer nodded patiently.

"And again, the speed is decreasing"—Goladan consulted his figures—"at the rate of twenty-four dines per segment. Since the orbit appears to bear directly upon the star Mina, and the decrease in speed is of a certain arbitrary origin, we must conclude that the object is a spaceship."

Roymer smiled.

"Very good, lieutenant." Like a tiny nova, Goladan began to glow and expand.

A good man, thought Roymer tolerantly, his is a race of good men. They have been two million years in achieving space flight; a certain adolescence is to be expected.

"Would you call Mind-Search, please?" Roymer asked.

Goladan sped away, to return almost immediately with the heavy-headed non-human Trian, chief of the Mind-Search Section.

Trian cocked an eyelike thing at Roymer, with grave inquiry.

"Yes, commander?"

The abrupt change in course was noticeable only on the viewplate, as the stars slid silently by. The patrol vessel veered off, swinging around and into the desert, settled into a parallel course with the strange new craft, keeping a discreet distance of—approximately—a light-year.

The scanners brought the object into immediate focus, and Goladan grinned with pleasure. A spaceship, yes, Alien, too. Undoubtedly a primitive race. He voiced these thoughts to Roymer.

"Yes," the commander said, staring at the strange,

small, projectilelike craft. "Primitive type. It is to be wondered what they are doing in the desert."

Goladan assumed an expression of intense curiosity.

"Trian," said Roymer pleasantly, "would you contact?"

The huge head bobbed up and down once and then stared into the screen. There was a moment of profound silence. Then Trian turned back to stare at Roymer, and there was a distinctly human expression of surprise in his eyelike things.

"Nothing," came the thought. "I can detect no presence at all."

Roymer raised an eyebrow.

"Is there a barrier?"

"No"—Trian had turned to gaze back into the screen—"a barrier I could detect. But there is nothing at all. There is no sentient activity on board that vessel."

Trian's word had to be taken, of course, and Roymer was disappointed. A spaceship empty of life—Roymer shrugged. A derelict, then. But why the decreasing speed? Pre-set controls would account for that, of course, but why? Certainly, if one abandoned a ship, one would not arrange for it to—

He was interrupted by Trian's thought:

"Excuse me, but there is nothing. May I return to my quarters?"

Roymer nodded and thanked him, and Trian went ponderously away. Goladan said:

"Shall we prepare to board it, sir?"

"Yes."

And then Goladan was gone to give his proud orders.

Roymer continued to stare at the primitive vessel which hung on the plate. Curious. It was very interesting, always, to come upon derelict ships. The stories that were old, the silent tombs that had been drifting perhaps, for millions of years in the deep sea of space. In the beginning Roymer had hoped that the ship would be manned, and alien, but—nowadays, contact with an isolated race was rare, extremely rare. It was not to be hoped for, and he would be content with this, this undoubtedly empty, ancient ship.

And then, to Roymer's complete surprise, the ship at which he was staring shifted abuptly, turned on its axis, and flashed off like a live thing upon a new course.

When the defrosters activated and woke him up, Jansen lay for a while upon the steel table, blinking. As always with the freeze, it was difficult to tell at first whether anything had actually happened. It was like a quick blink and no more, and then you were lying, feeling exactly the same, thinking the same thoughts even, and if there was anything at all different it was maybe that you were a little numb. And yet in the blink time took a great leap, and the months went by like—Jansen smiled—like fenceposts.

He raised a languid eye to the red bulb in the ceiling. Out. He sighed. The freeze had come and gone. He felt vaguely cheated, reflected that this time, before the freeze, he would take a little nap.

He climbed down from the table, noted that Cohn had already gone to the control room. He adjusted himself to the thought that they were approaching a new sun, and it came back to him suddenly that this would be the last one, now they would go home.

Well then, let this one have planets. To have come all this way, to have been gone from home for eleven years, and yet to find nothing—

He was jerked out of the old feeling of despair by a lurch of the ship. That would be Cohn taking her off the auto. And now, he thought, we will go in and run out the telescope and have a look, and there won't be a thing.

Wearily, he clumped off over the iron deck, going up to the control room. He had no hope left now, and he had been so hopeful at the beginning. As they are all hopeful, he thought, as they have been hoping now for three hundred years. And they will go on hoping, for a little while, and then men will become hard to get, even with the freeze, and then the starships won't go out any more. And Man will be doomed to the System for the rest of his days.

Therefore, he asked humbly, silently, let this one have planets.

Up in the dome of the control cabin, Cohn was bent

over the panel, pouring power into the board. He looked up, nodded briefly as Jansen came in. It seemed to both of them that they had been apart for five minutes.

"Are they all hot yet?" asked Jansen.

"No, not yet."

The ship had been in deep space with her ports thrown open. Absolute cold had come in and gone to the core of her, and it was always a while before the ship was reclaimed and her instruments warmed. Even now there was a sharp chill in the air of the cabin.

Jansen sat down idly, rubbing his arms.

"Last time around, I guess."

"Yes," said Cohn, and added laconically, "I wish Weizsäcker was here."

Jansen grinned. Weizsäcker, poor old Weizsäcker. He was long dead and it was a good thing, for he was the most maligned human being in the System.

For a hundred years his theory on the birth of planets, that every sun necessarily gave birth to a satellite family, had been an accepted part of the knowledge of Man. And then, of course, there had come space flight.

Jansen chuckled wryly. Lucky man, Weizsäcker. Now, two hundred years and a thousand stars later, there had been discovered just four planets. Alpha Centauri had one: a barren, ice-crusted mote no larger than the Moon; and Pollux had three, all dead lumps of cold rock and iron. None of the other stars had any at all. Yes, it would have been a great blow to Weizsäcker.

A hum of current broke into Jansen's thought as the telescope was run out. There was a sudden beginning of light upon the screen.

In spite of himself and the wry, hopeless feeling that had been in him, Jansen arose quickly, with a thin trickle of nervousness in his arms. There is always a chance, he thought, after all, there is always a chance. We have only been to a thousand suns, and in the Galaxy a thousand suns are not anything at all. So there is always a chance.

Cohn, calm and methodical, was manning the radar.

Gradually, condensing upon the center of the screen, the image of the star took shape. It hung at last, huge and yellow and flaming with an awful brilliance, and the prominences of the rim made the vast circle uneven. Because the ship was close and the filter was in, the stars of the background were invisble, and there was nothing but the one great sun.

Jansen began to adjust for observation.

The observation was brief.

They paused for a moment before beginning the tests, gazing upon the face of the alien sun. The first of their race to be here and to see, they were caught up for a time in the ancient, deep thrill of space and the unknown Universe.

They watched, and into the field of their vision, breaking in slowly upon the glaring edge of the sun's disk, there came a small black ball. It moved steadily away from the edge, in toward the center of the sun. It was unquestionably a planet in transit.

When the alien ship moved, Roymer was considerably rattled.

One does not question Mind-Search, he knew, and so there could not be any living thing aboard that ship. Therefore, the ship's movement could be regarded only as a peculiar aberration in the still-functioning drive. Certainly, he thought, and peace returned to his mind.

But it did pose an uncomfortable problem. Boarding that ship would be no easy matter, not if the thing was inclined to go hopping away like that, with no warning. There were two hundred years of conditioning in Roymer, it would be impossible for him to put either his ship or his crew into an unnecessarily dangerous position. And wavery, erratic spaceships could undoubtedly be classified as dangerous.

Therefore, the ship would have to be disabled.

Regretfully, he connected with Fire Control, put the operation into the hands of the Firecon officer and settled back to observe the results of the actions against the strange craft.

And the alien moved again.

Not suddenly, as before, but deliberately now, the thing turned once more from its course, and its speed decreased even more rapidly. It was still moving in upon

Mina, but now its orbit was tangential and no longer direct. As Roymer watched the ship come about, he turned up the magnification for a larger view, checked the automatic readings on the board below the screen. And his eyes were suddenly directed to a small, conical projection which had begun to rise up out of the ship, which rose for a short distance and stopped, pointed in on the orbit towards Mina at the center.

Roymer was bewildered, but he acted immediately. Firecon was halted, all protective screens were re-established, and the patrol ship back-tracked quickly into the protection of deep space.

There was no question in Roymer's mind that the movements of the alien had been directed by a living intelligence, and not by any mechanical means. There was also no doubt in Roymer's mind that there was no living being on board that ship. The problem was acute.

Roymer felt the scalp of his hairless head beginning to crawl. In the history of the galaxy, there had been dis-covered but five nonhuman races, yet never a race which did not betray its existence by the telepathic nature of its thinking. Roymer could not conceive of a people so alien that even the fundamental structure of their thought process was entirely different from the Galactics.

Extra-Galactics? He observed the ship closely and shook his head. No. Not an extra-Galactic ship certainly, much too primitive a type.

Extraspatial? His scalp crawled again.

Completely at a loss as to what to do, Roymer again contacted Mind-Search and requested that Trian be sent to him immediately.

Trian was preceded by a puzzled Goladan. The orders to alien contact, then to Firecon, and finally for a quick retreat, had affected the lieutenant deeply. He was a man accustomed to a strictly logical and somewhat ponderous course of events. He waited expectantly for some expla-nation to come from his usually serene commander.

Roymer, however, was busily occupied in tracking the alien's new course. An orbit about Mina, Roymer observed, with that conical projection laid on the star; a device of war; or some measuring instrument?

The stolid Trian appeared—walking would not quite describe how—and was requested to make another attempt at contact with the alien. He replied with his usual eerie silence and in a moment, when he turned back to Roymer, there was surprise in the transmitted thought.

"I cannot understand. There is life there now."

Roymer was relieved, but Goladan was blinking.

Trian went on, turning again to gaze at the screen.

"It is very remarkable. There are two life-beings. Human-type race. Their presence is very clear, they are"—he paused briefly—"explorers, it appears. But they were not there before. It is extremely unnerving."

So it is, Roymer agreed. He asked quickly: "Are they aware of us?"

"No. They are directing their attention on the star. Shall I contact?"

"No. Not yet. We will observe them first."

The alien ship floated upon the screen before them, moving in slow orbit about the star Mina.

Seven. There were seven of them. Seven planets, and three at least had atmospheres, and two might even be inhabitable. Jansen was so excited he was hopping around the control room. Cohn did nothing, but grin widely with a wondrous joy, and the two of them repeatedly shook hands and gloated.

"Seven!" roared Jansen. "Old lucky seven!"

Quickly then, and with extreme nervousness, they ran spectograph analyses of each of those seven fascinating worlds. They began with the central planets, in the favorable temperature belt where life conditions would be most likely to exist, and they worked outwards.

For reasons which were as much sentimental as they were practical, they started with the third planet of this fruitful sun. There was a thin atmosphere, fainter even than that of Mars, and no oxygen. Silently they went on to the fourth. It was cold and heavy, perhaps twice as large as Earth, had a thick envelope of noxious gases. They saw with growing fear that there was no hope there, and they turned quickly inwards toward the warmer area nearer the sun.

On the second planet—as Jansen put it—they hit the jackpot.

A warm, green world it was, of an Earthlike size and atmosphere; oxygen and water vapor lines showed strong and clear in the analysis.

"This looks like it," said Jansen, grinning again.

Cohn nodded, left the screen and went over to man the navigating instruments.

"Let's go down and take a look."

"Radio check first." It was the proper procedure. Jansen had gone over it in his mind a thousand times. He clicked on the receiver, waited for the tubes to function, and then scanned for contact. As they moved in toward the new planet he listened intently, trying all the lengths, waiting for any sound at all. There was nothing but the rasping static of open space.

"Well," he said finally, as the green planet grew large upon the screen, "if there's any race there, it doesn't have radio."

"Could be a young civilization."

"Or one so ancient and advanced that it doesn't *need* radio."

Jansen refused to let his deep joy be dampened. It was impossible to know what would be there. Now it was just as it had been three hundred years ago, when the first Earth ship was approaching Mars. And it will be like this—Jansen thought—in every other system to which we go. How can you picture what there will be? There is nothing at all in your past to give you a clue. You can only hope.

The planet was a beautiful green ball on the screen.

The thought which came out of Trian's mind was tinged with relief.

"I see how it was done. They have achieved a complete statis, a perfect state of suspended animation which they produce by an ingenious usage of the absolute zero of outer space. Thus, when they are—frozen, is the way they regard it—their minds do not function, and their lives are not detectable. They have just recently revived and are directing their ship."

Roymer digested the new information slowly. What kind of a race was this? A race which flew in primitive star ships, yet it had already conquered one of the greatest problems in Galactic history, a problem which had baffled the Galactics for millions of years. Roymer was uneasy.

"A very ingenious device," Trian was thinking, "they use it to alter the amount of subjective time consumed in their explorations. Their star ship has a very low maximum speed. Hence, without this—freeze—their voyage would take up a good portion of their lives."

"Can you classify the mind-type?" Roymer asked with growing concern.

Trian reflected silently for a moment.

"Yes," he said, "although the type is extremely unusual. I have never observed it before. General classification would be Human-Four. More specifically, I would place them at the Ninth level."

Roymer started. "The Ninth level?"

"Yes. As I say, they are extremely unusual."

Roymer was now clearly worried. He turned away and paced the deck for several moments. Abruptly, he left the room and went to the files of alien classification. He was gone for a long time, while Goladan fidgeted and Trian continued to gather information plucked across space from the alien minds. Roymer came back at last.

"What are they doing?"

"They are moving in on the second planet. They are about to determine whether the conditions are suitable there for an establishment of a colony of their kind."

Gravely, Roymer gave his orders to navigation. The patrol ship swung into motion, sped off swiftly in the direction of the second planet.

There was a single, huge blue ocean which covered an entire hemisphere of the new world. And the rest of the surface was a young jungle, wet and green and empty of any kind of people, choked with queer growths of green and orange. They circled the globe at a height of several thousand feet, and to their amazement and joy, they never saw a living thing; not a bird or a rabbit or the alien equivalent, in fact nothing alive at all. And so they stared in happy fascination.

"This is it," Jansen said again, his voice uneven.

"What do you think we ought to call it?" Cohn was speaking absently. "New Earth? Utopia?"

Together they watched the broken terrain slide by beneath them.

"No people at all. It's ours." And after a while Jansen said: "New Earth. That's a good name."

Cohn was observing the features of the ground intently.

"Do you notice the kind of . . . circular appearance of most of those mountain ranges? Like on the Moon, but grown over and eroded. They're all almost perfect circles.'

Pulling his mind away from the tremendous visions he had of the colony which would be here, Jansen tried to look at the mountains with an objective eye. Yes, he realized with faint surprise, they were round, like Moon craters.

"Peculiar," Cohn muttered. "Not natural, I don't think. Couldn't be. Meteors not likely in this atmosphere. What in—?"

Jansen jumped. "Look there," he cried suddenly, "a round lake!"

Off toward the northern pole of the planet, a lake which was a perfect circle came slowly into view. There was no break in the rim other than that of a small stream which flowed in from the north.

"That's not natural," Cohn said briefly, "someone built that."

They were moving on to the dark side now, and Cohn turned the ship around. The sense of exhilaration was too new for them to be let down, but the strange sight of a huge number of perfect circles, existing haphazardly like the remains of great splashes on the surface of the planet, was unnerving.

It was the sight of one particular crater, a great barren hole in the midst of a wide red desert, which rang a bell in Jansen's memory, and he blurted:

"A war! There was a war here. That one there looks just like a fusion bomb crater."

Cohn stared, then raised his eyebrows.

"I'll bet you're right."

"A bomb crater, do you see? Pushes up hills on all sides in a circle, and kills—" A sudden, terrible thought hit Jansen. Radioactivity. Would there be radioactivity here?

While Cohn brought the ship in low over the desert, he tried to calm Jansen's fears.

"There couldn't be much. Too much plant life. Jungles all over the place. Take it easy, man."

"But there's not a living thing on the planet. I'll bet that's why there was a war. It got out of hand, the radioactivity got everything. We might have done this to Earth!"

They glided in over the flat emptiness of the desert, and the counters began to click madly.

"That's it," Jansen said conclusively, "still radioactive. It might not have been too long ago."

"Could have been a million years, for all we know."

"Well, most places are safe, apparently. We'll check before we go down."

As he pulled the ship up and away, Cohn whistled.

"Do you suppose there's really not a living thing? I mean, not a bug or a germ or even a virus? Why, it's like a clean new world, a nursery!" He could not take his eyes from the screen.

They were going down now. In a very little while they would be out and walking in the sun. The lust of the feeling was indescribable. They were Earthmen freed forever from the choked home of the System, Earthmen gone out to the stars, landing now upon the next world of their empire.

Cohn could not control himself.

"Do we need a flag?" he said grinning. "How do we claim this place?"

"Just set her down, man," Jansen roared.

Cohn began to chuckle.

"Oh, brave new world," he laughed, "that has *no* people in it."

"But why do we have to contact them?" Goladan asked impatiently. "Could we not just—"

Roymer interrupted without looking at him.

"The law requires that contact be made and the situation explained before action is taken. Otherwise it would be a barbarous act."

Goladan brooded.

The patrol ship hung in the shadow of the dark side, tracing the alien by its radioactive trail. The alien was going down for a landing on the daylight side.

Trian came forward with the other members of the Alien Contact Crew, reported to Roymer, "The aliens have landed."

"Yes," said Roymer, "we will let them have a little time. Trian, do you think you will have any difficulty in the transmission?"

"No. Conversation will not be difficult. Although the confused and complex nature of their thought-patterns does make their inner reactions somewhat obscure. But I do not think there will be any problem."

"Very well. You will remain here and relay the messages."

"Yes."

The patrol ship flashed quickly up over the north pole, then swung inward toward the equator, circling the spot where the alien had gone down. Roymer brought his ship in low and with the silence characteristic of a Galactic, landed her in a wooded spot a mile east of the alien. The Galactics remained in their ship for a short while as Trian continued his probe for information. When at last the Alien Contact Crew stepped out, Roymer and Goladan were in the lead. The rest of the crew faded quietly into the jungle.

As he walked through the young orange brush, Roymer regarded the world around him. Almost ready for repopulation, he thought, in another hundred years the radiation will all be gone, and we will come back. One by one the worlds of that war will be reclaimed.

He felt Trian's directions pop into his mind.

"You are approaching them. Proceed with caution. They are just beyond the next small rise. I think you had better wait, since they are remaining close to their ship."

Roymer sent back a silent yes. Motioning Goladan to

be quiet, Roymer led the way up the last rise. In the jungle around him the Galactic crew moved silently.

The air was perfect; there was no radiation. Except for the wild orange color of the vegetation, the spot was a Garden of Eden. Jansen felt instinctively that there was no danger here, no terrible blight or virus or any harmful thing. He felt a violent urge to get out of his spacesuit and run and breathe, but it was forbidden. Not on the first trip. That would come later, after all the tests and experiments had been made and the world pronounced safe.

One of the first things Jansen did was get out the recorder and solemnly claim this world for the Solar Federation, recording the historic words for the archives of Earth. And he and Cohn remained for a while by the air lock of their ship, gazing around at the strange yet familiar world into which they had come.

"Later on we'll search for ruins," Cohn said. 'Keep an eye out for anything that moves. It's possible that there are some of them left and who knows what they'll look like. Mutants, probably, with five heads. So keep an eye open."

"Right."

Jansen began collecting samples of the ground, of the air, of the nearer foliage. The dirt was Earth-dirt, there was no difference. He reached down and crumbled the soft moist sod with his fingers. The flowers may be a little peculiar—probably mutated, he thought—but the dirt is honest to goodness dirt, and I'll bet the air is Earth-air.

He rose and stared into the clear open blue of the sky, feeling again an almost overpowering urge to throw open his helmet and breathe, and as he stared at the sky and at the green and orange hills, suddenly, a short distance from where he stood, a little old man came walking over the hill.

They stood facing each other across the silent space of a foreign glade. Roymer's face was old and smiling; Jansen looked back at him with absolute astonishment.

After a short pause, Roymer began to walk out onto

the open soil, with Goladan following, and Jansen went
for his heat gun.

"Cohn!" he yelled, in a raw brittle voice, "Cohn!"

And as Cohn turned and saw and froze, Jansen heard
words being spoken in his brain. They were words coming
from the little old man.

"Please do not shoot," the old man said, his lips
unmoving.

"No, don't shoot," Cohn said quickly. "Wait. Let him
alone." The hand of Cohn, too, was at his heat gun.

Roymer smiled. To the two Earth-men his face was
incredibly old and wise and gentle. He was thinking: had
I been a nonhuman they would have killed me.

He sent a thought back to Trian. The Mind-Searcher
picked it up and relayed it into the brains of the Earthmen, sending it through their cortical centers and then up
into their conscious minds, so that the words were heard
in the language of Earth. "Thank you," Roymer said
gently. Jansen's hand held the heat gun leveled on
Roymer's chest. He stared, not knowing what to say.

"Please remain where you are," Cohn's voice was hard
and steady.

Roymer halted obligingly. Goladan stopped at his
elbow, peering at the Earthmen with mingled fear and
curiosity. The sight of fear helped Jansen very much.

"Who are you?" Cohn said clearly, separating the
words.

Roymer folded his hands comfortably across his chest,
he was still smiling.

"With your leave, I will explain our presence."

Cohn just stared.

"There will be a great deal to explain. May we sit down
and talk?"

Trian helped with the suggestion. They sat down.

The sun of the new world was setting, and the conference went on. Roymer was doing most of the talking. The
Earthmen sat transfixed.

It was like growing up suddenly, in the space of a
second.

The history of Earth and of all Mankind just faded and
dropped away. They heard of great races and worlds

beyond number, the illimitable government which was the Galactic Federation. The fiction, the legends, the dreams of a thousand years had come true in a moment, in the figure of a square little old man who was not from Earth. There was a great deal for them to learn and accept in the time of a single afternoon, on an alien planet.

But it was just as new and real to them that they had discovered an uninhabited, fertile planet, the first to be found by Man. And they could not help but revolt from the sudden realization that the planet might well be someone else's property—that the Galactics owned everything worth owning.

It was an intolerable thought.

"How far," asked Cohn, as his heart pushed up in his throat, "does the Galactic League extend?"

Roymer's voice was calm and direct in their minds.

"Only throughout the central regions of the galaxy. There are millions of stars along the rim which have not yet been explored."

Cohn relaxed, bowed down with relief. There was room then, for Earthmen.

"This planet. Is it part of the Federation?"

"Yes," said Roymer, and Cohn tried to mask his thought. Cohn was angry, and he hoped that the alien could not read his mind as well as he could talk to it. To have come this far—

"There was a race here once," Roymer was saying, "a humanoid race which was almost totally destroyed by war. This planet has been uninhabitable for a very long time. A few of its people who were in space at the time of the last attack were spared. The Federation established them elsewhere. When the planet is ready, the descendants of those survivors will be brought back. It is their home."

Neither of the Earthmen spoke.

"It is surprising," Roymer went on, "that your home world is in the desert. We had thought that there were no habitable worlds—"

"The desert?"

"Yes. The region of the galaxy from which you have come is that which we call the desert. It is an area almost entirely devoid of planets. Would you mind telling me which star is your home?"

Cohn stiffened.

"I'm afraid our government would not permit us to disclose any information concerning our race."

"As you wish. I am sorry you are disturbed. I was curious to know—" He waved a negligent hand to show that the information was unimportant. We will get it later, he thought, when we decipher their charts. He was coming to the end of the conference, he was about to say what he had come to say.

"No doubt you have been exploring the stars about your world?"

The Earthmen both nodded. But for the question concerning Sol, they long ago would have lost all fear of this placid old man and his wide-eyed, silent companion.

"Perhaps you would like to know," said Roymer, "why your area is a desert."

Instantly, both Jansen and Cohn were completely absorbed. This was it, the end of three hundred years of searching. They would go home with the answer.

Roymer never relaxed.

"Not too long ago," he said, "approximately thirty thousand years by your reckoning, a great race ruled the desert, a race which was known as the Antha, and it was not a desert then. The Antha ruled hundreds of worlds. They were perhaps the greatest of all the Galactic peoples; certainly they were as brilliant a race as the galaxy has ever known.

"But they were not a good race. For hundreds of years, while they were still young, we tried to bring them into the Federation. They refused, and of course we did not force them. But as the years went by the scope of their knowledge increased amazingly; shortly they were the technological equals of any other race in the galaxy. And then the Antha embarked upon an era of imperialistic expansion.

"They were superior, they knew it and were proud. And so they pushed out and enveloped the races and worlds of the area now known as the desert. Their rule was a tyranny unequaled in Galactic history."

The Earthmen never moved, and Roymer went on.

"But the Antha were not members of the Federation, and, therefore, they were not answerable for their acts. We could only stand by and watch as they spread their vicious rule from world to world. They were absolutely ruthless.

"As an example of their kind of rule, I will tell you of their crime against the Apectans.

"The planet of Apectus not only resisted the Antha, but somehow managed to hold out against their approach for several years. The Antha finally conquered and then, in retaliation for the Apectans' valor, they conducted the most brutal of their mass experiments.

"They were a brilliant people. They had been experimenting with the genes of heredity. Somehow they found a way to alter the genes of the Apectans, who were humanoids like themselves, and they did it on a mass scale. They did not choose to exterminate the race, their revenge was much greater. Every Apectan born since the Antha invasion, has been born without one arm."

Jansen sucked in his breath. It was a very horrible thing to hear, and a sudden memory came into his brain. Caesar did than, he thought. He cut off the right hands of the Gauls. Peculiar coincidence. Jansen felt uneasy.

Roymer paused for a moment.

"The news of what happened to the Apectans set the Galactic peoples up in arms, but it was not until the Antha attacked a Federation world that we finally moved against them. It was the greatest war in the history of Life.

"You will perhaps understand how great a people the Antha were when I tell you that they alone, unaided, dependent entirely upon their own resources, fought the rest of the Galactics, and fought them to a standstill. As the terrible years went by we lost whole races and planets—like this one, which was one the Antha destroyed—and yet we could not defeat them.

"It was only after many years, when a Galactic invented the most dangerous weapon of all, that we won. The invention—of which only the Galactic Council has knowledge—enabled us to turn the suns of the Antha into novae, at long range. One by one we destroyed the Antha worlds. We hunted them through all the planets of the desert; for the first time in history the edict of the Federation was death, death for an entire race. At last there were no longer any habitable worlds where the Antha had been. We burned their worlds, and ran them down in space. Thirty thousand years ago, the civilization of the Antha perished."

Roymer had finished. He looked at the Earthmen out of grave, tired old eyes.

Cohn was staring in open-mouth fascination, but Jansen—unaccountably felt a chill. The story of Caesar remained uncomfortably in his mind. And he had a quick, awful suspicion.

"Are you sure you got all of them?"

"No. Some surely must have escaped. There were too many in space, and space is without limits."

Jansen wanted to know: "Have any of them been heard of since?"

Roymer's smile left him as the truth came out. "No. Not until now."

There were only a few more seconds. He gave them time to understand. He could not help telling them that he was sorry, he even apologized. And then he sent the order with his mind.

The Antha died quickly and silently, without pain.

Only thirty thousand years, Roymer was thinking, but thirty thousand years, and they came back out to the stars. They have no memory now of what they were or what they have done. They started all over again, the old history of the race has been lost, and in thirty thousand years they came all the way back.

Roymer shook his head with sad wonder and awe. The most brilliant people of all.

Goladan came in quietly with the final reports.

"There are no charts," he grumbled, "no maps at all. We will not be able to trace them to their home star."

Roymer did not know, really, what was right, to be disappointed or relieved. We cannot destroy them now, he thought, not right away. He could not help being relieved. Maybe this time there will be a way, and they will not have to be destroyed. They could be—

He remembered the edict—the edict of death. The Antha had forged it for themselves and it was just. He realized that there wasn't much hope.

The reports were on his desk and he regarded them with a wry smile. There was indeed no way to trace them back. They had no charts, only a regular series of course-check coordinates which were preset on their home planet and which were not decipherable. Even at this stage of their civilization they had already anticipated the consequences of having their ship fall into alien hands. And this although they lived in the desert.

Goladan startled him with an anxious question:

"What can we do?"

Roymer was silent.

We can wait, he thought. Gradually, one by one, they will come out of the desert, and when they come we will be waiting. Perhaps one day we will follow one back and destroy their world, and perhaps before then we will find a way to save them.

Suddenly, as his eyes wandered over the report before him and he recalled the ingenious mechanism of the freeze, a chilling, unbidden thought came into his brain.

And perhaps, he thought calmly, for he was a philosophical man, they will come out already equipped to rule the galaxy.

A DEATH IN THE HOUSE

by Clifford D. Simak

Old Mose Abrams was out hunting cows when he found the alien. He didn't know it was an alien, but it was alive and it was in a lot of trouble and Old Mose, despite everything the neighbors said about him, was not the kind of man who could bear to leave a sick thing out there in the woods.

It was a horrid-looking thing, green and shiny, with some purple spots on it, and it was repulsive even twenty feet away. And it stank.

It had crawled, or tried to crawl, into a clump of hazel brush, but hadn't made it. The head part was in the brush and the rest lay out there naked in the open. Every now and then the parts that seemed to be arms and hands clawed feebly at the ground, trying to force itself deeper in the brush, but it was too weak; it never moved an inch.

It was groaning, too, but not too loud—just the kind of keening sound a lonesome wind might make around a wide, deep eave. But there was more in it than just the sound of winter wind; there was a frightened, desperate note that made the hair stand up on Old Mose's nape.

Old Mose stood there for quite a spell, making up his mind what he ought to do about it, and a while longer after that working his courage, although most folks off-hand would have said that he had plenty. But this was the sort of situation that took more than just ordinary screwed-up courage. It took a lot of foolhardiness.

But this was a wild, hurt thing and he couldn't leave it there, so he walked up to it and knelt down, and it was pretty hard to look at, though there was a sort of fascination in its repulsiveness that was hard to figure out—as if it were so horrible that it dragged one to it. And it stank in a way that no one had ever smelled before.

Mose, however, was not finicky. In the neighborhood, he was not well known for fastidity. Ever since his wife had died almost ten years before, he had lived alone on his untidy farm and the housekeeping that he did was the scandal of all the neighbor women. Once a year, if he got around to it, he sort of shoveled out the house, but the rest of the year he just let things accumulate.

So he wasn't upset as some might have been with the way the creature smelled. But the sight of it upset him, and it took him quite a while before he could bring himself to touch it, and when he finally did, he was considerably surprised. He had been prepared for it to be either cold or slimy, or maybe even both. But it was neither. It was warm and hard and it had a clean feel to it, and he was reminded of the way a green corn stalk would feel.

He slid his hand beneath the hurt thing and pulled it gently from the clump of hazel brush and turned it over so he could see its face. It hadn't any face. It had an enlargement at the top of it, like a flower on top of a stalk, although its body wasn't any stalk, and there was a fringe around this enlargement that wiggled like a can of worms, and it was then that Mose almost turned around and ran.

But he stuck it out.

He squatted there, staring at the no-face with the fringe of worms, and he got cold all over and his stomach doubled up on him and he was stiff with fright—and the fright got worse when it seemed to him that the keening of the thing was coming from the worms.

Mose was a stubborn man. One had to be stubborn to run a runty farm like this. Stubborn and insensitive in a lot of ways. But not insensitive, of course, to a thing in pain.

Finally he was able to pick it up and hold it in his arms and there was nothing to it, for it didn't weigh much. Less than a half-grown shoat, he figured.

He went up the woods path with it, heading back for home, and it seemed to him the smell of it was less. He was hardly scared at all and he was warm again and not cold all over.

For the thing was quieter now and keening just a little. And although he could not be sure of it, there were times when it seemed as if the thing were snuggling up to him, the way a scared and hungry baby will snuggle to any grown person that comes and picks it up.

Old Mose reached the buildings and he stood out in the yard a minute, wondering whether he should take it to the barn or house. The barn, of course, was the natural place for it, for it wasn't human—it wasn't even as close to human as a dog or cat or sick lamb would be.

He didn't hesitate too long, however. He took it into the house and laid it on what he called a bed, next to the kitchen stove. He got it straightened out all neat and orderly and pulled a dirty blanket over it, and then went to the stove and stirred up the fire until there was some flame.

Then he pulled up a chair beside the bed and had a good, hard, wondering look at this thing he had brought home. It had quietened down a lot and seemed more comfortable than it had out in the woods. He tucked the blanket snug around it with a tenderness that surprised himself. He wondered what he had that it might eat, and even if he knew, how he'd manage feeding it, for it seemed to have no mouth.

"But you don't need to worry none," he told it. "Now that I got you under a roof, you'll be all right. I don't know too much about it, but I'll take care of you the best I can."

By now it was getting on toward evening, and he looked out the window and saw that the cows he had been hunting had come home by themselves.

"I got to go get the milking done and the other chores," he told the thing lying on the bed, "but it won't take me long. I'll be right back."

Old Mose loaded up the stove so the kitchen would stay warm and he tucked the thing in once again, then got his milk pails and went down to the barn.

He fed the sheep and pigs and horses and he milked the cows. He hunted eggs and shut the chicken house. He pumped a tank of water.

Then he went back to the house.

It was dark now and he lit the oil lamp on the table, for he was against electricity. He'd refused to sign up when REA had run out the line and a lot of the neighbors had gotten sore at him for being unco-operative. Not that he cared, of course.

He had a look at the thing upon the bed. It didn't seem to be any better, or any worse, for that matter. If it had been a sick lamb or an ailing calf, he could have known right off how it was getting on, but this thing was different. There was no way to tell.

He fixed himself some supper and ate it and wished he knew how to feed the thing. And he wished, too, that he knew how to help it. He'd got it under shelter and he had it warm, but was that right or wrong for something like this? He had no idea.

He wondered if he should try to get some help, then felt squeamish about asking help when he couldn't say exactly what had to be helped. But then he wondered how he would feel himself if he were in a far, strange country, all played out and sick, and no one to get him any help because they didn't know exactly what he was.

That made up his mind for him and he walked over to the phone. But should he call a doctor or a veterinarian? He decided to call the doctor because the thing was in the house. If it had been in the barn, he would have called the veterinarian.

He was on a rural line and the hearing wasn't good and he was halfway deaf, so he didn't use the phone too often. He had told himself at times it was nothing but another aggravation and there had been a dozen times he had threatened to have it taken out. But now he was glad he hadn't.

The operator got old Doctor Benson and they couldn't hear one another too well, but Mose finally made the doctor understand who was calling and that he needed him and the doctor said he'd come.

With some relief, Mose hung up the phone and was just standing there, not doing anything, when he was struck by the thought that there maybe others of these things down there in the woods. He had no idea what they were or what they might be doing or where they might be

going, but it was pretty evident that the one upon the bed
was some sort of stranger from a very distant place. It
stood to reason that there might be more than one of
them, for far traveling was a lonely business and anyone
—or anything—would like to have some company along.

He got the lantern down off the peg and lit it and went
stumping out the door. The night was as black as a stack
of cats and the lantern light was feeble, but that made not
a bit of difference, for Mose knew this farm of his like the
back of his hand.

He went down the path into the woods. It was a spooky
place, but it took more than woods at night to spook Old
Mose. At the place where he had found the thing, he
looked around, pushing through the brush and holding
the lantern high so he could see a bigger area, but he
didn't find another one of them.

He did find something else, though—a sort of outsize
birdcage made of metal lattice work that had wrapped
itself around an eight-inch hickory tree. He tried to pull it
loose, but it was jammed so tight that he couldn't budge
it.

He sighted back the way it must have come. He could
see where it had plowed its way through the upper
branches of the trees, and out beyond were stars, shining
bleakly with the look of far away.

Mose had no doubt that the thing lying in his bed beside
the kitchen stove had come in this birdcage contraption.
He marveled some at that, but he didn't fret himself too
much, for the whole thing was so unearthly that he knew
he had little chance of pondering it out.

He walked back to the house and he scarcely had the
lantern blown out and hung back on its peg than he heard
a car drive up.

The doctor, when he came up to the door, became a
little grumpy at seeing Old Mose standing there.

"You don't look sick to me," the doctor said. "Not
sick enough to drag me clear out here tonight."

"I ain't sick," said Mose.

"Well, then," said the doctor, more grumpily than
ever, "what did you mean by phoning me?"

"I got someone who is sick," said Mose. "I hope you

can help him. I would have tried myself, but I don't know how to go about it."

The doctor came inside and Mose shut the door behind him.

"You got something rotten in here?" asked the doctor.

"No, it's just the way he smells. It was pretty bad at first, but I'm getting used to it by now."

The doctor saw the thing lying on the bed and went over to it. Old Mose heard him sort of gasp and could see him standing there, very stiff and straight. Then he bent down and had a good look at the critter on the bed.

When he straightened up and turned around to Mose, the only thing that kept him from being downright angry was that he was so flabbergasted.

"Mose," he yelled, "what *is* this?"

"I don't know," said Mose. "I found it in the woods and it was hurt and wailing and I couldn't leave it there."

"You think it's sick?"

"I know it is," said Mose. "It needs help awful bad. I'm afraid it's dying."

The doctor turned back to the bed again and pulled the blanket down, then went and got the lamp so that he could see. He looked the critter up and down, and he prodded it with a skittish finger, and he made the kind of mysterious clucking sound that only doctors make.

Then he pulled the blanket back over it again and took the lamp back to the table.

"Mose," he said, "I can't do a thing for it."

"But you're a doctor!"

"A human doctor, Mose. I don't know what this thing is, but it isn't human. I couldn't even guess what is wrong with it, if anything. And I wouldn't know what could be safely done for it even if I could diagnose its illness. I'm not even sure it's an animal. There are a lot of things about it that argue it's a plant."

Then the doctor asked Mose straight out how he came to find it and Mose told him exactly how it happened. But he didn't tell him anything about the birdcage, for when he thought about it, it sounded so fantastic that he couldn't bring himself to tell it. Just finding the critter and having it here was bad enough, without throwing in the birdcage.

"I tell you what," the doctor said. "You got something here that's outside all human knowledge. I doubt there's ever been a thing like this seen on Earth before. I have no idea what it is and I wouldn't try to guess. If I were you, I'd get in touch with the university up at Madison. There might be someone there who could get it figured out. Even if they couldn't they'd be interested. They'd want to study it."

Mose went to the cupboard and got the cigar box almost full of silver dollars and paid the doctor. The doctor put the dollars in his pocket, joshing Mose about his eccentricity.

But Mose was stubborn about his silver dollars. "Paper money don't seem legal somehow," he declared. "I like the feel of silver and the way it clinks. It's got authority."

The doctor left and he didn't seem as upset as Mose had been afraid he might be. As soon as he was gone, Mose pulled up a chair and sat down beside the bed.

It wasn't right, he thought, that the thing should be so sick and no one to help—no one who knew any way to help it.

He sat in the chair and listened to the ticking of the clock, loud in the kitchen silence, and the crackling of the wood burning in the stove.

Looking at the thing lying on the bed, he had an almost fierce hope that it could get well again and stay with him. Now that its birdcage was all banged up, maybe there'd be nothing it could do but stay. And he hoped it would, for already the house felt less lonely.

Sitting in the chair between the stove and bed, Mose realized how lonely it had been. It had not been quite so bad until Towser died. He had tried to bring himself to get another dog, but he never had been able to. For there was no dog that would take the place of Towser and it had seemed unfaithful to even try. He could have gotten a cat, of course, but that would remind him too much of Molly; she had been very fond of cats, and until the time she died, there had always been two or three of them under- foot around the place.

But now he was alone. Alone with his farm and his

stubbornness and his silver dollars. The doctor thought, like all the rest of them, that the only silver Mose had was in the cigar box in the cupboard. There wasn't one of them who knew about the old iron kettle piled plumb full of them, hidden underneath the floor boards of the living room. He chuckled at the thought of how he had them fooled. He'd give a lot to see his neighbors' faces if they could only know. But he was not the one to tell them. If they were to find it out, they'd have to find it out themselves.

He nodded in the chair and finally he slept, sitting upright, with his chin resting on his chest and his crossed arms wrapped around himself as if to keep him warm.

When he woke, in the dark before the dawn, with the lamp flickering on the table and the fire in the stove burned low, the alien had died.

There was no doubt of death. The thing was cold and rigid and the husk that was its body was rough and drying out—as a corn stalk in the field dries out, whipping in the wind once the growing had been ended.

Mose pulled the blanket up to cover it, and although this was early to do the chores, he went out by lantern light and got them done.

After breakfast, he heated water and washed his face and shaved, and it was the first time in years he'd shaved any day but Sunday. Then he put on his one good suit and slicked down his hair and got the old jalopy out of the machine shed and drove into town.

He hunted up Eb Dennison, the town clerk, who also was the secretary of the cemetery association.

"Eb," he said, "I want to buy a lot."

"But you've got a lot," protested Eb.

"That plot," said Mose, "is a family plot. There's just room for me and Molly."

"Well then," asked Eb, "why another one? You have no other members of the family."

"I found someone in the woods," said Mose. "I took him home and he died last night. I plan to bury him."

"If you found a dead man in the woods," Eb warned him, "you better notify the coroner and sheriff."

"In time I may," said Mose, not intending to. "Now how about that plot?"

Washing his hands of the affair entirely, Eb sold him the plot.

Having bought his plot, Mose went to the undertaking establishment run by Albert Jones.

"Al," he said, "there's been a death out at the house. A stranger I found out in the woods. He doesn't seem to have anyone and I aim to take care of it."

"You got a death certificate?" asked Al, who subscribed to none of the niceties affected by most funeral parlor operators.

"Well, no, I haven't."

"Was there a doctor in attendance?"

"Doc Benson came out last night."

"He should have made you one out last night."

He phoned Doctor Benson and talked with him a while and got red around the gills. He finally slammed down the phone and turned on Mose.

"I don't know what you're trying to pull off," he fumed, "but Doc tells me this thing of yours isn't even human. I don't take care of dogs or cats or—"

"This ain't no dog or cat."

"I don't care what it is. It's got to be human for me to handle it. And don't go trying to bury it in the cemetery, because it's against the law."

Considerably discouraged, Mose left the undertaking parlor and trudged slowly up the hill toward the town's one and only church.

He found the minister in his study working on a sermon. Mose sat down in a chair and fumbled his battered hat around and around in his work-scarred hands.

"Parson," he said, "I'll tell you the story from the first to the last," and he did. He added, "I don't know what it is. I guess no one else does, either. But it's dead and in need of decent burial and that's the least that I can do. I can't bury it in the cemetery, so I suppose I'll have to find a place for it on the farm. I wonder if you can bring yourself to come out and say a word or two."

The minister gave the matter some deep consideration.

"I'm sorry, Mose" he said at last. "I don't believe I can. I am not sure at all the church would approve of it."

"This thing may not be human," said Old Mose, "but it is one of God's critters."

The minister thought some more, and did some wondering out loud, but made up his mind finally that he couldn't do it.

So Mose went down the street to where his car was waiting and drove home, thinking about what heels some humans are.

Back at the farm again, he got a pick and shovel and went into the garden, and there, in one corner of it, he dug a grave. He went out to the machine shed to hunt up some boards to make the thing a casket, but it turned out that he had used the last of the lumber to patch up the hog pen.

Mose went to the house and dug around in a chest in one of the back rooms which had not been used for years, hunting for a sheet to use as a winding shroud, since there would be no casket. He couldn't find a sheet, but he did unearth an old white linen table cloth. He figured that would do, so he took it to the kitchen.

He pulled back the blanket and looked at the critter lying there in death and a sort of lump came into his throat at the thought of it—how it had died so lonely and so far from home without a creature of its own to spend its final hours with. And naked, too, without a stitch of clothing and with no possesion, with not a thing to leave behind as a remembrance of itself.

He spread the table cloth out on the floor beside the bed and lifted the thing and laid it on the table cloth. As he laid it down, he saw the pocket in it—if it was a pocket—a sort of slitted flap in the center of what could be its chest. He ran his hand across the pocket area. There was a lump inside it. He crouched for a long moment beside the body, wondering what to do.

Finally he reached his fingers into the flap and took out the thing that bulged. It was a ball, a little bigger than a tennis ball, made of cloudy glass—or, at least, it looked like glass. He squatted there, staring at it, then took it to the window for a better look.

There was nothing strange at all about the ball. It was just a cloudy ball of glass and it had a rough, dead feel about it, just as the body had.

He shook his head and took it back and put it where he'd found it and wrapped the body securely in the cloth. He carried it to the garden and put it in the grave. Standing solemnly at the head of the grave, he said a few short words and then shoveled in the dirt.

He had meant to make a mound above the grave and he had intended to put up a cross, but at the last he didn't do either one of these. There would be snoopers. The word would get around and they'd be coming out and hunting for the spot where he had buried this thing he had found out in the woods. So there must be no mound to mark the place and no cross as well. Perhaps it was for the best, he told himself, for what could he have carved or written on the cross?

By this time it was well past noon and he was getting hungry, but he didn't stop to eat, because there were other things to do. He went out into the pasture and caught up Bess and hitched her to the stoneboat and went down into the woods.

He hitched her to the birdcage that was wrapped around the tree and she pulled it loose as pretty as you please. Then he loaded it on the stoneboat and hauled it up the hill and stowed it in the back of the machine shed, in the far corner by the forge.

After that, he hitched Bess to the garden plow and gave the garden a cultivating that it didn't need so it would be fresh dirt all over and no one could locate where he'd dug the grave.

He was just finishing the plowing when Sheriff Doyle drove up and got out of the car. The sheriff was a soft-spoken man, but he was no dawdler. He got right to the point.

"I hear," he said, "you found something in the woods."

"That I did," said Mose.

"I hear it died on you."

"Sheriff, you heard right."

"I'd like to see it, Mose."

"Can't. I buried it. And I ain't telling where."

"Mose," the sheriff said, "I don't want to make you trouble, but you did an illegal thing. You can't go finding people in the woods and just bury them when they up and die on you."

"You talk to Doc Benson?"

The sheriff nodded. "He said it wasn't any kind of thing he'd ever seen before. He said it wasn't human."

"Well then," said Mose, "I guess that lets you out. If it wasn't human, there could be no crime against a person. And if it wasn't owned, there ain't any crime against property. There's been no one around to claim they owned the thing, is there?"

The sheriff rubbed his chin. "No, there hasn't. Maybe you're right. Where did you study law?"

"I never studied law. I never studied nothing. I just use common sense."

"Doc said something about the folks up at the university might want a look at it."

"I tell you, sheriff," said Mose. "This thing came here from somewhere and it died. I don't know where it came from and I don't know what it was and I don't hanker none to know. To me it was just a living thing that needed help real bad. It was alive and it had its dignity and in death it commanded some respect. When the rest of you refused it decent burial, I did the best I could. And that is all there is to it."

"All right, Mose," the sheriff said, "if that's how you want it."

He turned around and stalked back to the car. Mose stood beside old Bess hitched to her plow and watched him drive away. He drove fast and reckless as if he might be angry.

Mose put the plow away and turned the horse back to the pasture and by now it was time to do chores again.

He got the chores all finished and made himself some supper and after supper sat beside the stove, listening to the ticking of the clock, loud in the silent hours, and the crackle of the fire.

All night long the house was lonely.

The next afternoon, as he was plowing corn, a reporter came and walked up the row with him and talked with him when he came to the end of the row. Mose didn't like this reporter much. He was too flip and he asked some funny questions, so Mose clammed up and didn't tell him much.

A few days later, a man showed up from the university and showed him the story the reporter had gone back and written. The story made fun of Mose.

"I'm sorry," the professor said. "These newspapermen are unaccountable. I wouldn't worry too much about anything they write."

"I don't," Mose told him.

The man from the university asked a lot of questions and made quite a point about how important it was that he should see the body.

But Mose only shook his head. "It's at peace," he said. "I aim to leave it that way."

The man went away disgusted, but still quite dignified.

For several days there were people driving by and dropping in, the idly curious, and there were some neighbors Mose hadn't seen for months. But he gave them all short shrift and in a little while they left him alone and he went on with his farming and the house stayed lonely.

He thought again that maybe he should get a dog, but he thought of Towser and he couldn't do it.

One day, working in the garden, he found the plant that grew out of the grave. It was a funny-looking plant and his first impulse was to root it out.

But he didn't do it, for the plant intrigued him. It was a kind he'd never seen before and he decided he would let it grow, for a while at least, to see what kind it was. It was a bulky, fleshy plant, with heavy, dark-green, curling leaves, and it reminded him in some ways of the skunk cabbage that burgeoned in the woods come spring.

There was another visitor, the queerest of the lot. He was a dark and intense man who said he was the president of a flying saucer club. He wanted to know if Mose had talked with the thing he'd found out in the woods and seemed terribly disappointed when Mose told him he hadn't. He wanted to know if Mose had found a vehicle the creature might have traveled in and Mose lied to him about it. He was afraid, the wild way the man was acting, that he might demand to search the place, and if he had, he'd likely have found the birdcage hidden in the machine shed back in the corner by the forge. But the man got to lecturing Mose about withholding vital information.

Finally Mose had taken all he could of it, so he stepped into the house and picked up the shotgun from behind the door. The president of the flying saucer club said goodbye rather hastily and got out of there.

Farm life went on as usual, with the corn laid by and the haying started and out in the garden the strange plant kept on growing and now was taking shape. Old Mose couldn't believe his eyes when he saw the sort of shape it took and he spent long evening hours just standing in the garden, watching it and wondering if his loneliness were playing tricks on him.

The morning came when he found the plant standing at the door and waiting for him. He should have been surprised, of course, but he really wasn't, for he had lived with it, watching it of eventide, and although he had not dared admit it even to himself, he had known what it was.

For here was the creature he'd found in the woods, no longer sick and keening, no longer close to death, but full of life and youth.

It was not the same entirely, though. He stood and looked at it and could see the differences—the little differences that might have been those between youth and age, or between a father and a son, or again the differences expressed in an evolutionary pattern.

"Good morning," said Mose, not feeling strange at all to be talking to the thing. "It's good to have you back."

The thing standing in the yard did not answer him. But that was not important; he had not expected that it would. The one important thing was that he had something he could talk to.

"I'm going out to do the chores," said Mose. "You want to tag along?"

It tagged along with him and it watched him as he did the chores and he talked to it, which was a vast improvement over talking to himself.

At breakfast, he laid an extra plate for it and pulled up an extra chair, but it turned out the critter was not equipped to use a chair, for it wasn't hinged to sit.

Nor did it eat. That bothered Mose at first, for he was hospitable, but he told himself that a big, strong, strapping youngster like this one knew enough to take care of itself, and he probably didn't need to worry too much about how it got along.

After breakfast, he went out to the garden, with the critter accompanying him, and sure enough, the plant was gone. There was a collapsed husk lying on the ground, the outer covering that had been the cradle of the creature at his side.

Then he went to the machine shed and the creature saw the birdcage and rushed over to it and looked it over minutely. Then it turned around to Mose and made a sort of pleading gesture.

Mose went over to it and laid his hands on one of the twisted bars and the critter stood beside him and laid its hands on, too, and they pulled together. It was no use. They could move the metal some, but not enough to pull it back in shape again.

They stood and looked at one another, although looking may not be the word, for the critter had no eyes to look with. It made some funny motions with its hands, but Mose couldn't understand. Then it lay down on the floor and showed him how the birdcage ribs were fastened to the base.

It took a while for Mose to understand how the fastening worked and he never did know exactly why it did. There wasn't, actually, any reason that it should work that way.

First you applied some pressure, just the right amount at the exact and correct angle, and the bar would move a little. Then you applied some more pressure, again the exact amount and at the proper angle, and the bar would move some more. You did this three times and the bar came loose, although there was, God knows, no reason why it should.

Mose started a fire in the forge and shoveled in some coal and worked the bellows while the critter watched. But when he picked up the bar to put it in the fire, the critter got between him and the forge and wouldn't let him near. Mose realized then he couldn't—or wasn't supposed to—heat the bar to straighten it and he never questioned the entire rightness of it. For, he told himself, this thing should surely know the proper way to do it.

So he took the bar over to the anvil and started hammering it back into shape again, cold, without the use of fire, while the critter tried to show him the shape that it should be. It took quite a while, but finally it was straightened out to the critter's satisfaction.

Mose figured they'd have themselves a time getting the bar back in place again, but it slipped on as slick as could be.

Then they took off another bar and this one went faster, now that Mose had the hang of it.

But it was hard and grueling labor. They worked all day and only straightened out five bars.

It took four solid days to get the bars on the birdcage hammered into shape and all the time the hay was waiting to be cut.

But it was all right with Mose. He had someone to talk to and the house had lost its loneliness.

When they got the bars back in place, the critter slipped into the cage and starting fooling with a dingus on the roof of it that looked like a complicated basket. Mose, watching, figured that the basket was some sort of control.

The critter was discouraged. It walked around the shed looking for something and seemed unable to find it. It came back to Mose and made its despairing, pleading gesture. Mose showed it iron and steel; he dug into a carton where he kept bolts and clamps and bushings and scraps of metal and other odds and ends, finding brass and copper and even some aluminium, but it wasn't any of these.

And Mose was glad—a bit ashamed for feeling glad, but glad all the same.

For it had been clear to him that when the birdcage was all ready, the critter would be leaving him. It had been impossible for Mose to stand in the way of the repair of the cage, or to refuse to help. But now that it apparently couldn't be, he found himself well pleased.

Now the critter would have to stay with him and he'd

have someone to talk to and the house would not be lonely. It would be welcome, he told himself, to have folks again. The critter was almost as good a companion as Towser.

Next morning, while Mose was fixing breakfast, he reached up in the cupboard to get the box of oatmeal and his hand struck the cigar box and it came crashing to the floor. It fell over on its side and the lid came open and the dollars went free-wheeling all around the kitchen.

Out of the corner of his eye, Mose saw the critter leaping quickly in pursuit of one of them. It snatched it up and turned to Mose, with the coin held between its fingers, and a sort of thrumming noise was coming out of the nest of worms on top of it.

It bent and scooped up more of them and cuddled them and danced a sort of jig, and Mose knew, with a sinking heart, that it had been silver the critter had been hunting.

So Mose got down on his hands and knees and helped the critter gather up all the dollars. They put them back in the cigar box and Mose picked up the box and gave it to the critter.

The critter took it and hefted it and had a disappointed look. Taking the box over to the table, it took the dollars out and stacked them in neat piles and Mose could see it was very disappointed.

Perhaps, after all, Mose thought, it had not been silver the thing had been hunting for. Maybe it had made a mistake in thinking that the silver was some other kind of metal.

Mose got down the oatmeal and poured it into some water and put it on the stove. When it was cooked and the coffee was ready, he carried his breakfast to the table and sat down to eat.

The critter still was standing across the table from him, stacking and restacking the piles of silver dollars. And now it showed him with a hand held above the stacks, that it needed more of them. This many stacks, it showed him, and each stack so high.

Mose sat stricken, with a spoon full of oatmeal halfway to its mouth. He thought of all those other dollars, the iron kettle packed with them, underneath the floor boards in the living room. And he couldn't do it; they were the only thing he had—except the critter now. And he could not give them up so the critter could go and leave him too.

He ate his bowl of oatmeal without tasting it and drank two cups of coffee. And all the time the critter stood there and showed him how much more it needed.

"I can't do it for you," Old Mose said. "I've done all you can expect of any living being. I found you in the woods and I gave you warmth and shelter. I tried to help you, and when I couldn't, at least I gave you a place to die in. I buried you and protected you from all those other people and I did not pull you up when you started growing once again. Surely you can't expect me to keep on giving endlessly."

But it was no good. The critter could not hear him and he did not convince himself.

He got up from the table and walked into the living room with the critter trailing him. He loosened the floor boards and took out the kettle, and the critter, when it saw what was in the kettle, put its arms around itself and hugged in happiness.

They lugged the money out to the machine shed and Mose built a fire in the forge and put the kettle in the fire and started melting down that hard-saved money.

There were times he thought he couldn't finish the job, but he did.

The critter got the basket out of the birdcage and put it down beside the forge and dipped out the molten silver with an iron ladle and poured it here and there into the basket, shaping it in place with careful hammer taps.

It took a long time, for it was exacting work, but finally it was done and the silver almost gone. The critter lugged the basket back into the birdcage and fastened it in place.

It was almost evening now and Mose had to go and do the chores. He half expected the thing might haul out the birdcage and be gone when he came back to the house. And he tried to be sore at it for its selfishness—it had taken from him and had not tried to pay him back—it had not, so far as he could tell, even tried to thank him. But he made a poor job of being sore at it.

It was waiting for him when he came from the barn carrying two pails full of milk. It followed him inside the house and stood around and he tried to talk to it. But he didn't have the heart to do much talking. He could not forget that it would be leaving, and the pleasure of its present company was lost in his terror of the loneliness to come.

For now he didn't even have his money to help ward off the loneliness.

As he lay in bed that night, strange thoughts came creeping in upon him—the thought of an even greater loneliness than he had ever known upon this runty farm, the terrible, devastating loneliness of the empty wastes that lay between the stars, a driven loneliness while one hunted for a place or person that remained a misty thought one could not define, but which it was most important one should find.

It was a strange thing for him to be thinking, and quite suddenly he knew it was no thought of his, but of this other that was in the room with him.

He tried to raise himself, he fought to raise himself, but he couldn't do it. He held his head up a moment, then fell back upon the pillow and went sound asleep.

Next morning, after Mose had eaten breakfast, the two of them went to the machine shed and dragged the birdcage out. It stood there, a weird alien thing, in the chill brightness of the dawn.

The critter walked up to it and started to slide between two of the bars, but when it was halfway through, it stepped out again and moved over to confront Old Mose.

"Good-bye, friend," said Mose. "I'll miss you."

There was a strange stinging in his eyes.

The other held out its hand in farewell, and Mose took it and there was something in the hand he grasped, something round and smooth that was transferred from its hand to his.

The thing took its hand away and stepped quickly to the birdcage and slid between the bars. The hands reached for the basket and there was a sudden flicker and the birdcage was no longer there.

Mose stood lonely in the barnyard, looking at the place

where there was no birdcage and remembering what he had felt or thought—or been told?—the night before as he lay in bed.

Already the critter would be there, out between the stars, in that black and utter loneliness, hunting for a place or thing or person that no human mind could grasp.

Slowly Mose turned around to go back to the house, to get the pails and go down to the barn to get the milking done.

He remembered the object in his hand and lifted his still-clenched fist in front of him. He opened his fingers and the little crystal ball lay there in his palm—and it was exactly like the one he'd found in the slitted flap in the body he had buried in the garden. Except that one had been dead and cloudy and this one had the living glow of a distant-burning fire.

Looking at it, he had the strange feeling of a happiness and comfort such as he had seldom known before, as if there were many people with him and all of them were friends.

He closed his hand upon it and the happiness stayed on—and it was all wrong, for there was not a single reason that he should be happy. The critter finally had left him and his money was all gone and he had no friends, but still he kept on feeling good.

He put the ball into his pocket and stepped spryly for the house to get the milking pails. He pursed up his whiskered lips and began to whistle and it had been a long, long time since he had even thought to whistle.

Maybe he was happy, he told himself, because the critter had not left without stopping to take his hand and try to say good-bye.

And a gift, no matter how worthless it might be, how cheap a trinket, still had a basic value in simple sentiment. It had been many years since anyone had bothered to give him a gift.

It was dark and lonely and unending in the depths of space with no Companion. It might be long before another was obtainable.

It perhaps was a foolish thing to do, but the old

creature had been such a kind savage, so fumbling and so pitiful and eager to help. And one who travels far and fast must likewise travel light. There had been nothing else to give.

FIREWATER

by William Tenn

The hairiest, dirtiest and oldest of the three visitors from Arizona scratched his back against the plastic of the web-foam chair. "Insinuations are lavender nearly," he remarked by way of opening the conversation.

His two companions—the thin young man with dripping eyes, and the woman whose good looks were marred chiefly by incredibly decayed teeth—giggled and relaxed. The thin young man said "Gabble, gabble, honk!" under his breath, and the other two nodded emphatically.

Greta Seidenheim looked up from the tiny stenographic machine resting on a pair of the most exciting knees her employer had been able to find in Greater New York. She swiveled her blond beauty at him. "That too, Mr. Hebster?"

The president of Hebster Securities, Inc., waited until the memory of her voice ceased to tickle his ears; he had much clear thinking to do. Then he nodded and said resonantly, "That too, Miss Seidenheim. Close phonetic approximations of the gabble-honk and remember to indicate when it sounds like a question and when like an exclamation."

He rubbed his recently manicured fingernails across the desk drawer containing his fully loaded Parabellum. Check. The communication buttons with which he could summon any quantity of Hebster Securities personnel up to the nine hundred working at present in the Hebster Building lay some eight inches from the other hand. Check. And there were the doors here, the doors there, behind which his uniformed bodyguard stood poised to burst in at a signal which would blaze before them the moment his right foot came off the tiny spring set in the floor. *And* check.

Algernon Hebster could talk business—even with Primeys.

Courteously, he nodded at each one of his visitors from Arizona; he smiled ruefully at what the dirty shapeless masses they wore on their feet were doing to the calf-deep rug that had been woven specially for his private office. He had greeted them when Miss Seidenheim had escorted them in. They had laughed in his face.

"Suppose we rattle off some introductions. You know me. I'm Hebster, Algernon Hebster—you asked for me specifically at the desk in the lobby. If it's important to the conversation, my secretary's name is Greta Seidenheim. And you, sir?"

He had addressed the old fellow, but the thin young man leaned forward in his seat and held out a taut, almost transparent hand. "Names?" he inquired. "Names are round if not revealed. Consider names. How many names? Consider names, *reconsider* names!"

The woman leaned forward too, and the smell from her diseased mouth reached Hebster even across the enormous space of his office. "Rabble and reaching and all the upward clash," she intoned, spreading her hands as if in agreement with an obvious point. "Emptiness derogating itself into infinity—"

"Into duration," the older man corrected.

"Into infinity," the woman insisted.

"Gabble, gabble, honk?" the young man queried bitterly.

"Listen!" Hebster roared. "When I asked for—"

The communicator buzzed and he drew a deep breath and pressed a button. His receptionist's voice boiled out rapidly, fearfully:

"I remember your orders, Mr. Hebster, but those two men from the UM Special Investigating Commission are here again and they look as if they mean business. I mean they look as if they'll make trouble."

"Yost and Funatti?"

"Yes, sir. From what they said to each other, I think they know you have three Primeys in there. They asked me what are you trying to do—deliberately inflame the

Firsters? They said they're going to invoke full supra-
national powers and force an entry if you don't—"

"Stall them."

"But, Mr. Hebster, the *UM Special Investigating*—"

"Stall them, I said. Are you a receptionist or a swinging
door? Use your imagination, Ruth. You have a nine-
hundred-man organization and a ten-million-dollar
corporation at your disposal. You can stage any kind of
farce in that outer office you want—up to and including
the deal where some actor made up to look like me walks
in and drops dead at their feet. Stall them and I'll nod a
bonus at you. *Stall them.*" He clicked off, looked up.

His visitors, at least, were having a fine time. They had
turned to face each other in a reeking triangle of gibber-
ish. Their voices rose and fell argumentatively,
pleadingly, decisively; but all Algernon Hebster's ears
could register of what they said were very many sounds
similar to *gabble* and an occasional, indisputable *honk!*

His lips curled contempt inward. Humanity prime!
These messes? Then he lit a cigarette and shrugged. Oh,
well. Humanity prime. And business is business.

Just remember they're not supermen, he told himself.
*They may be dangerous, but they're not supermen. Not
by a long shot. Remember that epidemic of influenza that
almost wiped them out, and how you diddled those two
other Primeys last month. They're not supermen, but
they're not humanity either. They're just different.*

He glanced at his secretary and approved. Greta
Seidenheim clacked away on her machine as if she were
recording the curtest, the tritest of business letters. He
wondered what system she was using to catch the
intonations. Trust Greta, though, she'd do it.

"Gabble, honk! Gabble, gabble, gabble, honk, honk.
Gabble, honk, gabble, gabble, honk? Honk."

What had precipitated all this conversation? He'd only
asked for their names. Didn't they use names in Arizona?
Surely, they knew that it was customary here. They
claimed to know at least as much as he about such
matters.

Maybe it was something else that had brought them to
New York this time—maybe something about the Aliens?

He felt the short hairs rise on the back of his neck and he smoothed them down self-consciously.

Trouble was it was so *easy* to learn their language. It was such a very simple matter to be able to understand them in these talkative moments. Almost as easy as falling off a log—or jumping off a cliff.

Well, his time was limited. He didn't know how long Ruth could hold the UM investigators in his outer office. Somehow he had to get a grip on the meeting again without offending them in any of the innumerable, highly dangerous ways in which Primeys could be offended.

He rapped the desk top—gently. The gabble-honk stopped short at the hyphen. The woman rose slowly.

"On this question of names," Hebster began doggedly, keeping his eyes on the woman, "since you people claim—"

The woman writhed agonizingly for a moment and sat down on the floor. She smiled at Hebster. With her rotted teeth, the smile had all the brilliance of a dead star.

Hebster cleared his throat and prepared to try again.

"If you want names," the older man said suddenly, "you can call me Larry."

The president of Hebster Securities shook himself and managed to say "Thanks" in a somewhat weak but not too surprised voice. He looked at the thin young man.

"You can call me Theseus." The young man looked sad as he said it.

"Theseus? Fine!" One thing about Primeys when you started clicking with them, you really moved along. But *Theseus!* Wasn't that just like a Primey? Now the woman, and they could begin.

They were all looking at the woman, even Greta with a curiosity which had sneaked up past her beauty-parlor glaze.

"Name," the woman whispered to herself. "Name a name."

Oh, no, Hebster groaned. *Let's not stall here.*

Larry evidently had decided that enough time had been wasted. He made a suggestion to the women. "Why not call yourself Moe?"

The young man—Theseus, it was now—also seemed to

get interested in the problem. "Rover's a good name," he announced helpfully.

"How about Gloria?" Hebster asked desperately.

The woman considered. "Moe, Rover, Gloria," she mused. "Larry, Theseus, Seidenheim, Hebster, me." She seemed to be running a total.

Anything might come out, Hebster knew. But at least they were not acting snobbish any more; they were talking down on his level now. Not only no gabble-honk, but none of this sneering double-talk which was almost worse. At least they were making sense—of a sort.

"For the purposes of this discussion," the woman said at last, "my name will be . . . will be—My name *is* S.S. Lusitania."

"Fine!" Hebster roared, letting the word he'd kept bubbling on his lips burst out. "That's a *fine* name. Larry, Theseus and . . . er, S.S. Lusitania. Fine bunch of people. Sound. Let's get down to business. You came here on business, I take it?"

"Right," Larry said. "We heard about you from two others who left home a month ago to come to New York. They talked about you when they got back to Arizona."

"They did, eh? I hoped they would."

Theseus slid off his chair and squatted next to the woman who was making plucking motions at the air. "They talked about you," he repeated. "They said you treated them very well, that you showed them as much respect as a thing like you could generate. They also said you cheated them."

"Oh, well, Theseus," Hebster spread his manicured hands. "I'm a businessman."

"You're a businessman," S.S. Lusitania agreed, getting to her feet stealthily and taking a great swipe with both hands at something invisible in front of her face. "And here, in this spot, at this moment, so are we. You can have what we've brought, but you'll pay for it. And don't think you can cheat *us*."

Her hands, cupped over each other, came down to her waist. She pulled them apart suddenly and a tiny eagle fluttered out. It flapped toward the fluorescent panels glowing in the ceiling. Its flight was hampered by the

heavy, striped shield upon its breast, by the bunch of
arrows it held in one claw, by the olive branch it grasped
with the other. It turned is miniature bald head and
gasped at Algernon Hebster, then began to drift rapidly
down to the rug. Just before it hit the floor, it
disappeared.

Hebster shut his eyes, remembering the strip of bunting
that had fallen from the eagle's beak when it had turned
to gasp. There had been words printed on the bunting,
words too small to see at the distance, but he was sure the
words would have read "*E Pluribus Unum*." He was as
certain of that as he was of the necessity of acting unconcerned over the whole incident, as unconcerned as the
Primeys. Professor Kleimbocher said Primeys were
mental drunkards. But why did they give everyone else
the D.T.'s?

He opened his eyes. "Well," he said, "what have you
to sell?"

Silence for a moment. Theseus seemed to forget the
point he was trying to make; S.S. Lusitania stared at
Larry.

Larry scratched his right side through heavy, stinking
cloth.

"Oh, an infallible method for defeating anyone who
attempts to apply the *reductio ad absurdum* to a reasonable proposition you advance." He yawned smugly and
began scratching his left side.

Hebster grinned because he was feeling so good. "No.
Can't use it."

"Can't use it?" The old man was trying hard to look
amazed. He shook his head. He stole a sideways glance at
S.S. Lusitania.

She smiled again and wriggled to the floor. "Larry still
isn't talking a language you can understand, Mr.
Hebster," she cooed, very much like a fertilizer factory
being friendly. "We came here with something we know
you need badly. Very badly."

"Yes?" *They're like those two Primeys last month*,
Hebster exulted: *they don't know what's good and what
isn't. Wonder if their masters would know. Well, and if*

they did—who does business with Aliens?

"We ... have," she spaced the words carefully, trying pathetically for a dramatic effect, "a new shade of red, but not merely that. Oh, *no*! A new shade of red, and a full set of color values derived from it! A complete set of color values derived from this one shade of red, Mr. Hebster! Think what a non-objectivist painter can do with such a—"

"Don't sell me, lady. Theseus, do you want to have a go now?"

Theseus had been frowning at the green foundation of the desk. He leaned back, looking satisfied. Hebster realized abruptly that the tension under his right foot had disappeared. Somehow, Theseus had become cognizant of the signal-spring set in the floor; and, somehow, he had removed it.

He had disintegrated it without setting off the alarm to which it was wired.

Giggles from three Primey throats and a rapid exchange of "gabble-honk." Then they all knew what Theseus had done and how Hebster had tried to protect himself. They weren't angry, though—and they didn't sound triumphant. Try to understand Primey behavior!

No need to get unduly alarmed—the price of dealing with these characters was a nervous stomach. The rewards, on the other hand—

Abruptly, they were businesslike again.

Theseus snapped out his suggestion with all the finality of a bazaar merchant making his last, absolutely the last offer. "A set of population indices which can be correlated with—"

"No, Theseus," Hebster told him gently.

Then, while Hebster sat back and enjoyed, temporarily forgetting the missing coil under his foot, they poured out more, desperately, feverishly, waving in and out of each other's sentences.

"A portable neutron stabilizer for high altit—"

"More than fifty ways of saying 'however' without—"

"... So that every housewife can do an *entrechat* while cook—"

"... Synthetic fabric with the drape of silk and manufactura—"

"... Decorative pattern for bald heads using the follicles as—"

"... Complete and utter refutation of all pyramidologists from—"

"All right!" Hebster roared, "*All right!* That's enough!"

Greta Seidenheim almost forgot herself and sighed with relief. Her stenographic machine had been sounding like a centrifuge.

"Now," said the executive. "What do you want in exchange?"

"One of those we said is the one you want, eh?" Larry muttered. "Which one—the pyramidology refutation? That's it, I betcha."

S.S. Lusitania waved her hands contemptuously. "Bishop's miters, you fool! The new red color values excited him. The new—"

Ruth's voice came over the communicator. "Mr. Hebster, Yost and Funatti are back. I stalled them, but I just received word from the lobby receptionist that they're back and on their way upstairs. You have two minutes, maybe three. And they're so mad they almost look like Firsters themselves!"

"Thanks. When they climb out of the elevator, do what you can without getting too illegal." He turned to his guests. "Listen—"

They had gone off again.

"Gabble, gabble, honk, honk, honk? Gabble, honk, *gabble*, gabble! Gabble, honk, gabble, honk, gabble, honk, honk."

Could they honestly make sense out of these throat-clearings and half-sneezes? Was it really a language as superior to all previous languages of man as ... as the Aliens were supposed to be to man himself? Well, at least they could communicate with the Aliens by means of it. And the Aliens, the Aliens—

He recollected abruptly the two angry representatives of the world state who were hurtling towards his office.

"Listen, friends. You came here to sell. You've shown me your stock, and I've seen something I'd like to buy. *What* exactly is immaterial. The only question now is what you want for it. And let's make it fast. I have some other business to transact."

The woman with the dental nightmare stamped her foot. A cloud no larger than a man's hand formed near the ceiling, burst and deposited a pailful of water on Hebster's fine custom-made rug.

He ran a manicured forefinger around the inside of his collar so that his bulging neck veins would not burst. Not right now, anyway. He looked at Greta and regained confidence from the serenity with which she waited for more conversation to transcribe. There was a model of business precision for you. The Primeys might pull what one of them had in London two years ago, before they were barred from all metropolitan areas—increased a housefly's size to that of an elephant—and Greta Seidenheim would go on separating fragments of conversation into the appropriate shorthand symbols.

With all their power, why didn't they *take* what they wanted? Why trudge wearisome miles to cities and attempt to smuggle themselves into illegal audiences with operators like Hebster, when most of them were caught easily and sent back to the reservation and those that weren't were cheated unmercifully by the "straight" humans they encountered? Why didn't they just blast their way in, take their weird and pathetic prizes and toddle back to their masters? For that matter, why didn't their masters— But Primey psych was Primey psych— not for this world, nor of it.

"We'll tell you what we want in exchange," Larry began in the middle of a honk. He held up a hand on which the length of the fingernails was indicated graphically by the grime beneath them and began to tot up the items, bending a digit for each item. "First, a hundred paper-bound copies of Melville's 'Moby Dick.' Then, twenty-five crystal radio sets, with earphones; two earphones for each set. Then, two Empire State Buildings or three Radio Cities, whichever is more convenient. We want those with foundations intact. A reasonably good copy of the 'Hermes' statue by Praxiteles. And an electric toaster, *circa* 1941. That's about all, isn't it, Theseus?"

Theseus bent over until his nose rested against his knees.

Hebster groaned. The list wasn't as bad as he'd expected—remarkable the way their masters always yearned for the electric gadgets and artistic achievements of Earth—but he had so little time to bargain with them. *Two* Empire State Buildings!

"Mr. Hebster," his receptionist chattered over the communicator. "Those SIC men—I managed to get a crowd out in the corridor to push toward their elevator when it came to this floor, and I've locked the . . . I mean I'm trying to . . . but I don't think—Can you—"

"Good girl! You're doing fine!"

"Is that all we want, Theseus?" Larry asked again. "Gabble?"

Hebster heard a crash in the outer office and footsteps running across the floor.

"See here, Mr. Hebster," Theseus said at last, "if you don't want to buy Larry's *reductio ad absurdum* exploder, and you don't like my method of decorating bald heads for all its innate artistry, how about a system of musical notation—"

Somebody tried Hebster's door, found it locked. There was a knock on the door, repeated most immediately with more urgency.

"He's *already* found something he wants," S.S. Lusitania snapped. "Yes, Larry, that was the complete list."

Hebster plucked a handful of hair from his already receding forehead. "Good! Now, look, I can give you everything but the two Empire State Buildings and the three Radio Cities."

"*Or* the three Radio Cities," Larry corrected. "Don't try to cheat us! Two Empire State Buildings *or* three Radio Cities. Whichever is more convenient. Why . . . isn't it worth that to you?"

"Open this door!" a bull-mad voice yelled. "Open this door in the name of United Mankind!"

"Miss Seidenheim, open the door," Hebster said

loudly and winked at his secretary who rose, stretched and began a thoughtful, slow-motion study in the direction of the locked panel. There was a crash as of a pair of shoulders being thrown against it. Hebster knew that his office door could withstand a medium-sized tank. But there was a limit even to delay when it came to fooling around with the UM Special Investigating Commission. Those boys knew their Primeys and their Primey-dealers; they were empowered to shoot first and ask questions afterwards—as the questions occurred to them.

"It's not a matter of whether it's worth my while," Hebster told them rapidly as he shepherded them to the exit behind his desk. "For reasons I'm sure you aren't interested in. I just can't give away two Empire State Buildings and/or three Radio Cities with foundations intact—not at the moment. I'll give you the rest of it, and—"

"Open this door or we start blasting it down!"

"Please, gentlemen, please," Greta Seidenheim told them sweetly. "You'll kill a poor working girl who's trying awfully hard to let you in. The lock's stuck." She fiddled with the door knob, watching Hebster with a trace of anxiety in her fine eyes.

"And to replace those items," Hebster was going on. "I will—"

"What I mean," Theseus broke in, "is this. You know the greatest single difficulty composers face in the twelve-tone technique?"

"I can offer you," the executive continued doggedly, sweat bursting out of his skin like spring freshets, "complete architectural blueprints of the Empire State Building and Radio City, plus five . . . no, I'll make it ten . . . scale models of each. And you get the rest of the stuff you asked for. That's it. Take it or leave it. Fast!"

They glanced at each other, as Hebster threw the exit door open and gestured to the five liveried bodyguards waiting near his private elevator. "*Done*," they said in unison.

"Good!" Hebster almost squeaked. He pushed them through the doorway and said to the tallest of the five men: "Nineteenth floor!"

He slammed the exit shut just as Miss Seidenheim opened the outer office door. Yost and Funatti, in the bottle-green uniform of the UM, charged through. Without pausing, they ran to where Hebster stood and plucked the exit open. They could all hear the elevator descending.

Funatti, a little, olive-skinned man, sniffed. "Primeys," he muttered. "He had Primeys here, all right. Smell that unwash, Yost?"

"Yeah," said the bigger man. "Come on. The emergency stairway. We can track that elevator!"

They holstered their service weapons and clattered down the metal-tipped stairs. Below, the elevator stopped.

Hebster's secretary was at the communicator. "Maintenance!" She waited. "Maintenance, automatic locks on the nineteenth floor exit until the party Mr. Hebster just sent down gets to a lab somewhere else. And keep apologizing to those cops until then. Remember, they're SIC."

"Thanks, Greta," Hebster said, switching to the personal now that they were alone. He plumped into his desk chair and blew out gustily: "There must be easier ways of making a million."

She raised two perfect blond eyebrows. "Or of being an absolute monarch right inside the parliament of man?"

"If they wait long enough," he told her lazily, "I'll *be* the UM, modern global government and all. Another year or two might do it."

"Aren't you forgetting one Vandermeer Dempsey? His huskies also want to replace the UM. Not to mention their colorful plans for you. And there are an awful, awful lot of them."

"They don't worry me, Greta. *Humanity First* will dissolve overnight once that decrepit old demagogue gives up the ghost." He stabbed at the communicator button. "Maintenance! Maintenance, that party I sent down arrived at a safe lab yet?"

"No, Mr. Hebster. But everything's going all right. We sent them up to the twenty-fourth floor and got the SIC men re-routed downstairs to the personnel levels. Uh, Mr. Hebster—about the SIC. We take your orders and all that, but none of us wants to get in trouble with the Special Investigating Commission. According to the latest laws, it's practically a capital offense to obstruct 'em.''

"Don't worry," Hebster told him. "I've never let one of my employees down yet. The boss fixes everything is the motto here. Call me when you've got those Primeys safely hidden and ready for questioning.''

He turned back to Greta. "Get that stuff typed before you leave and into Professor Kleimbocher's hands. He thinks he may have a new angle on their gabble-honk.''

She nodded. "I wish you could use recording apparatus instead of making me sit over an old-fashioned click-box.''

"So do I. But Primeys enjoy reaching out and putting a hex on electrical apparatus—when they aren't collecting it for the Aliens. I had a raft of wire and tape recorders busted in the middle of Primey interviews before I decided that human stenos were the only answer. And a Primey may get around to bollixing them some day.''

"Cheerful thought. I must remember to dream about the possibility some cold night. Well, I should complain," she muttered as she went into her own little office, "Primey hexes built this business and pay my salary as well as supply me with the sparkling little knick-nacks I love so well.''

That was not quite true, Hebster remembered as he sat waiting for the communicator to buzz the news of his recent guests' arrival in a safe lab. Something like ninety-five per cent of Hebster Securities had been built out of Primey gadgetry extracted from them in various fancy deals, but the base of it all had been the small investment bank he had inherited from his father, back in the days of the Half-War—the days when the Aliens had first appeared on Earth.

The fearfully intelligent dots swirling in their variously shaped multicolored bottles were completely outside the pale of human understanding. There had been no way at all to communicate with them for a time.

A humorist had remarked back in those early days that the Aliens came not to bury man, not to conquer or enslave him. They had a truly dreadful mission—to ignore him!

No one knew, even today, what part of the galaxy the Aliens came from. Or why. No one knew what the total of their small visiting population came to. Or how they operated their wide-open and completely silent spaceships. The few things that had been discovered about them on the occasions when they deigned to swoop down and examine some human enterprise, with the aloof amusement of the highly civilized tourist, had served to confirm a technological superiority over Man that strained and tore the capacity of his richest imagination. A sociological treatise Hebster had read recently suggested that they operated from concepts as far in advance of modern science as a meteorologist sowing a drought-struck area with dry ice was beyond the primitive agriculturist blowing a ram's horn at the heavens in a frantic attempt to wake the slumbering gods of rain.

Prolonged, infinitely dangerous observation had revealed, for example, that the dots-in-bottles seemed to have developed past the need for prepared tools of any sort. They worked directly on the material itself, shaping it to need, evidently creating and destroying matter at will!

Some humans had communicated with them—

They didn't stay human.

Men with superb brains had looked into the whirring flickering settlements established by the outsiders. A few had returned with tales of wonders they had realized dimly and not quite seen. Their descriptions always sounded as if their eyes had been turned off at the most crucial moments or a mental fuse had blown just this side of understanding.

Others—such celebrities as a President of Earth, a three-time winner of the Nobel Prize, famous poets—had evidently broken through the fence somehow. These, however, were the ones who didn't return. They stayed in the Alien settlements of the Gobi, the Sahara, the

American Southwest. Barely able to fend for themselves, despite newly-acquired and almost unbelievable powers, they shambled worshipfully around the outsiders speaking, with weird writhings of larynx and nasal passage, what was evidently a human approximation of their masters' language—a kind of pidgin Alien. Talking with a Primey, someone had said, was like a blind man trying to read a page of Braille originally written for an octopus.

And that these bearded, bug-ridden, stinking derelicts, these chattering wrecks drunk and sodden on the logic of an entirely different life-form, were the heavy yellow cream of the human race didn't help people's egos any.

Humans and Primeys despised each other almost from the first; humans for Primey subservience and helplessness in human terms, Primeys for human ignorance and ineptness in Alien terms. And, except when operating under Alien orders and through barely legal operators like Hebster, Primeys didn't communicate with humans any more than their masters did.

When institutionalized, they either gabble-honked themselves into an early grave or, losing patience suddenly, they might dissolve a path to freedom right through the walls of the asylum and any attendants who chanced to be in the way. Therefore the enthusiasm of sheriff and deputy, nurse and orderly, had waned considerably and the forcible incarceration of Primeys had almost ceased.

Since the two groups were so far apart psychologically as to make mating between them impossible, the ragged miracle-workers had been honored with the status of a separate classification:

Humanity Prime. Not better than humanity, not necessarily worse—but different, and dangerous.

What made them that way? Hebster rolled his chair back and examined the hole in the floor from which the alarm spring had spiraled. Theseus had disintegrated it—*how?* With a thought? Telekinesis, say, applied to all the molecules of the metal simultaneously, making them move rapidly and at random. Or possibly he had merely moved the spring somewhere else. Where? In space? In hyperspace? In time? Hebster shook his head and pulled himself back to the efficiently smooth and sanely useful desk surface.

"Mr. Hebster?" the communicator inquired abruptly, and he jumped a bit, "this is Margritt of General Lab 23B. Your Primeys just arrived. Regular check?"

Regular check meant drawing them out on every conceivable technical subject by the nine specialists in the general laboratory. This involved firing questions at them with the rapidity of a police interrogation, getting them off balance and keeping them there in the hope that a useful and unexpected bit of scientific knowledge would drop.

"Yes," Hebster told him. "Regular check. But first let a textile man have a whack at them. In fact let him take charge of the check."

A pause. "The only textile man in this section is Charlie Verus."

"Well?" Hebster asked in mild irritation. "Why put it like that? He's competent I hope. What does personnel say about him?"

"Personnel says he's competent."

"Then there you are. Look, Margritt, I have the SIC running around my building with blood in its enormous eye. I don't have time to muse over your departmental feuds. Put Verus on."

"Yes, Mr. Hebster. Hey Bert! Get Charlie Verus. Him."

Hebster shook his head and chuckled. These technicians! Verus was probably brilliant and nasty.

The box crackled again: "Mr. Hebster? Mr. Verus." The voice expressed boredom to the point of obvious affectation. But the man was probably good despite his neuroses. Hebster Securities, Inc., had a first-rate personnel department.

"Verus? Those Primeys, I want you to take charge of the check. One of them knows how to make a synthetic fabric with the drape of silk. Get that first and then go after anything else they have."

"Primeys, Mr. Hebster?"

"I said Primeys, Mr. Verus. You are a textile technician,

please to remember, and not the straight or ping-pong half of a comedy routine. Get humping. I want a report on that synthetic fabric by tomorrow. Work all night if you have to."

"Before we do, Mr. Hebster, you might be interested in a small piece of information. There is *already* in existence a synthetic which falls better than silk—"

"I know," his employer told him shortly. "Cellulose acetate. Unfortunately, it has a few disadvantages: low melting point, tends to crack; separate and somewhat inferior dyestuffs have to be used for it; poor chemical resistance. Am I right?"

There was no immediate answer, but Hebster could feel the dazed nod. He went on. "Now, we also have protein fibers. They dye well and fall well, have the thermoconductivity control necessary for wearing apparel, but don't have the tensile strength of synthetic fabrics. An *artificial* protein fiber might be the answer: it would drape as well as silk, might be we could use the acid dyestuffs we use on silk which result in shades that dazzle female customers and cause them to fling wide their pocketbooks. There are a lot of *ifs* in that, I know, but one of those Primeys said something about a synthetic with the drape of silk, and I don't think he'd be sane enough to be referring to cellulose acetate. Nor nylon, orlon, vinyl choloride, or anything else we already have and use."

"You've looked into textile problems, Mr. Hebster."

"I have. I've looked into everything to which there are big gobs of money attached. And now suppose you go look into those Primeys. Several million women are waiting breathlessly for the secrets concealed in their beards. Do you think, Verus, that with the personal and scientific background I've just given you it's possible you might now get around to doing the job you are paid to do?"

"Um-m-m. Yes."

Hebster walked to the office closet and got his hat and coat. He liked working under pressure; he liked to see people jump up straight whenever he barked. And now, he liked the prospect of relaxing.

He grimaced at the webfoam chair that Larry had used. No point in having it resquirted. Have a new one made.

"I'll be at the University," he told Ruth on his way out. "You can reach me through Professor Kleimbocher. But don't, unless it's very important. He gets unpleasantly annoyed when he's interrupted."

She nodded. Then, very hesitantly: "Those two men —Yost and Funatti—from the Special Investigating Commission? They said no one would be allowed to leave the building."

"Did they now?" he chuckled. "I think they were angry. They've been that way before. But unless and until they can hang something on me—And Ruth, tell my bodyguard to go home, except for the man with the Primeys. He's to check with me, wherever I am, every two hours."

He ambled out, being careful to smile benevolently at every third executive and fifth typist in the large office. A private elevator and entrance was all very well for an occasional crisis, but Hebster like to taste his successes in as much public as possible.

It would be good to see Kleimbocher again. He had a good deal of faith in the linguistic approach; grants from his corporation had tripled the size of the university's philology department. After all, the basic problem between man and Primey as well as man and Alien was one of communication. Any attempt to learn their science, to adjust their mental processes and logic into safer human channels, would have to be preceded by understanding.

It was up to Kleimbocher to find that understanding, not him. "I'm Hebster," he thought. "I *employ* the people who solve problems. And then I make money off them."

Somebody got in front of him. Somebody else took his arm. "I'm Hebster," he repeated automatically, but out loud. "*Algernon* Hebster."

"Exactly the Hebster we want," Funatti said holding tightly on to his arm. "'You don't mind coming along with us?"

"Is this an arrest?" Hebster asked the larger Yost who now moved aside to let him pass. Yost was touching his holstered weapon with dancing fingertips.

The SIC man shrugged. "Why ask such questions?" he countered. "Just come along and be sociable, kind of. People want to talk to you."

He allowed himself to be dragged through the lobby ornate with murals by radical painters and nodded appreciation at the doorman who, staring right through his captors, said enthusiastically, "Good *afternoon*, Mr. Hebster." He made himself fairly comfortable on the back seat of the dark green SIC car, a late model Hebster Monowheel.

"Surprised to see you minus your bodyguard." Yost, who was driving, remarked over his shoulder.

"Oh, I gave them the day off."

"As soon as you were through with the Primeys? No," Funatti admitted, "we never did find out where you cached them. That's one big building you own, mister. And the UM Special Investigating Commission is notoriously understaffed."

"Not forgetting it's also notoriously underpaid," Yost broke in.

"I couldn't forget that if I tried," Funatti assured him. "You know, Mr. Hebster, I wouldn't have sent my bodyguard off if I'd been in your shoes. Right now there's something about five times as dangerous as Primeys after you. I mean Humanity Firsters."

"Vandermeer Dempsey's crackpots? Thanks, but I think I'll survive."

"That's all right. Just don't give any long odds on the proposition. Those people have been expanding fast and furious. *The Evening Humanitarian* alone has a tremendous circulation. And when you figure their weekly newspapers, their penny booklets and throwaway handbills, it adds up to an impressive amount of propaganda. Day after day they bang away editorially at the people who're making money off the Aliens and Primeys. Of course, they're really hitting at the UM, like always, but if an ordinary Firster met you on the street, he'd be as likely to cut your heart out as not. Not interested? Sorry. Well, maybe you'll like this. *The Evening Humanitarian* has a cute name for you."

Yost guffawed. "Tell him, Funatti."

The corporation president looked at the little man inquiringly.

"They call you," Funatti said with great savoring deliberation, "they call you an interplanetary pimp!"

Emerging at last from the crosstown underpass, they sped up the very latest addition to the strangling city's facilities —the East Side Air-Floating Super-Duper Highway, known familiarly as Dive-Bomber Drive. At the Forty-Second Street offway, the busiest road exit in Manhattan, Yost failed to make a traffic signal. He cursed absent-mindedly and Hebster found himself nodding the involuntary passenger's agreement. They watched the elevator section dwindling downward as the cars that were to mount the highway spiraled up from the right. Between the two, there rose and fell the steady platforms of harbor traffic while, stacked like so many decks of cards, the pedestrian stages awaited their turn below.

"Look! Up there, straight ahead! See it?"

Hebster and Funatti followed Yost's long, waggling forefinger with their eyes. Two hundred feet north of the offway and almost a quarter of a mile straight up, a brown object hung in obvious fascination. Every once in a while a brilliant blue dot would enliven the heavy murk imprisoned in its bell-jar shape only to twirl around the side and be replaced by another.

"Eyes? You think they're eyes?" Funatti asked, rubbing his small dark fists against each other futilely. "I know what the scientists say—that every dot is equivalent to one person and the whole bottle is like a family or a city, maybe. But how do they know? It's a theory, a guess. *I* say they're eyes."

Yost hunched his great body half out of the open window and shaded his vision with his uniform cap against the sun. "Look at it," they heard him say, over his shoulder. A nasal twang, long-buried, came back into his voice as heaving emotion shook out its cultivated accents. "A-setting up there, a-staring and a-staring. So all-fired interested in how we get on and off a busy highway! Won't pay us no never mind when we try to talk to it, when we try to find out what it wants, where it comes from, who it is. Oh, no! It's too superior to talk to the likes of us! But it can watch us, hours on end, days without end, light and dark, winter and summer; it can watch us going about our business; and every time we dumb two-legged animals try to do something *we* find complicated, along comes a blasted 'dots-in-bottle' to watch and sneer and—"

"Hey there, man," Funatti leaned forward and tugged at his partner's green jerkin. "Easy! We're SIC, on business."

"All the same," Yost grunted wistfully, as he plopped back into his seat and pressed the power button, "I wish I had Daddy's little old M-1 Garand right now." They bowled forward, smoothed into the next long elevator section and started to descend. "It would be worth the risk of getting *pinged*."

And this was a UM man, Hebster reflected with acute discomfort. Not only UM, at that, but member of a special group carefully screened for their lack of anti-Primey prejudice, sworn to enforce the reservation laws without discrimination and dedicated to the proposition that Man could somehow achieve equality with Alien.

Well, how much dirt-eating could people do? People without a business sense, that is. His father had hauled himself out of the pick-and-shovel brigade hand over hand and raised his only son to maneuver always for greater control, to search always for that extra percentage of profit.

But others seemed to have no such abiding interest, Algernon Hebster knew regretfully.

They found it impossible to live with achievements so abruptly made inconsequential by the Aliens. To know with certainty that the most brilliant strokes of which they were capable, the most intricate designs and clever careful workmanship, could be duplicated—and surpassed—in an instant's creation by the outsiders and was of interest to them only as a collector's item. The feeling of inferiority is horrible enough when imagined; but when it isn't feeling but *knowledge*, when it is inescapable and thoroughly demonstrable, covering every aspect of constructive activity, it becomes unbearable and maddening.

No wonder men went berserk under hours of unwinking Alien scrutiny—watching them as they marched in a colorfully uniformed lodge parade, or fished through a hole in the ice, as they painfully maneuvered a giant transcontinental jet to a noiseless landing or sat in sweating, serried rows chanting to a single, sweating man to "knock it out of the park and sew the whole thing up!" No wonder they seized rusty shotgun or gleaming rifle and sped shot after vindictive shot into a sky poisoned by the contemptuous curiosity of a brown, yellow or vermillion "bottle."

Not that it made very much difference. It did give a certain release to nerves backed into horrible psychic corners. But the Aliens went right on watching, as if all this shooting and uproar, all these imprecations and weapon-wavings, were all part of the self-same absorbing show they had paid to witness and were determined to see through if for nothing else than the occasional amusing fluff some member of the inexperienced cast might commit.

The Aliens weren't injured, and the Aliens didn't feel attacked. Bullets, shells, buckshot, arrows, pebbles from a slingshot—all Man's miscellany of anger passed through them like the patient and eternal rain coming in the opposite direction. Yet the Aliens had solidity somewhere in their strange bodies. One could judge that by the way they intercepted light and heat. And also—

Also by the occasional *ping*.

Every once in a while, someone would evidently have hurt an Alien slightly. Or more probably just annoyed it by some unknown concomitant of rifle-firing or javelin-throwing.

There would be the barest suspicion of a sound—as if a guitarist had lunged at a string with his fingertip and decided against it one motor impulse too late. And, after this delicate and hardly-heard *ping*, quite unspectacularly, the rifleman would be weaponless. He would be standing there sighting stupidly up along his empty curled fingers, elbow cocked out and shoulder hunched in, like a large oafish child who had forgotten when to end the game. Neither his rifle nor a fragment of it would ever be found. And—gravely, curiously, intently—the Alien would go on watching.

The *ping* seemed to be aimed chiefly at weapons. Thus, occasionally, a 155 mm. howitzer was *pinged*, and also, occasionally, unexpectedly, it might be a muscular arm, curving back with another stone, that would disappear to the accompaniment of a tiny elfin note. And yet sometimes—could it be that the Alien, losing interest, had become careless in its irritation?—the entire man, murderously violent and shrieking, would *ping* and be no more.

It was not as if a counter-weapon were being used, but a thoroughly higher order or reply, such as a slap to an insect bite. Hebster, shivering, recalled the time he had seen a black tubular Alien swirl its amber dots over a new substreet excavation, seemingly entranced by the spectacle of men scrabbling at the earth beneath them.

A red-headed Sequoia of Irish labor had looked up from Manhattan's stubborn granite just long enough to shake the sweat from his eyelids. So doing, he had caught sight of the dot-pulsing observer and paused to snarl and lift his pneumatic drill, rattling it in noisy, if functionless, bravado at the sky. He had hardly been noticed by his mates, when the long, dark, speckled representative of a race beyond the stars turned end over end once and *ping*ed.

The heavy drill remained upright for a moment, then dropped as if it had abruptly realized its master was gone. Gone? Almost, he had never been. So thorough had his disappearance been, so rapid, with so little flicker had he been snuffed out—harming and taking with him nothing else—that it had amounted to an act of gigantic and positive noncreation.

No, Hebster decided, making threatening gestures at the Aliens was suicidal. Worse, like everything else that had been tried to date, it was useless. On the other hand, wasn't the *Humanity First* approach a complete neurosis? What *could* you do?

He reached into his soul for an article of fundamental faith, found it. "I can make money," he quoted to himself. "That's what I'm good for. That's what I can always do."

As they spun to a stop before the dumpy, brown-brick armory that the SIC had appropriated for its own use, he had a shock. Across the street was a small cigar store, the only one on the block. Brand names which had decorated the plate-glass window in all the colors of the copyright had been supplanted recently by great gilt slogans. Familiar slogans they were by now—but this close to a UM office, the Special Investigating Commission itself?

At the top of the window, the proprietor announced his affiliation in two huge words that almost screamed their hatred across the street:

HUMANITY FIRST!

Underneath these, in the exact center of the window, was the large golden initial of the organization, the wedded letters HF arising out of the huge, symbolic safety razor.

And under that, in straggling script, the theme repeated, reworded and sloganized:

"Humanity first, last and all the time!"

The upper part of the door began to get nasty:

"Deport the Aliens! Send them back to wherever they came from!"

And the bottom of the door made the store-front's only concession to business:

"Shop here! Shop Humanitarian!"

"Humanitarian!" Funatti nodded bitterly beside Hebster. "Ever see what's left of a Primey if a bunch of Firsters catch him without SIC protection? Just about enough to pick up with a blotter. I don't imagine you're too happy about boycott-shops like that?"

Hebster managed a chuckle as they walked past the saluting, green-uniformed guards. "There aren't very many Primey-inspired gadgets having to do with tobacco. And if there were, one *Shop Humanitarian* outfit isn't going to break me."

But it is, he told himself disconsolately. It is going to break me—if it means what it seems to. Organization membership is one thing and so is planetary patriotism, but business is something else.

Hebster's lips moved slowly, in half-remembered catechism: Whatever the proprietor believes in or does not believe in, he has to make a certain amount of money out of that place if he's going to keep the door free of bailiff stickers. He can't do it if he offends the greater part of his possible clientele.

Therefore, since he's still in business and, from all outward signs, doing quite well, it's obvious that he doesn't have to depend on across-the-street UM personnel. Therefore, there must be a fairly substantial trade to offset this among entirely transient customers who not only don't object to his Firstism but are willing to forego the interesting new gimmicks and lower prices in standard items that Primey technology is giving us.

Therefore, it is entirely possible—from this one extremely random but highly significant sample—that the newspapers I read have been lying and the socio-economists I employ are incompetent. It is entirely possible that the buying public, the only aspect of the public in which I have the slightest interest, is beginning a shift in general viewpoint which will profoundly affect its purchasing orientation.

It is possible that the entire UM economy is now at the top of a long slide into Humanity First domination, the secure zone of fanatic blindness demarcated by men like Vandermeer Dempsey. The highly usurious, commercially speculative economy of Imperial Rome made a similar transition in the much slower historical pace of two millennia ago and became, in three brief centuries, a static unbusinesslike world in which banking was a sin and wealth which had not been inherited was gross and dishonorable.

Meanwhile, people may already have begun to judge manufactured items on the basis of morality instead of usability, Hebster realized, as dim mental notes took their stolid place beside forming conclusions. He remembered a folderful of brilliant explanation Market Research had sent up last week dealing with unexpected consumer resistance to the new Evvakleen dishware. He had dismissed the pages of carefully developed thesis—to the effect that women were unconsciously associating the product's name with a certain Katherine Evvakios who had recently made the front page of every tabloid in the world by dint of some fast work with a breadknife on the throats of her five children and two lovers—with a yawning smile after examining its first brightly colored chart.

"Probably nothing more than normal housewifely suspicion of a radically new idea," he had muttered, "after washing dishes for years, to be told it's no longer necessary! She can't believe her Evvakleen dish is still the same after stripping the outermost film of molecules after a meal. Have to hit that educational angle a bit harder—maybe tie it in with the expendable molecules lost by the skin during a shower."

He'd penciled a few notes on the margin and flipped the whole problem onto the restless lap of Advertising and Promotion.

But then there had been the seasonal slump in furniture —about a month ahead of schedule. The surprising lack of interest in the Hebster Chubbichair, an item which should have revolutionized men's sitting habits.

Abruptly, he could remember almost a dozen unaccountable disturbances in the market recently, and all in consumer goods. That fits, he decided; any change in buying habits wouldn't be reflected in heavy industry for at least a year. The machine tools plants would feel it before the steel mills; the mills before the smelting and refining combines; and the banks and big investment houses would be the last of the dominoes to topple.

With its capital so thoroughly tied up in research and new production, his business wouldn't survive even a temporary shift of this type. Hebster Securities, Inc. could go like a speck of lint being blown off a coat collar.

Which is a long way to travel from a simple little cigar

store. Funatti's jitters about growing Firstist sentiment are contagious! he thought.

If only Kleimbocher could crack the communication problem! If we could talk to the Aliens, find some sort of place for ourselves in their universe. The Firsters would be left without a single political leg!

Hebster realized they were in a large, untidy, map-spattered office and that his escort was saluting a huge, even more untidy man who waved their hands down impatiently and nodded them out of the door. He motioned Hebster to a choice of seats. This consisted of several long walnut-stained benches scattered about the room.

P. Braganza, said the desk nameplate with ornate Gothic flow. P. Braganza had a long, twirlable and tremendously thick mustache. Also, P. Braganza needed a haircut badly. It was as if he and everything in the room had been carefully designed to give the maximum affront to Humanity Firsters. Which, considering their crew-cut, closely-shaven, "Cleanliness is next to Manliness" philosophy, meant that there was a lot of gratuitous unpleasantness in this office when a raid on a street demonstration filled it with jostling fanatics, antiseptically clean and dressed with bare-bone simplicity and neatness.

"So you're worrying about Firster effect on business?"

Hebster looked up, startled.

"No, I don't read your mind," Braganza laughed through tobacco-stained teeth. He gestured at the window behind his desk. "I saw you jump just the littlest bit when you noticed that cigar store. And then you stared at it for two full minutes. I knew what you were thinking about."

"Extremely perceptive of you, " Hebster remarked dryly.

The SIC official shook his head in a violent negative. "No, it wasn't. It wasn't a bit perceptive. I knew what you were thinking about because I sit up here day after day staring at that cigar store and thinking exactly the same thing. Braganza, I tell myself, that's the end of your job. That's the end of scientific world government. Right there on that cigar-store window."

He glowered at his completely littered desk top for a moment. Hebster's instincts woke up—there was a sales talk in the wind. He realized the man was engaged in the unaccustomed exercise of looking for a conversational gambit. He felt an itch of fear crawl up his intestines. Why should the SIC, whose power was almost above law and certainly above governments, be trying to dicker with him?

Considering his reputation for asking questions with the snarling end of a rubber hose, Braganza was being entirely too gentle, too talkative, too friendly. Hebster felt like a trapped mouse into whose disconcerted ear a cat was beginning to pour complaints about the dog upstairs.

"Hebster, tell me something. What are your goals?"

"I beg your pardon?"

"What do you want out of life? What do you spend your days planning for, your nights dreaming about? Yost likes the girls and wants more of them. Funatti's a family man, five kids. He's happy in his work because his job's fairly secure, and there are all kinds of pensions and insurance policies to back up his life."

Braganza lowered his powerful head and began a slow, reluctant pacing in front of the desk.

"Now, I'm a little different. Not that I mind being a glorified cop. I appreciate the regularity with which the finance office pays my salary, of course; and there are very few women in this town who can say that I have received an offer of affection from them with outright scorn. But the one thing for which I would lay down my life is United Mankind. *Would* lay down my life? In terms of blood pressure and heart strain you might say I've already done it. Braganza, I tell myself, you're a lucky dope. You're working for the first world government in human history. Make it count."

He stopped and spread his arms in front of Hebster. His unbuttoned green jerkin came apart awkwardly and exposed the black slab of hair on his chest. "That's me. That's basically all there is to Braganza. Now if we're to talk sensibly I have to know as much about you. I ask—what are your goals?"

The President of Hebster Securities, Inc., wet his lips. "I am afraid I'm even less complicated."

"That's all right," the other man encouraged. "Put it any way you like."

"You might say that before everything else I am a businessman. I am interested chiefly in becoming a better businessman, which is to say a bigger one. In other words, I want to be richer than I am."

Braganza peered at him intently. "And that's all?"

"All? Haven't you ever heard it said that money isn't everything, but that what it isn't it can buy?"

"It can't buy me."

Hebster examined him coolly. "I don't know if you're a sufficiently desirable commodity. I buy what I need, only occasionally making an exception to please myself."

"I don't like you." Braganza's voice had become thick and ugly. "I never liked your kind and there's no sense being polite. I might as well stop trying. I tell you straight out—I think your guts stink."

Hebster rose. "In that case, I believe I should thank you for—"

"Sit *down!* You were asked here for a reason. I don't see any point to it, but we'll go through the motions. Sit down."

Hebster sat. He wondered idly if Braganza received half the salary he paid Greta Seidenheim. Of course, Greta was talented in many different ways and performed several distinct and separately useful services. No, after tax and pension deductions, Braganza was probably fortunate to receive one third of Greta's salary.

He noticed that a newspaper was being proffered him. He took it. Branganza grunted, clumped back behind his desk and swung his swivel chair around to face the window.

It was a week-old copy of *The Evening Humanitarian*. The paper had lost the "voice-of-a-small-but-highly-articulate-minority" look, Hebster remembered from his last reading of it, and acquired the feel of publishing big business. Even if you cut in half the circulation claimed by the box in the upper left-hand corner, that still gave them three million paying readers.

In the upper right-hand corner, a red-bordered box exhorted the faithful to "*Read Humanitarian!*" A green streamer across the top of the first page announced that "*Making sense is human—to gibber, Prime!*"

But the important item was in the middle of the page. A cartoon.

Half-a-dozen Primeys wearing long, curved beards and insane, tongue-lolling grins, sat in a rickety wagon. They held reins attached to a group of straining and portly gentlemen dressed—somewhat simply—in high silk hats. The fattest and ugliest of these, the one in the lead, had a bit between his teeth. The bit was labeled "*crazy-money*" and the man, "Algernon Hebster."

Crushed and splintering under the wheels of the wagon were such varied items as a "Home Sweet Home" framed motto with a piece of wall attached, a clean-cut youngster in a Boy Scout uniform, a streamlined locomotive and a gorgeous young woman with a squalling infant under each arm.

The caption inquired starkly: "Lords of Creation—Or *Serfs?*"

"This paper seems to have developed into a fairly filthy scandal sheet," Hebster mused out loud. "I shouldn't be surprised if it makes money."

"I take it then," Braganza asked without turning around from his contemplation of the street, "that you haven't read it very regularly in recent months?"

"I am happy to say I have not."

"That was a mistake."

Hebster stared at the clumped locks of black hair. "Why?" he asked carefully.

"Because it *has* developed into a thoroughly filthy and extremely successful scandal sheet. You're its chief scandal." Braganza laughed. "You see these people look upon Primey dealing as more of a sin than a crime. And, according to that morality, you're close to Old Nick himself!"

Shutting his eyes for a moment, Hebster tried to understand people who imagined such a soul-satisfying and beautiful concept as profit to be a thing of dirt and crawling maggots. He sighed. "I've thought of Firstism as a religion myself."

That seemed to get the SIC man. He swung around excitedly and pointed with both forefingers. "I tell you that you are right! It crosses all boundaries—incompatible and warring creeds are absorbed into it. It is willful, witless denial of a highly painful fact—that there are intellects abroad in the universe which are superior to our own. And the denial grows in strength every day that we are unable to contact the Aliens. If, as seems obvious, there is no respectable place for humanity in this galactic civilization, why, say men like Vandermeer Dempsey, then let us preserve our self-conceit at the least. Let's stay close to and revel in the things that are undeniably human. In a few decades, the entire human race will have been sucked into this blinkered vacuum."

He rose and walked around the desk again. His voice had assumed a terribly earnest, tragically pleading quality. His eyes roved Hebster's face as if searching for a pin-point of weakness, an especially thin spot in the frozen calm.

"Think of it," he asked Hebster. "Periodic slaughters of scientists and artists who, in the judgment of Dempsey, have pushed out too far from the conventional center of so-called humanness. An occasional *auto-da-fé* in honor of a merchant caught selling Primey goods—"

"I shouldn't like that," Hebster admitted, smiling. He thought a moment. "I see the connection you're trying to establish with the cartoon in *The Evening Humanitarian*."

"Mister, I shouldn't have to. They want your head on the top of a long stick. They want it because you've become a symbol of dealing successfully for your own ends, with these stellar foreigners, or at least their human errand-boys and chambermaids. They figure that maybe they can put a stop to Primey-dealing generally if they put a bloody stop to you. And I tell you this—maybe they are right."

"What exactly do you propose?" Hebster asked in a low voice.

"That you come in with us. We'll make an honest man of you—officially. We want you directing our investigation;

except that the goal will not be an extra buck but all-important interracial communication and eventual interstellar negotiation."

The president of Hebster Securities, Inc., gave himself a few minutes on that one. He wanted to work out a careful reply. And he wanted time—above all, he wanted time!

He was so close to a well-integrated and world-wide commercial empire! For ten years, he had been carefully fitting the component industrial kingdoms into place, establishing suzerainty in this production network and squeezing a little more control out of that economic satrapy. He had found delectable tidbits of power in the dissolution of his civilization, endless opportunities for wealth in the shards of his race's self-esteem. He required a bare twelve months now to consolidate and coordinate. And suddenly—with the open-mouthed shock of a Jim Fiske who had cornered gold on the Exchange only to have the United States Treasury defeat him by releasing enormous quantities from the Government's own hoard—suddenly, Hebster realized he wasn't going to have the time. He was too experienced a player not to sense that a new factor was coming into the game, something outside his tables of actuarial figures, his market graphs and cargo loading indices.

His mouth was clogged with the heavy nausea of unexpected defeat. He forced himself to answer:

"I'm flattered. Braganza, I *really* am flattered. I see that Dempsey has linked us—we stand or fall together. But—I've always been a loner. With whatever help I can buy, I take care of myself. I'm not interested in any goal but the extra buck. First and last, I'm a businessman."

"Oh, stop it!" the dark man took a turn up and down the office angrily. "This a planet-wide emergency. There are times when you can't be a businessman."

"I deny that. I can't conceive of such a time."

Braganza snorted. "You can't be a businessman if you're strapped to a huge pile of blazing faggots. You can't be a businessman if people's minds are so thoroughly controlled that they'll stop eating at their leader's command. You can't be a businessman, my slavering, acquisitive friend, if demand is so well in hand that it ceases to exist."

"That's impossible!" Hebster had leaped to his feet. To his amazement, he heard his voice climbing up the scale to hysteria. "There's *always* demand. Always! The trick is to find what new form it's taken and then fill it!"

"Sorry! I didn't mean to make fun of your religion."

Hebster drew a deep breath and sat down with infinite care. He could almost feel his red corpuscles simmering.

Take it easy, he warned himself, take it easy! This is a man who must be won, not antagonized. They're changing the rules of the market, Hebster, and you'll need every friend you can buy.

Money won't work with this fellow. But there are *other* values—

"Listen to me, Braganza. We're up against the psycho-social consequences of an extremely advanced civilization hitting a comparatively barbarous one. Are you familiar with Professor Kleimbocher's Firewater Theory?"

"That the Aliens' logic hits us mentally in the same way as whiskey hit the North American Indian? And the Primeys, representing our finest minds, are the equivalent of those Indians who had the most sympathy with the white man's civilization? Yes. It's a strong analogy. Even carried to the Indians who, lying sodden with liquor in the streets of frontier towns, helped create the illusion of the treacherous, lazy, kill-you-for-a-drink aborigines while being so thoroughly despised by their tribesmen that they didn't dare go home for fear of having their throats cut. I've always felt—"

"The only part of that I want to talk about," Hebster interrupted, "is the firewater concept. Back in the Indian villages, an ever-increasing majority became convinced that firewater and gluttonous paleface civilization were synonymous, that they must rise and retake their land forcibly, killing in the process as many drunken renegades as they came across. This group can be equated with the Humanity Firsters. Then there was a minority who recognized the white men's superiority in numbers and weapons, and desperately tried to find a way of coming to terms with his civilization—terms that would not include his booze. For them read the UM. Finally, there was my kind of Indian."

Braganza knitted voluminous eyebrows and hitched himself up to a corner of the desk. "Hah?" he inquired. "What kind of Indian were *you*, Hebster?"

"The kind who had enough sense to know that the paleface had not the slightest interest in saving him from slow and painful cultural anemia. The kind of Indian, also, whose instincts were sufficiently sound so that he was scared to death of innovations like firewater and wouldn't touch the stuff to save himself from snake bite. But the kind of Indian—"

"Yes? Go on!"

"The kind who was fascinated by the strange transparent container in which the firewater came! Think how covetous an Indian potter might be of the whiskey bottle, something which was completely outside the capacity of his painfully acquired technology. Can't you see him hating, despising and terribly afraid of the smelly amber fluid, which toppled the most stalwart warriors, yet wistful to possess a bottle minus contents? That's about where I see myself, Braganza—the Indian whose greedy curiosity shines through the murk of hysterical clan politics and outsiders' contempt like a lambent flame. I want the new kind of container somehow separated from the firewater."

Unblinkingly, the great dark eyes stared at his face. A hand came up and smoothed each side of the arched mustachio with long, unknowing twirls. Minutes passed.

"Well. Hebster as our civilization's noble savage," the SIC man chuckled at last, "it almost feels right. But what does it mean in terms of the overall problem?"

"I've told you," Hebster said wearily, hitting the arm of the bench with his open hand, "that I haven't the slightest interest in the overall problem."

"And you only want the bottle. I heard you. But you're not a potter, Hebster—you haven't an elementary particle of craftsman's curiosity. All of that historical romance you spout—you don't care if your world drowns in its own agonized juice. You just want a profit."

"I never claimed an altruistic reason. I leave the general solution to men whose minds are good enough to juggle its complexities—like Kleimbocher."

"Think somebody like Kleimbocher could do it?"

"I'm almost certain he will. That was our mistake from the beginning—trying to break through with historians and psychologists. Either they've become limited by the study of human societies or—well, this is personal, but I've always felt that the science of the mind attracts chiefly those who've already experienced grave psychological difficulty. While they might achieve such an understanding of themselves in the course of their work as to become better adjusted eventually than individuals who had less problems to begin with, I'd still consider them too essentially unstable for such an intrinsically shocking experience as establishing *rapport* with an Alien. Their internal dynamics inevitably make Primeys of them."

Braganza sucked at a tooth and considered the wall behind Hebster. "And all this, you feel, wouldn't apply to Kleimbocher?"

"No, not a philology professor. He has no interest, no intellectual roots in personal and group instability. Kleimbocher's a comparative linguist—a technician, really—a specialist in basic communication. I've been out to the university and watched him work. His approach to the problem is entirely in terms of his subject—communicating with the Aliens instead of trying to understand them. There's been entirely too much intricate speculation about Alien consciousness, sexual attitudes and social organization, about stuff from which we will derive no tangible and immediate good. Kleimbocher's completely pragmatic."

"All right. I follow you. Only he went Prime this morning."

Hebster paused, a sentence dangling from his dropped jaw. "Professor Kleimbocher? *Rudolf* Kleimbocher?" he asked idiotically. "But he was so close . . . he almost had it . . . an elementary signal dictionary . . . he was about to—"

"He *did*. About nine forty-five. He'd been up all night with a Primey one of the psych professors had managed to hypnotize and gone home unusually optimistic. In the middle of his first class this morning, he interrupted himself in a lecture on medieval cyrillic to ... to gabble-honk. He sneezed and wheezed at the students for about ten minutes in the usual Primey pattern of initial irritation, then, abruptly giving them up as hopeless, worthless idiots, he levitated himself in that eerie way they almost always do at first. Banged his head against the ceiling and knocked himself out. I don't know what it was, fright, excitement, respect for the old boy perhaps, but the students neglected to tie him up before going for help. By the time they'd come back with the campus SIC man, Kleimbocher had revived and dissolved one wall of the Graduate School to get out. Here's a snapshot of him about five hundred feet in the air, lying on his back with his arms crossed behind his head, skimming west at twenty miles an hour."

The executive studied the little paper rectangle with blinking eyes. "You radioed the air force to chase him, of course."

"What's the use? We've been through *that* enough times. He'd either increase his speed and generate a tornado, drop like a stone and get himself smeared all over the countryside or materialize stuff like wet coffee grounds and gold ingots inside the jets of the pursuing plane. Nobody's caught a Primey yet in the first flush of ... whatever they do feel at first. And we might stand to lose anything from a fairly expensive hunk of aircraft, including pilot, to a couple of hundred acres of New Jersey topsoil."

Hebster groaned. "But the eighteen years of research that he represented!"

"Yeah. That's where we stand. Blind Alley umpteen hundred thousand or thereabouts. Whatever the figure is, it's awfully close to the end. If you can't crack the Alien on a straight linguistic basis, you can't crack the Alien at all, period, end of paragraph. Our most powerful weapons affect them like bubble pipes, and our finest minds are good for nothing better than to serve them in low, fawning idiocy. But the Primeys are all that's left. We might be able to talk sense to the Man if not the Master."

"Except that Primeys, by definition, don't talk sense."

Braganza nodded. "But since they were human— *ordinary* human—to start with, they represent a hope. We always knew we might some day have to fall back on our only real contact. That's why the Primey protective laws are so rigid; why the Primey reservation compounds surrounding Alien settlements are guarded by our military detachments. The lynch spirit has been evolving into the pogrom spirit as human resentment and discomfort have been growing. Humanity First is beginning to feel strong enough to challenge United Mankind. And honestly, Hebster, at this point neither of us know which would survive a real fight. But you're one of the few who have talked to Primeys, worked with them—"

"Just on business."

"Frankly, that much of a start is a thousand times further along than the best that we've been able to manage. It's so blasted ironical that the only people who've had any conversation at all with the Primeys aren't even slightly interested in the imminent collapse of civilization! Oh, well. The point is that in the present political picture, you sink with us. Recognizing this, my people are prepared to forget a great deal and document you back into respectability. How about it?"

"Funny," Hebster said thoughtfully. "It can't be knowledge that makes miracle-workers out of fairly sober scientists. They all start shooting lightnings at their families and water out of rocks far too early in Primacy to have had time to learn new techniques. It's as if by merely coming close enough to the Aliens to grovel, they immediately move into position to tap a series of cosmic laws more basic than cause and effect."

The SIC man's face slowly deepened into purple. "Well, are you coming in, or aren't you? Remember Hebster, in these times, a man who insists on business as usual is a traitor to history."

"I think Kleimbocher *is* the end," Hebster nodded to

himself. "Not much point in chasing Alien mentality if you're going to lose your best men on the way. I say let's forget all this nonsense of trying to live as equals in the same universe with Aliens. Let's concentrate on human problems and be grateful that they don't come into our major population centers and tell us to shove over."

The telephone rang. Braganza had dropped back into his swivel chair. He let the instrument squeeze out several piercing sonic bubbles while he clicked his strong square teeth and maintained a carefully-focused glare at his visitor. Finally, he picked it up, and gave it the verbal minima:

"Speaking. He is here. I'll tell him. 'Bye."

He brought his lips together, kept them pursed for a moment and then, abruptly, swung around to face the window.

"Your office, Hebster. Seems your wife and son are in town and have to see you on business. She the one you divorced ten years ago?"

Hebster nodded at his back and rose once more. "Probably wants her semiannual alimony dividend bonus. I'll have to go. Sonia never does office morale any good."

This meant trouble, he knew. "Wife-and-son" was executive code for something seriously wrong with Hebster Securities, Inc. He had not seen his wife since she had been satisfactorily maneuvered into giving him control of his son's education. As far as he was concerned, she had earned a substantial income for life by providing him with a well-mothered heir.

"Listen!" Braganza said sharply as Hebster reached the door. He still kept his eyes studiously on the street. "I tell you this: you don't want to come in with us. All right! You're a businessman first and world citizen second. All right! But keep your nose clean, Hebster. If we catch you the slightest bit off base from now on, you'll get hit with everything. We'll not only pull the most spectacular trial this corrupt old planet has ever seen, but somewhere along the line, we'll throw you and your entire organization to the wolves. We'll see to it that *Humanity*

First pulls the Hebster Tower down around your ears."

Hebster shook his head, licked his lips. "*Why*? What would that accomplish?"

"Hah! It would give a lot of us here the craziest kind of pleasure. But it would also relieve us temporarily of some of the mass pressure we've been feeling. There's always the chance that Dempsey would lose control of his hotter heads, that they'd go on a real gory rampage, make with the sound and the fury sufficiently to justify full deployment of troops. We could knock off Dempsey and all of the big-shot Firsters then, because John Q. United Mankind would have seen to his own vivid satisfaction and injury what a dangerous mob they are."

"This," Hebster commented bitterly, "is the idealistic, legalistic world government!"

Braganza's chair spun around to face Hebster and his fist came down on the desk top with all the crushing finality of a magisterial gavel. "No, it is not! It is the SIC, a plenipotentiary and highly practical bureau of the UM, especially created to organize a relationship between Alien and human. Furthermore, it's the SIC in a state of the greatest emergency when the reign of law and world government may topple at a demagogue's belch. Do you think"—his head snaked forward belligerently, his eyes slitted to thin lines of purest contempt—"that the career and fortune, even the life, let us say, of as openly selfish a slug as you, Hebster, would be placed above that of the representative body of two billion *socially* operating human beings?"

The SIC official thumped his sloppily buttoned chest. "Braganza, I tell myself now, you're lucky he's too hungry for his blasted profit to take you up on that offer. Think how much fun it's going to be to sink a hook into him when he makes a mistake at last! To drop him onto the back of *Humanity First* so that they'll run amuck and destroy themselves! Oh, get out, Hebster. I'm through with you."

He had made a mistake, Hebster reflected as he walked out of the armory and snapped his fingers at a gyrocab. The SIC was the most powerful single government agency

in a Primey-infested world; offending them for a man in
his position was equivalent to a cab driver delving into the
more uncertain aspects of a traffic cop's ancestry in the
policeman's popeyed presence.

But what could he do? Working with the SIC would
mean working under Braganza—and since maturity,
Algernon Hebster had been quietly careful to take orders
from no man. It would mean giving up a business which,
with a little more work and a little more time, might somehow still become the dominant combine on the plant.
And worst of all, it would mean acquiring a social orientation to replace the calculating businessman's viewpoint
which was the closest thing to a soul he had ever known.

The doorman of his building preceded him at a rapid
pace down the side corridor that led to his private elevator
and flourished aside for him to enter. The car stopped on
the twenty-third floor. With a heart that had sunk so deep
as to have practically foundered, Hebster picked his way
along the wide-eyed clerical stares that lined the corridor.
At the entrance to General Laboratory 23B, two tall men
in the gray livery of his personal bodyguard moved apart
to let him enter. If they had been recalled after having
been told to take the day off, it meant that a full-dress
emergency was being observed. He hoped that it had been
declared in time to prevent any publicity leakage.

It had, Greta Seidenheim assured him. "I was down here
applying the clamps five minutes after the fuss began.
Floors twenty-one through twenty-five are closed off and
all outside lines are being monitored. You can keep your
employees an hour at most past five o'clock—which gives
you a maximum of two hours and fourteen minutes."

He followed her green-tipped fingernail to the far
corner of the lab where a body lay wrapped in murky
rags. Theseus. Protruding from his back was the
yellowed ivory handle of quite an old German S.S.
dagger, 1942 edition. The silver swastika on the hilt had
been replaced by an ornate symbol—an HF. Blood had
soaked Theseus' long matted hair into an ugly red rug.

A dead Primey, Hebster thought, staring down hopelessly. In *his* building, in the laboratory to which the
Primey had been spirited two or three jumps ahead of

Yost and Funatti. This was capital offense material—if the courts ever got a chance to weigh it.

"Look at the dirty Primey-lover!" a slightly familiar voice jeered on his right. "He's scared! Make money out of *that*, Hebster!"

The corporation president strolled over to the thin man with the knobby, completely shaven head who was tied to an unused steampipe. The man's tie, which hung outside his laboratory smock, sported an unusual ornament about halfway down. It took Hebster several seconds to identify it. A miniature gold safety razor upon a black "3."

"He's a third echelon official of *Humanity First!*"

"He's also Charlie Verus of Hebster Laboratories," an extremely short man with a corrugated forehead told him. "My name is Margritt, Mr. Hebster, Dr. J. H. Margritt. I spoke to you on the communicator when the Primeys arrived."

Hebster shook his head determinedly. He waved back the other scientists who were milling around him self-consciously. "How long have third echelon officials, let alone ordinary members of *Humanity First*, been receiving salary checks in my laboratories?"

"I don't know." Margritt shrugged up at him. "Theoretically no Firsters can be Hebster employees. Personnel is supposed to be twice as efficient as the SIC when it comes to sifting background. They probably are. But what can they do when an employee joins *Humanity First* after he passed his probationary period? These proselyting times you'd need a complete force of secret police to keep tabs on all the new converts!"

"When I spoke to you earlier in the day, Margritt, you indicated disapproval of Verus. Don't you think it was your duty to let me know I had a Firster official about to mix it up with Primeys?"

The little man beat a violent negative back and forth with his chin. "I'm paid to supervise research, Mr. Hebster, not to co-ordinate your labor relations nor vote your political ticket!"

Contempt—the contempt of the creative researcher for the businessman-entrepreneur who paid his salary and was now in serious trouble—flickered behind every word he spoke. Why, Hebster wondered irritably, did people so despise a man who made money? Even the Primeys back in his office, Yost and Funatti, Braganza, Margritt—who had worked in his laboratories for years. It was his only talent. Surely, as such, it was as valid as a pianist's?

"I've never like Charlie Verus," the lab chief went on, "but we never had reason to suspect him of Firstism! He must have hit the third echelon rank about a week ago, eh, Bert?"

"Yeah," Bert agreed from across the room. "The day he came in an hour late, broke every Florence flask in the place and told us all dreamily that one day we might be very proud to tell our grandchildren that we'd worked in the same lab with Charles Bolop Verus."

"Personally," Margritt commented, "I thought he might have just finished writing a book which proved that the Great Pyramid was nothing more than a prophecy in stone of our modern textile designs. Verus was that kind. But it probably was his little safety razor that tossed him up so high. I'd say he got the promotion as a sort of payment in advance for the job he finally did today."

Hebster ground his teeth at the carefully hairless captive who tried, unsuccessfully, to spit in his face; he hurried back to the door where his private secretary was talking to the bodyguard who had been on duty in the lab.

Beyond them, against the wall, stood Larry and S.S. Lusitania conversing in a low-voiced and anxious gabble-honk. They were evidently profoundly disturbed. S.S. Lusitania kept plucking tiny little elephants out of her rags which, kicking and trumpeting tinnily, burst like malformed bubbles as she dropped them on the floor. Larry scratched his tangled beard nervously as he talked, periodically waving a hand at the ceiling which was already studded with fifty or sixty replicas of the dagger buried in Theseus. Hebster couldn't help thinking anxiously of what could have happened to his building if the Primeys had been able to act human enough to defend themselves.

"Listen, Mr. Hebster," the bodyguard began, "I was told not to—"

"Save it," Hebster rapped out. "This wasn't your fault. Even Personnel isn't to blame. Me and my experts deserve to have our necks chopped for falling so far behind the times. We can analyze any trend but the one which will make us superfluous. Greta! I want my roof helicopter ready to fly and my personal stratojet at LaGuardia alerted. Move, girl! And *you* . . . Williams is it?" he queried, leaving forward to read the bodyguard's name on his badge, "Williams, pack these two Primeys into my helicopter upstairs and stand by for a fast take-off."

He turned. "Everyone else!" he called. "You will be allowed to go home at six. You will be paid one hour's overtime. Thank you."

Charlie Verus started to sing as Hebster left the lab. By the time he reached the elevator, several of the clerks in the hallway had defiantly picked up the hymn. Hebster paused outside the elevator as he realized that fully one-fourth of the clerical personnel, male and female, were following Verus' cracked and mournful but terribly earnest tenor.

> *Mine eyes have seen the coming of*
> *the glory of the shorn:*
> *We will overturn the cess-pool*
> *where the Primey slime is born,*
> *We'll be wearing cleanly garments*
> *as we face a human morn—*
> *The First are on the march!*
> *Glory, glory, hallelujah,*
> *Glory, glory, hallelujah . . .*

If it was like this in Hebster Securities, he thought wryly as he came into his private office, how fast was *Humanity First* growing among the broad masses of people? Of course, many of those singing could be put down as sympathizers rather than converts, people who were suckers for choral groups and vigilante posses—but how much more momentum did an organization have to generate to acquire the name of political juggernaut?

The only encouraging aspect was the SIC's evident awareness of the danger and the unprecedented steps they were prepared to take as countermeasure.

Unfortunately, the unprecedented steps would take place upon Hebster.

He now had a little less than two hours, he reflected, to squirm out of the most serious single crime on the books of present World Law.

He lifted one of his telephones. "Ruth," he said. "I want to speak to Vandermeer Dempsey. Get me through to him personally."

She did. A few moments later he heard the famous voice, as rich and slow and thick as molten gold. "Hello Hebster, Vandermeer Dempsey speaking." He paused as if to draw breath, then went on sonorously: "*Humanity—may it always be ahead, but, ahead or behind, Humanity!*" He chuckled. "Our newest. What we call our telephone toast. Like it?"

"Very much," Hebster told him respectfully, remembering that this former video quizmaster might shortly be church and state combined. "Er ... Mr. Dempsey, I notice you have a new book out, and I was wondering—"

"Which one? 'Anthropolitics'?"

"That's it. A fine study! You have some very quotable lines in the chapter headed, 'Neither More Nor Less Human.' "

A raucous laugh that still managed to bubble heavily. "Young man, I have quotable lines in every chapter of every book! I maintain a writer's assembly line here at headquarters that is capable of producing up to fifty-five memorable epigrams on any subject upon ten minutes' notice. Not to mention their capacity for political metaphors and two-line jokes with sexy implications! But you wouldn't be calling me to discuss literature, however good a job of emotional engineering I have done in my little text. What is it about, Hebster? Go into your pitch."

"Well," the executive began, vaguely comforted by the Firster chieftain's cynical approach and slightly annoyed at the openness of his contempt, "I had a chat today with your friend and my friend, P. Braganza."

"I know."

"You do? How?"

Vandermeer Dempsey laughed again, the slow, good-natured chortle of a fat man squeezing the curves out of a rocking chair. "Spies, Hebster, *spies*. I have them everywhere practically. This kind of politics is twenty per cent espionage, twenty per cent organization and sixty per cent waiting for the right moment. My spies tell me everything you do."

"They didn't by any chance tell you what Braganza and I discussed?"

"Oh, they did, young man, they did!" Dempsey chuckled a carefree scale exercise. Hebster remembered his pictures: the head like a soft and enormous orange, gouged by a brilliant smile. There was no hair anywhere on the head—all of it, down to the last eyelash and follicled wart, was removed regularly through electrolysis. "According to my agents, Braganza made several strong representations on behalf of the Special Investigating Commission which you rightly spurned. Then, somewhat out of sorts, he announced that if you were henceforth detected in the nefarious enterprises which every one knows have made you one of the wealthiest men on the face of the Earth, he would use you as bait for our anger. I must say I admire the whole ingenious scheme immensely."

"And you're not going to bite," Hebster suggested. Greta Seidenheim entered the office and made a circular gesture at the ceiling. He nodded.

"On the contrary, Hebster, we *are* going to bite. We're going to bite with just a shade more vehemence than we're expected to. We're going to swallow this provocation that the SIC is devising for us and go on to make a world-wide revolution out of it. We *will*, my boy."

Hebster rubbed his left hand back and forth across his lips. "Over my dead body!" He tried to chuckle himself and managed only to clear his throat. "You're right about the conversation with Braganza, and you may be right about how you'll do when it gets down to paving stones and baseball bats. But, if you'd like to have the whole thing a lot easier, there is a little deal I have in mind—"

"Sorry, Hebster my boy. No deals. Not on this. Don't you see we really *don't* want to have it easier? For the same reason, we pay our spies nothing despite the risks they run and the great growing wealth of *Humanity First*. We found that the spies we acquired through conviction worked harder and took many more chances than those forced into our arms by economic pressure. No, we desperately need *L'affaire Hebster* to inflame the populace. We need enough excitement running loose so that it transmits to the gendarmerie and the soldiery, so that conservative citizens who normally shake their heads at a parade will drop their bundles and join the rape and robbery. Enough such citizens and Terra goes *Humanity First*."

"Heads you win, tails I lose."

The liquid gold of Dempsey's laughter poured. "I see what you mean, Hebster. Either way, UM or HF, you wind up a smear-mark on the sands of time. You had your chance when we asked for contributions from public-spirited businessmen four years ago. Quite a few of your competitors were able to see the valid relationship between economics and politics. Woodran of the Underwood Investment Trust is a first echelon official today. Not a single one of *your* top executives wears a razor. But, even so, whatever happens to you will be mild compared to the Primeys."

"The Aliens may object to their body-servants being mauled."

"There are no Aliens!" Dempsey replied in a completely altered voice. He sounded as if he had stiffened too much to be able to move his lips.

"No Aliens? Is that your latest line? You don't mean that!"

"There are only Primeys—creatures who have resigned from human responsibility and are therefore able to do many seemingly miraculous things, which real humanity refuses to do because of the lack of dignity involved. But there are no Aliens. Aliens are a Primey myth."

Hebster grunted. "That is the ideal way of facing an unpleasant fact. Stare right through it."

"If you insist on talking about such illusions as

Aliens," the rustling and angry voice cut in, "I'm afraid we can't continue the conversation. You're evidently going Prime, Hebster."

The line went dead.

Hebster scraped a finger inside the mouthpiece rim. "He believes his own stuff!" he said in an awed voice. "For all of the decadent urbanity, he has to have the same reassurance he gives his followers—the horrible, superior thing just isn't there!"

Greta Seidenheim was waiting at the door with his briefcase and both their coats. As he came away from the desk, he said, "I won't tell you not to come along, Greta, but—"

"Good," she said, swinging along behind him. "Think we'll make it to–wherever we're going?"

"Arizona. The first and largest Alien settlement. The place our friends with the funny names come from."

"What can you do there that you can't do here?"

"Frankly, Greta, I don't know. But it's a good idea to lose myself for a while. Then again, I want to get in the area where all this agony originates and take a close look; I'm an off-the-cuff businessman; I've done all of my important figuring on the spot."

There was bad news waiting for them outside the helicopter. "Mr. Hebster," the pilot told him tonelessly while cracking a dry stick of gum, "the stratojet's been seized by the SIC. Are we still going? If we do it in this thing, it won't be very far or very fast."

"We're still going," Hebster said after a moment's hesitation.

They climbed in. The two Primeys sat on the floor in the rear, sneezing conversationally at each other. Williams waved respectfully at his boss. "Gentle as lambs," he said. "In fact, they made one. I had to throw it out."

The large pot-bellied craft climbed up its rope of air and started forward from the Hebster Building.

"There must have been a leak," Greta muttered angrily. "They heard about the dead Primey. Somewhere in the organization there's a leak that I haven't been able to find. The SIC heard about the dead Primey and now they're hunting us down. Real efficient, I am!"

Hebster smiled at her grimly. She *was* very efficient. So was Personnel and a dozen other subdivisions of the organization. So was Hebster himself. But these were functioning members of a normal business designed for stable times. *Political* spies! If Dempsey could have spies and saboteurs all over Hebster Securities, why couldn't Braganza? They'd catch him before he had even started running; they'd bring him back before he could find a loophole.

They'd bring him back for trial, perhaps, for what in all probability would be known to history as the Bloody Hebster Incident. The incident that had precipitated a world revolution.

"Mr. Hebster, they're getting restless," Williams called out. "Should I relax 'em out, kind off?"

Hebster sat up sharply, hopefully. "No," he said. "Leave them alone!" He watched the suddenly agitated Primeys very closely. This was the odd chance for which he'd brought them along! Years of haggling with Primeys had taught him a lot about them. They were good for other things than sheer gimmick-craft.

Two specks appeared on the windows. They enlarged sleekly into jets with SIC insignia.

"Pilot!" Hebster called, his eyes on Larry who was pulling painfully at his beard. "Get away from the controls! Fast! Did you hear me? That was an *order! Get away from those controls!*"

The man moved off reluctantly. He was barely in time. The control board dissolved into rattling purple shards behind him. The vanes of the gyro seemed to flower into indigo saxophones. Their ears rang with supersonic frequencies as they rose above the jets on a spout of unimaginable force.

Five seconds later they were in Arizona.

They piled out of their weird craft into a sage-cluttered desert.

"I don't ever want to know what my windmill was turned into," the pilot commented, "or what was used to push it along—but how did the Primey come to understand the cops were after us?"

"I don't think he knew that," Hebster explained, "but he was sensitive enough to know he was going home, and that somehow those jets were there to prevent it. And so he functioned, in terms of his interests, in what was almost a human fashion. He protected himself!"

"Going home," Larry said. He'd been listening very closely to Hebster, dribbling from the right-hand corner of his mouth as he listened. "Haemostat, hammersdarts, hump. Home is where the hate is. Hit is where the hump is. Home and locks the door."

S.S. Lusitania had started on one leg and favored them with her peculiar fleshy smile. "Hindsight," she suggested archly, "is no more than home site. Gabble, honk?"

Larry started after her, some feet off the ground. He walked the air slowly and painfully as if the road he traveled were covered with numerous small boulders, all of them pitilessly sharp.

"Good-bye, people," Hebster said. "I'm off to see the wizard with my friends in greasy gray here. Remember, when the SIC catches up to your unusual vessel—stay close to it for that purpose, by the way—it might be wise to refer to me as someone who forced you into this. You can tell them I've gone into the wilderness looking for a solution, figuring that if I went Prime I'd still be better off than as a punching bag whose ownership is being hotly disputed by such characters as P. Braganza and Vandermeer Dempsey. I'll be back with my mind or on it."

He patted Greta's cheek on the wet spot; then he walked deftly away in pursuit of S.S. Lusitania and Larry. He glanced back once and smiled as he saw them looking curiously forlorn, especially Williams, the chunky young man who earned his living by guarding other people's bodies.

The Primeys followed a route of sorts, but it seemed to have been designed by someone bemused by the motions of an accordion. Again and again it doubled back upon itself, folded across itself, went back a hundred yards and started all over again.

This was Primey country—Arizona, where the first and largest Alien settlement had been made. There were mighty few humans in this corner of the southwest any more—just the Aliens and their coolies.

"Larry," Hebster called as an uncomfortable thought struck him. "Larry! Do ... do your masters know I'm coming?"

Missing his step as he looked up at Hebster's peremptory question, the Primey tripped and plunged to the ground. He rose, grimaced at Hebster and shook his head. "You are not a businessman," he said. "Here there can be no business. Here there can be only humorous what-you-might-call-worship. The movement to the universal, the inner nature—The realization, complete and eternal, of the partial and evanescent that alone enables ... that alone enables—" His clawed fingers writhed into each other, as if he were desperately trying to pull a communicable meaning out of the palms. He shook his head with a slow rolling motion from side to side.

Hebster saw with a shock that the old man was crying. Then going Prime had yet another similarity to madness! It gave the human an understanding of something thoroughly beyond himself, a mental summit he was constitutionally incapable of mounting. It gave him a glimpse of some psychological promised land, then buried him, still yearning, in his own inadequacies. And it left him at last bereft of pride in his realizable accomplishments with a kind of myopic half-knowledge of where he wanted to go but with no means of getting there.

"When I first came," Larry was saying haltingly, his eyes squinting into Hebster's face, as if he knew what the businessman was thinking, "when first I tried to know ... I mean the charts and textbooks I carried here, my statistics, my plotted curves were so useless. All playthings I found, disorganized, based on shadow-thought. And then, Hebster, to watch real-thought, real-control! You'll see the joy—You'll serve beside us, you will! Oh, the enormous lifting—"

His voice died into angry incoherencies as he bit into his fist. S.S. Lusitania came up, still hopping on one foot.

"Larry," she suggested in a very soft voice, "gabble-honk Hebster away?"

He looked surprised, then nodded. The two Primeys linked arms and clambered laboriously back up to the invisible road from which Larry had fallen. They stood facing him for a moment, looking like a weird, ragged, surrealistic version of Tweedledee and Tweedledum.

Then they disappeared and darkness fell around Hebster as if it had been knocked out of the jar. He felt under himself cautiously and sat down on the sand which retained all the heat of daytime Arizona.

Now!

Suppose an Alien came. Suppose an Alien asked him point-blank what it was that he wanted. That would be bad. Algernon Hebster, businessman extraordinary—slightly on the run, at the moment, of course—didn't know what he wanted; not with reference to Aliens.

He didn't want them to leave, because the Primey technology he had used in over a dozen industries was essentially an intepretation and adaptation of Alien methods. He didn't want them to stay because whatever was orderly in his world was dissolving under the acids of their omnipresent superiority.

He also knew that he personally did not want to go Prime.

What was left then? Business? Well, there was Braganza's question. What does a businessman do when demand is so well controlled that it can be said to have ceased to exist?

Or what does he do in a case like the present, when demand might be said to be nonexistent, since there was nothing the Aliens seemed to want of Man's puny hoard?

"He *finds* something they want," Hebster said out loud.

How? *How?* Well, the Indian still sold his decorative blankets to the paleface as a way of life, as a source of income. And he insisted on being paid in cash—not firewater. If *only*, Hebster thought, he could somehow contrive to meet an Alien—he'd find out soon enough what its needs were, what was basically desired.

And then as the retort-shaped, the tube-shaped, the

bell-shaped bottles materialized all around him, he understood! They had been forming the insistent questions in his mind. And they weren't satisfied with the answers he had found thus far. They liked answers. They liked answers very much indeed. If he was interested, there was always a way—

A great dots-in-bottle brushed his cortex and he screamed. "No! I don't *want* to!" he explained desperately.

Ping! went the dots-in-bottle and Hebster grabbed at his body. His continuing flesh reassured him. He felt very much like the girl in Greek mythology who had begged Zeus for the privilege of seeing him in the full regalia of his godhood. A few moments after her request had been granted, there had been nothing left of the inquisitive female but a fine feathery ash.

The bottles were swirling in and out of each other in a strange and intricate dance from which there radiated emotions vaguely akin to curiosity, yet partaking of amusement and rapture.

Why rapture? Hebster was positive he had caught that note, even allowing for the lack of similarity between mental patterns. He ran a hurried dragnet through his memory, caught a few corresponding items and dropped them after a brief, intensive examination. What was he trying to remember—what was his supremely efficient businessman's instincts trying to remind him of?

The dance became more complex, more rapid. A few bottles had passed under his feet and Hebster could see them, undulating and spinning some ten feet below the surface of the ground as if their presence had made the Earth a transparent as well as permeable medium. Completely unfamiliar with all matters Alien as he was, not knowing—not caring!—whether they danced as an expression of the counsel they were taking together, or as a matter of necessary social ritual, Hebster was able none the less to sense an approaching climax. Little crooked lines of green lightning began to erupt between the huge bottles. Something exploded near his left ear. He rubbed his face fearfully and moved away. The bottles followed, maintaining him in the imprisoning sphere of their frenzied movements.

Why *rapture?* Back in the city, the Aliens had had a terribly studious air about them as they hovered, almost motionless, above the works and lives of mankind. They were cold and careful scientists and showed not the slightest capacity for . . . for—

So he had something. At last he had something. But what do you do with an idea when you can't communicate it and can't act upon it yourself?

Ping!

The previous invitation was being repeated, more urgently. *Ping! Ping! Ping!*

"No!" he yelled and tried to stand. He found he couldn't. "I'm not . . . I don't want to go Prime!"

There was detached, almost divine laughter.

He felt that awful scrabbling inside his brain as if two or three entities were jostling each other within it. He shut his eyes hard and thought. He was close, he was very close. He had an idea, but he needed time to formulate it—a little while to figure out just exactly what the idea was and just exactly what to do with it!

Ping, ping, ping! Ping, ping, ping!

He had a headache. He felt as if his mind were being sucked out of his head. He tried to hold on to it. He couldn't.

All right, then. He relaxed abruptly, stopped trying to protect himself. But with his mind and his mouth, he yelled. For the first time in his life and with only a partially formed conception of whom he was addressing the desperate call to, Algernon Hebster screamed for help.

"I can do it!" he alternately screamed and thought. "Save money, save time, save whatever it is you want to save, whoever you are and whatever you call yourself—I can help you save! Help me, *help me—We* can do it—but *hurry*. Your problem can be solved—Economize. The balance-sheet—*help*—"

The words and frantic thoughts spun in and out of each other like the contracting rings of Aliens all around him. He kept screaming, kept the focus on his mental images, while, unbearably, somewhere inside him, a gay and jocular force began to close a valve on his sanity.

Suddenly, he had absolutely no sensation. Suddenly, he knew dozens of things he had never dreamed he could know and had forgotten a thousand times as many. Suddenly, he felt that every nerve in his body was under control of his forefinger. Suddenly, he—

Ping, ping, ping! Ping! Ping! PING! PING! PING! PING!

". . . Like that," someone said.

"What, for example?" someone else asked.

"Well, they don't even lie normally. He's been sleeping like a human being. They twist and moan in their sleep, the Primeys do, for all the world like habitual old drunks. Speaking of moans, here comes our boy."

Hebster sat up on the army cot, rattling his head. The fears were leaving him, and, with the fears gone, he would no longer be hurt. Braganza, highly concerned and unhappy, was standing next to his bed with a man who was obviously a doctor. Hebster smiled at both of them, manfully resisting the temptation to drool out a string of nonsense syllables.

"Hi, fellas," he said. "Here I come, ungathering nuts in May."

"You don't mean to tell me you communicated!" Braganza yelled. "You communicated and didn't go Prime!"

Hebster raised himself on an elbow and glanced out past the tent flap to where Greta Seidenheim stood on the other side of a port-armed guard. He waved his fist at her, and she nodded a wide-open smile back.

"Found me lying in the desert like a waif, did you?"

"*Found* you!" Braganza spat. "You were brought in by Primeys, man. First time in history they ever did that. We've been waiting for you to come to in the serene faith that once you did, everything would be all right."

The corporation president rubbed his forehead. "It will be, Braganza, it will be. Just Primeys, eh? No Aliens helping them?"

"*Aliens!*" Braganza swallowed. "What led you to believe—What gave you reason to hope that . . . that *Aliens* would help the Primeys bring you in?"

"Well, perhaps I shouldn't have used the word 'help.'

But I did think there would be a few Aliens in the group that escorted my unconscious body back to you. Sort of an honor guard, Braganza. It would have been a real nice gesture, don't you think?"

The SIC man looked at the doctor who had been following the conversation with interest. "Mind stepping out for a minute," he suggested.

He walked behind the man and dropped the tent flap into place. Then he came around to the foot of the army cot and pulled on his mustache vigorously. "Now, see here, Hebster, if you keep up this clowning, so help me I will slit your belly open and snap your intestines back in your face! *What happened?*"

"What happened?" Hebster laughed and stretched slowly, carefully, as if he were afraid of breaking the bones of his arm. "I don't think I'll ever be able to answer that question completely. And there's a section of my mind that's very glad that I won't. This much I remember clearly: I had an idea. I communicated it to the proper and interested party. We concluded—this party and I—a tentative agreement as agents, the exact terms of the agreement to be decided by our principals and its complete ratification to be contingent upon their accept-ance. Furthermore, we—All right, Braganza, all right! I'll tell it straight. Put down that folding chair. Remember, I've just been through a pretty unsettling experience!"

"Not any worse than the world is about to go through," the official growled. "While you've been out on your three-day vacation, Dempsey's been organizing a full-dress revolution every place at once. He's been very careful to limit it to parades and verbal fireworks so that we haven't been able to make with the riot squads, but it's pretty evident that he's ready to start using muscle. Tomorrow might be it; he's spouting on a world-wide video hookup and it's the opinion of the best experts we have available that his tag line will be the signal for action. Know what their slogan is? It concerns Verus who's been indicted for murder; they claim he'll be a martyr."

"And you were caught with your suspicions down.

How many SIC men turned out to be Firsters?"

Braganza nodded. "Not too many, but more than we expected. More than we could afford. He'll do it, Dempsey will, unless you've hit the real thing. Look, Hebster," his heavy voice took on a pleading quality, "don't play with me any more. Don't hold my threats against me; there was no personal animosity in them, just a terrible, fearful worry over the world and its people and the government I was supposed to protect. If you still have a gripe against me, I, Braganza, give you leave to take it out of my hide as soon as we clear this mess up. But let me know where we stand first. A lot of lives and a lot of history depend on what you did out there in that patch of desert."

Hebster told him. He began with the extraterrestrial *Walpurgis Nacht*. "Watching the Aliens slipping in and out of each other in that cock-eyed and complicated rhythm, it struck me how different they were from the thoughtful dots-in-bottles hovering over our busy places, how different all creatures are in their home environments—and how hard it is to get to know them on the basis of their company manners. And then I realized that this place wasn't their home."

"Of course. Did you find out which part of the galaxy they come from?"

"That's not what I mean. Simply because we have marked this area off—and others like it in the Gobi, in the Sahara, in Central Australia—as a reservation for those of our kind whose minds have crumbled under the clear, conscious and certain knowledge of inferiority, we cannot assume that the Aliens around whose settlements they have congregated have necessarily settled themselves."

"*Huh?*" Braganza shook his head rapidly and batted his eyes.

"In other words we have made an assumption on the basis of the Aliens' very evident superiority to ourselves. But that assumption—and therefore that superiority—was in our own terms of what is superior and inferior, and not the Aliens'. And it especially might not apply to those Aliens on . . . the reservation."

The SIC man took a rapid walk around the tent. He beat a great fist into an open sweaty palm. "I'm beginning to, just beginning to—"

"That's what I was doing at that point, just beginning to. Assumptions that don't stand up under the structure they're supposed to support have caused the ruin of more close-thinking businessmen than I would like to face across any conference table. The four brokers, for example, who, after the market crash of 1929—"

"All right," Braganza broke in hurriedly, taking a chair near the cot. "Where did you go from there?"

"I still couldn't be certain of anything; all I had to go on were a few random thoughts inspired by extra-substantial adrenalin secretions and, of course, the strong feeling that these particular Aliens weren't acting the way I had become accustomed to expect Aliens to act. They reminded me of something, of somebody. I was positive that once I got that memory tagged, I'd have most of the problem solved. And I was right."

"How were you right? What was the memory?"

"Well, I hit it backwards, kind of. I went back to Professor Kleimbocher's analogy about the paleface inflicting firewater on the Indian. I've always felt that somewhere in that analogy was the solution. And suddenly, thinking of Professor Kleimbocher and watching those powerful creatures writhing their way in and around each other, suddenly I knew what was wrong. Not the analogy, but our way of using it. We'd picked it up by the hammer head instead of the handle. The paleface gave firewater to the Indian all right—but he got something in return."

"What?"

"Tobacco. Now there's nothing very much wrong with tobacco if it isn't misused, but the first white men to smoke probably went as far overboard as the first Indians to drink. And both booze and tobacco have this in common—they make you awfully sick if you use too much for your initial experiment. See, Braganza? These Aliens out here in the desert reservation are *sick*. They have hit something in our culture that is as psychologically indigestible to them as ... well, whatever they have that sticks in our mental gullet and causes ulcers among us. They've been put into a kind of isolation in our desert areas until the problem can be licked."

"Something that's as indigestible psychologically— What could it be, Hebster?"

The businessman shrugged irritably. "I don't know. And I don't want to know. Perhaps it's just that they can't let go of a problem until they've solved it—and they can't solve the problems of mankind's activity because of mankind's inherent and basic differences. Simply because we can't understand them, we had no right to assume that they could and did understand us."

"That wasn't all, Hebster. As the comedians put it—everything we can do, they can do better."

"Then why did they keep sending Primeys in to ask for those weird gadgets and impossible gimcracks?"

"They could duplicate anything we made."

"Well, maybe that is it," Hebster suggested. "They could duplicate it, but could they design it? They show every sign of being a race of creatures who never had to make very much for themselves; perhaps they evolved fairly early into animals with direct control over matter, thus never having had to go through the various stages of artifact design. This, in our terms, is a tremendous advantage; but it inevitably would have concurrent disadvantages. Among other things, it would mean a minimum of art forms and a lack of basic engineering knowledge of the artifact itself if not of the directly activated and altered material. The fact is I was right, as I found out later.

"For example. Music is not a function of theroretical harmonics, of complete scores in the head of a conductor or composer—these come later, much later. Music is first and foremost a function of the particular instrument, the reed pipe, the skin drum, the human throat—it is a function of tangibles which a race operating upon electrons, positrons and mesons would never encounter in the course of its construction. As soon as I had that, I had the other flaw in the analogy—the assumption itself."

"You mean the assumption that we are necessarily inferior to the Aliens?"

"Right, Braganza. They can do a lot that we can't do,

but vice very much indeed versa. How many special racial talents we possess that they don't is a matter of pure conjecture—and may continue to be for a good long time. Let the theoretical boys worry that one a century from now, just so they stay away from it at present."

Braganza fingered a button on his green jerkin and stared over Hebster's head. "No more scientific investigation of them, eh?"

"Well, we can't right now and we have to face up that mildly unpleasant situation. The consolation is that they have to do the same. Don't you see? It's not a basic inadequacy. We don't have enough facts and can't get enough at the moment through normal channels of scientific observation because of the implicit psychological dangers to both races. Science, my forward-looking friend, is a complex of interlocking theories, *all derived from observation*.

"Remember, long before you had any science of navigation you had coast-hugging and river-hopping traders who knew how the various currents affected their leaky little vessels, who had learned things about the relative dependability of the moon and the stars—without any interest at all in integrating these scraps of knowledge into broader theories. Not until you have a sufficiently large body of these scraps, and are able to distinguish the preconceptions from the actual observations, can you proceed to organize a science of navigation without running the grave risk of drowning while you conduct your definitive experiments.

"A trader isn't interested in theories. He's interested only in selling something that glitters for something that glitters even more. In the process, painlessly and imperceptibly, he picks up bits of knowledge which gradually reduce the area of unfamiliarity. Until one day there are enough bits of knowledge on which to base a sort of preliminary understanding, a working hypothesis. And then, some Kleimbocher of the future, operating in an area no longer subject to the sudden and unexplainable mental disaster, can construct meticulous and exact laws out of the more obviously valid hypotheses."

"I might have known it would be something like this,

if you came back with it, Hebster! So their theorists and our theorists had better move out and the traders move in. Only how do we contact their traders—if they have any such animals?"

The corporation president sprang out of bed and began dressing. "They have them. Not a Board of Director type perhaps—but a business-minded Alien. As soon as I realized that the dots-in-bottles were acting, relative to their balanced scientific colleagues, very like our own high IQ Primeys, I knew I needed help. I needed someone I could tell about it, someone on their side who had as great a stake in an operating solution as I did. There had to be an Alien in the picture somewhere who was concerned with profit and loss statements, with how much of a return you get out of a given investment of time, personnel, material and energy. I figured with him I could talk—*business*. The simple approach: what have you got that we want and how little of what we have will you take for it. No attempts to understand completely incompatible philosophies. There had to be that kind of character somewhere in the expedition. So I shut my eyes and let out what I fondly hoped was a telepathic *yip* channeled to him. I was successful.

"Of course, I might not have been successful if he hadn't been searching desperately for just that sort of *yip*. He came buzzing up in a rousing United States Cavalry-routs-the-red-skins type of rescue, stuffing my dripping psyche back into my subconscious and hauled me up into some sort of never-never-ship. I've been in this interstellar version of Mohammed's coffin, suspended between Heaven and Earth, for three days while he alternately bargained with me and consulted the home office about developments.

"We dickered the way I do with Primeys—by running down a list of what each of us could offer and comparing it with what we wanted; each of us trying to get a little more than we gave to the other guy, in our own terms, of course. Buying and selling are intrinsically simple processes; I don't imagine our discussions were very much different from those between a couple of Phoenician sailors and the blue-painted Celtic inhabitants of early Britain."

"And this . . . this business-Alien never suggested the possibility of taking what they wanted—"

"By force? No, Braganza, not once. Might be they're too civilized for such shenanigans. Personally, I think the big reason is that they don't have any idea of what it is they do want from us. We represent a fantastic enigma to them—a species which uses matter to alter matter, producing objects which, while intended for similar functions, differ enormously from each other. You might say that we ask the question '*how!*' about their activities; and they want to know the '*why?*' about ours. Their investigators have compulsions even greater than ours. As I understand it, the intelligent races they've encountered up to this point are all comprehensible to them since they derive from parallel evolutionary paths. Every time one of their researchers gets close to the answer of why we wear various colored clothes even in climates where clothing is unnecessary, he slips over the edges and splashes.

"Of course, that's why this opposite number of mine was so worried. I don't know his exact status—he may be anything from the bookkeeper to the business-manager of the expedition—but it's his bottle-neck if the outfit continues to be uneconomic. And I gathered that not only has his occupation kind of barred him from doing the investigation his unstable pals were limping back from into the asylums he's constructed here in the deserts, but those of them who've managed to retain their sanity constantly exhibit a healthy contempt for him. They feel, you see, that their function is that of the expedition. He's strictly supercargo. Do you think it bothers them one bit," Hebster snorted, "that he has a report to prepare, to show how his expedition stood up in terms of a balance sheet—"

"Well, you did manage to communicate on that point, at least," Braganza grinned. "Maybe traders using the simple, earnestly chiseling approach will be the answer. You've certainly supplied us with more basic data already than years of heavily subsidized research. Hebster I want you to go on the air with this story you told me and show a couple of Primey Aliens to the video public."

"Uh-uh. You tell 'em. You can use the prestige. I'll think a message to my Alien buddy along the private channel he's keeping open for me, and he'll send you a couple of human-happy dots-in-bottles for the telecast. I've got to whip back to New York and get my entire outfit to work on a really encyclopedic job."

"Encyclopedic?"

The executive pulled his belt tight and reached for a tie. "Well, what else would you call the first edition of the Hebster Interstellar Catalogue of all Human Activity and Available Artifacts, prices available upon request with the understanding that they are subject to change without notice?"

HIDING PLACE

by Poul Anderson

Captain Bahadur Torrance received the news as befitted a Lodgemaster in the Federated Brotherhood of Spacemen. He heard it out, interrupting only with a few knowledgeable questions. At the end, he said calmly, "Well done, Freeman Yamamura. Please keep this to yourself till further notice. I'll think about what's to be done. Carry on." But when the engineer officer had left the cabin—the news had not been the sort you tell on the intercom—he poured himself a triple whisky, sat down, and stared emptily at the viewscreen.

He had traveled far, seen much, and been well rewarded. However, promotion being swift in his difficult line of work, he was still too young not to feel cold at hearing his death sentence.

The screen showed such a multitude of stars, hard and winter-brilliant, that only an astronaut could recognize individuals. Torrance sought past the Milky Way until he identified Polaris. Then Valhalla would lie so-and-so-many degrees away, in that direction. Not that he could see a type-G sun at this distance, without optical instruments more powerful than any aboard the *Hebe G.B.* But he found a certain comfort in knowing his eyes were sighted toward the nearest League base (houses, ships, humans, nestled in a green valley on Freya) in this almost uncharted section of our galactic arm. Especially when he didn't expect to land there, ever again.

The ship hummed around him, pulsing in and out of four-space with a quasi-speed that left light far behind and yet was still too slow to save him.

Well ... it became the captain to think first of the others. Torrance sighed and stood up. He spent a moment checking his appearance; morale was important,

never more so than now. Rather than the ususal gray
coverall of shipboard, he preferred full uniform: blue
tunic, white cape and culottes, gold braid. As a citizen of
Ramanujuan planet, he kept a turban on his dark aqui-
line head, pinned with the Ship-and-Sunburst of the
Polesotechnic League.

He went down a passageway to the owner's suite. The
steward was just leaving, a tray in his hand. Torrance
signaled the door to remain open, clicked his heels and
bowed. "I pray pardon for the interruption, sir," he said.
"May I speak privately with you? Urgent."

Nicholas van Rijn hoisted the two-liter tankard which
had been brought him. His several chins quivered under
the stiff goatee; the noise of his gulping filled the room,
from the desk littered with papers to the Huy Brasealian
jewel-tapestry hung on the opposite bulkhead. Something by Mozart lilted out of a taper. Blond, big-eyed,
and thoroughly three-dimensional, Jeri Kofoed curled on
a couch, within easy reach of him where he sprawled in his
lounger. Torrance, who was married but had been away
from home for some time, forced his gaze back to the
merchant.

"Ahhh!" Van Rijn banged the empty mug down on a
table and wiped foam from his mustaches. "Pox and
pestilence, but the first beer of the day is good! Something with it is so quite cool and—um—by damn, what
word do I want?" He thumped his sloping forehead with
one hairy fist. "I get more absent in the mind every week.
Ah, Torrance, when you are too a poor old lonely fat man
with all powers failing him, you will look back and
remember me and wish you was more good to me. But
then is too late." He sighed like a minor tornado and
scratched the pelt on his chest. In the near tropic
temperature at which he insisted on maintaining his
quarters, he need wrap only a sarong about his huge
body. "Well, what begobbled stupiding is it I must be
dragged from my all-too-much work to fix up for you,
ha?"

His tone was genial. He had, in fact, been in a good
mood ever since they escaped the Adderkops. (Who
wouldn't be? For a mere space yacht, even an armed one

with ultrapowered engines, to get away from three cruisers was more than an accomplishment; it was nearly a miracle. Van Rijn still kept four grateful candles burning before his Martian sandroot statuette of St. Dismas.) True, he sometimes threw cockery at the steward when a drink arrived later than he wished, and he fired everybody aboard ship at least once a day. But that was normal.

Jeri Kofoed arched her brows. "Your first beer, Nicky?" she murmured. "Now really! Two hours ago—"

"*Ja*, but that was before midnight time. If not Greenwich midnight, then surely on some planet somewhere, *nie*? So is a new day." Van Rijn took his churchwarden off the table and began stuffing it. "Well, sit down, Captain Torrance, make yourself to be comfortable and lend me your lighter. You look like a dynamited custard, boy. All you youngsters got no stamina. When I was a working spaceman, by Judas, we made solve our own problems. These days, death and damnation, you come ask me how to wipe your noses! Nobody has any guts but me." He slapped his barrel belly. "So what is be-jingle-bang gone wrong now?"

Torrance wet his lips. "I'd rather speak to you alone, sir."

He saw the color leave Jeri's face. She was no coward. Frontier planets, even the pleasant ones like Freya, didn't breed that sort. She had come along on what she knew would be a hazardous trip because a chance like this—to get an in with the merchant prince of the Solar Spice & Liquors Company, which was one of the major forces within the whole Polesotechnic League—was too good for an opportunistic girl to refuse. She had kept her nerve during the fight and the subsequent escape, though death came very close. But they were still far from her planet, among unknown stars, with the enemy hunting them.

"So go in the bedroom," van Rijn ordered her.

"Please," she whispered. "I'd be happier hearing the truth."

The small black eyes, set close to van Rijn's hook nose, flared. "Foulness and fulminate!" he bellowed. "What is this poppies with cocking? When I say frog, by billy damn, you jump!"

She sprang to her feet, mutinous. Without rising, he slapped her on the appropriate spot. It sounded like a pistol going off. She gasped, choked back an indignant screech, and stamped into the inner suite. Van Rijn rang for the steward.

"More beer this calls for," he said to Torrance. "Well, don't stand there making bug's eyes! I got no time for fumblydiddles, even if you overpaid loafers do. I got to make revises of all price schedules on pepper and nutmeg for Freya before we get there. Satan and stenches! At least ten percent more that idiot of a factor could charge them, and not reduce volume of sales. I swear it! All good saints, hear me and help a poor old man saddled with oatmeal-brained squatpots for workers!"

Torrance curbed his temper with an effort. "Very well, sir. I just had a report from Yamamura. You know we took a near miss during the fight, which hulled us at the engine room. The converter didn't seem damaged, but after patching the hole, the gang's been checking to make sure. And it turns out that about half the circuitry for the infrashield generator was fused. We can't replace more than a fraction of it. If we continue to run at full quasi-speed, we'll burn out the whole converter in another fifty hours."

"Ah, s-s-so." Van Rijn grew serious. The snap of the lighter, as he touched it to his pipe, came startlingly loud. "No chance of stopping altogether to make fixings? Once out of hyperdrive, we would be much too small a thing for the bestinkered Adderkops to find. Hey?"

"No, sir. I said we haven't enough replacement parts. This is a yacht, not a warship."

"Hokay, we must continue in hyperdrive. How slow must we go, to make sure we come within calling distance of Freya before our engine burns out?"

"One-tenth of top speed. It'd take us six months."

"No, my captain friend, not that long. We never reach Valhalla star at all. The Adderkops find us first."

"I suppose so. We haven't got six months' stores aboard anyway." Torrance stared at the deck. "What occurs to me is, well, we could reach one of the nearby stars. There barely might be a planet with an industrial civilization, whose people could eventually be taught to make the circuits we need. A habitable planet, at least—maybe . . .''

"*Nie!*" Van Rijn shook his head till the greasy black ringlets swirled about his shoulders. "All us men and one woman, for life on some garbagey rock where they have not even wine grapes? I'll take an Adderkop shell and go out like a gentleman, by damn!" The steward appeared. "Where you been snoozing? Beer, with God's curses on you! I need to make thinks! How you expect I can think with a mouth like a desert at midsummer?"

Torrance chose his words carefully. Van Rijn would have to be reminded that the captain, in space, was the final boss. And yet the old devil must not be antagonized, for he had a record of squirming between the horns of dilemmas. "I'm open to suggestions, sir, but I can't take the responsibility of courting enemy attack."

Van Rijn rose and lumbered about the cabin, fuming obscenities and volcanic blue clouds. As he passed the shelf where St. Dismas stood, he pinched the candles out in a marked manner. That seemed to trigger something in him. He turned about and said, "Ha! Industrial civilizations, *ja*, maybe. Not only the pest-begotten Adderkops ply this region of space. Gives some chance perhaps we can come in detection range of an un-beat-up ship, *nie*? You go get Yamamura to jack up our detector sensitivities till we can feel a gnat twiddle its wings back in my Djakarta office on Earth, so lazy the cleaners are. Then we go off this direct course and run a standard naval search pattern at reduced speed."

"And if we find a ship? Could belong to the enemy, you know."

"That chance we take."

"In all events, sir, we'll lose time. The pursuit will gain on us while we follow a search-helix. Especially if we spend days persuading some nonhuman crew who've never heard of the human race that we have to be taken to Valhalla immediately if not sooner."

"We burn that bridge when we come to it. You have might be a more hopeful scheme?"

"Well . . ." Torrance pondered awhile, blackly.

The steward came in with a fresh tankard. Van Rijn
snatched it.

"I think you're right, sir," said Torrance. "I'll go
and—"

"Virginal!" bellowed Van Rijn.

Torrance jumped. "What?"

"Virginal! That's the word I was looking for. The first
beer of the day, you idiot!"

The cabin door chimed. Torrance groaned. He'd been
hoping for some sleep, at least, after more hours on deck
than he cared to number. But when the ship prowled
through darkness, seeking another ship which might or
might not be out there, and the hunters drew closer . . .
"Come in."

Jeri Kofoed entered. Torrance gaped, sprang to his
feet, and bowed. "Freelady! What—what—what a
surprise! Is there anything I can do?"

"Please." She laid a hand on his. Her gown was of
shimmerite and shameless in cut, because van Rijn hadn't
provided any different sort, but the look she gave
Torrance had nothing to do with that. "I had to come,
Lodgemaster. If you've any pity at all, you'll listen to
me."

He waved her to a chair, offered cigarettes, and struck
one for himself. The smoke, drawn deep into his lungs,
calmed him a little. He sat down on the opposite side of
the table. "If I can be of help to you, Freelady Kofoed,
you know I'm happy to oblige. Uh . . . Freeman van Rijn
. . ."

"He's asleep. Not that he has any claims on me. I
haven't signed a contract or any such thing." Her
irritation gave way to a wry smile. "Oh, admitted, we're
all his inferiors, in fact as well as in status. I'm not
contravening his wishes, not really. It's just that he won't
answer my questions, and if I don't find out what's going
on I'll have to start screaming."

Torrance weighed a number of factors. A private
explanation, in more detail than the crew had required,
might indeed be best for her. "As you wish, Freelady,"
he said, and related what had happened to the converter.

"We can't fix it ourselves," he concluded. "If we continued traveling at high quasi-speed, we'd burn it out before we arrived; and then, without power, we'd soon die. If we proceed slowly enough to preserve it, we'd need half a year to reach Valhalla, which is more time than we have supplies for. Though the Adderkops would doubtless track us down within a week or two."

She shivered. "Why? I don't understand." She stared at her glowing cigarette end for a moment, until a degree of composure returned, and with it a touch of humor. "I may pass for a fast, sophisticated girl on Freya, Captain. But you know even better than I, Freya is a jerkwater planet on the very fringe of human civilization. We've hardly any spatial traffic, except the League merchant ships, and they never stay long in port. I really know nothing about military or political technology. No one told me this was anything more important than a scouting mission, because I never thought to inquire. Why should the Adderkops be so anxious to catch us?"

Torrance considered the total picture before framing a reply. As a spaceman of the League, he must make an effort before he could appreciate how little the enemy actually meant to colonists who seldom left their home world. The name "Adderkop" was Freyan, a term of scorn for outlaws who'd been booted off the planet a century ago. Since then, however, the Freyans had had no direct contact with them. Somewhere in the unexplored deeps beyond Valhalla, the fugitives had settled on some unknown planet. Over the generations, their numbers grew, and the numbers of their warships. But Freya was still too strong for them to raid, and had no extra-planetary enterprises of her own to be harried. Why should Freya care?

Torrance decided to explain systematically, even if he must repeat the obvious. "Well," he said, "the Adderkops aren't stupid. They keep somewhat in touch with events, and know the Polesotechnic League wants to expand its operations into this region. They don't like that. It'd mean the end of their attacks on planets which can't fight back, their squeezing of tribute and their overpriced trade. Not that the League is composed of

saints; we don't tolerate that sort of thing, but merely
because freebooting cuts into the profits of our member
companies. So the Adderkops undertook not to fight a
full-dress war against us, but to harass our outposts till we
gave it up as a bad job. They have the advantage of
knowing their own sector of space, which we hardly do at
all. And we were, indeed, at the point of writing this
whole region off and trying someplace else. Freeman van
Rijn wanted to make one last attempt. The opposition to
this was so great that he had to come here and lead the
expedition himself.

"I suppose you know what he did: used an unholy skill
at bribery and bluff, at extracting what little information
the prisoners we'd taken possessed, at fitting odd facts
together. He got a clue to a hitherto untried segment. We
flitted there, picked up a neutrino trail, and followed it to
a human-colonized planet. As you know, it's almost
certainly their own home world.

"If we bring back that information, there'll be no more
trouble with the Adderkops. Not after the League sends
in a few Star-class battleships and threatens to bombard
their planet. They realize as much. We were spotted;
several warcraft jumped us; we were lucky to get away.
Their ships are obsolete, and so far we've shown them a
clean pair of heels. But I hardly think they've quit hunting
for us. They'll send their entire fleet cruising in search.
Hyperdrive vibrations transmit instantaneously, and can
be detected out to about one light-year distance. So if any
Adderkop observes our 'wake' and homes in on it—with
us crippled—that's the end."

She drew hard on her cigarette, but remained otherwise
calm. "What are your plans?"

"A countermove. Instead of trying to make Freya—
uh—I mean, we're proceeding in a search-helix at
medium speed, straining our own detectors. If we discover another ship, we'll use the last gasp of our engines
to close in. If it's an Adderkop vessel, well, perhaps
we can seize it or something; we do have a couple of light
guns in our turrets. It may be a nonhuman craft, though.
Our intelligence reports, interrogation of prisoners,
evaluation of explores' observations et cetera, indicate

that three or four different species in this region possess the hyperdrive. The Adderkops themselves aren't certain about all of them. Space is so damned huge.''

"If it does turn out to be nonhuman?''

"Then we'll do what seems indicated.''

"I see.'' Her bright head nodded. She sat for a while, unspeaking, before she dazzled him with a smile. "Thanks, Captain. You don't know how much you've helped me.''

Torrance suppressed a foolish grin. "A pleasure, Freelady.''

"I'm coming to Earth with you. Did you know that? Freeman van Rijn has promised me a very good job.''

He always does, thought Torrance.

Jeri leaned closer. "I hope we'll have a chance on the Earthward trip to get better acquainted, Captain. Or even right now.''

The alarm bell chose that moment to ring.

The *Hebe G.B.* was a yacht, not a buccaneer frigate. When Nicholas van Rijn was aboard, though, the distinction sometimes got a little blurred. Thus she had more legs than most ships, detectors of uncommon sensitivity, and a crew experienced in the tactics of overhauling.

She was able to get a bearing on the hyperemission of the other craft long before her own vibrations were observed. Pacing the unseen one, she established the set course it was following, then poured on all available juice to intercept. If the stranger had maintained quasi-velocity, there would have been contact in three or four hours. Instead, its wake indicated a sheering off, an attempt to flee. The *Hebe G.B.* changed course too, and continued gaining on her slower quarry.

"They're afraid of us,'' decided Torrance. "And they're not running back toward the Adderkop sun. Which two facts indicate they're not Adderkops themselves, but do have reason to be scared of strangers.'' He nodded, rather grimly, for during the preliminary investigations he had inspected a few backward planets which the bandit nation had visited.

Seeing that the pursuer kept shortening her distance, the pursued turned off their hyperdrive. Reverting to intrinsic sublight velocity, converter throttled down to minimal output, their ship became an infinitesimal speck in an effectively infinite space. The maneuver often works; after casting about futilely for a while, the enemy gives up and goes home. The *Hebe G.B.*, though, was prepared. The known superlight vector, together with the instant of cutoff, gave her computers a rough idea of where the prey was. She continued to that volume of space and then hopped about in a well-designed search pattern, reverting to normal state at intervals to sample the neutrino haze which any nuclear engine emits. Those nuclear engines known as stars provided most; but by statistical analysis, the computers presently isolated one feeble nearby source. The yacht went thither . . . and wan against the glittering sky, the other ship appeared in her screens.

It was several times her size, a cylinder with bluntly rounded nose and massive drive cones, numerous housings for auxiliary boats, a single gun turret. The principles of physics dictate that the general conformation of all ships intended for a given purpose shall be roughly the same. But any spaceman could see that this one had never been built by members of Technic civilization.

Fire blazed. Even with the automatic stopping-down of his viewscreen, Torrance was momentarily blinded. Instruments told him that the stranger had fired a fusion shell which his own robogunners had intercepted with a missile. The attack had been miserably slow and feeble. This was not a warcraft in any sense; it was no more a match for the *Hebe G.B.* than the yacht was for one of the Adderkops chasing her.

"Hokay, now we got that foolishness out of the way and we can talk business," said Van Rijn. "Get them on the telecom and develop a common language. Fast! Then explain we mean no harm but want just a lift to Valhalla." He hesitated before adding, with a distinct wince, "We can pay well."

"Might prove difficult, sir," said Torrance. "Our ship

is identifiably human-built, but chances are that the only humans they've ever met are Adderkops.''

"Well, so if it makes needful, we can board them and force them to transport us, *nie*? Hurry up, for Satan's sake! If we wait too long here, like bebobbled snoozers, we'll get caught.''

Torrance was about to point out they were safe enough. The Adderkops were far behind the swifter Terrestrial ship. They could have no idea that her hyperdrive was now cut off; when they began to suspect it, they could have no measurable probability of finding her. Then he remembered that the case was not so simple. If the parleying with these strangers took unduly long—more than a week, at best—Adderkop squadrons would have penetrated this general region and gone beyond. They would probably remain on picket for months, which the humans could not do for lack of food. When a hyperdrive did start up, they'd detect it and run down this awkward merchantman with ease. The only hope was to hitch a ride to Valhalla *soon*, using the head start already gained to offset the disadvantage of reduced speed.

"We're trying all bands, sir," he said. "No response so far." He frowned worriedly. "I don't understand. They must know we've got them cold, and they must have picked up our calls and realize we want to talk. Why don't they respond? Wouldn't cost them anything."

"Maybe they abandoned ship," suggested the communications officer. "They might have hyperdriven lifeboats.''

"No." Torrance, shook his head. "We'd have spotted that ... Keep trying, Freeman Betancourt. If we haven't gotten an answer in an hour, we'll lay alongside and board.''

The receiver screens remained blank. But at the end of the grace period, when Torrance was issuing space armor, Yamamura reported something new. Neutrino output had increased from a source near the stern of the alien. Some process involving moderate amounts of energy was being carried out.

Torrance clamped down his helmet. "We'll have a look at that.''

He posted a skeleton crew—van Rijn himself, loudly protesting, took over the bridge—and led his boarding party to the main air lock. Smooth as a gliding shark (the old swine was a blue-ribbon spaceman after all, the captain realized in some astonishment), the *Hebe G.B.* clamped on a tractor beam and hauled herself toward the bigger vessel.

It disappeared. Recoil sent the yacht staggering.

"Beelzebub and botulism!" snarled van Rijn. "He went back into hyper, ha? We see about that!" The ulcerated converter shrieked as he called upon it, but the engines were given power. On a lung and a half, the Terrestrial ship again overtook the foreigner. Van Rijn phased in so casually that Torrance almost forgot this was a job considered difficult by master pilots. He evaded a frantic pressor beam and tied his yacht to the larger hull with unshearable bands of force. He cut off his hyperdrive again, for the converter couldn't take much more. Being within the force-field of the alien, the *Hebe G.B.* was carried along, though the "drag" of extra mass reduced quasi-speed considerably. If he had hoped the grappled vessel would quit and revert to normal state, he was disappointed. The linked hulls continued plunging faster than light toward an unnamed constellation.

Torrance bit back an oath, summoned his men, and went outside.

He had never forced entry on a hostile craft before, but assumed it wasn't much different from burning his way into a derelict. Having chosen his spot, he set up a balloon tent to conserve air; no use killing the alien crew. The torches of his men spewed flame; blue actinic sparks fountained backward and danced through zero gravity. Meanwhile the rest of the squad stood by with blasters and grenades.

Beyond, the curves of the two hulls dropped off to infinity. Without compensating electronic viewscreens, the sky was weirdly distorted by aberration and Doppler effect, as if the men were already dead and beating through the other existence toward Judgment. Torrance held his mind firmly to practical worries. Once inboard, the nonhumans made prisoner, how was he to communicate? Especially if he first had to gun down several of them . . .

The outer shell was peeled back. He studied the inner structure of the plate with fascination. He'd never seen anything like it before. Surely this race had developed space travel quite independently of mankind. Though their engineering must obey the same natural laws, it was radically different in detail. What was that tough but corky substance lining the inner shell? And was the circuitry embedded in it, for he didn't see any elsewhere?

The last defense gave way. Torrance swallowed hard and shot a flashbeam into the interior. Darkness and vacuum met him. When he entered the hull, he floated, weightless; artificial gravity had been turned off. The crew was hiding someplace and . . .

And . . .

Torrance returned to the yacht in an hour. When he came on the bridge, he found van Rijn seated by Jeri. The girl started to speak, took a closer look at the captain's face, and clamped her teeth together.

"Well?" snapped the merchant peevishly.

Torrance cleared his throat. His voice sounded unfamiliar and faraway to him. "I think you'd better come have a look, sir."

"You found the crew, wherever the sputtering hell they holed up? What are they like? What kind of ship is this we've gotten us, ha?"

Torrance chose to answer the last question first. "It seems to be an interstellar animal collector's transport vessel. The main hold is full of cages—environmentally controlled compartments, I should say—with the damnedest assortment of creatures I've ever seen outside Luna City Zoo."

"So what the pox is that to me? Where is the collector himself, and his fig-plucking friends?"

"Well, sir." Torrance gulped. "We're pretty sure by now they're hiding from us. Among the other animals."

A tube was run between the yacht's main lock and the entry cut into the other ship. Through this, air was pumped and electric lines were strung, to illuminate the prize. By some fancy juggling with the gravitic generator of the *Hebe G.B.*, Yamamura supplied about one-fourth Earth-weight to the foreigner, though he couldn't get the direction uniform and its decks felt canted in wildly varying degrees.

Even under such conditions, van Rijn walked ponderously. He stood with a salami in one hand and a raw onion in the other, glaring around the captured bridge. It could only be that, though it was in the bows rather than the waist. The viewscreens were still in operation, smaller than human eyes found comfortable, but revealing the same pattern of stars, surely by the same kind of optical compensators. A control console made a semicircle at the forward bulkhead, too big for a solitary human to operate. Yet presumably the designer had only had one pilot in mind, for a single seat had been placed in the middle of the arc.

Had been. A short metal post rose from the deck. Similar structures stood at other points, and boltholes showed where chairs were once fastened to them. But the seats had been removed.

"Pilot sat there at the center, I'd guess, when they weren't simply running on automatic," Torrance hazarded. "Navigator and communications officer . . . here and here? I'm not sure. Anyhow, they probably didn't use a copilot, but that chair bollard at the after end of the room suggests that an extra officer sat in reserve, ready to take over."

Van Rijn munched his onion and tugged his goatee. "Pestish big, this panel," he said. "Must be a race of bloody-be-damned octopussies, ha? Look how complicated."

He waved the salami around the half circle. The console, which seemed to be of some fluorocarbon polymer, held very few switches or buttons, but scores of flat luminous plates, each about twenty centimeters square. Some of them were depressed. Evidently these were the controls. Cautious experiment had shown that a stiff push was needed to budge them. The experiment had ended then and there, for the ship's cargo lock had opened and a good deal of air was lost before Torrance slapped the plate he had been testing hard enough to make the hull reseal itself. One should not tinker with the atomic-powered unknown, most especially not in galactic space.

"They must be strong like horses, to steer by this system without getting exhausted," went on van Rijn. "The size of everything tells likewise, *nie*?"

"Well, not exactly, sir," said Torrance. "The view-screens seem made for dwarfs. The meters even more so." He pointed to a bank of instruments, no larger than buttons, on each of which a single number glowed. (Or letter, or ideogram, or what? They looked vaguely Old Chinese.) Occasionally a symbol changed value. "A human couldn't use these long without severe eyestrain. Of course, having eyes better adapted to close work than ours doesn't prove they are not giants. Certainly that switch couldn't be reached from here without long arms, and it seems meant for big hands." By standing on tiptoe, he touched it himself, an outsize double-pole affair set overhead, just above the pilot's hypothetical seat.

The switch fell open.

A roar came from aft. Torrance lurched backward under a sudden force. He caught at a shelf on the after bulkhead to steady himself. Its thin metal buckled as he clutched. "Devilfish and dunderheads!" cried van Rijn. Bracing his columnar legs, he reached up and shoved the switch back into position. The noise ended. Normality returned. Torrance hastened to the bridge doorway, a tall arch, and shouted down the corridor beyond: "It's okay! Don't worry! We've got it under control!"

"What the blue blinking blazes happened?" demanded van Rijn, in somewhat more high-powered words.

Torrance mastered a slight case of the shakes. "Emergency switch, I'd say." His tone wavered. "Turns on the gravitic field full speed ahead, not wasting any force on acceleration compensators. Of course, we being in hyperdrive, it wasn't very effective. Only gave us a— uh—less than one-G push, intrinsic. In normal state we'd have accelerated several Gs, at least. It's for quick getaways and . . . and . . ."

"And you, with brains like fermented gravy and

bananas for fingers, went ahead and yanked it open!''

Torrance felt himself redden. ''How was I to know, sir? I must've applied less than half a kilo of force. Emergency switches aren't hair-triggered, after all. Considering how much it takes to move one of those control plates, who'd have thought the switch would respond to so little?''

Van Rijn took a closer look. ''I see now there is a hook to secure it by,'' he said. ''Must be they use that when the ship's on a high-gravity planet.'' He peered down a hole near the center of the panel, about one centimeter in diameter and fifteen deep. At the bottom a small key projected. ''This must be another special control, ha? Safer than that switch. You would need thin-nosed pliers to make a turning of it.'' He scratched his pomaded curls. ''But then, why is not the pliers hanging handy? I don't see even a hook or bracket or drawer for them.''

''I don't care,'' said Torrance. ''When the whole interior's been stripped—There's nothing but a slagheap in the engine room, I tell you—fused metal, carbonized plastic ... bedding, furniture, anything they thought might give us a clue to their identity, all melted down in a jury-rigged cauldron. They used their own converter to supply heat. That was the cause of the neutrino flux Yamamura observed. They must have worked like demons.''

''But they did not destroy all needful tools and machines, surely? Simpler then they should blow up their whole ship, and us with it. I was sweating like a hog, me, for fear they would do that. Not so good a way for a poor sinful old man to end his days, blown into radioactive stinks three hundred light-years from the vineyards of Earth.''

''N-n-no. As far as we can tell from a cursory examination, they didn't sabotage anything absolutely vital. We can't be sure, of course. Yamamura's gang would need weeks just to get a general idea of how this ship is put together, let alone the practical details of operating it. But I agree, the crew isn't bent on suicide. They've got us more neatly trapped than they know, even. Bound helplessly through space—toward their home star, maybe. In any event, almost at right angles to the course we want.''

Torrance led the way out. "Suppose we go have a more thorough look at the zoo, sir," he went on. "Yamamura talked about setting up some equipment . . . to help us tell the crew from the animals!"

The main hold comprised almost half the volume of the great ship. A corridor below, a catwalk above, ran through a double row of two-decker cubicles. These numbered ninety-six, and were identical. Each was about five meters on a side, with adjustable fluorescent plates in the ceiling and a springy, presumably inert plastic on the floor. Shelves and parallel bars ran along the side walls, for the benefit of creatures that liked jumping or climbing. The rear wall was connected to well-shielded machines. Yamamura didn't dare tamper with these, but said they obviously regulated atmosphere, temperature, gravity, sanitation, and other environmental factors within each "cage." The front wall, facing on corridor and catwalk, was transparent. It held a stout air lock, almost as high as the cubicle itself, motorized but controlled by simple wheels inside and out. Only a few compartments were empty.

The humans had not strung fluoros in this hold, for it wasn't necessary. Torrance and Van Rijn walked through shadows, among monsters; the simulated light of a dozen different suns streamed around them: red, orange, yellow, greenish, and harsh electric blue.

A thing like a giant shark, save that tendrils fluttered about its head, swam in a water-filled cubicle among fronded seaweeds. Next to it was a cageful of tiny flying reptiles, their scales aglitter in prismatic hues, weaving and dodging through the air. On the opposite side, four mammals crouched among yellow mists—beautiful creatures, the size of a bear, vividly tiger-striped, walking mostly on all fours but occasionally standing up; then you noticed the retractable claws between stubby fingers, and the carnivore jaws on the massive heads. Farther on, the humans passed half a dozen sleek red beasts like six-legged otters, frolicking in a tank of water provided for them. The environmental machines must have decided this was their feeding time, for a hopper spewed chunks of proteinaceous material into a trough and the animals lollopped over to rip it with their fangs.

"Automatic feeding," Torrance observed. "I think probably the food is synthesized on the spot, according to the specifications of each individual species as determined by biochemical methods. For the crew, also. At least, we haven't found anything like a galley."

Van Rijn shuddered. "Nothing but synthetics? Not even a little glass Genever before dinner?" He brightened. "Ha, maybe here we find a good new market. And until they learn the situation, we can charge them triple prices."

"First," clipped Torrance, "we've got to find them."

Yamamura stood near the middle of the hold, focussing a set of instruments on a certain cage. Jeri stood by, handing him what he asked for, plugging and unplugging at a small powerpack. Van Rijn hove into view. "What goes on, anyhows?" he asked.

The chief engineer turned a patient brown face to him. "I've got the rest of the crew examining the shop in detail, sir," he said. "I'll join them as soon as I've gotten Freelady Kofoed trained at this particular job. She can handle the routine of it while the rest of us use our special skills to . . ." His words trailed off. He grinned ruefully. "To poke and prod gizmos we can't possibly understand in less than a month of work, with our limited research tools."

"A month we have not got," said van Rijn. "You are here checking conditions inside each individual cage?"

"Yes, sir. They're metered, of course, but we can't read the meters, so we have to do the job ourselves. I've haywired this stuff together, to give an approximate value of gravity, atmospheric pressure and composition, temperature, illumination spectrum, and so forth. It's slow work, mostly because of all the arithmetic needed to turn the dial readings into such data. Luckily, we don't have to test every cubicle, or even most of them."

"No," said van Rijn. "Even to a union organizer, obvious this ship was never made by fishes or birds. In fact, some kind of hands is always necessary."

"Or tentacles." Yamamura nodded at the compartment before him. The light within was dim red. Several black creatures could be seen walking restlessly about. They had stumpy-legged quadrupedal bodies, from which torsos rose, centaur fashion, toward heads armored in some bony material. Below the faceless heads were six thick, ropy arms, set in triplets. Two of these ended in three boneless but probably strong fingers.

"I suspect these are our coy friends," said Yamamura. "If so, we'll have a deuce of a time. They breathe hydrogen under high pressure and triple gravity, at a temperature of seventy below."

"Are they the only ones who like that kind of weather?" asked Torrance.

Yamamura gave him a sharp look. "I see what you're getting at, Skipper. No, they aren't. In the course of putting this apparatus together and testing it, I've already found three other cubicles where conditions are similar. And in those, the animals are obviously just animals, snakes and so on, which couldn't possibly have built this ship."

"But then these octopus-horses can't be the crew, can they?" asked Jeri timidly. "I mean, if the crew were collecting animals from other planets, they wouldn't take home animals along, would they?"

"They might," said van Rijn. "We have a cat and a couple parrots aboard the *Hebe G.B., nie?* Or, there are many planets with very similar conditions of the hydrogen sort, just like Earth and Freya are much-alike oxygen planets. So that proves nothings." He turned toward Yamamura, rather like a rotating globe himself. "But see here, even if the crew did pump out the air before we boarded, why not check their reserve tanks? If we find air stored away just like these diddlers here are breathing . . ."

"I thought of that," said Yamamura. "In fact, it was almost the first thing I told the men to look for. They've located nothing. I don't think they'll have any success, either. Because what they did find was an adjustable catalytic manifold. At least, it looks as if it should be, though we'd need days to find out for certain. Anyhow, my guess is that it renews exhausted air and acts as a chemosynthesizer to replace losses from a charge of simple inorganic compounds. The crew probably bled the ship's atmosphere into space before we boarded. When we go away, if we do, they'll open the door of their particular cage a crack, so its air can trickle out. The environmental adjuster will automatically force the chemosynthesizer to replace this. Eventually the ship'll be full of enough of their kind of gas for them to venture forth and adjust things more precisely." He shrugged. "That's assuming they even need to. Perhaps Earth-type conditions suit them perfectly well."

"Uh, yes," said Torrance. "Suppose we look around some more, and line up the possibly intelligent species."

Van Rijn trundled along with him. "What sort intelligence they got, these bespattered aliens?" he grumbled. "Why try this stupid masquerade in the first places?"

"It's not too stupid to have worked so far," said Torrance dryly. "We're being carried along on a ship we don't know how to stop. They must hope we'll either give up and depart, or else that we'll remain baffled until the ship enters their home region. At which time, quite probably a naval vessel—or whatever they've got—will detect us, close in, and board us to check up on what's happened."

He paused before a compartment. "I wonder . . ."

The quadruped within was the size of an elephant, though with a more slender build, indicating a lower gravity than Earth's. Its skin was green and faintly scaled, a ruff of hair along the back. The eyes with which it looked out were alert and enigmatic. It had an elephant-like trunk, terminating in a ring of pseudodactyls which must be as strong and sensitive as human fingers.

"How much could a one-armed race accomplish?" mused Torrance. "About as much as we, I imagine, if not quite as easily. And sheer strength would compensate. That trunk could bend an iron bar."

Van Rijn grunted and went past a cubicle of feathered ungulates. He stopped before the next. "Now here are some beasts might do," he said. "We had one like them on Earth once. What they called it? Quintilla? No, gorilla. Or chimpanzee, better, of gorilla size."

Torrance felt his heart thud. Two adjoining sections

each held four animals of a kind which looked extremely hopeful. They were bipedal, short-legged and long-armed. Standing two meters tall, with a three-meter arm span, one of them could certainly operate that control console alone. The wrists, thick as a man's thighs, ended in proportionate hands, four-digited including a true thumb. The three-toed feet were specialized for walking, like man's feet. Their bodies were covered with brown fleece. Their heads were comparatively small, rising almost to a point, with massive snouts and beady eyes under cavernous brow ridges. As they wandered aimlessly about, Torrance saw that they were divided among males and females. On the sides of each neck he noticed two lumens closed by sphincters. The light upon them was the familiar yellowish white of a Sol-type star.

He forced himself to say, "I'm not sure. Those huge jaws must demand corresponding maxillary muscles, attaching to a ridge on top of the skull. Which'd restrict the cranial capacity."

"Suppose they got brains in their bellies," said van Rijn.

"Well, some people do," murmured Torrance. As the merchant choked, he added in haste, "No, actually, sir, that's hardly believable. Neural paths would get too long and so forth. Every animal I know of, if it has a central nervous system at all, keeps the brain close to the principal sense organs, which are usually located in the head. To be sure, a relatively small brain, within limits, doesn't mean these creatures are not intelligent. Their neurons might well be more efficient than ours."

"Humph and hassenpfeffer!" said van Rijn. "Might, might, might!" As they continued among strange shapes; "We can't go too much by atmosphere or light, either. If hiding, the crew could vary conditions quite a bit from their norm without hurting themselves. Gravity, too, by twenty or thirty percent."

"I hope they breathe oxygen, though—hoy!" Torrance stopped. After a moment, he realized what was so eerie about the several forms under the orange glow. They were chitinous-armored, not much bigger than a squarish military helmet and about the same shape. Four stumpy

legs projected from beneath to carry them awkwardly
about on taloned feet, also a pair of short tentacles ending
in a bush of cilia. There was nothing special about them,
as extraterrestrial animals go, except the two eyes which
gazed from beneath each helmet: as large and somehow
human as—well—the eyes of an octopus.

"Turtles," snorted van Rijn. "Armadillos at most."

"There can't be any harm in letting Jer—Freelady
Kofoed check their environment too," said Torrance.

"It can waste time."

"I wonder what they eat. I don't see any mouths."

"Those tentacles look like capillary suckers. I bet they
are parasites, or overgrown leeches, or something else
like one of my competitors. Come along."

"What do we do after we've established which species
could possibly be the crew?" said Torrance. "Try to
communicate with each in turn?"

"Not much use, that. They hide because they don't
want to communicate. Unless we can prove to them we
are not Adderkops . . . but hard to see how."

"Wait! Why'd they conceal themselves at all, if they've
had contact with the Adderkops? It wouldn't work."

"I think I tell you that, by damn," said van Rijn. "To
give them a name, let us call this unknown race the
Eksers. So. The Eksers been traveling space for some
time, but space is so big they never bumped into humans.
Then the Adderkop nation arises, in this sector where
humans never was before. The Eksers hear about this
awful new species which has gotten into space also. They
land on primitive planets where Adderkops have made
raids, talk to natives, maybe plant automatic cameras
where they think raids will soon come, maybe spy on
Adderkop camps from afar or capture a lone Adderkop
ship. So they know what humans look like, but not much
else. They do not want humans to know about them, so
they shun contact; they are not looking for trouble. Not
before they are well prepared to fight a war, at least.
Hell's sputtering griddles! Torrance, we have got to
establish our bona fides with this crew, so they take us to
Freya and afterward go tell their leaders all humans are
not so bad as the slime-begotten Adderkops. Otherwise,

maybe we wake up one day with some planets attacked by Eksers, and before the fighting ends, we have spent billions of credits.'' He shook his fists in the air and bellowed like a wounded bull. ''It is our duty to prevent this!''

''Our first duty is to get home alive, I'd say,'' Torrance answered curtly. ''I have a wife and kids.''

''Then stop throwing sheepish eyes at Jeri Kofoed. I saw her first.''

The search turned up one more possibility. Four organisms the length of a man and the build of thick-legged caterpillars dwelt under greenish light. Their bodies were dark blue, spotted with silver. A torso akin to that of the tentacled centauroids, but stockier, carried two true arms. The hands lacked thumbs, but six fingers arranged around a three-quarter circle could accomplish much the same things. Not that adequate hands prove effective intelligence; on Earth, not only simians but a number of reptiles and amphibia boast as much, even if a man has the best, and man's apish ancestors were as well equipped in this respect as we are today. However, the round flat-faced heads of these beings, the large bright eyes beneath feathery antennae of obscure function, the small jaws and delicate lips, all looked promising.

Promising of what? thought Torrance.

Three Earth-days later, he hurried down a central corridor toward the Ekser engine room.

The passage was a great hemicylinder lined with the same rubbery gray plastic as the cages, making footfalls silent and spoken words weirdly unresonant. But a deeper vibration went through it, the almost subliminal drone of the hyperengine, driving the ship into darkness toward an unknown star, and announcing their presence to any hunter straying within a light-year of them. The fluoros strung by the humans were far apart, so that one passed through bands of humming shadow. Doorless rooms opened off the hallway. Some were still full of supplies, and however peculiar the shape of tools and containers might be, however unguessable their purpose, this was a reassurance that one still lived, was not yet a ghost

aboard the Flying Dutchman. Other cabins, however had
been inhabited. And their bareness made Torrrance's
skin crawl.

Nowhere did a personal trace remain. Books, both
codex and micro, survived, but in the finely printed sym-
bology of a foreign planet. Empty places in the shelves
suggested that all illustrated volumes had been sacrificed.
Certainly he could see where pictures stuck on the walls
had been ripped down. In the big private cabins, in the
still larger one which might have been a saloon, as well as
in the engine room and workshop and bridge, only the
bollards to which furniture had been bolted were left.
Long low niches and small cubbyholes were built into the
cabin bulkheads, but when bedding had been thrown into
a white-hot cauldron, how could a man guess which were
the bunks ... if either kind were? Clothing, ornaments,
cooking and eating utensils, everything was destroyed.
One room must have been a lavatory, but the facilities
had been ripped out. Another might have been used for
scientific studies, presumably of captured animals, but
was so gutted that no human was certain.

By God you've got to admire them, Torrance thought.
Captured by beings whom they had every reason to think
of as conscienceless monsters, the aliens had not taken
the easy way out, the atomic explosion that would annihi-
late both crews. They might have, except for the chance
of this being a zoo ship. But given a hope of survival, they
snatched it, with an imaginative daring few humans could
have matched. Now they sat in plain view, waiting for the
monsters to depart—without wrecking their ship in mere
spitefulness—or for a naval vessel of their own to rescue
them. They had no means of knowing their captors were
not Adderkops, or that this sector would soon be filled
with Adderkop squadrons; the bandits rarely ventured
even this close to Valhalla. Within the limits of available
information, the aliens were acting with complete logic.
But the nerve it took!

I wish we could identify them and make friends,
thought Torrance. *The Eksers would be damned good
friends for Earth to have. Or Ramanujan, or Freya, or
the entire Polesotechnic League.* With a lopsided grin:

I'll bet they'd be nowhere near as easy to swindle as Old Nick thinks. They might well swindle him. That I'd love to see!

My reason is more personal, though, he thought with a return of bleakness. *If we don't clear up this misunderstanding soon, neither they nor we will be around. I mean soon. If we have another three or four days of grace, we're lucky.*

The passage opened on a well, with ramps curving down either side to a pair of automatic doors. One door led to the engine room, Torrance knew. Behind it, a nuclear converter powered the ship's electrical system, gravitic cones, and hyperdrive; the principles on which this was done were familiar to him, but the actual machines were engines cased in metal and in foreign symbols. He took the other door, which opened on a workshop. A good deal of the equipment here was identifiable, however distorted to his eyes: lathe, drill press, oscilloscope, crystal tester. Much else was mystery. Yamamura sat at an improvised workbench, fitting together a piece of electronic apparatus. Several other devices, haywired on breadboards, stood close by. His face was shockingly haggard, and his hands trembled. He'd been laboring this whole time, stimpills holding him awake.

As Torrance approached, the engineer was talking with Betancourt, the communications man. The entire crew of the *Hebe G.B.* were under Yamamura's direction, in a frantic attempt to outflank the Eksers by learning on their own how to operate this ship.

"I've identified the basic electrical arrangement, sir," Betancourt was saying. "They don't tap the converter directly like us; evidently they haven't developed our stepdown methods. Instead, they use a heat exchanger to run an extremely large generator—yeah, the same thing you guessed was an armature-type dynamo—and draw AC for the ship off that. Where DC is needed, the AC passes through a set of rectifier plates which, by looking at 'em, I'm sure must be copper oxide. They're bare, behind a safety screen, though so much current goes through that they're too hot to look at close up. It all seems kind of primitive to me."

"Or else merely different," sighed Yamamura. "We use a light-element fusion converter, one of whose advantages is that it can develop electric current directly. They may have perfected a power plant which utilizes moderately heavy elements with small positive packing fractions. I remember that was tried on Earth a long while ago, and given up as impractical. But maybe the Eksers are better engineers than us. Such a system would have the advantage of needing less refinement of fuel— which'd be a real advantage to a ship knocking about among unexplored planets. Maybe enough to justify that clumsy heat exchanger and rectifier system. We simply don't know."

He stared head-shakingly at the wires he was soldering. "We don't know a damn thing," he said. Seeing Torrance: "Well, carry on, Freeman Betancourt. And remember, *festina lente*."

"For fear of wrecking the ship?" asked the captain.

Yamamura nodded. "The Eksers would've known a small craft like ours couldn't generate a big enough hyperforce field to tug their own ship home," he replied. "So they'll have made sure no prize crew could make off with it. Some of the stuff may be booby-trapped to wreck itself if it isn't handled just right; and how'd we ever make repairs? Hence we're proceeding with the utmost caution. So cautiously that we haven't a prayer of figuring out the controls before the Adderkops find us."

"It keeps the crew busy, though."

"Which is useful. Uh-huh. Well, sir, I've about got my basic apparatus set up. Everything seems to test okay. Now, let me know which animal you want to investigate first." As Torrance hesitated, the engineer explained: "I have to adapt the equipment for the creature in question, you see. Especially if it's a hydrogen breather."

Torrance shook his head. "Oxygen. In fact, they live under conditions so much like ours that we can walk right into their cages. The gorilloids. That's what Jeri and I have named them. Those woolly, two-meter-tall bipeds with the ape faces."

Yamamura made an ape face of his own. "Brutes that powerful? Have they shown any sign of intelligence?"

"No. But then, would you expect the Eksers to? Jeri Kofoed and I have been parading in front of the cages of the possible species, making signs, drawing pictures, everything we could think of, trying to get the message across that we are not Adderkops and the genuine article is chasing us. No luck, of course. All the animals did give us an interested regard, though, except the gorilloids . . . which may or may not prove anything."

"What animals, now? I've been so blinking busy—"

"Well, we call 'em the tiger apes, the tentacle centaurs, the elephantoid, the helmet beasts, and the caterpiggles. That's stretching things, I know; the tiger apes and the helmet beasts are highly improbable, to say the least, and the elephantoid isn't much more convincing. The gorilloids have the right size and the most effective-looking hands, and they're oxygen breathers, as I said, so we may well take them first. Next in order of likelihood, I'd guess, are the caterpiggles and the tentacle centaurs. But the caterpiggles, though oxygen breathers, are from a high-gravity planet; their air pressure would give us narcosis in no time. The tentacle centaurs breathe hydrogen. In either case, we'd have to work in space armor."

"The gorilloids will be quite bad enough, thank you kindly."

Torrance looked at the workbench. "What exactly do you plan to do?" he asked. "I've been too busy with my own end of this affair to learn any details of yours."

"I've adapted some things from the medical kit," said Yamamura. "A sort of ophthalmoscope, for example, because the ship's instruments use color codes and finely printed symbols, so that the Eksers are bound to have eyes at least as good as ours. Then this here's a nervous-impulse tracer. It detects synaptic flows and casts a three-dimensional image into yonder crystal box, shows us the whole nervous system functioning as a set of luminous traces. By correlating this with gross anatomy, we can roughly identify the sympathetic and parasympathetic systems—or their equivalents—I hope. And the brain. And, what's really to the point, the degrees of brain activity more or less independent of the other nerve paths. That is, whether the animal is thinking."

He shrugged. "It tests out fine on me. Whether it'll work on a nonhuman, especially in a different sort of atmosphere, I do not know. I'm sure it'll develop bugs."

"'We can but try'" quoted Torrance wearily.

"I suppose Old Nick is sitting and thinking," said Yamamura in an edged voice. "I haven't seen him for quite some time."

"He's not been helping Jeri and me either," said Torrance. "Told us our attempt to communicate was futile until we could prove to the Eksers that we know who they are. And even after that, he said, the only communication at first will be by gestures made with a pistol."

"He's probably right."

"He's not right! Logically, perhaps, but not psychologically. Or morally. He sits in his suite with a case of brandy and a box of cigars. The cook, who could be down here helping you, is kept aboard the yacht to fix him his damned gourmet meals. You'd think he didn't care if we're blown out of the sky!"

He remembered his oath of fealty, his official position, and so on and so on. They felt nonsensical, here on the edge of extinction. But habit was strong. He swallowed and said harshly, "Sorry. Please ignore what I said. When you're ready, Freeman Yamamura, we'll test the gorilloids."

Six men and Jeri stood by in the passage with drawn blasters. Torrance hoped fervently they wouldn't have to shoot. He hoped even more that if they did have to, he'd still be alive.

He gestured to the four crewmen at his back. "Okay, boys." He wet his lips. His heart thuttered. Being a captain and a Lodgemaster was very fine until moments like this came, when you must make a return for your special privileges.

He spun the outside control wheel. The airlock motor hummed and opened the doors. He stepped through, into a cage of gorilloids.

Pressure differentials weren't enough to worry about, but after all this time at one-fourth G, to enter a field only ten percent less than Earth's was like a blow. He lurched, almost fell, gasped in an air warm and thick and full of unnamed stenches. Sagging back against the wall, he stared across the floor at the four bipeds. Their brown fleecy bodies loomed unfairly tall, up and up to the coarse faces. Eyes overshadowed by brows glared at him. He clapped a hand on his stun pistol. He didn't want to shoot it, either. No telling what supersonics might do to a non-human nervous system; and if these were in truth the crewfolk, the worst thing he could do was inflict serious injury on one of them. But he wasn't used to being small and frail. The knurled handgrip was a comfort.

A male growled deep in his chest, and advanced a step. His pointed head thrust forward, the sphincters in his neck opened and shut like sucking mouths; his jaws gaped to show the white teeth.

Torrance backed toward a corner. "I'll try to attract that one in the lead away from the others," he called softly. "Then get him."

"Aye." A spacehand, a stocky slant-eyed nomad from Altai, uncoiled a lariat. Behind him, the other three spread a net woven for this purpose.

The gorilloid paused. A female hooted. The male seemed to draw resolution from her. He waved the others back with a strangely humanlike gesture and stalked toward Torrance.

The captain drew his stunner, pointed it shakily, re-sheathed it, and held out both hands. "Friends," he croaked.

His hope that the masquerade might be dropped became suddenly ridiculous. He sprang back toward the air lock. The gorilloid snarled and snatched at him. Torrance wasn't fast enough. The hand ripped his shirt open and left a bloody trail on his breast. He went to hands and knees, stabbed with pain. The Altaian's lasso whirled and snaked forth. Caught around the ankles, the gorilloid crashed. His weight shook the cubicle.

"*Get him! Watch out for his arms! Here—*"

Torrance staggered back to his feet. Beyond the melee, where four men strove to wind a roaring, struggling monster in a net, he saw the remaining three creatures.

They were crowded into the opposite corner, howling in basso. The compartment was like the inside of a drum.

"Get him out," choked Torrance. "Before the others charge."

He aimed his stunner again. If intelligent, they'd know this was a weapon. They might attack anyway . . . Deftly, the man from Altai roped an arm, snubbed his lariat around the gargantuan torso, and made it fast by a slip knot. The net came into position. Helpless in cords of wire-strong fiber, the gorilloid was dragged to the entrance. Another male advanced, step by jerky step. Torrance stood his ground. The animal ululation and human shouting surfed about him, within him. His wound throbbed. He saw with unnatural clarity the muzzle full of teeth that could snap his head off, the little dull eyes turned red with fury, the hands so much like his own but black-skinned, four-fingered, and enormous . . .

"All clear, Skipper!"

The gorilloid lunged. Torrance scrambled through the air-lock chamber. The giant followed. Torrance braced himself in the corridor and aimed his stun pistol. The gorilloid halted, shivered, looked around in something resembling bewilderment, and retreated. Torrance closed the airlock.

Then he sat down and trembled.

Jeri bent over him. "Are you okay?" she breathed. "Oh! You've been hurt!"

"Nothing much," he mumbled. "Gimme a cigarette."

She took one from her belt pouch and said with a crispness he admired, "I suppose it is just a bruise and a deep scratch. But we'd better check it, anyway, and sterilize. Might be infected."

He nodded but remained where he was until he had finished the cigarette. Farther down the corridor, Yamamura's men got their captive secured to a steel framework. Unharmed but helpless, the brute yelped and tried to bite as the engineer approached with his equipment. Returning him to the cubicle afterward was likely to be almost as tough as getting him out.

Torrance rose. Through the transparent wall, he saw a female gorilloid viciously pulling something to shreds, and realized he had lost his turban when he was knocked over. He sighed. "Nothing much we can do till Yamamura gives us a verdict," he said. "Come on, let's go rest awhile."

"Sick bay first," said Jeri firmly. She took his arm. They went to the entry hole, through the tube, and into the steady half-weight of the *Hebe G.B.* which van Rijn preferred. Little was said while Jeri got Torrance's shirt off, swabbed the wound with universal disinfectant, which stung like hell, and bandaged it. Afterward he suggested a drink.

They entered the saloon. To their surprise, and to Torrance's displeasure, van Rijn was there. He sat at the inlaid mahogany table, dressed in snuff-stained lace and his usual sarong, a bottle in his right and a Trichinopoly cigar in his left. A litter of papers lay before him.

"Ah, so," he said, glancing up. "What gives?"

"They're testing a gorilloid now." Torrance flung himself into a chair. Since the steward had been drafted for the capture party, Jeri went after drinks. Her voice floated back, defiant:

"Captain Torrance was almost killed in the process. Couldn't you at least come watch, Nick?"

"What use I should watch, like some tourist with haddock eyes?" scoffed the merchant. "I make no skeletons about it, I am too old and fat to help chase large economy-size apes. Nor am I so technical I can twiddle knobs for Yamamura." He took a puff of his cigar and added complacently, "Besides, that is not my job. I am no kind of specialist, I have no fine university degrees, I learned in the school of hard knockers. But what I learned is how to make them do things for me, and then how to make something profitable from their doings."

Torrance breathed out, long and slow. With the tension eased, he was beginning to feel immensely tired. "What're you checking over?" he asked.

"Reports of engineer studies on the Ekser ship," said van Rijn. "I told everybody should take full notes on what they observed. Somewhere in those notes is maybe a clue we can use. If the gorilloids are not the Eksers, I mean. The gorilloids are possible, and I see no way to eliminate them except by Yamamura's checkers.''

Torrance rubbed his eyes. "They're not entirely plausible," he said. "Most of the stuff we've found seems meant for big hands. but some of the tools, especially, are so small that—oh, well, I suppose a nonhuman might be as puzzled by an assortment of our own tools. Does it really make sense that the same race would use sledge hammers and etching needles?''

Jeri came back with two stiff Scotch-and-sodas. His gaze followed her. In a tight blouse and half knee-length skirt, she was worth following. She sat down next to him rather than van Rijn, whose jet eyes narrowed.

However, the older man spoke mildly. "I would like if you should list for me, here and now, the other possibilities, with your reasons for thinking of them. I have seen them too, natural, but my own ideas are not all clear yet and maybe something that occurs to you would joggle my head.''

Torrance nodded. One might as well talk shop, even though he'd been over this ground a dozen times before with Jeri and Yamamura.

"Well," he said, "the tentacle centaurs appear very likely. You know the ones I mean. They live under red light and about half again Earth's gravity. A dim sun and a low temperature must make it possible for their planet to retain hydrogen, because that's what they breathe, hydrogen and argon. You know how they look: bodies sort of like rhinoceri, torsos with bone-plated heads and fingered tentacles. Like the gorilloids, they're big enough to pilot this ship easily.

"All the rest are oxygen breathers. The ones we call caterpiggles—the long, many-legged, blue-and-silver ones, with the peculiar hands and the particularly intelligent-looking faces—they're from an oddball world. It must be big. They're under three Gs in their cage, which can't be a red herring for this length of time. Body fluid adjustment would go out of kilter, if they're used to much lower weight. Nevertheless, their planet has oxygen and nitrogen rather than hydrogen, under a dozen Earth-atmospheres' pressure. The temperature is rather high, fifty degrees. I imagine their world, though of nearly Jovian mass, is so close to its sun that the hydrogen was boiled off, leaving a clear field for evolution similar to Earth's.

"The elephantoid comes from a planet with only about half our gravity. He's the single big fellow with a trunk ending in fingers. He gets by in air too thin for us, which indicates the gravity in his cubicle isn't faked either."

Torrance took a long drink. "The others live under pretty terrestroid conditions," he resumed. "For that reason, I wish they were more probable. But actually, except for the gorilloids, they seem like long shots. The helmet beasts—"

"What's that?" asked van Rijn.

"Oh, you remember," said Jeri. "Those eight or nine things like humpbacked turtles, not much bigger than your head. They crawl around on clawed feet, waving little tentacles that end in filaments. They blot up food through those, soupy stuff the machines dump into their trough. They haven't anything like effective hands—the tentacles could only do a few very simple things—but we gave them some time because they do seem to have better developed eyes than parasites usually do."

"Parasites don't evolve intelligence," said van Rijn. "They got better ways to make a living, by damn. Better make sure the helmet beasts really are parasites—in their home environments—and got no hands tucked under those shells, before you quite write them off. Who else you got?"

"The tiger apes," said Torrance. "Those striped carnivores built something like bears. They spend most of their time on all fours, but they do stand and walk on their hind legs sometimes, and they do have hands. Clumsy, thumbless ones, with retractable claws, but on all their limbs. Are four hands without thumbs as good as two with? I don't know. I'm too tired to think."

"And that's the lot, ha?" Van Rijn tilted the bottle to his lips. After a prolonged gurgling he set it down, belched, and blew smoke through his majestic nose. "Who's to try next, if the gorilloids flunk?"

"It better be the caterpiggles, in spite of the air pressure," said Jeri. "Then ... oh ... the tentacle centaurs, I suppose. Then maybe the—"

"Horse maneuvers!" Van Rijn's fist struck the table. The bottle and glasses jumped. "How long it takes to catch and check each specimen? Hours, *nie?* And in between times, takes many more hours to adjust the apparatus and chase out the hiccups it develops under a new set of conditions. Also, Yamamura will collapse if he can't sleep soon, and who else we got can do this? All the whiles, the forstunken Adderkops get closer. We have not got time for that method! If the gorilloids don't pan out, then only logic will help us: We must deduce from the facts we have who the Eksers are."

"Go ahead." Torrance drained his glass. "I'm going to take a nap."

Van Rijn purpled. "That's right!" he huffed. "Be like everybody elses. Loaf and play, dance and sing, enjoy yourselfs the liver-long day. Because you always got poor old Nicholas van Rijn there, to heap the work and worry on his back. Oh, dear St. Dismas, why can't you at least make some *one* other person in this whole universe do something useful?"

Torrance was awakened by Yamamura. The gorilloids were not the Eksers. They were color blind and incapable of focusing on the ship's instruments; their brains were small, with nearly the whole mass devoted to purely animal functions. He estimated their intelligence as equal to a dog's.

The captain stood on the bridge of the yacht, because it was a familiar place, and tried to accustom himself to being doomed.

Space had never seemed so beautiful as now. He was not well acquainted with the local constellations, but his trained gaze identified Perseus, Auriga, Taurus, not much distorted since they lay in the direction of Earth (and of Ramanujan, where gilt towers rose out of mists to catch the first sunlight, blinding against blue Mount Gandhi). A few individuals could also be picked out: ruby Betelgeuse, amber Spica, the pilot stars by which he had steered through his whole working life. Otherwise the sky was aswarm with small frosty fires, across blackness unclouded and endless. The Milky Way girdled it with cool silver, a nebula glowed faint and green, another galaxy spiraled on the mysterious edge of visibility. He thought less about the planets he had trod, even his own, than about this faring between them which was soon to terminate. For end it would, in a burst of violence too swift to be felt. Better go out thus cleanly when the Adderkops came, than into their dungeons.

He stubbed out his cigarette. Returning, his hand caressed the dear shapes of controls. He knew each switch and knob as well as he knew his own fingers. This ship was his—in a way, himself. Not like that other, whose senseless control board needed a giant and a dwarf, whose emergency switch fell under a mere slap if it wasn't hooked in place, whose—

A light footfall brought him twisting around. Irrationally, so strained was he, his heart flew up within him. When he saw it was Jeri, he eased his muscles, but the pulse continued quick in his blood.

She advanced slowly. The overhead light gleamed on her yellow hair and in the blue of her eyes. But she avoided his glance, and her mouth was not quite steady.

"What brings you here?" he asked. His tone fell even more soft than he had intended.

"Oh . . . the same as you." She stared out the view-screen. During the time since they captured the alien ship, or it captured them, a red star off the port bow had visibly grown. Now it burned baleful as they passed, a light-year distant. She grimaced and turned her back to it. "Yamamura is readjusting the test apparatus," she said thinly. "No one else knows enough about it to help him, but he has the shakes so bad from exhaustion he can scarcely do the job himself. Old Nick just sits in his suite, smoking and drinking. He's gone through that bottle already, and started another. I couldn't breathe in there any longer; it was too smoky. And he won't say a word. Except to himself, in Malay or something. I couldn't stand it."

"We may as well wait," said Torrance. "We've done everything we can, till time to check a caterpiggle. We'll have to do that spacesuited, in their own cage, and hope they don't attack us."

She slumped. "Why bother?" she said. "I know the situation as well as you. Even if the caterpiggles are the Eksers, under those conditions we'll need a couple of days to prove it. I doubt if we have that much time left. If we start toward Valhalla two days from now, I'll bet we're detected and run down before we get there. Certainly, if the caterpiggles are only animals too, we'll never get time to test a third species. Why bother?"

"We've nothing else to do," said Torrance.

"Yes, we do. Not this ugly, futile squirming about, like cornered rats. Why can't we accept that we're going to die, and use the time to . . . to be human again?"

Startled, he looked back from the sky to her. "What do you mean?"

Her lashes fluttered downward. "I suppose that would depend on what we each prefer. Maybe you'll want to, well, get your thoughts in order or something."

"How about you?" he asked through his heartbeat.

"I'm not a thinker." She smiled forlornly. "I'm afraid I'm just a shallow sort of person. I'd like to enjoy life while I have it." She half turned from him. "But I can't find anyone I'd like to enjoy it with."

He, or his hands, grabbed her bare shoulders and spun her around to face him. She felt silken under his palms. "Are you sure you can't?" he said roughly. She closed her eyes and stood with face tilted upward, lips half parted. He kissed her. After a second she responded.

After a minute, Nicholas van Rijn appeared in the doorway.

He stood an instant, pipe in hand, gun belted to his waist, before he flung the churchwarden shattering to the deck. "So!" he bellowed.

"Oh!" wailed Jeri.

She disengaged herself. A tide of rage mounted in Torrance. He knotted his fists and started toward van Rijn.

"So!" repeated the merchant. The bulkheads seemed to quiver with his voice. "By louse-bitten damn, this is a fine thing for me to come on. Satan's tail in a mousetrap! I sit hour by hour sweating my brain to the bone for the sake of your worthless life, and all whiles you, you illegitimate spawn of a snake with dandruff and a cheese mite, here you are making up to my own secretary hired with my own hard-earned money! Gargoyles and *Götter-dämmerung!* Down on your knees and beg my pardon, or I mash you up and sell you for dogfood!''

Torrance stopped, a few centimeters from van Rijn. He was slightly taller than the merchant, if less bulky, and at least thirty years younger. "Get out," he said in a strangled voice.

Van Rijn turned puce and gobbled at him.

"Get out," repeated Torrance. "I'm still the captain of this ship. I'll do what I damned well please, without interference from any loud-mouthed parasite. Get off the bridge, or I'll toss you out on your fat bottom!"

The color faded in van Rijn's cheeks. He stood motionless for whole seconds. "Well, by damn," he whispered at last. "By damn," he whispered at last. "By damn and death, cubical. He has got the nerve to talk back."

His left fist came about in a roundhouse swing. Torrance blocked it, though the force nearly threw him off his feet. His own left smacked the merchant's stomach, sank a short way into fat, encountered the muscles, and rebounded bruised. Then van Rijn's right fist clopped. The cosmos exploded around Torrance. He flew up in the air, went over backward, and lay where he fell.

When awareness returned, van Rijn was cradling his head and offering brandy which a tearful Jeri had fetched. "Here, boy. Go slow there. A little nip of this, ha? That goes good. There, now, you only lost one tooth and we get that fixed at Freya. You can even put it on expense account. There, that makes you feel more happy, *nie?* Now, girl, Jarry, Jelly, whatever your name is, give me that stimpill. Down the hatchworks, boy. And then, upsy-rosy, onto your feet. You should not miss the fun."

One-handed, van Rijn heaved Torrance erect. The captain leaned awhile on the merchant, until the stimpill removed aches and dizziness. Then, huskily through swollen lips, he asked, "What's going on? What d'you mean?"

"Why, I know who the Eksers are. I came to get you,

and we fetch them from their cage." Van Rijn nudged
Torrance with a great splay thumb and whispered almost
as softly as a hurricane, "Don't tell anyone or I have too
many fights, but I like a brass-bound nerve like you got.
When we get home, I think you transfer off this yacht to
command of a trading squadron. How you like that, ha?
But come, we still got a damn plenty of work to do."

Torrance followed him in a daze through the small ship
and the tube, into the alien, down a corridor and a ramp
to the zoological hold. Van Rijn gestured at the spacemen
posted on guard lest the Eksers make a sally. They drew
their guns and joined him, their weary slouch jerking to
alertness when he stopped before an air lock.

"Those?" sputtered Torrance. "But—I thought—"

"You thought what they hoped you would think," said
van Rijn grandly. "The scheme was good. Might have
worked, not counting the Adderkops, except that
Nicholas van Rijn was here. Now, then. We go in and
carry them all out, making a good show of our weapons.
I hope we need not get too tough with them. I expect not,
when we explain by drawings how we understand their
secret. Then they should take us to Valhalla, as we can
show by those pretty astronautical diagrams Captain
Torrance has already prepared. They will cooperate
under threats, as prisoners, at first. But on the voyage, we
can use the standard means to establish alimentary communications . . . no, terror and taxes, I mean rudimentary . . . anyhows, we get the idea across that all humans
are not Adderkops and we want to be friends and sell
them things. Hokay? We go!"

He marched through the air lock, scooped up a helmet
beast, and bore it kicking out of its cage.

Torrance didn't have time for anything en route except
his work. First the entry hole in the prize must be sealed,
while supplies and equipment were carried over from the
Hebe G.B. Then the yacht must be cast loose under her
own hyperdrive; in the few hours before her converter
quite burned out, she might draw an Adderkop in chase.
Then the journey commenced, and though the Eksers laid
a course as directed, they must be constantly watched lest

they try some suicidal stunt. Every spare moment must be devoted to the urgent business of achieving a simple common language with them. Torrance must also supervise his crew, calm their fears, and maintain a detector-watch for enemy vessels. If any had been detected, the humans would have gone off hyperdrive and hoped they could lie low. None were, but the strain was considerable.

Occasionally he slept.

Thus he got no chance to talk to van Rijn at length. He assumed the merchant had had a lucky hunch, and let it go at that.

Until Valhalla was a tiny yellow disc, outshining every other star; a League patrol ship closed on them; and, explanation being made, it gave them escort as they moved at sublight speed toward Freya.

The patrol captain intimated he'd like to come aboard. Torrance stalled him. "When we're in orbit, Freeman Agilik, I'll be delighted. But right now, things are pretty disorganized. You can understand that, I'm sure."

He switched off the alien telecom he had now learned to operate. "I'd better go below and clean up," he said. "Haven't had a bath since we abandoned the yacht. Carry on, Freeman Lafarge." He hesitated. "And—uh—Freeman Jukh-Barklakh."

Jukh grunted something. The gorilloid was too busy to talk, squatting where a pilot seat should have been, his big hands slapping control plates as he edged the ship into a hyperbolic path. Barklakh, the helmet beast on his shoulders, who had no vocal cords of his own, waved a tentacle before he dipped it into the protective shaft to turn a delicate adjustment key. The other tentacle remained buried on its side of the gorilloid's massive neck, drawing nourishment from the bloodstream, receiving sensory impulses, and emitting the motor-nerve commands of a skilled space pilot.

At first the arrangement had looked vampirish to Torrance. But though the ancestors of the helmet beasts might once have been parasites on the ancestors of the gorilloids, they were no longer. They were symbionts. They supplied the effective eyes and intellect, while the big animals supplied strength and hands. Neither species was good for much by itself; in combination, they were something rather special. Once he got used to the idea, Torrance found the sight of a helmet beast using its claws to climb up a gorilloid no more unpleasant than a man in a historical stereopic mounting a horse. And once the helmet beasts were used to the idea that these humans were not enemies, they showed a positive affection for them.

Doubtless they're thinking what lovely new specimens we can sell them for their zoo, reflected Torrance. He slapped Barklakh on the shell, patted Jukh's fur, and left the bridge.

A sponge bath of sorts and fresh garments took the edge off his weariness. He thought he'd better warn van Rijn, and knocked at the cabin which the merchant had curtained off as his own.

"Come in," boomed the bass voice. Torrance entered a cubicle blue with smoke. Van Rijn sat on an empty brandy case, one hand holding a cigar, the other holding Jeri, who was snuggled on his lap.

"Well, sit down, sit down," he roared cordially. "You find a bottle somewhere under those dirty clothes in the corner."

"I stopped by to tell you, sir, we'll have to receive the captain of our escort when we're in orbit around Freya, which'll be soon. Professional courtesy, you know. He's naturally anxious to meet the Eks—uh—the Togru-Kon-Tanakh."

"Hokay, pipe him aboard, lad." Van Rijn scowled. "Only make him bring his own bottle, and not take too long. I want to land, me; I'm sick of space. I think I'll run barefoot over the soft cool acres and acres of Freya, by damn!"

"Maybe you'd like to change clothes?" hinted Torrance.

"Ooh!" squeaked Jeri, and ran off to the cabin she sometimes occupied. Van Rijn leaned back against the wall, hitched up his sarong and crossed his shaggy legs as he said: "If that captain comes to meet the Eksers, let him meet the Eksers. I stay comfortable like I am. And I will not entertain him with how I figured out who they were.

That I keep exclusive, for sale to what news syndicate bids highest. Understand?''

His eyes grew unsettlingly sharp. Torrance gulped. ''Yes, sir.''

''Good. Now do sit down, boy. Help me put my story in order. I have not your fine education, I was a poor lonely hard-working old man from I was twelve, so I would need some help making my words as elegant as my logic.''

''Logic?'' echoed Torrance, puzzled. He tilted the flask, chiefly because the tobacco haze in here made his eyes smart. ''I thought you guessed—''

''What? You know me so little as that? No, no, by damn. Nicholas van Rijn never guesses. I *knew*.'' He reached for the bottle, took a hefty swig, and added magnanimously, ''That is, after Yamamura found the gorilloids alone could not be the peoples we wanted. Then I sat down and uncluttered my brains and thought it over.

''See, it was simple eliminations. The elephantoid was out right away. Only one of him. Maybe, in emergency, one could pilot this ship through space—but not land it, and pick up wild animals, and care for them, and all else. Also, if somethings go wrong, he is helpless.''

Torrance nodded. ''I did consider it from the spaceman's angle,'' he said. ''I was inclined to rule out the elephantoid on that ground. But I admit I didn't see the animal-collecting aspect made it altogether impossible that this could be a one-being expedition.''

''He was pretty too big anyhow,'' said van Rijn. ''As for the tiger apes, like you, I never took them serious. Maybe their ancestors was smaller and more biped, but this species is reverting to quadruped again. Animals do not specialize in being everything. Not brains and size and carnivore teeth and cat claws, all to once.

''The caterpiggles looked hokay till I remembered that time you accidental turned on the bestonkered emergency acceleration switch. Unless hooked in place, what such a switch would not be except in special cases, it fell rather easy. So easy that its own weight would make it drop open under three Earth gravities. Or at least there would always be serious danger of this. Also, that shelf you bumped into—they wouldn't build shelves so light on high-gravity planets.''

He puffed his cigar back to furnace heat. "Well, might be the tentacle centaurs,'' he continued. "Which was bad for us, because hydrogen and oxygen explode. I checked hard through the reports on the ship, hoping I could find something that would eliminate them. And by damn, I did. For this I will give St. Dismas an altar cloth, not too expensive. You see, the Eksers is kind enough to use copper oxide rectifiers, exposed to the air. Copper oxide and hydrogen, at a not very high temperature such as would soon develop from strong electricking, they make water and pure copper. Poof, no more rectifier. Therefore ergo, this ship was not designed for hydrogen breathers.'' He grinned. "You has had so much high scientific education you forgot your freshlyman chemistry.''

Torrance snapped his fingers and swore at himself.

"By eliminating, we had the helmet beasts,'' said van Rijn. "Only they could not possible be the builders. True, they could handle certain tools and controls, like that buried key, but never all of it. And they are too slow and small. How could they ever stayed alive long enough to invent spaceships? Also, animals that little don't get room for real brains. And neither armored animals nor parasites ever get much. Nor do they get good eyes. And yet the helmet beasts seemed to have very good eyes, as near as we could tell. They looked like human eyes, anyhows.

"I remembered there was both big and little cubbyholes in these cabins. Maybe bunks for two kinds of sleeper? And I thought, is the human brain a turtle just because it is armored in bone? A parasite just because it lives off blood from other places? Well, maybe some people I could name but won't, like Juan Harleman of the Venusian Tea & Coffee Growers, Inc., has parasite turtles for brains. But not me. So there I was. Q.,'' said van Rijn smugly, "E.D.''

Hoarse from talking, he picked up the bottle. Torrance sat a few minutes more, but as the other seemed disinclined to conversation, he got up to go.

Jeri met him in the doorway. In a slit and topless blue

gown which fitted like a coat of lacquer, she was a fourth-order stunblast. Torrance stopped in his tracks. Her gaze slid slowly across him, as if reluctant to depart.

"Mutant sea-otter coats," murmured van Rijn dreamily. "Martian firegems. An apartment in the Stellar Towers."

She scampered to him and ran her fingers through his hair. "Are you comfortable, Nicky, darling?" she purred. "Can't I do something for you?"

Van Rijn winked at Torrance. "Your technique, that time on the bridge—I watched and it was lousy," he said to the captain. "Also, you are not old and fat and lonesome; you have a happy family for yourself."

"Uh—yes," said Torrance. "I do." He let the curtain drop and returned to the bridge.

FINAL CONTACT
by J. A. Pollard

The science fiction writer was a man, of course, and, as she'd expected, intelligent, creative, and a whiz at dealing with machines. She could tell that by thumbing through the first five pages of his new book: "Turn the indicator panel right-side up, you asshole, or I'll cram it down your throat." "Sure boss!" Thaxter double-flipped the instrument, inserted the duplex, dapper-ray otis tube and grinned. And he never used the tired, old, "he said, she said, he shouted." That was impressive, really. Paragraphs flowed. Style. It showed an attempt at literacy.

But nothing like my own. No assholes there!

The theater entrance was crowded, with more people coming. They oogled in, craning around for the writer, stopped to buy tickets, then thinned out slowly past the little table where he sat.

You're not impressive looking. Grey mostly, bags under eyes. Also grey. Hair thin on top. Slightly overweight ... like most sedentary people. What're your hands like? Not terribly neat. Not exactly chewed.

Margery Rollins looked at her manicured nails which she'd buffed to a sheen that evening.

Why? Why did I do that? Reminds me of my mother. Nobody buffs their nails any more. No one but us "oldies." Must be the same age as me. Fifty if he's a day.

She pulled in her tummy slightly, an unnecessary action, pushed up her thick brown hair. *You may be a highly successful science fiction writer with a movie credit, mister, but a beauty you ain't.* She chuckled, somebody pushed her from behind, she stumbled slightly, found herself gazing at a pair of wide green eyes reflected from a glassed-in movie poster. Ghostly before a scarecrow, a tin man, a lion, and a little girl dancing down a yellow brick road, the eyes with their long lashes swept the high cheekbones shyly, glanced up again. The face was delicate, the small mouth opened.

My God! It's me!

She found herself at the crowd's edge in front of his table. The theater entrance opened into a small hallway which in turn opened into a café, all of it small, friendly, *artsy*. Double doors to the movie section swung to their right. The smell of popcorn, heating cider, and coffee made her think of syrup dribbling down a dish of pudding.

He hardly glanced at her. No expectancy. No question. No interest. Nothing.

What the devil do I say?

"Ah . . . This is your newest book?" *What else?* And sudden gushing: "I **love** your writing! I **love** *Oh Christ, I'm gushing!* I **love** . . . "

"Where d'ya want it signed?"

Because it seemed she had her money out and was placing it beside a money box.

It Came From Outer Space?

"Oh yes, ah . . . "

A beautiful blonde women, about thirty-four. And a half. Dressed in a tan suit. High heels. Hair long like a girl's but nicely curled. Blonde woman hovered behind his chair like a . . .

"Is this your wife?"

She can't be!

"I'm a writer too." *Did I actually say that? Damn it all!*

Someone had taken her money, passed over the book. Someone was bending down asking him, "How do you get all your ideas?" and everybody was leaning in, ready to hear molten lava, and he just kept signing. Just kept signing on, one book after the other, never looking at anyone, mumbling incomprehensibles; and his aura was one of cynicism on a leash.

People purchased left and right. Margery held her book, wondering what on earth she'd bought it for, and the blonde woman glanced in her direction for a moment between handing him books and taking in money. She was a goddess: Demeter nurturing, possibly, a bit of

Hera. Yes, Hera certainly: that air of possessiveness . . .
like wild bee's honey so thick and soporific nothing could
wash it off, nothing could unglue him from her apron
strings. Bit of fright, too, as if he might suddenly do
something bearlike.

Margery leaned in, found her mouth asking, "Do you
like this movie version of your book?"

"Goddam sons of bitches screwed it up."

"But you did the screenplay."

He never stopped signing.

"Good for the thirteen-year-olds."

*What I want is a glint of eyeball, but you're not going
to give it to me.*

Hera hovered closer.

The movie, of course, was about an alien and an earthling
but who's really the alien? having to cooperate. Which
wasn't easy for the earthman. *Man.* "You asshole! Goddam
asshole, now you've done it! Now you've got us trapped! You
fucking frog!" And they fought with laser guns and then
with sticks and finally with rocks because their airships
crashed: metal, fire, fuel screaming all over the place, and
sound, like earthquakes!

*Why do aliens usually look like reptiles? Or is a reptile
about as alien to a human as we can imagine?*

She opened the new book after she'd seen the movie,
stumbling into the café along with a few other shell-
shocked victims, then closed it and looked at the cover. A
reptile! Big dinosaur handling high technology. *Fancy
that! Nothing like what I would have imagined! No, lady,
and you're not much published either. Sweet, fantasy
stuff just doesn't make it with the hard core buffs these
days. You're lacking something, sweetie. Shall I ask
Barnaby Rudge? Big winner of all those awards? No.
Make you sound like a leech or . . . a dimwit. Well, maybe
you are.*

And in the hush, basking, as if there were no time to spend,
no future coming, wings spread wide against the grass, she
waited . . .

Yeh, that's my style.

A page fell open and he was describing what he'd

written: "My editor called and said 'funchbunk.' So, not being able to resist, I accepted and hit the research books. What resulted was what he bought, though at first I thought the idea was about as interesting as watching the Mediterranean drain."

Since when have I experienced an editor who called me?

"Hey, Barnaby! Hey! Howsa boy?" Whack whack on the shoulder.

The writer actually looked up.

"Christamighty where the hell you been keeping yourself?"

"So where'd you get the idea for this movie?"

Two men guffawing from the depths of mutual world-view.

"I don'wanna see it, Barn. Probably all about contact. Alien contact."

"That's right. How'dja guess? Magic is the word! Contact! Anybody'll buy it!"

"This your wife?"

"Never mind her, howsyer own book?"

"I'm stuck, goddamit. Need a brain storming session!"

"How about tonight?"

Margery Rollins stood up. *Males together! He can write, oh, he can write!* She wiped her mouth gently with her napkin, creased the book's cover with her nicely buffed fingernails, and left it on the table.

He's arrogant and utterly lacking in tenderness. But it fits, she thought. *Anybody who writes about a lot of men swearing while they fight one another with a lot of carefully described hardware has to be. And he's published! That is some strange kind of contact!*

It was nine-thirty and dark. People were still swarming into the theater to see their celebrity and watch his movie. Margery eased out, wondering for the hundredth time if she'd be an escapee should there ever be a fire, thinking for the hundredth time about interior exit doors, and if someone really unlocked them during performances. *Bodies piled up at the doors. Plenty of time to escape if only* ... yes, that was her type of fantasy, some of the not-so-friendly.

She paused before going to her car, jangling keys and running sentences over her imagination as she always did, polishing words, picking out character names. Oo-dup crouched in the roadway waiting for the alien. He could smell the lavender, crushed and mangled where his boots had trod. And he could see the bright gold of the buttercups bending. "If only," he thought . . . *yes, if only* . . . "if only contact would be easy!"

It never is, love.

She looked up at the sky. Black, and all the city lights blotting out the stars. *Oh, you silly lady, thinking this successful writer might have read one of yours! Thinking he might even smile while you paid him your money! Silly, silly lady!*

Light for a moment was blinding, but only for an instant. She paused, half way to her car, waiting for the other vehicle to park or pull away. But there was no sound of tires and no automobile.

Funny.

She reached her car and the man was standing close beside it.

Determined gent. What's he doing beside my car? Odd shine to him. Wonder where he's been?

"Good evening."

"Good evening."

He stood there like a rock, unmoving.

"Um . . . I'm going to move my car. Don't get run over, ha ha!"

Still didn't move. She came on briskly. *Don't panic. Nothing ever happens at this theater. The crowd's too artsy. You don't get the leather-jacket variety who only think with their tails out here.*

"Nice evening, isn't it? Come to see Barnaby Rudge no doubt? He's in there, signing his latest book." *Yes God bless him.*

"You feel hostile to this person."

Margery jumped.

"How on earth could you tell?"

"I read your mind."

"Of course you did!" *Is this a crazy?*

"You think I'm mad."

My God!
"Don't be afraid."
"I'm not!"
She was.
"Where are you going?"
"What do you want to know for?" *Look! I'm angry! I've just come out of a rather ego-destroying experience and I'm drained and want to be left alone. Alone, do you hear? Because that man in there, that successful, typical, insensitive male in there ... like James, actually ...*
"Your mate?"
Margery sagged against her car. For a moment she was dizzy with despair and shock. And fright. Then she gathered herself.
"I don't know who you are, or **what** you are, mister, but, yes, James was my mate, as you so cleverly put it. My swamping, enveloping, suffocating husband (and she suddenly screamed it) **who never let me be myself in twenty years of being married!**"
She was massively ashamed of shouting. "If it's any of your business."
"It's **all** my business."
Her dander was definitely up.
"And who gave you the go-ahead? And besides," she added, "I'm all right since the divorce. I'm perfectly, happily, individually, gratefully, deliriously, relieved and free at last ... **and I am not lonesome!**"
It was all true.
"**Do you understand me? Free at last!**"
"Free?"
"To write! To walk! To think! To be ... myself!"
He leaned down suddenly and thrust his face at her. "And haven't you always been ... yourself?"
"Are you kidding? With a man to wait on? Who criticizes every line ..."
She suddenly shook herself, jangled her keys defiantly, jammed them into the lock.
"And now, mister ..."
He put his hand over hers. *My gawd! I never thought of ...*

"You wanted to be free of your mate? You did not like serving your mate?"

"Why do you keep calling James my mate, as if it were something sacred . . ."

It was! It was! And he smashed it! Suffocating me! Never even seeing . . . me! What I was! What I am!

She straightened herself. *I'm really letting it go! I'm letting all that hostility go right here in this car park with this strange man . . . whose hand is still holding my hand . . .*

"Take your hand off my hand, please, before I . . ." *before you what, stupid? Shout? Kick him in the shins? Everybody's inside watching the movie.* Something hot seemed to flood her chest while her legs turned to rubber!

Her gaze swept the area of parked cars, came back to him. *He's huge. I've never seen so large a man!* She thought for a moment she would stop breathing, clutched her throat.

The sound of a train whistle blared so that they both started and looked over the roof of her car at the line of railroad tracks which edged the parking lot. And suddenly Margery found herself fleeing towards the tracks. *I can put the train between him and me!* But he had caught her hand and his voice, high and somewhat muffled, as if he couldn't get the words out easily, *like an old victrola* commanded, "Stop, Margery!"

How can he possibly know my name? I've never given him my name!

"Is it sacred, the name-giving? Don't run away! Come back!" And he was pulling at her.

She shook her hand, trying to dislodge his fingers, straining away, and they wrestled slightly while terror burst into her like a sword thrust. He dropped her fingers.

It's like a bad movie! It's like that damned movie back there in that theater and the script all written by some insensitive wacko . . . oh damn it. Damn it!

The whistle sounded louder. She fled across the tracks. *Train to my right, nothing but black tracks further on. What'll I do after the train passes? Where'll I hide? Warehouses over there? Will there be anything open? Just a bunch of streets and not even a doorway? What if I scream? What do the experts say to do, scream or be quiet? Isn't that what they want you to do, those men who hurt women? Don't they want you to cry and beg and . . .*

It wasn't she who was screaming. The sound came from behind her.

Margery stopped and whirled about. In the diffused city light and the extra shine from the big bulb at the theater's entrance, and in the light of the one-eyed locomotive bearing down like a thundering buffalo she could see the man. He was crouching in the middle of the tracks.

What are you doing there?

Something in his attitude arrested her. The train was bearing down, the whistle blasting, and the man was bent nearly double in the middle of the tracks directly before it, *looking at the ground.*

"Get off the tracks!" *I'm flying! I think I must be flying!* Because she found herself beside him shouting. "Get out of the way! You'll be run over!"

"My foot is caught!"

His face turned towards her for an instant, pale, grimacing, gruesome in its terror. A very odd face. *My God! Who wrote this script?*

The engine appeared claustrophobically near now, momentous in the brilliance of its single light and the blackness and sound behind it. All of night seemed to be rushing at them with a malevolent inescapable will.

What am I doing here? She knelt calmly by his foot and saw, in the terrible gleam of that single eye bearing down upon them, that he had wedged the toe of his shoe under a rail, between two of the wooden carriers; and she saw that he wouldn't be able to pull it out.

"Get away!"

"Shut up!" *James always hated me like this.*

"Save yourself!"

Let mother do it for you.

He put his hands down, tugging at her, pushing her away, but she slapped him viciously, suddenly swore, screaming, "Why do you insist on wearing lacings like these anyway? I've never seen any like them!" *I've never seen so many!* It was a high, heeled, hiking boot and the laces seemed to wind up his leg forever.

"Get away!"

A rush of air slammed into them. A gigantic brittle sun, cold and hideous poured down. He shouted loudly, giving her a spinning shove; but she had the lacings in her hand, she grasped his ankle, his foot was coming out, and, as he pushed, she grabbed his arm and pulled with all her might. *We're dead!*

They rolled together hard, his body hitting hers. There was a long interval of wind and noise. *I wonder if I've lost my legs?*

"You haven't."

His hand had taken hers again. She began to breathe.

"You've saved my life!"

In the darkness she couldn't see his face, only that it loomed above her, that the hand held hers, that feeling was beginning to come into her body again, like a vacationer returning home.

"Are you all right?" *Poor man. Nearly lost his foot.* "You have your foot?"

"I've only lost my boot."

"Thank God! Thank God!"

She sat up, suddenly laughing. *How wonderful that is!* Pictures of feet in shoes, feet severed, blood, lacings, boots. She waved her arms, wriggled her toes, looked up at the sky and laughed. "How wonderful that is!"

And he was laughing. "Let me help you up. You are so happy!"

"Yes!" They leaned together for a moment, then, as if drawn by a magnet, returned to the tracks. The boot was gone.

"Where could it have got to?"

The rails were trembling. They could see the red lights of the train far away down the tracks. The whole night seemed to be humming. And it was important, then, to find the boot.

"Dragged," she said. "The high top did it. The engine must have picked it up, dragged it off . . ."

Your body. Could have been your body!

They found the boot down the tracks, quite shredded. She began to cry. *The boot is cut!*

She couldn't stop crying. *What if you'd been in it?*

"I'm not. You saved my life."

She found herself standing by her car again, shaking, apologizing, looking for a handkerchief. "So sorry! Oh, it's all my fault!"

"You saved my life!"

They were back at the beginning, his odd voice strained, sounding like an old victrola, staring at the ruined boot. But this time she gave him her hand.

"Whoever you are," she said, and a warmth flooded her chest again, only it was exultant, fierce, like a hearth-fire, "whoever you are, I would give you your life a thousand times over just to see you standing there ... holding that ... **boot**!" She giggled foolishly. "Whoever you are ..." She put her key into the lock, turned it easily, and opened the door. "... whatever you are doing, know that life is beautiful and that only the way I'm feeling now is ... proper!"

I think I'll hug the world!

She reached across, took his face in both hands, and kissed him on each shadowy, satin-smooth cheek. *May whatever rules this universe be good to you!*

She got in and drove away.

"You know that I can't stay any longer."

"Yes. I know. But it doesn't make me happy."

He ruffled the big wings that hid most of the time under an over-coat, and crossed his legs—the boot, the repaired boot, laced up tightly, showing his elegant ankles before the swell of calf.

"And I suppose I shan't be pregnant."

"It apears we are ..."

He smiled, the odd sheen of his not-quite-human features glinting.

"... intraspecifically infertile."

"And yet ..."

She dropped her robe and waited. "Has it only been a scientific research project for you?"

"Your emotions hurt."

"I would be ... shattered!"

His look radiated tenderness.

"What do you think, earth woman, my lovely earth creature who saved my life?"

"You read my mind so why ask questions?" She waved her arms, suddenly ran to him. "What will you tell them, darling? That we are apes who leave our litter everywhere? That we're going to blow up our whole planet? That we've poisoned a lot of it already? That it's best to introduce a small bacterium, kill the ape, and save the other species? What's your final assessment? How can I live without you?"

He swept off the couch, wings flaring, reaching for her. She was like a bird, he thought, something infinitely soft that needed nesting. And how would it be possible for their males, who didn't understand their own females, to deal with aliens?

She wept. "Oh, do not leave me! I'm in love with you!"

"As I with you!"

He put his wings about her.

"Women are a separate species with vastly different needs. When your men can understand you, they might begin to learn about the universe."

Oh sure. Right on. That's how you'd write it, kid. Too bad it couldn't happen!

PROOF
by Hal Clement

Kron held his huge freighter motionless, feeling forward for outside contact. The tremendous interplay of magnetic and electrostatic fields just beyond the city's edge was as clearly perceptible to his senses as the city itself—a milewide disk ringed with conical field towers, stretching away behind and to each side. The ship was poised between two of the towers; immediately behind it was the field from which Kron had just taken off. The area was covered with cradles of various forms—cup-shaped receptacles which held city craft like Kron's own; long, boat-shaped hollows wherein reposed the cigarlike vessels which plied between the cities; and towering skeleton frameworks which held upright the slender double cones that hurtled across the dark, lifeless regions between stars.

Beyond the landing field was the city proper; the surface of the disk was covered with geometrically shaped buildings—cones, cylinders, prisms, and hemispheres, jumbled together.

Kron could "see" all this as easily as a human being in an airplane can see New York; but no human eyes could have perceived this city, even if a man could have existed anywhere near it. The city, buildings and all, glowed a savage, white heat; and about and beyond it—a part of it, to human eyes—raged the equally dazzling, incandescent gases of the solar photosphere.

The freighter was preparing to launch itself into that fiery ocean; Kron was watching the play of the artificial reaction fields that supported the city, preparatory to plunging through them at a safe moment.

There was considerable risk of being flattened against the edge of the disk if an inauspicious choice was made,

but Kron was an experienced flier, and slipped past the
barrier with a sudden, hurtling acceleration that would
have pulped any body of flesh and bone. The outer fringe
of the field flung the globe sharply downward; then it was
free, and the city was dwindling above them.

Kron and four others remained at their posts; the rest
of the crew of thirty relaxed, their spherical bodies lying
passive in the cuplike rests distributed through the ship,
bathing in the fierce radiance on which those bodies fed,
and which was continually streaming from a three-inch
spheroid at the center of the craft. That an artificial
source of energy should be needed in such an environment may seem strange, but to these creatures the outer
layers of the Sun were far more inhospitable to life than is
the stratosphere of Earth to human beings.

They had evolved far down near the solar core, where
pressures and temperatures were such that matter existed
in the "collapsed" state characteristic of the entire mass
of white dwarf stars. Their bodies were simply constructed: a matrix of close-packed electrons—really an
unimaginably dense electrostatic field, possessing quasi-
solid properties—surrounded a core of neutrons, com-
pacted to the ultimate degree. Radiation of sufficient
energy, falling on the "skin", was stabilized, altered to
the pattern and structure of neutrons; the tiny particles of
neutronium which resulted were borne along a circula-
tory system—of magnetic fields, instead of blood—to the
nucleus, where it was stored.

The race had evolved to the point where no material
appendages were needed. Projected beams and fields of
force were their limbs, powered by the annihilation of
some of their own neutron substance. Their strange
senses gave them awareness not only of electromagnetic
radiation, permitting them to "see" in a more or less
normal fashion, but also of energies still undreamed of by
human scientists. Kron, now hundreds of miles below the
city, was still dimly aware of its location, though radio
waves, light, and gamma rays were all hopelessly fogged
in the clouds of free electrons. At his goal, far down in the
solar interior, "seeing" conditions would be worse—
anything more than a few hundred yards distant would

be quite indetectable even to him.

Poised beside Kron, near the center of the spheroidal Sunship, was another being. Its body was ovoid in shape, like that of the Solarian, but longer and narrower, while the ends were tipped with pyramidal structures of neutronium, which projected through the "skin." A second, fainter static aura outside the principal surface enveloped the creature; and as the crew relaxed in their cups, a beam of energy from this envelope impinged on Kron's body. It carried a meaning, transmitting a clear thought from one being to the other.

"I still find difficulty in believing my senses," stated the stranger. "My own worlds revolve about another which is somewhat similar to this; but such a vast and tenuous atmosphere is most unlike conditions at home. Have you ever been away from Sol?"

"Yes," replied Kron, "I was once on the crew of an interstellar projectile. I have never seen your star, however; my acquaintance with it is entirely through hearsay. I am told it consists almost entirely of collapsed matter, like the core of our own; but there is practically no atmosphere. Can this be so? I should think, at the temperature necessary for life, gases would break free of the core and form an envelope."

"They tend to do so, of course," returned the other, "but our surface gravity is immeasurably greater than anything you have here; even your core pull is less, since it is much less dense than our star. Only the fact that our worlds are small, thus causing a rapid diminution of gravity as one leaves them, makes it possible to get a ship away from them at all; atoms, with only their original velocities, remain within a few miles of the surface.

"But you remind me of my purpose on this world—to check certain points of a new theory concerning the possible behavior of aggregations of normal atoms. That was why I arranged a trip on your flier; I have to make density, pressure, temperature, and a dozen other kinds of measurements at a couple of thousand different levels, in your atmosphere. While I'm doing it, would you mind telling me why you make these regular trips—and why, for that matter, you live so far above your natural level?

I should think you would find life easier below, since there would be no need to remain in sealed buildings or to expend such a terrific amount of power in supporting your cities?''

Kron's answer was slow.

"We make the journeys to obtain neutronium. It is impossible to convert enough power from the immediate neighborhood of the cities to support them; we must descend periodically for more, even though our converters take so much as to lower the solar temperature considerably for thousands of miles around each city.

"The trips are dangerous—you should have been told that. We carry a crew of thirty, when two would be enough to man this ship, for we must fight, as well as fly. You spoke truly when you said that the lower regions of Sol are our natural home; but for aeons we have not dared to make more than fleeting visits, to steal the power which is life to us.

"Your little worlds have been almost completely subjugated by your people, Sirian; they never had life forms sufficiently powerful to threaten seriously your domination. But Sol, whose core alone is far larger than the Sirius B pair, did develop such creatures. Some are vast, stupid, slow-moving, or immobile; others are semi-intelligent, and rapid movers; all are more than willing to ingest the ready-compacted neutronium of another living being.''

Kron's tale was interrupted for a moment, as the Sirian sent a ray probing out through the ship's wall, testing the physical state of the inferno beyond. A record was made, and the Solarian resumed.

"We, according to logical theory, were once just such a race—of small intelligence, seeking the needs of life among a horde of competing organisms. Our greatest enemy was a being much like ourselves in size and power—just slightly superior in both ways. We were somewhat ahead in intelligence, and I suppose we owe them some thanks—without the competition they provided, we should not have been forced to develop our minds to their present level. We learned to cooperate in fighting them, and from that came the discovery that many of us together could handle natural forces that a single individual could not even approach, and survive. The creation of force effects that had no counterpart in nature was the next step; and, with the understanding of them, our science grew.

"The first cities were of neutronium, like those of today, but it was necessary to stablize the neutrons with fields of energy; at core temperature, as you know, neutronium is a gas. The cities were spherical and much smaller than our present ones. For a long time, we managed to defend them.

"But our enemies evolved, too; not in intelligence, but in power and fecundity. With overspecialization of their physical powers, their mentalities actually degenerated; they became little more than highly organized machines, driven, by an age-old enmity toward our race, to seek us out and destroy us. Their new powers at last enabled them to neutralize, by brute force, the fields which held our cities in shape; and then it was that, from necessity, we fled to the wild, inhospitable upper regions of Sol's atmosphere. Many cities were destroyed by the enemy before a means of supporting them was devised; many more fell victims to forces which we generated, without being able to control, in the effort. The dangers of our present-day trips seem trivial beside those our ancestors braved, in spite of the fact that ships not infrequently fail to return from their flights. Does that answer your question?"

The Sirian's reply was hesitant. "I guess it does. You of Sol must have developed far more rapidly than we, under that drive; your science, I know, is superior to ours in certain ways, although it was my race which first developed space flight."

"You had greater opportunities in that line," returned Kron. "Two small stars, less than a diameter apart, circling a larger one at a distance incomparably smaller than the usual interstellar interval, provided perfect ground for experimental flights; between your world and mine, even radiation requires some hundred and thirty rotations to make the journey, and even the nearest other star is almost half as far.

"But enough of this—history is considered by too

many to be a dry subject. What brings you on a trip with a power flier? You certainly have not learned anything yet which you could not have been told in the city."

During the conversation, the Sirian had periodically tested the atmosphere beyond the hull. He spoke rather absently, as though concentrating on something other than his words.

"I would not be too sure of that, Solarian. My measurements are of greater delicacy than we have ever before achieved. I am looking for a very special effect, to substantiate or disprove an hypothesis which I have recently advanced—much to the detriment of my prestige. If you are interested, I might explain: laugh afterward if you care to—you will not be the first.

"The theory is simplicity itself. It has occurred to me that matter—ordinary substances like iron and calcium —might actually take on solid form, like neutronium, under the proper conditions. The normal gas, you know, consists of minute particles traveling with considerable speed in all directions. There seems to be no way of telling whether or not these atoms exert appreciable forces on one another; but it seems to me that if they were brought closely enough together, or slowed down sufficiently, some such effects might be detected."

"How, and why?" asked Kron. "If the forces are there, why should they not be detectable under ordinary conditions?"

"Tiny changes in velocity due to mutual attraction or repulsion would scarcely be noticed when the atomic speeds are of the order of hundreds of kilometers per second," returned the Sirian. "The effects I seek to detect are of a different nature. Consider, please. We know the sizes of the various atoms, from their radiations. We also know that under normal conditions, a given mass of any particular gas fills a certain volume. If, however, we surround this gas with an impenetrable container and exert pressure, that volume decreases. We would expect that decrease to be proportional to the pressure, except for an easily determined constant due to the size of the atoms, if no interatomic forces existed; to detect such forces, I am making a complete series of pressure-density tests, more delicate than any heretofore, from the level of your cities down to the neutron core of your world.

"If we could reduce the kinetic energy of the atoms—slow down their motions of translation—the task would probably be simpler; but I see no way to accomplish that. Perhaps, if we could negate nearly all of that energy, the interatomic forces would actually hold the atoms in definite relative positions, approximating the solid state. It was that somewhat injudicious and perhaps too imaginative suggestion which caused my whole idea to be ridiculed on Sirius."

The ship dropped several hundred miles in the few seconds after Kron answered; since gaseous friction is independent of change in density, the high pressures of the regions being penetrated would be no bar to high speed of flight. Unfortunately, the viscosity of a gas does increase directly as the square root of its temperature; and at the lower levels of the Sun, travel would be slow.

"Whether or not our scientists will listen to you, I cannot say," said Kron finally. "Some of them are a rather imaginative crowd, I guess, and none of them will ignore any data you may produce.

"I do not laugh, either. My reason will certainly interest you, as your theory intrigues me. It is the first time anyone has accounted even partly for the things that happened to us on one of my flights."

The other members of the crew shifted slightly on their cradles; a ripple of interest passed through them, for all had heard rumors and vague tales of Kron's time in the space carrier fleets. The Sirian settled himself more comfortably; Kron dimmed the central globe of radiance a trifle, for the outside temperature was now considerably higher, and began the tale.

"This happened toward the end of my career in space. I had made many voyages with the merchant and passenger vessels, had been promoted from the lowest ranks, through many rotations, to the post of independent captain. I had my own cruiser—a special long-period explorer, owned by the Solarian government. She was shaped like our modern interstellar carriers, consisting of two cones, bases together, with the field ring just forward of their meeting point. She was larger than most, being designed to carry fuel for exceptionally long flights.

"Another cruiser, similar in every respect, was under the command of a comrade of mine, named Akro; and the two of us were commissioned to transport a party of scientists and explorers to the then newly discovered Fourth System, which lies, as you know, nearly in the plane of the solar equator, but about half again as distant as Sirius.

"We made good time, averaging nearly half the speed of radiation, and reached the star with a good portion of our hulls still unconsumed. We need not have worried about that, in any case; the star was denser even than the Sirius B twins, and neutronium was very plentiful. I restocked at once, plating my inner walls with the stuff until they had reached their original thickness, although experience indicated that the original supply was ample to carry us back to Sol, to Sirius, or to Procyon B.

"Akro, at the request of the scientists, did not refuel. Life was present on the star, as it seems to be on all stars where the atomic velocities and the density are high enough; and the biologists wanted to bring back specimens. That meant that room would be needed, and if Akro replated his walls to normal thickness, that room would be lacking—as I have mentioned, these were special long-range craft, and a large portion of their volume consisted of available neutronium.

"So it happened that the other ship left the Fourth System with a low, but theoretically sufficient, stock of fuel, and half a dozen compartments filled with specimens of alien life. I kept within detection distance at all times, in case of trouble, for some of those life forms were as dangerous as those of Sol, and, like them, all consumed neutronium. They had to be kept well under control to safeguard the very walls of the ship, and it is surprisingly difficult to make a wild beast, surrounded by food, stay on short rations.

"Some of the creatures proved absolutely unmanageable; they had to be destroyed. Others were calmed by lowering the atomic excitation of their compartments, sending them into a stupor; but the scientists were reluctant to try that in most cases, since not all of the beings could stand such treatment.

"So, for nearly four hundred solar rotations, Akro practically fought his vessel across space—fought successfully. He managed on his own power until we were within a few hundred diameters of Sol; but I had to help him with the landing—or try to, for the landing was never made.

"It may seem strange, but there is a large volume of space in the neighborhood of this Sun which is hardly ever traversed. The normal landing orbit arches high over one of the poles of rotation, enters atmosphere almost tangentially somewhere between that pole and the equator, and kills as much as remains of the ship's velocity in the outer atmospheric layers. There is a minimum of magnetic interference that way, since the flier practically coasts along the lines of force of the solar magnetic field.

"As a result, few ships pass through the space near the plane of the solar equator. One or two may have done so before us, and I know of several that searched the region later; but none encountered the thing which we found.

"About the time we would normally have started correcting our orbits for a tangential landing, Akro radiated me the information that he could not possibly control his ship any farther with the power still available to him. His walls were already so thin that radiation loss, ordinarily negligible, was becoming a definite menace to his vessel. All his remaining energy would have to be employed in keeping the interior of his ship habitable.

"The only thing I could do was to attach our ships together with an attractor beam, and make a nearly perpendicular drop to Sol. We would have to take our chances with magnetic and electrostatic disturbances in the city-supporting fields which cover so much of the near-equatorial zones, and try to graze the nucleus of the Sun instead of its outer atmosphere, so that Akro could replenish his rapidly failing power.

"Akro's hull was radiating quite perceptibly now; it made an easy target for an attractor. We connected without difficulty, and our slightly different linear velocities

caused us to revolve slowly about each other, pivoting on
the center of mass of our two ships. I cut off my driving
fields, and we fell spinning toward Sol.

"I was becoming seriously worried about Akro's
chances of survival. The now-alarming energy loss
through his almost consumed hull threatened to exhaust
his supply long before we reached the core; and we were
still more than a hundred diameters out. I could not give
him any power; we were revolving about each other at a
distance of about one-tenth of a solar diameter. To lessen
that distance materially would increase our speed of
revolution to a point where the attractor could not over-
come centrifugal force; and I had neither power nor time
to perform the delicate job of exactly neutralizing our
rotary momentum without throwing us entirely off
course. All we could do was hope.

"We were somewhere between one hundred and one
hundred and fifty diameters out when there occurred the
most peculiar phenomenon I have ever encountered. The
plane of revolution of our two ships passed near Sol, but
was nearly perpendicular to the solar equator; at the time
of which I speak, Akro's ship was almost directly between
my flier and the Sun. Observations had just shown that we
were accelerating Sunward at an unexpectedly high pace,
when a call came from Akro.

"'Kron! I am being pulled away from your attractor!
There is a large mass somewhere near, for the pull is
gravitational, but it emits no radiation that I can detect.
Increase your pull, if you can; I cannot possibly free
myself alone.'

"I did what I could, which was very little. Since we did
not know the location of the disturbing dark body, it was
impossible to tell just what I should do to avoid bringing
my own or Akro's vessel too close. I think now that if I
had released him immediately he would have swung clear,
for the body was not large, I believe. Unfortunately, I did
the opposite, and nearly lost my own ship as well. Two of
my crew were throwing as much power as they could
convert and handle into the attractor, and trying to hold it
on the still easily visible hull of Akro's ship; but the
motions of the latter were so peculiar that aiming was a

difficult task. They held the ship as long as we could see it; but quite suddenly the radiations by means of which we perceived the vessel faded out, and before we could find a band which would get through, the sudden cessation of our centripetal acceleration told us that the beam had slipped from its target.

"We found that electromagnetic radiations of wavelengths in the octave above H-alpha would penetrate the interference, and Akro's hull was leaking energy enough to radiate in that band. When we found him however, we could scarcely believe our senses; his velocity was now nearly at right angles to his former course, and his hull radiation had become far weaker. What terrific force had caused this acceleration, and what strange field was blanketing the radiation, were questions none of us could answer.

"Strain as we might, not one of us could pick up an erg of radiant energy that might emanate from the thing that had trapped Akro. We could only watch, and endeavor to plot his course relative to our own, at first. Our ships were nearing each other rapidly, and we were attempting to determine the time and distance of closest approach, when we were startled by the impact of a communicator beam. Akro was alive! The beam was weak, very weak, showing what an infinitesimal amount of power he felt he could spare. His words were not encouraging.

"'Kron! You may as well cut your attractor, if you are still trying to catch me. No power that I dare supply seems to move me perceptibly in any direction from this course. We are badly shocked, for we hit something that felt almost solid. The walls, even, are strained, and may go at any time.'

"'Can you perceive anything around you?' I returned. 'You seem to us to be alone in space, though something is absorbing most of your radiated energy. There must be energies in the cosmos of which we have never dreamed, simply because they did not affect our senses. What do your scientists say?'

"'Very little,' was the answer. 'They have made a few tests, but they say that anything they project is absorbed without reradiating anything useful. We seem to be in a sort of energy vacuum—it takes everything and returns nothing.'

"This was the most alarming item yet. Even in free space, we had been doubtful of Akro's chances of survival; now they seemed reduced to the ultimate zero.

"Meanwhile, our ships were rapidly approaching each other. As nearly as my navigators could tell, both vessels were pursuing almost straight lines in space. The lines were nearly perpendicular but did not lie in a common plane; their minimum distance apart was about one one-thousandth of a solar diameter. His velocity seemed nearly constant, while I was accelerating Sunward. It seemed that we would reach the near-intersection point almost simultaneously, which meant that my ship was certain to approach the energy vacuum much too closely. I did not dare to try to pull Akro free with an attractor; it was only too obvious that such an attempt could only end in disaster for both vessels. If he could not free himself, he was lost.

"We could only watch helplessly as the point of light marking the position of Akro's flier swept closer and closer. At first, as I have said, it seemed perfectly free in space; but as we looked, the region around it began to radiate feebly. There was nothing recognizable about the vibrations, simply a continuous spectrum, cut off by some interference just below the H-alpha wavelength and, at the other end, some three octaves higher. As the emission grew stronger, the visible region around the stranded ship grew larger, fading into nothingness at the edges. Brighter and broader the patch of radiance grew, as we swept toward it.''

That same radiance was seriously inconveniencing Gordon Aller, who was supposed to be surveying for a geological map of northern Australia. He was camped by the only water hole in many miles, and had stayed up long after dark preparing his cameras, barometer, soil kit, and other equipment for the morrow's work.

The arrangement of instruments completed, he did not at once retire to his blankets. With his back against a smooth rock, and a short, blackened pipe clenched in his teeth, he sat for some time, pondering. The object of his musing does not matter to us; though his eyes were directed heavenward, he was sufficiently accustomed to the southern sky to render it improbable that he was paying much attention to its beauties.

However that may be, his gaze was suddenly attracted to the zenith. He had often seen stars which appeared to move when near the edge of his field of vision—it is a common illusion; but this one continued to shift as he turned his eyes upward.

Not far from Achernar was a brilliant white point, which brightened as Aller watched it. It was moving slowly northward, it seemed; but only a moment was needed for the man to realize that the slowness was illusory. The thing was slashing almost vertically downward at an enormous speed, and must strike Earth not far from his camp.

Aller was not an astronomer and had no idea of astronomical distances or speeds. He may be forgiven for thinking of the object as traveling perhaps as fast as a modern fighting plane, and first appearing at a height of two or three miles. The natural conclusion from this belief was that the crash would occur within a few hundred feet of the camp. Aller paled; he had seen pictures of the Devil's Pit in Arizona.

Actually, of course, the meteor first presented itself to his gaze at a height of some eighty miles, and was then traveling at a rate of many miles per second relative to Earth. At that speed, the air presented a practically solid obstacle to its flight, and the object was forced to a fairly constant velocity of ten or twelve hundred yards a second while still nearly ten miles from Earth's surface. It was at that point that Aller's eyes caught up with, and succeeded in focusing upon, the celestial visitor.

That first burst of light had been radiated by the frightfully compressed and heated air in front of the thing; as the original velocity departed, so did the dazzling light. Aller got a clear view of the meteor at a range of less than five miles, for perhaps ten seconds before the impact. It was still incandescent, radiating a bright cherry-red; this must have been due to the loss from within, for so brief a contact even with such highly heated air could not have warmed the Sunship's neutronium walls a measurable fraction of a degree.

Aller felt the ground tremble as the vessel struck. A geyser of earth, barely visible in the reddish light of the hull, spouted skyward, to fall back seconds later with a long-drawn-out rumble. The man stared at the spot, two miles away, which was still giving off a faint glow. Were "shooting stars" as regularly shaped as that? He had seen a smooth, slender body, more than a hundred feet in length, apparently composed of two cones of unequal length, joined together at the bases. Around the longer cone, not far from the point of juncture, was a thick bulging ring; no further details were visible at the distance from which he had observed. Aller's vague recollections of meteorites, seen in various museums, brought images of irregular, clinkerlike objects before his mind's eye. What, then, could this thing be?

He was not imaginative enough to think for a moment of any possible extraterrestrial source for an aircraft; when it did occur to him that the object was of artificial origin, he thought more of some experimental machine produced by one of the more progressive Earth nations.

At the thought, Aller strapped a first-aid kit to his side and set out toward the crater, in the face of the obvious fact that nothing human could possibly have survived such a crash. He stumbled over the uneven terrain for a quarter of a mile and then stopped on a small rise of ground to examine more closely the site of the wreck.

The glow should have died by this time, for Aller had taken all of ten muniutes to pick his way those few hundred yards; but the dull-red light ahead had changed to a brilliant orange radiance against which the serrated edges of the pit were clearly silhouetted. No flames were visible; whence came the increasing heat? Aller attempted to get closer, but a wave of frightfully hot air blistered his face and hands and drove him back. He took up a station near his former camp, and watched.

If the hull of the flier had been anywhere near its normal thickness, the tremendous mass of neutronium would have sunk through the hardest of rocks as though they were liquid. There was, however, scarcely more than a paper thickness of the substance at any part of the walls; and an upthrust of adamantine volcanic rock not far beneath the surface of the desert proved thick enough to absorb the Sunship's momentum and to support its still enormous weight. Consequently, the ship was covered only by a thin layer of powdered rock which had fallen back into the crater. The disturbances arising from the now extremely rapid loss of energy from Akro's ship were, as a result, decidedly visible from the surface.

The hull, though thin, was still intact; but its temperature was now far above the melting point of the surrounding rocks. The thin layer of pulverized material above the ship melted and flowed away almost instantly, permitting free radiation to the air above; and so enormous is the specific heat of neutronium that no perceptible lowering of hull temperature occurred.

Aller, from his point of observation, saw the brilliant fan of light that sprang from the pit as the flier's hull was exposed—the vessel itself was invisible to him, since he was only slightly above the level of the crater's mouth. He wondered if the impact of the "meteor" had released some pent-up volcanic energy, and began to doubt, quite justifiably, if he was at a safe distance. His doubts vanished and were replaced by certainty as the edges of the crater began to glow dull red, then bright orange, and slowly subsided out of sight. He began packing the most valuable items of his equipment, while a muted, continuous roaring and occasional heavy thuds from the direction of the pit admonished him to hasten.

When he straightened up, with the seventy-pound pack settled on his shoulders, there was simply a lake of lava where the crater had been. The fiery area spread even as he watched; and without further delay he set off on his own back trail. He could see easily by the light diffused from the inferno behind him; and he made fairly good time, considering his burden and the fact that he had not slept since the preceding night.

The rock beneath Akro's craft was, as we have said, extremely hard. Since there was relatively free escape upward for the constantly liberated energy, this stratum melted very slowly, gradually letting the vessel sink deeper into the earth. What would have happened if Akro's power supply had been greater is problematical; Aller can tell us only that some five hours after the landing, as he was resting for a few moments near the top of a rocky hillock, the phenomenon came to a cataclysmic end.

A quivering of the earth beneath him caused the surveyor to look back toward his erstwhile camp. The lake of lava, which by this time was the better part of a mile in breadth, seemed curiously agitated. Aller, from his rather poor vantage point, could see huge bubbles of pasty lava hump themselves up and burst, releasing brilliant clouds of vapor. Each cloud illuminated earth and sky before cooling to invisibility, so that the effect was somewhat similar to a series of lightning flashes.

For a short time—certain no longer than a quarter of a minute—Aller was able to watch as the activity increased. Then a particularly violent shock almost flung him from the hilltop, and at nearly the same instant the entire volume of molten rock fountained skyward. For an instant it seemed to hang there, a white, raging pillar of liquid and gas; then it dissolved, giving way before the savage thrust of the suddenly released energy below. A tongue of radiance, of an intensity indescribable in mere words, stabbed upward, into and through the lava, volatilizing instantly. A dozen square miles of desert glowed white, then an almost invisible violet, and disappeared in superheated gas. Around the edges of this region, great gouts of lava and immense fragments of solid rock were hurled to all points of the compass.

Radiation exerts pressure; at the temperature found in the cores of stars, that pressure must be measured in thousands of tons per square inch. It was this thrust, rather than the by no means negligible gas pressure of the boiling lava, which wrought most of the destruction.

Aller saw little of what occurred. When the lava was hurled upward, he had flung an arm across his face to protect his eyes from the glare. That act unquestionably saved his eyesight as the real flash followed; as it was, his body was seared and blistered through his clothing. The second, heavier, shock knocked his feet from under him, and he half crawled, half rolled down to the comparative shelter of the little hill. Even here, gusts of hot air almost cooked him; only the speed with which the phenomenon ended saved his life.

Within minutes, both the temblors and hot winds had ceased; and he crawled painfully to the hilltop again to gaze wonderingly at the five-mile-wide crater, ringed by a pile of tumbled, still-glowing rock fragments.

Far beneath that pit, shards of neutronium, no more able to remain near the surface than the steel pieces of a wrecked ocean vessel can float on water, were sinking through rock and metal to a final resting place at Earth's heart.

"The glow spread as we watched, still giving no clue to the nature of the substance radiating it," continued Kron. "Most of it seemed to originate between us and Akro's ship; Akro himself said that but little energy was being lost on the far side. His messages, during that last brief period as we swept by our point of closest approach, were clear—so clear that we could almost see, as he did, the tenuous light beyond the ever-thinning walls of his ship; the light that represented but a tiny percentage of the energy being sucked from the hull surface.

"We saw, as though with his own senses, the tiny perforation appear near one end of the ship; saw it extend, with the speed of thought, from one end of the hull to the other, permitting the free escape of all the energy in a single instant; and, from our point of vantage, saw the glowing area where the ship had been suddenly brightened, blazing for a moment almost as brightly as a piece of Sun matter.

"In that moment, every one of us saw the identifying frequencies as the heat from Akro's disrupted ship raised the substance which had trapped him to an energy level which permitted atomic radiation. Every one of us recognized the spectra of iron, of calcium, of carbon, and of silicon and a score of the other elements—Sirian, I tell you that that 'trapping field' was *matter*—matter in such a state that it could not radiate, and could offer resistance to other bodies in exactly the fashion of a solid. I thought, and have always thought, that some strange field of force held the atoms in their 'solid' positions; you have convinced me that I was wrong. The 'field' was the sum of the interacting atomic forces which you are trying to detect. The energy level of that material body was so low that those forces were able to act without interference. The condition you could not conceive of reaching artificially actually exists in nature!''

''You go too fast, Kron,'' responded the Sirian. ''Your first idea is far more likely to be the true one. The idea of unknown radiant or static force fields is easy to grasp; the one you propose in its place defies common sense. My theories called for some such conditions as you described, granted the one premise of a sufficiently low energy level; but a place in the real Universe so devoid of energy as to absorb that of a well-insulated interstellar flier is utterly inconceivable. I have assumed your tale to be true as to details, though you offer neither witnesses nor records to support it; but I seem to have heard that you have somewhat of a reputation as an entertainer, and you seem quick-witted enough to have woven such a tale on the spot, purely from the ideas I suggested. I compliment you on the tale, Kron; it was entrancing; but I seriously advise you not to make anything more out of it. Shall we leave it at that, my friend?''

''As you will,'' replied Kron.

SCIENTIFIC METHOD

by Chad Oliver

The first step in the scientific method involves the observation of facts and the formulation of The Problem . . .

The man named Reda Dani did not, of course, think of himself as an alien.

There was no doubt in *his* mind that he was a human being, a moderately dubious distinction that he shared with all his fellow citizens on Capella IV.

The only aliens mixed up in the affair were from Earth.

Naturally enough, considering the circumstances, Reda Dani was nobody's fool. He was quite well aware of the meaning of ethnocentrism, to say nothing of plain old-fashioned egotism. He knew that what you chose to define as "alien" varied with where you happened to be sitting.

That didn't make his problem any easier, however.

Unhappily, he turned his attention to his pipe. The damned thing had gone out again. Somewhat fatalistically, he knocked out a soggy lump of unburned tobacco into a desk vaporizer, refilled his pipe and lit it. He blew a cloud of smoke in the general direction of the air purifier and felt a little better.

He walked over to the viewscreen and took a look. The system of Sol was close. Too close.

He felt worse again; the palms of his hands began to sweat.

"I wish the whole planet would drop dead," Reda Dani said, not without bitterness.

"Take it easy," advised Hago Vere, the semantics man. "If you blow your top, we might as well all pick up our marbles and go home. Anyhow, you're mixing your metaphors, or something.''

"I wish you would drop dead also," Reda Dani informed him, puffing on his pipe.

"Civil war," said Hago Vere. "A great beginning. You're supposed to be a co-ordinator, or don't you read your own propaganda? You could be shot at sunrise, except that there isn't any sunrise."

"A great pity," Reda Dani conceded, smiling. "I'm okay, really, as far as I know. Just blowing off steam. It's just that it's getting close—you know."

"I know, Reda."

Both men fell silent. The ship throbbed around them with the high, taut power of the overdrive. Reda Dani smoked his pipe carefully, nursing it along. His hands were still sweating.

It *was* a nasty problem.

Nasty because it had never been faced before.

Nasty because there was no known solution.

Nasty because it *had* to be solved.

He went over it again, step by step.

The world of Capella IV—his world—was quite similar to Earth. It was, in fact, almost identical. This was largely a coincidence, since the Aurigae system, of which Capella was a part, happened to be a binary. Capella was a good sixteen times as big as Sol, though of the same general type.

It was a coincidence that had consequences, however.

Life had evolved on Capella IV in much the same way it had on Earth. All of the details were not precisely the same, but there was a part-for-part correspondence of general stages. Capella IV had its aquatic forms, its amphibians, its reptiles, its mammals. It had its own primate chain, culminating finally in *Homo sapiens*—an erect biped, pleased with its brain, clever with its hands, variable in its color.

The people of Capella IV had gone out into space. They wanted to find out whether or not they had neighbors.

They had.

The galaxy teemed with life.

But not with "neighbors," unless mere physical proximity were the only criterion of neighborliness. They found that life could take many forms. They discovered how absolutely *different* life might be. There was no basis at all for getting together; they had nothing in common.

It wasn't that the life-forms were hostile. Hardly. They didn't even have a *concept* of hostility, or of friendliness. They were *different*.

Alien. Isolated. Eventually, they had contacted the Earth. They had found a life-form physically indistinguishable from themselves, and one with a fairly similar civilization.

The people of Earth had cobalt bombs and interplanetary travel.

The people of Capella IV had force fields and interstellar overdrive.

It was a neat situation.

For twenty-five years, the two peoples surveyed each other, discussed each other, sparred with each other. They exchanged telephotos and information. They staged demonstrations of strength. They probed and speculated, wondered and guessed.

For twenty-five years.

They were, of course, scared to death of each other. The people from Capella IV were afraid of the bomb, which they didn't have. The people from Earth were afraid of the overdrive, which they didn't have—for the overdrive meant that the Capella ships could attack and then retreat to the stars where they could not be followed.

Neither side could be *sure* it understood the other.

They had never dared to meet face to face. Until now.

Reda Dani frowned glumly at his cold pipe, which had gone out again. He tapped the refuse into the vaporizer and put the pipe away. He stared into the viewscreen, hypnotically.

He could see Earth now, far away and lonely.

He closed his eyes.

Who would Earth send?

They had finally decided to take a chance, these two peoples separated by forty-two light-years and a sea of emptiness. They had agreed to meet—one man from each planet, unarmed.

It had to be in the system of Sol, for there was no way for a man from Earth to get to Capella. They had chosen a tiny chamber on Mars for the meeting. Each group had built exactly half of it, and each group had inspected it one hundred times. They had taken turns to make certain that the workers never met.

That little compromise had taken ten years to work out.

Who would Earth send?

One man from each culture, meeting in a little room on a planet without life of its own. One man, carrying a responsibility almost too fantastic to be real.

If the meeting failed, if someone made a mistake—

It might hinge on a little thing, a nothing-thing. How could you tell? "John Smith" was a common name on Earth, but to a man from Capella IV it was unbearably funny, as well as illogical. On Capella IV, they had systematic names, given in adulthood, which placed each person according to status and role by the pattern of alternating morphemes—Reda Dani, Hago Vere, Hada Nire. *This* seemed funny to the men of Earth, who, in turn, named a baby practically anything that suited their fancy, within the limits of their values and their prejudices.

Even assuming good intentions on both sides, the little things could be dangerous.

If you had to pick one individual to represent your entire species in a game of life and death, who would you pick?

Who *could* you pick?

The man named Reda Dani looked into the viewscreen, staring at the stars and the planets and the darkness.

That was his problem. That was the problem, too, that had to be faced by a man on Earth, a man like himself. A man who even now must be wondering, watching, trying to decide—

Who would Earth send?

There was no answer.

He could only wait.

After the formulation of the problem, the next step, in strict chronology, involves the working out of the hypothesis, or trial solution. Passing this by for the moment, however, we turn to what is actually the third step, the testing of the hypothesis in experience, or The Experiment . . .

Svend Graves walked steadily through the sand canyon and listened to his breathing in the oxygen mask. It was slow and even, neither excited nor lethargic, and he smiled with satisfaction. He had been worried, but now he knew he was not going to be afraid.

He was ready.

The cold wind moaned and whispered through the sand tunnels and twisted valleys, whining out on the cold desert beyond, losing itself in fine clouds of gray, driven sand. It wrapped icy fingers around Svend Graves as he walked, plucking at his sleeves, singing songs that were sad with the ice of despair . . .

Mars.

It had never known a life of its own. It was barren, sterile, its only meaning given to it by the dreams and thoughts of a people over forty-eight million miles away.

Svend Graves felt a curious, warm pride. *His* people.

Mars.

First, perhaps, it had been a campfire in the sky. It had been a cold fire that gave no warmth, a miracle to be watched and feared by some early man who scarcely knew fire of any kind. He had listened to the night talking around him, and he had wondered what manner of man would build his sky-fire so far away, and what songs he might sing around it.

Then it had become Mars, the god of war.

Finally, it had become a planet, one of several, orbited around the sun. The planet, with time, had become a symbol, a lure, an invitation. It had challenged the men of Earth to travel into the sea of night that washed their shores.

And they had come.

And this was the reality, at least for now. A cold desert of shifting sands and sculptured canyons, forever silent save for the sigh of the winds.

Neutral ground. A meeting place. Svend Graves came out of the sand canyon and into the desert, his feet slipping slightly on the uncertain floor of the planet. Ahead of him, waiting all alone in the middle of a great plain, was the tiny building that housed a room for two.

It was time.

Coming out of the desert from the other side, half hidden by the drifting curtains of reddish sand, he saw a dark figure moving slowly toward the building.

The two men from different star-systems stood in the cubicle and stared at each other.

They were close enough to touch, but they did not touch.

The room was antiseptically plain. It had dull gray walls and a single overhead light. It had a small gray table in the exact center of the room, and two hard gray chairs, one at each end of the table. There was an air-conditioning unit in one corner, and no other machinery of any kind within a two-hundred mile radius.

No one was taking any chances.

The room was just what it seemed to be—a room, and nothing more.

Svend Graves kept a smile on his face. It had first been determined, of course, that smiles meant the same thing in both cultures. His job was three fold: he had to make a good impression, he had to protect the secrets of his people, and he had to evaluate the other man.

He examined the man from Capella IV courteously but thoroughly. The man from Capella IV examined him the same way.

Svend Graves couldn't see very much. The other man was dressed in what appeared to be a light spacesuit, complete with helmet. He was definitely humanoid in construction —he had two arms and two legs and one head. Behind the glass in his helmet, he seemed to have a rather pleasant face.

There was a long, awkward silence.

Svend Graves shrugged. He reached up and took off his oxygen mask. He sniffed the air and it was good. No tricks so far, then. He noticed that the other man was smiling, but he made no attempt to remove his helmet. He just stood there.

"Do you mind if I smoke?" asked Svend Graves. It seemed to him as though his voice went off in the silence like a bomb.

"Not at all," replied the other man instantly. His voice was low and well-modulated, crystal-clear through his helmet speaker.

Svend Graves fished out a cigarette and lit it. He blew smoke through his nose, being careful to keep it away from the alien.

"My name is Svend Graves," he said.

"My name is Hada Nire," the other said.

Neither laughed.

Neither volunteered any more information.

The silence filled the room.

Evidently he's just going to respond to my cues, Svend Graves thought. *It's up to me to direct the interview.*

He sat down in one of the chairs. The other man did not hesitate but lowered himself into the other one, still not making any move to take off either his helmet or his spacesuit.

They eyed each other across the table.

"Well, Mr. Nire, where do we go from here?" asked Svend Graves, reflecting that it was really quite decent of the aliens to agree to the use of English during the first meeting.

Hada Nire chuckled pleasantly. "An excellent question, Svend Graves," he said. "I must apologize for my seeming reticence. The circumstances under which we meet—"

He waved a spacesuited arm, vaguely.

Careful, thought Svend Graves. *Could that be a psychological probe?* He said: "Not at all, my friend. It is as much my fault as it is yours. I hope I may express the wish that we can meet again one of these days, and speak as man to man."

"That is also my wish," the other man said. "This is a difficult situation for both of us. I feel as though I were under a microscope."

"Me too," agreed Svend Graves.

They indulged in some highly tentative exploratory conversation, and they laughed rather too much over the mutual clumsiness of the situation. Their talk was, if not friendly, at least cordial.

Then the silence came again.

They sat across the table from each other in the little gray room, wondering.

When the agreed-upon termination time arrived, neither of them had said much of consequence.

They both stood up, Hada Nire still in his spacesuit and helmet. There was tension in the room. It wasn't exactly fear, nor was it hope, and yet it included both of these.

They both felt it.

"I know we're both thinking the same thing," Svend Graves said slowly. "I can't speak with much authority, but just as a man. I hope that this is a beginning, not an ending."

The other man nodded. "I hope that both of our peoples will be blessed with understanding. *Understanding*. That is a good word. Next to a sense of humor, it is what we need the most."

They walked to the door together. Svend Graves stopped and put on his oxygen mask, and then they went outside. They paused, and Svend Graves put out his hand. Hada Nire took it gently in his spacesuit glove, and they shook hands, Earth-style. Then the other man waved briefly and set out across the desert for the rendezvous with his ship.

Svend Graves watched him go, trying to register all the data, no matter how unimportant. Then he turned and walked through the sands that were old when Earth was young, back into the wind-blasted canyons, his hands in his pockets.

He did not look back.

As previously indicated, we have left out a step in our scientific method, a step between the problem and the experiment. The step did occur, of course, and we go back for it now. Between the problem and the experiment comes the trial solution, or The Hypothesis . . .

Reda Dani was worried.

He puffed on his pipe and failed to get any smoke. Why was it, he wondered, that a culture that could devise an overdrive for interstellar flight could not invent a pipe that would stay lit? He toyed with the notion of dropping the whole pipe into the vaporizer, but rejected the notion. Primarily to prove a point to himself, he refilled the mutinous artifact and tried again.

He wiped his hands nervously and checked his watch.

Four hours to zero. Time for the final check.

He walked through the great ship, his stomach a cold knot inside of him. The question he had lived with for years crawled endlessly through his brain, a monstrous worm twisted into a mocking interrogation mark—

Had he made the right decision?

The problem of picking a single man to represent your culture in a crucial situation was virtually beyond solution, and Reda Dani knew it. He had wrestled with it so long that he knew every angle, every consideration, every argument.

The only thing he didn't know for sure was the answer.

He listened to his heels clicking down the corridor and knew that it was too late to back down now. They would have to go through with it.

It was no great task to think of someone you knew who was gifted along one particular line—a mathematician, an artist, a sociologist. It was not even inordinately difficult to find individuals who might have talent and training in all three fields. Conceivably, some fantastic individual, somewhere, somehow, might be an expert in ten fields, or even twenty.

Unfortunately, that wasn't good enough.

There was, certainly, an excellent possibility that any good man could successfully represent his people in the coming encounter; maybe a diplomat could do it. The catch was that "an excellent possibility" wasn't adequate for *this* situation. There was too much at stake.

You had to be *sure*.

Easy enough to state, but how did you go about it? You needed a representative who was capable of responding to any imaginable trickery or force. Unpleasant as it was, you had to plan on the possibility that the people of Earth would not keep faith. You had to be ready to take advantage of either the worst or the best—whichever offered itself.

The characteristics of the required representative could be listed briefly. One, he had to make a good impression. Two, he had to be prepared for anything, insofar as possible, so that he could not be outwitted. Three, he had to be able to make a complete and accurate report back to his superiors; no one person, naturally, could be entrusted with the power of decision in such a case. Fourth and last, he had to have some sort of built-in defense mechanism, so that he could not possibly be made to reveal any classified information, no matter what pressures were brought to bear.

Of course, no such human being existed.

Once you accepted that fact, there was only one thing to do.

Reda Dani passed through the security check and into the special control room, his pipe still going. He hoped that was a good omen.

It had better be.

He nodded to his co-workers and looked around. The control room was ready.

There was a large, spherical screen that filled the entire center of the chamber—blank now. Around the screen were fifty chairs, each with a small control panel on one arm. The potential occupants of the chairs milled around in a fog of blue smoke and fast conversation—semantics experts, philosophers, chemists, anthropologists, psychologists, generals, writers, doctors, corporation managers, diplomats.

Above the spherical screen, placed so that the observer could look down into it, was another chair, completely surrounded by integration controls that co-ordinated the information from below.

Reda Dani looked at it, nervously. His chair.

He climbed up into it and settled himself. He clamped on his headphones and switched on the master control panel.

He put down his pipe, reluctantly, and picked up an auxillary phone.

"Trial run," he said.

The others took their places, silent now, and cut in their sets. The spherical screen flashed white and came to life. It showed four rather drab green walls, a ceiling, a floor.

A storeroom.

Reda Dani steadied his hands and moved his fingers over the control panel. There wasn't a sound. Gradually, the scene in the spherical screen shifted, swaying very slightly, just as a view does through the eyes of a walking man.

There was a door. It opened and shut.

A corridor, long and featureless, moving up and down. Another door—

A polite knock. The door of the special control room clicked open. The view in the screen switched to the room they were sitting in. Reda Dani saw himself clearly, pale and nervous over the control panel.

A spacesuited figure came into the room, carefully. Behind the glass in his helmet could be seen a rather pleasant face with an easy smile.

He stopped, respectfully.

"My name is Hada Nire," the figure said in a well-modulated voice. It spoke in English. "May I be of some assistance?"

There was a buzz of approval from the assembled men.

Reda Dani relaxed a little.

There was no denying it—the robot was well made.

Reda Dani began to worry in earnest again after they landed the ship just outside the restricted area on Mars.

They started the spacesuited assemblage of radio controls, tri-di, and testing apparatus toward the tiny building in the desert where the meeting was to take place. Reda Dani sat tensely in his chair, watching every move in the spherical screen. The robot walked gracefully through the shifting sands. He *looked* convincing.

But he wasn't human, of course.

What if they find out? Reda Dani asked himself. *What if I've thrown away our only chance, just out of fear?*

The problem was exactly analogous to hunting for a house to live in. If you couldn't find precisely what you wanted, at the price you could afford to pay, there was only one course of action open to you.

Build your own.

The thing they had called Hada Nire wasn't really a robot; he was not a mechanical man with a mind of his own. Rather, he was an integrated synthesis of fifty remote minds—fifty men, each with a control panel, each able to take over in any conceivable situation, each seeing out of his eyes in the spherical screen and hearing every word by radio.

Hada Nire, whatever else he may have been, was no fool.

Reda Dani watched him, step by step, on automatic now. He saw him walk through the desert. He saw the little building come into view before him.

Beyond the building, a dark figure. Walking.

The man from Earth.

Who had *they* sent?''

The final step in the scientific method is known as the solution. From the solution, if all has gone well, may often be derived certain General Principles . . .

Ralph Hawley paced up and down the evaluation room, alternately staring at his watch and smoking cigarettes in short, jerky puffs. The others sat nervously in their chairs, watching him.

"What's he doing?" he asked again. "Where in the living hell can he *be*?"

Lee Gomez, by profession a philosopher and by temperament not given to impatience or, indeed, to haste in any known form, said, "Park yourself, Ralph. Svend isn't overdue yet, and he's no doubt doing just what he's supposed to be doing—to wit, contacting our non-Earthly friends."

"Ummmm," Ralph Hawley said, hooking his thumbs in his suspenders. Then, sensing the inadequacy of the phrase, he added: "Three cheers for Svend, he's true blue."

Damn Gomez anyway—he was right entirely too often, and Hawley knew it, and it annoyed him.

"My professional opinion," put in Dr Weinstein, "is that we are all suffering from a none-too-rare scientific malady. I don't wish to be quoted on this, gentlemen, but my diagnosis is *Gestaltus adrenalinfusorium*—wholesale jitters. As a remedy, I propose a spot of medicinal brandy."

Ralph Hawley ran a hand through his lank, graying hair. "Not yet, Doc. Not that we all can't use a snort or two."

He continued his pacing, which was in itself highly unusual. Ralph Hawley, under normal circumstances, was anything but a nervous man. He was tall, rather spare, with a pleasantly horse-like face. He was addicted to sloppy clothes, infrequent speech, and relaxed movements. By trade, he was a social psychologist working in the field of mass communications, and he was the last person in the world that he himself would have selected to head the project.

"Where *is* he?" he asked again, lighting another cigarette. A red light flashed. A buzzer sounded.

A speaker said: "Svend Graves has entered the ship. He has not been harmed. He reports a non-antagonistic contact with some complications. As instructed we have sent him on to the evaluation room. This is Major Bernatzik, Intelligence."

A knock at the door. A pause.

The door opened and Svend Graves walked in. Every eye in the room was on him. He took it well, never losing his poise for an instant.

"I'm quite all right," he said calmly. "You can relax."

No one relaxed.

Svend Graves walked up to Ralph Hawley, smiling. "It all went off like clockwork, Ralph," he said. "I couldn't get a good look at their man, but there was no trouble. I'm ready to give a full report, from the beginning."

"That won't be necessary, Svend," Ralph Hawley said.

"I beg your pardon?"

Ralph Hawley sighed. Then, quickly, he reached out and turned Svend Graves off.

Hawley stripped off Svend's shirt and opened the panel

in his chest. He took out the cameras, the recorders, the analyzers, the dials, the data cards.

"Print these up and get a reading," he told the specialists.

The thing that had been Svend Graves stood motionless in the center of the room, looking at nothing.

It was four hours later.

The last film had been studied, the last card interpreted, the last sentence broken down and evaluated.

There was a long, shocked silence.

"Well, I'll be damned," Ralph Hawley said finally.

There was a chorus of voices:

"They didn't *trust* us!"

"They tried to trick us!"

"They sent a remote-controlled robot—"

"Of all the crummy stunts—"

Ralph Hawley sat down in a chair.

"Don't you see what this means?" he said.

The others saw it too.

"They tried the identical trick on us that we tried on them," a psychologist said. "Roughly identical, anyway."

"They worked out the same basic solution to the same problem," an anthropologist said.

"They're our kind, damn them," said Gomez, the philosopher. "Look at them—insecure, scared, tricky, smart, capable, baby-faced liars."

Ralph Hawley closed his eyes.

There was only one basic solution to the problem of course, if you assumed that the two cultures saw the problem in the same terms. No human being could be saddled with a job like that; it was unthinkable. And so the aliens had sent a robot, and Earth had sent—

Svend Graves.

An artificial humanoid mechanism, twenty years in the making, designed to perform with inhuman skill in a contact situation. Designed to believe it was a human being, so that it had no part to play. Designed with builtin recording devices, skilled behavior patterns—but lacking classified data.

A robot and an android.

Two representatives from two *very* similar cultures.

"Gentlemen," said Ralph Hawley, "we are equals."

The red light flashed again.

The speaker said: "Hawley, we've got Reda Dani on the line. He's calling from the alien ship. Says he wants to talk to you."

"Put him on in here," Hawley said.

The communicator in the room came to life. Reda Dani looked at him and smiled.

Ralph Hawley smiled back.

"I see we didn't fool you," Reda Dani said.

"No. And I guess we didn't fox you any, either."

"No," agreed Reda Dani. "Damned clever, though."

"Thank you. That stunt of yours was pretty neat, too."

A pause.

"Look, Ralph," Reda Dani said. "This isn't getting us anywhere. Why not come on over yourself? The drinks are on me, and maybe we can get some *real* talking done."

Ralph Hawley didn't hesitate. "You've made yourself a deal, Reda," he said. "See you in half an hour."

He switched off the communicator.

The other specialists were laughing and clapping each other on the back.

The tension was gone. They had not failed.

The others gathered in a knot around him as he stepped into the port of the space shuttle that would carry him to Redi Dani's ship.

Everyone was trying to shake his hand and wish him well.

Just before he left, an aide appeared with a case of Hawley's own liquor, which was respectfully loaded aboard the shuttle.

"I thought Reda asked you to have a drink on *him*," Gomez objected. "Why take your own liquor?"

Ralph Hawley grinned.

"A man can't be too careful," he said, and closed the port behind him.

FIRST CONTACT
by Murray Leinster

Tommy Dort went into the captain's room with his last pair of stereophotos and said:

"I'm through, sir. These are the last two pictures I can take."

He handed over the photographs and looked with professional interest at the visiplates which showed all space outside the ship. Subdued, deep-red lighting indicated the controls and such instruments as the quartermaster on duty needed for navigation of the spaceship *Llanvabon*. There was a deeply cushioned control chair. There was the little gadget of oddly angled mirrors—remote descendant of the back-view mirrors of twentieth century motorists—which allowed a view of all the visiplates without turning the head. And there were the huge plates which were so much more satisfactory for a direct view of space.

The *Llanvabon* was a long way from home. The plates which showed every star of visual magnitude and could be stepped up to any desired magnification, portrayed stars of every imaginable degree of brilliance, in the startlingly different colors they showed outside of atmosphere. But every one was unfamiliar. Only two constellations could be recognized as seen from Earth, and they were shrunken and distorted. The Milky Way seemed vaguely out of place. But even such oddities were minor compared to a sight in the forward plates.

There was a vast, vast mistiness ahead. A luminous mist. It seemed motionless. It took a long time for any appreciable nearing to appear in the vision plates, though the spaceship's velocity indicator showed an incredible speed. The mist was the Crab Nebula, six light-years long, three and a half light years thick, with outward-reaching members that in the telescopes of Earth gave it some resemblance to the creature for which it was named. It was a cloud of gas, infinitely tenuous, reaching half again as far as from Sol to its nearest neighbor-sun. Deep within it burned two stars; a double star; one component the familiar yellow of the sun of Earth, the other an unholy white.

Tommy Dort said meditatively:

"We're heading into a deep, sir?"

The skipper studied the last two plates of Tommy's taking, and put them aside. He went back to his uneasy contemplation of the vision plates ahead. The *Llanvabon* was decelerating at full force. She was a bare half light-year from the nebula. Tommy's work was guiding the ship's course, now, but the work was done. During all the stay of the exploring ship in the nebula, Tommy Dort would loaf. But he'd more than paid his way so far.

He had just completed a quite unique first—a complete photographic record of the movement of a nebula during a period of four thousand years, taken by one individual with the same apparatus and with control exposures to detect and record any systematic errors. It was an achievement in itself worth the journey from Earth. But in addition, he had also recorded four thousand years of the history of a double star, and four thousand years of the history of a star in the act of degenerating into a white dwarf.

It was not that Tommy Dort was four thousand years old. He was, actually, in his twenties. But the Crab Nebula is four thousand light-years from Earth, and the last two pictures had been taken by light which would not reach Earth until the sixth millennium A.D. On the way here—at speeds incredible multiples of the speed of light—Tommy Dort had recorded each aspect of the nebula by the light which had left it from forty centuries since to a bare six months ago.

The *Llanvabon* bored on through space. Slowly, slowly, slowly, the incredible luminosity crept across the vision plates. It blotted out half the universe from view. Before was glowing mist, and behind was a star-studded emptiness. The mist shut off three-fourths of all the stars. Some few of the brightest shone dimly through it near its edge, but only a few. Then there was only an irregularly shaped patch of darkness astern against which stars shone unwinking. The *Llanvabon* dived into the nebula, and it seemed as if it bored into a tunnel of darkness with walls of shining fog.

Which was exactly what the spaceship was doing. The most distant photographs of all had disclosed structural features in the nebula. It was not amorphous. It had form. As the *Llanvabon* drew nearer, indications of structure grew more distinct, and Tommy Dort had argued for a curved approach for photographic reasons. So the spaceship had come up to the nebula on a vast logarithmic curve, and Tommy had been able to take successive photographs from slightly different angles and get stereopairs which showed the nebula in three dimensions; which disclosed billowings and hollows and an actually complicated shape. In places, the nebula displayed convolutions like those of a human brain. It was into one of those hollows that the spaceship now plunged. They had been called "deeps" by analogy with crevasses in the ocean floor. And they promised to be useful.

The skipper relaxed. One of a skipper's functions, nowadays, is to think of things to worry about, and then worry about them. The skipper of the *Llanvabon* was conscientious. Only after a certain instrument remained definitely nonregistering did he ease himself back in his seat.

"It was just barely possible," he said heavily, "that those deeps might be nonluminous gas. But they're empty. So we'll be able to use overdrive as long as we're in them."

It was a light-year-and-a-half from the edge of the nebula to the neighborhood of the double star which was its heart. That was the problem. A nebula is a gas. It is so thin that a comet's tail is solid by comparison, but a ship traveling on overdrive—above the speed of light—does not want to hit even a merely hard vacuum. It needs pure emptiness, such as exists between the stars. But the *Llanvabon* could not do much in this expanse of mist if it was limited to speeds a merely hard vacuum will permit.

The luminosity seemed to close in behind the spaceship, which slowed and slowed and slowed. The overdrive went off with the sudden *pinging* sensation which goes all over a person when the overdrive field is released.

Then, almostly instantly, bells burst into clanging, strident uproar all through the ship. Tommy was almost deafened by the alarm bell which rang in the captain's room before the quartermaster shut it off with a flip of his hand. But other bells could be heard ringing throughout the rest of the ship, to be cut off as automatic doors closed one by one.

Tommy Dort stared at the skipper. The skipper's hands clenched. He was up and staring over the quartermaster's shoulder. One indicator was apparently having convulsions. Others strained to record their findings. A spot on the diffusedly bright mistiness of a bow-quartering visiplate grew brighter as the automatic scanner focused on it. That was the direction of the object which had sounded collision-alarm. But the object locator itself—. According to its reading, there was one solid object some eighty thousand miles away—an object of no great size. But there was another object whose distance varied from extreme range to zero, and whose size shared its impossible advance and retreat.

"Step up the scanner," snapped the skipper.

The extra-bright spot on the scanner rolled outward, obliterating the undifferentiated image behind it. Magnification increased. But nothing appeared. Absolutely nothing. Yet the radio locator insisted that something monstrous and invisible made lunatic dashes toward the *Llanvabon*, at speeds which inevitably implied collision, and then fled coyly away at the same rate.

The visiplate went up to maximum magnification. Still nothing. The skipper ground his teeth. Tommy Dort said meditatively:

"D'you know, sir, I saw something like this on a liner on the Earth-Mars run once, when we were being located by another ship. Their locator beam was the same frequency as ours, and every time it hit, it registered like something monstrous, and solid."

"That," said the skipper savagely, "is just what's happening now. There's something like a locator beam on us. We're getting that beam and our own echo besides. But the other ship's invisible! Who is out here in an invisible ship with locator devices? Not men, certainly!"

He pressed the button in his sleeve communicator and snapped:

"Action stations! Man all weapons! Condition of extreme alert in all departments immediately!"

His hands closed and unclosed. He stared again at the visiplate which showed nothing but a formless brightness.

"Not men?" Tommy straightened sharply. "You mean—"

"How many solar systems in our galaxy?" demanded the skipper bitterly. "How many planets fit for life? And how many kinds of life could there be? If this ship isn't from Earth—and it isn't—it has a crew that isn't human. And things that aren't human but are up to the level of deep-space travel in their civilization could mean anything!"

The skipper's hands were actually shaking. He would not have talked so freely before a member of his own crew, but Tommy Dort was of the observation staff. And even a skipper whose duties include worrying may sometimes need desperately to unload his worries. Sometimes, too, it helps to think aloud.

"Something like this has been talked about and speculated about for years," he said softly. "Mathematically, it's been an odds-on bet that somewhere in our galaxy there'd be another race with a civilization equal to or further advanced than ours. Nobody could ever guess where or when we'd meet them. But it looks like we've done it now!"

Tommy's eyes were very bright.

"D'you suppose they'll be friendly, sir?"

The skipper glanced at the distance indicator. The phantom object still made its insane, nonexistent swoops toward and away from the *Llanvabon*. The secondary indication of an object at eighty thousand miles stirred ever so slightly.

"It's moving," he said curtly. "Heading for us. Just

what we'd do if a strange spaceship appeared in our hunting grounds! Friendly? Maybe! We're going to try to contact them. We have to. But I suspect this is the end of this expedition. Thank God for blasters!''

The blasters are those beams of ravening destruction which take care of recalcitrant meteorites in a spaceship's course when the deflectors can't handle them. They are not designed as weapons, but they can serve as pretty good ones. They can go into action at five thousand miles, and draw on the entire power output of a whole ship. With automatic aim and a traverse of five degrees, a ship like the *Llanvabon* can come very close to blasting a hole through a small-sized asteroid which gets in its way. But not on overdrive, of course.

Tommy Dort had approached the bow-quartering visiplate. Now he jerked his head around.

"Blasters sir? What for?"

The skipper grimaced at the empty visiplate.

"Because we don't know what they're like and can't take a chance! I know!" he added bitterly. "We're going to make contacts and try to find out all we can about them—especially where they come from. I suppose we'll try to make friends—but we haven't much chance. We can't trust them the fraction of an inch. We daren't! They've locators. Maybe they've tracers better than any we have. Maybe they could trace us all the way home without our knowing it! We can't risk a nonhuman race knowing where Earth is unless we're sure of them! And how can we be sure? They could come to trade, of course—or they could swoop down on overdrive with a battle fleet that could wipe us out before we knew what happened. We wouldn't know which to expect, or when!''

Tommy's face was startled.

"It's all been thrashed out over and over, in theory," said the skipper. "Nobody's ever been able to find a sound answer, even on paper. But you know, in all their theorizing, no one considered the crazy, rank impossibility of a deep-space contact, with neither side knowing the other's home world! But we've got to find an answer in fact! What are we going to do about them? Maybe these creatures will be aesthetic marvels, nice and friendly and polite—and underneath with the sneaking brutal ferocity of a Japanese. Or maybe they'll be crude and gruff as a Swedish farmer—and just as decent underneath. Maybe they're something in between. But am I going to risk the possible future of the human race on a guess that it's safe to trust them? God knows it would be worth while to make friends with a new civilization! It would be bound to stimulate our own, and maybe we'd gain enormously. But I can't take chances. The one thing I won't risk is having them know how to find Earth! Either I know they can't follow me, or I don't go home! And they'll probably feel the same way!''

He pressed the sleeve-communicator button again.

''Navigation officers, attention! Every star map on this ship is to be prepared for instant destruction. This includes photographs and diagrams from which our course or starting point could be deduced. I want all astronomical data gathered and arranged to be destroyed in a split second, on order. Make it fast and report when ready!''

He released the button. He looked suddenly old. The first contact of humanity with an alien race was a situation which had been forseen in many fashions, but never one quite so hopeless of solution as this. A solitary Earth-ship and a solitary alien, meeting in a nebula which must be remote from the home planet of each. They might wish peace, but the line of conduct which best prepared a treacherous attack was just the seeming of friendliness. Failure to be suspicious might doom the human race,—and a peaceful exchange of the fruits of civilization would be the greatest benefit imaginable. Any mistake would be irreparable, but a failure to be on guard would be fatal.

The captain's room was very, very quiet. The bow-quartering visiplate was filled with the image of a very small section of the nebula. A very small section indeed. It was all diffused, featureless, luminous mist.

''There, sir!''

There was a small shape in the mist. It was far away. It was a black shape, not polished to mirror-reflection like the hull of the *Llanvabon*. It was bulbous—roughly pearshaped. There was much thin luminosity between, and no details could be observed, but it was surely no natural object. Then Tommy looked at the distance indicator and said quietly:

"It's headed for us at very high acceleration, sir. The odds are that they're thinking the same thing, sir, that neither of us will dare let the other go home. Do you think they'll try a contact with us, or let loose with their weapons as soon as they're in range?"

The *Llanvabon* was no longer in a crevasse of emptiness in the nebula's thin substance. She swam in luminesence. There were no stars save the two fierce glows in the nebula's heart. There was nothing but an all-enveloping light, curiously like one's imagining of underwater in the tropics of Earth.

The alien ship had made one sign of less than lethal intention. As it drew near the *Llanvabon*, it decelerated. The *Llanvabon* itself had advanced for a meeting and then come to a dead stop. Its movement had been a recognition of the nearness of the other ship. Its pausing was both a friendly sign and a precaution against attack. Relatively still, it could swivel on its own axis to present the least target to a slashing assault, and it would have a longer firing-time than if the two ships flashed past each other at their combined speeds.

The moment of actual approach, however, was tenseness itself. The *Llanvabon's* needle-pointed bow aimed at the alien bulk. A relay to the captain's room put a key under his hand which would fire the blaster with maximum power. Tommy Dort watched, his brow wrinkled. The aliens must be of a high degree of civilization if they had spaceships, and civilization does not develop without the development of foresight. These aliens must recognize all the implications of this first contact of two civilized races as fully as did the humans on the *Llanvabon*.

The possibility of an enormous spurt in the development of both, by peaceful contact and exchange of their separate technologies, would probably appeal to them as to the man. But when dissimilar human cultures are in contact, one must usually be subordinate or there is war.

But subordination between races arising on separate planets could not be peacefully arranged. Men, at least, would never consent to subordination, nor was it likely that any highly-developed race would agree. The benefits to be derived from commerce could never make up for a condition of inferiority. Some races—men, perhaps— would prefer commerce to conquest. Perhaps— perhaps!—these aliens would also. But some types even of human beings would have craved red war. If the alien ship now approaching the *Llanvabon* returned to its home base with news of humanity's existence and of ships like the *Llanvabon*, it would give its race the choice of trade or battle. They might want trade, or they might want war. But it takes two to make trade, and only one to make war. They could not be sure of men's peacefulness, nor could men be sure of theirs. The only safety for either civilization would lie in the destruction of one or both of the two ships here and now.

But even victory would not be really enough. Men would need to know where this alien race was to be found, for avoidance if not for battle. They would need to know its weapons, and its resources, and if it could be a menace and how it could be eliminated in case of need. The aliens would feel the same necessities concerning humanity.

So the skipper of the *Llanvabon* did not press the key which might possibly have blasted the other ship to nothingness. He dare not. But he dared not not fire either. Sweat came out on his face.

A speaker muttered. Someone from the range room.

"The other ship's stopped, sir. Quite stationary. Blasters are centered on it, sir."

It was an urging to fire. But the skipper shook his head, to himself. The alien ship was no more than twenty miles away. It was dead-black. Every bit of its exterior was an abysmal, nonreflecting sable. No details could be seen except by minor variations in its outline against the misty nebula.

"It's stopped dead, sir," said another voice. "They've sent a modulated short wave at us, sir. Frequency modulated. Apparently a signal. Not enough power to do any harm."

The skipper said through tight-locked teeth:

"They're doing something now. There's movement on the outside of their hull. Watch what comes out. Put the auxiliary blasters on it."

Something small and round came smoothly out of the oval outline of the black ship. The bulbous bulk moved.

"Moving away, sir," said the speaker. "The object they let out is stationary in the place they've left."

Another voice cut in:

"More frequency modulated stuff, sir. Unintelligible."

Tommy Dort's eyes brightened. The skipper watched the visiplate, with sweat-droplets on his forehead.

"Rather pretty, sir," said Tommy, meditatively. "If they sent anything toward us, it might seem a projectile or a bomb. So they came close, let out a lifeboat, and went away again. They figure we can send a boat or a man to make contact without risking our ship. They must think pretty much as we do."

The skipper said, without moving his eyes from the plate:

"Mr. Dort, would you care to go out and look the thing over? I can't order you, but I need all my operating crew for emergencies. The observation staff—"

"Is expendable. Very well, sir," said Tommy briskly. "I won't take a lifeboat, sir. Just a suit with a drive in it. It's smaller and the arms and legs will look unsuitable for a bomb. I think I should carry a scanner, sir."

The alien ship continued to retreat. Forty, eighty, four hundred miles. It came to a stop and hung there, waiting. Climbing into his atomic-driven spacesuit just within the *Llanvabon*'s air lock, Tommy heard the reports as they went over the speakers throughout the ship. That the other ship had stopped its retreat at four hundred miles was encouraging. It might not have weapons effective at a greater distance than that, and so felt safe. But just as the thought formed itself in his mind, the alien retreated precipitately still farther. Which, as Tommy reflected as he emerged from the lock, might be because the aliens had realized they were giving themselves away, or might be because they wanted to give the impression that they had done so.

He swooped away from the silvery-mirror *Llanvabon*, through a brightly glowing emptiness which was past any previous experience of the human race. Behind him, the *Llanvabon* swung about and darted away. The skipper's voice came in Tommy's helmet phones.

"We're pulling back, too, Mr. Dort. There is a bare possibility that they've some explosive atomic reaction they can't use from their own ship, but which might be destructive even as far as this. We'll draw back. Keep your scanner on the object."

The reasoning was sound, if not very comforting. An explosive which could destroy anything within twenty miles was theoretically possible, but humans didn't have it yet. It was decidedly safest for the *Llanvabon* to draw back.

But Tommy Dort felt very lonely. He sped through emptiness toward the tiny black speck which hung in incredible brightness. The *Llanvabon* vanished. Its polished hull would merge with the glowing mist at a relatively short distance, anyhow. The alien ship was not visible to the naked eye, either. Tommy swam in nothingness, four thousand light-years from home, toward a tiny black spot which was the only solid object to be seen in all of space.

It was a slightly distorted sphere, not much over six feet in diameter. It bounced away when Tommy landed on it, feet-first. There were small tentacles, or horns, which projected in every direction. They looked rather like the detonating horns of a submarine mine, but there was a glint of crystal at the tip-end of each.

"I'm here," said Tommy into his helmet phone.

He caught hold of a horn and drew himself to the object. It was all metal, dead-black. He could feel no texture through his space gloves, of course, but he went over and over it, trying to discover its purpose.

"Deadlock, sir," he said presently. "Nothing to report that the scanner hasn't shown you."

Then, through his suit, he felt vibrations. They translated themselves as clankings. A section of the rounded hull of the object opened out. Two sections. He worked his way around to look in and see the first nonhuman civilized beings that any man had ever looked upon.

But what he saw was simply a flat plate on which dim-red glows crawled here and there in seeming aimlessness. His helmet phones emitted a startled exclamation. The skipper's voice:

"Very good, Mr. Dort. Fix your scanner to look into that plate. They dumped out a robot with an infra-red visiplate for communication. Not risking any personnel. Whatever we might do would damage only machinery. Maybe they expect us to bring it on board—and it may have a bomb charge that can be detonated when they're ready to start for home. I'll send a plate to face one of its scanners. You return to the ship."

"Yes, sir," said Tommy. "But which way is the ship, sir?"

There were no stars. The nebula obscured them with its light. The only thing visible from the robot was the double star at the nebula's center. Tommy was no longer oriented. He had but one reference point.

"Head straight away from the double star," came the order in his helmet phone. "We'll pick you up."

He passed another lonely figure, a little later, headed for the alien sphere with a vision plate to set up. The two spaceships, each knowing that it dared not risk its own race by the slightest lack of caution, would communicate with each other through this small round robot. Their separate vision systems would enable them to exchange all the information they dared give, while they debated the most practical way of making sure that their own civilization would not be endangered by this first contact with another. The truly most practical method would be the destruction of the other ship in a swift and deadly attack—in self-defense.

II

The *Llanvabon*, thereafter, was a ship in which there were two separate enterprises on hand at the same time. She had come out from Earth to make close-range observations on the smaller component of the double star at the nebula's center. The nebula itself was the result of the most titanic explosion of which men have any knowledge. The explosion took place some time in the year 2946 B.C., before the first of the seven cities of long-dead Illium was even thought of. The light of that explosion reached Earth in the year 1054 A. D., and was duly recorded in ecclesiastic annals and somewhat more reliably by Chinese court astronomers. It was bright enough to be seen in daylight for twenty-three successive days. Its light—and it was four thousand light-years away—was brighter than that of Venus.

From these facts, astronomers could calculate nine hundred years later the violence of the detonation. Matter blown away from the center of the explosion would have traveled outward at the rate of two million three hundred thousand miles an hour; more than thirty-eight thousand miles a minute; something over six hundred thirty-eight miles per second. When twentieth-century telescopes were turned upon the scene of this vast explosion, only a double star remained—and the nebula. The brighter star of the doublet was almost unique in having so high a surface temperature that it showed no spectrum lines at all. It had a continuous spectrum. Sol's surface temperature is about 7,000° Absolute. That of the hot white star is 500,000 degrees. It has nearly the mass of the sun, but only one fifth its diameter, so that its density is one hundred seventy-three times that of water, sixteen times that of lead, and eight times that of iridium —the heaviest substance known on earth. But even this density is not that of a dwarf white star like the companion of Sirius. The white star in the Crab Nebula is an incomplete dwarf; it is a star still in the act of collapsing. Examination—including the survey of a four-thousand-year column of its light—was worth while. The *Llanvabon* had come to make that examination. But the finding of an alien spaceship upon a similar errand had implications which overshadowed the original purpose of the expedition.

A tiny bulbous robot floated in the tenuous nebular gas. The normal operating crew of the *Llanvabon* stood at their posts with a sharp alertness which was productive of tense nerves. The observation staff divided itself, and a part went half-heartedly about the making of the observations for which the *Llanvabon* had come. The other half applied itself to the problem the spaceship offered.

It represented a culture which was up to space travel on an interstellar scale. The explosion of a mere five thousand years since must have blasted every trace of life out of existence in the area now filled by the nebula. So the aliens of the black spaceship came from another solar system. Their trip must have been, like that of the Earth ship, for purely scientific purposes. There was nothing to be extracted from the nebula.

They were, then, at least near the level of human civilization, which meant that they had or could develop arts and articles of commerce which men would want to trade for, in friendship. But they would necessarily realize that the existence and civilization of humanity was a potential menace of their own race. The two races could be friends, but also they could be deadly enemies. Each, even if unwillingly, was a monstrous menace to the other. And the only safe thing to do with a menace is to destroy it.

In the Crab Nebula the problem was acute and immediate. The future relationship of the two races would be settled here and now. If a process for friendship could be established, one race, otherwise doomed, would survive and both would benefit immensely. But that process had to be established, and confidence built up, without the most minute risk of danger from treachery. Confidence would need to be established upon a foundation of necessarily complete distrust. Neither dared return to its own base if the other could do harm to its race. Neither dared risk any of the necessities to trust. The only safe thing for either to do was destroy the other or be destroyed.

But even for war, more was needed than mere destruction of the other. With interstellar traffic, the aliens must have atomic power and some form of overdrive for travel above the speed of light. With radio location and visiplates and short-wave communication they had, of

course, many other devices. What weapons did they
have? How widely extended was their culture? What were
their resources? Could there be a development of trade
and friendship, or were the two races so unlike that only
war could exist between them? If peace was possible, how
could it be begun?

The men on the *Llanvabon* needed facts—and so did
the crew of the other ship. They must take back every
morsel of information they could. The most important
information of all would be of the location of the other
civilization, just in case of war. That one bit of
information might be the decisive factor in an interstellar
war. But other facts would be enormously valuable.

The tragic thing was that there could be no possible
information which could lead to peace. Neither ship
could stake its own race's existence upon any conviction
of the good will or the honor of the other.

So there was a strange truce between the two ships. The
alien went about its work of making observations, as did
the *Llanvabon*. The tiny robot floated in bright emptiness. A scanner from the *Llanvabon* was focussed upon a
vision plate from the alien. A scanner from the alien
regarded a vision plate from the *Llanvabon*. Communication began.

It progressed rapidly. Tommy Dort was one of those who
made the first progress report. His special task on the
expedition was over. He had now been assigned to work
on the problem of communication with the alien entities.
He went with the ship's solitary psychologist to the
captain's room to convey the news of success. The
captain's room, as usual, was a place of silence and dull-
red indicator lights and the great bright visiplates on
every wall and on the ceiling.

"We've established fairly satisfactory communication,
sir," said the psychologist. He looked tired. His work on
the trip was supposed to be that of measuring personal
factors of error in the observation staff, for the reduction
of all observations to the nearest possible decimal to the
absolute. He had been pressed into service for which he
was not especially fitted, and it told upon him. "That

is, we can say almost anything we wish, to them, and can understand what they say in return. But of course we don't know how much of what they say is the truth.''

The skipper's eyes turned to Tommy Dort.

''We've hooked up some machinery,'' said Tommy, ''that amounts to a mechanical translator. We have vision plates, of course, and then short-wave beams direct. They use frequency-modulation plus what is probably variation in wave forms—like our vowel and consonant sounds in speech. We've never had any use for anything like that before, so our coils won't handle it, but we've developed a sort of code which isn't the language of either set of us. They shoot over short-wave stuff with frequency-modulation, and we record it as sound. When we shoot it back, it's reconverted into frequency-modulation.''

The skipper said, frowning:

''What wave-form changes short waves? How do you know?''

''We showed them our recorder in the vision plates, and they showed us theirs. They record the frequency-modulation direct. I think,'' said Tommy carefully, ''they don't use sound at all, even in speech. They've set up a communications room, and we've watched them in the act of communicating with us. They make no perceptible movement of anything that corresponds to a speech organ. Instead of a microphone, they simply stand near something that would work as a pick-up antenna. My guess, sir, is that they use microwaves for what you might call person-to-person conversation. I think they make short-wave trains as we make sounds.''

The skipper stared at him:

''That means they have telepathy?''

''M-m-m. Yes, sir,'' said Tommy. ''Also it means that we have telepathy too, as far as they are concerned. They're probably deaf. They've certainly no idea of using sound waves in air for communication. They simply don't use noises for any purpose.''

The skipper stored the information away.

''What else?''

"Well, sir," said Tommy doubtfully. "I think we're all set. We agreed on arbitrary symbols for objects, sir, by way of the visiplates, and worked out relationships and verbs and so on with diagrams and pictures. We've a couple of thousand words that have mutual meanings. We set up an analyzer to sort out their short-wave groups, which we feed into a decoding machine. And then the coding end of the machine picks out recordings to make the wave groups we want to send back. When you're ready to talk to the skipper of the other ship, sir, I think we're ready."

"H-m-m. What's your impression of their psychology?" The skipper asked the question of the psychologist.

"I don't know, sir," said the psychologist harassedly. "They seem to be completely direct. But they haven't let slip even a hint of the tenseness we know exists. They act as if they were simply setting up a means of communication for friendly conversation. But there is . . . well . . . an overtone—"

The psychologist was a good man at psychological mensuration, which is a good and useful field. But he was not equipped to analyze a completely alien thought-pattern.

"If I may say so, sir—" said Tommy uncomfortably.

"What?"

"They're oxygen breathers," said Tommy, "and they're not too dissimilar to us in other ways. It seems to me, sir, that paralled evolution has been at work. Perhaps intelligence evolves in parallel lines, just as . . . well . . . basic bodily functions. I mean," he added conscientiously, "any living being of any sort must ingest, metabolize, and excrete. Perhaps any intelligent brain must perceive, apperceive, and find a personal reaction. I'm sure I've detected irony. That implies humor, too. In short, sir, I think they could be likable."

The skipper heaved himself to his feet.

"H-m-m." He said profoundly. "We'll see what they have to say."

He walked to the communication room. The scanner for the vision plate in the robot was in readiness. The skipper walked in front of it. Tommy Dort sat down at the coding machine and tapped at the keys. Highly improbable noises came from it, went into a microphone, and governed the frequency-modulation of a signal sent through space to the other spaceship. Almost instantly the vision screen which with one relay—in the robot— showed the interior of the other ship lighted up. An alien came before the scanner and seemed to look inquisitively out of the plate. He was extraordinarily manlike, but he was not human. The impression he gave was of extreme baldness and somehow humorous frankness.

"I'd like to say," said the skipper heavily, "the appropriate things about this first contact of two dissimilar civilized races, and of my hopes that a friendly intercourse between the two peoples will result."

Tommy Dort hesitated. Then he shrugged and tapped expertly upon the coder. More improbable noises.

The alien skipper seemed to receive the message. He made a gesture which was wryly assenting. The decoder on the *Llanvabon* hummed to itself and word-cards dropped into the message frame. Tommy said dispassionately:

"He says, sir, 'That is all very well but is there any way for us to let each other go home alive? I would be happy to hear of such a way if you can contrive one. At the moment it seems to me that one of us must be killed.'"

III

The atmosphere was of confusion. There were too many questions to be answered all at once. Nobody could answer any of them. And all of them had to be answered.

The *Llanvabon* could start for home. The alien ship might or might not be able to multiply the speed of light by one more unit than the Earth vessel. If it could, the *Llanvabon* would get close enough to Earth to reveal its destination—and then have to fight. It might or might not win. Even if it did win, the aliens might have a communication system by which the *Llanvabon's* destination might have been reported to the aliens' home planet before battle was joined. But the *Llanvabon* might lose in such a fight. If she was to be destroyed, it would be better to be destroyed here, without giving any clue to where human beings might be found by a forewarned, forearmed alien battle fleet.

The black ship was in exactly the same predicament. It too, could start for home. But the *Llanvabon* might be faster, and an overdrive field can be trailed, if you set to work on it soon enough. The aliens, also, would not know whether the *Llanvabon* could report to its home base without returning. If the alien was to be destroyed, it also would prefer to fight it out here, so that it could not lead a probable enemy to its own civilization.

Neither ship, then, could think of flight. The course of the *Llanvabon* into the nebula might be known to the black ship, but it had been the end of a logarithmic curve, and the aliens could not know its properties. They could not tell from that from what direction the Earth ship had started. As of the moment, then, the two ships were even. But the question was and remained, "What now?"

There was no specific answer. The aliens traded information for information—and did not always realize what information they gave. The humans traded information for information—and Tommy Dort sweated blood in his anxiety not to give any clue to the whereabouts of Earth.

The aliens saw by infrared light, and the vision plates and scanners in the robot communication-exchange had to adapt their respective images up and down an optical octave each, for them to have any meaning at all. It did not occur to the aliens that their eyesight told that their sun was a red dwarf, yielding light of greatest energy just below the part of the spectrum visible to human eyes. But after that fact was realized on the *Llanvabon*, it was realized that the aliens, also, should be able to deduce the Sun's spectral type by the light to which men's eyes were best adapted.

There was a gadget for the recording of short-wave trains which was so casually in use among the aliens as a sound-recorder is among men. The humans wanted that, badly. And the aliens were fascinated by the mystery of sound. They were able to perceive noise, of course, just as a man's palm will perceive infrared light by the sensation of heat it produces, but they could no more differentiate pitch or tone-quality than a man is able to distinguish between two frequencies of heat-radiation even half an octave part. To them, the human science of sound was a remarkable discovery. They would find uses for noises which humans had never imagined—if they lived.

But that was another question. Neither ship could leave without first destroying the other. But while the flood of information was in passage, neither ship could afford to destroy the other. There was the matter of the outer coloring of the two ships. The *Llanvabon* was mirror-bright exteriorly. The alien ship was dead-black by visible light. It absorbed heat to perfection, and should radiate it away again as readily. But it did not. The black coating was not a "black body" color or lack of color. It was a perfect reflector of certain infrared wave lengths while simultaneously it fluoresced in just those wave bands. In practice, it absorbed the higher frequencies of heat, converted them to lower frequencies it did not radiate— and stayed at the desired temperature even in empty space.

Tommy Dort labored over his task of communications. He found the alien thought-processes not so alien that he could not follow them. The discussion of technics reached the matter of interstellar navigation. A star map was needed to illustrate the process. It would not have been logical to use a star map from the chart room—but from a star map one could guess the point from which the map was projected. Tommy had a map made specially, with imaginary but convincing star images upon it. He translated directions for its use by the coder and decoder. In return, the aliens presented a star map of their own before the visiplate. Copied instantly by photograph, the Nav officers labored over it, trying to figure out from what spot in the galaxy the stars and Milky Way would show at such an angle. It baffled them.

It was Tommy who realized finally that the aliens had made a special star map for their demonstration too, and that it was a mirror-image of the faked map Tommy had shown them previously.

Tommy could grin, at that. He began to like these aliens. They were not human, but they had a very human sense of the ridiculous. In course of time Tommy essayed a mild joke. It had to be translated into code numerals, these into quite cryptic groups of short-wave, frequency-modulated impulses, and these went to the other ship and into heaven knew what to become intelligible. A joke which went through such formalities would not seem likely to be funny. But the aliens did see the point.

There was one of the aliens to whom communication became as normal a function as Tommy's own code-handlings. The two of them developed a quite insane friendship, conversing by coder, decoder, and short-wave trains. When technicalities in the official message grew too involved, that alien sometimes threw in strictly nontechnical interpolations akin to slang. Often, they cleared up the confusion. Tommy, for no reason whatever, had filed a code-name of "Buck" which the decoder picked out regularly when this particular signed his own symbol to a message.

In the third week of communication, the decoder suddenly presented Tommy with a message in the message frame.

You are a good guy. It is too bad we have to kill each other.—Buck

Tommy had been thinking much the same thing. He tapped off the rueful reply;

We can't see any way out of it. Can you?

There was a pause, and the message frame filled up again.

If we could believe each other, yes. Our skipper would like it. But we can't believe you, and you can't believe us.

We'd trail you home if we got a chance, and you'd trail us. But we feel sorry about it—Buck.

Tommy Dort took the messages to the skipper.

"Look here, sir!" he said urgently. "These people are almost human, and they're likable cusses."

The skipper was busy about his important task of thinking things to worry about, and worrying about them. He said tiredly:

"They're oxygen breathers. Their air is twenty-eight percent oxygen instead of twenty, but they could do very well on Earth. It would be a highly desirable conquest for them. And we still don't know what weapons they've got or what they can develop. Would you tell them how to find Earth?"

"N-no," said Tommy, unhappily.

"They probably feel the same way," said the skipper dryly. "And if we did manage to make a friendly contact, how long would it say friendly? If their weapons were inferior to ours, they'd feel that for their own safety they had to improve them. And we, knowing they were planning to revolt, would crush them while we could— for our own safety! If it happened to be the other way about, they'd have to smash us before we could catch up to them."

Tommy was silent, but he moved restlessly.

"If we smash this black ship and get home," said the skipper, "Earth Government will be annoyed if we don't tell them where it came from. But what can we do? We'll be lucky enough to get back alive with our warning. It isn't possible to get out of those creatures any more information than we give them, and we surely won't give them our address! We've run into them by accident. Maybe—if we smash this ship—there won't be another contact for thousands of years. And it's a pity, because trade could mean so much! But it takes two to make a peace, and we can't risk trusting them. The only answer is to kill them if we can, and if we can't, to make sure that when they kill us they'll find out nothing that will lead them to Earth. I don't like it," added the skipper tiredly, "but there simply isn't anything else to do!"

IV

On the *Llanvabon*, the technicians worked frantically in two divisions. One prepared for victory, and the other for defeat. The one working for victory could do little. The main blasters were the only weapons with any promise. Their mountings were cautiously altered so that they were no longer fixed nearly dead ahead, with only a 5° traverse. Electronic controls which followed a radio-locator masterfinder would keep them trained with absolute precision upon a given target regardless of its maneuverings. More; a hitherto unsung genius in the engine room devised a capacity-storage system by which the normal full-output of the ship's engines could be momentarily accumulated and released in surges of stored power far above normal. In theory, the range of the blasters should be multiplied and their destructive power considerably stepped up. But there was not much more that could be done.

The defeat crew had more leeway. Star charts, navigational instruments carrying telltale notations, the photographic record Tommy Dort had made on the six-months' journey from Earth, and every other memorandum offering clues to Earth's position, were prepared for destruction. They were put in sealed files, and if any one of them was opened by one who did not know the exact, complicated process, the contents of all the files would flash into ashes and the ash be churned past any hope of restoration. Of course, if the *Llanvabon* should be victorious, a carefully not-indicated method of reopening them in safety would remain.

There were atomic bombs placed all over the hull of the ship. If its human crew should be killed without complete destruction of the ship, the atomic-power bombs should detonate if the *Llanvabon* was brought alongside the alien vessel. There were no ready-made atomic bombs on board, but there were small spare atomic-power units on board. It was not hard to trick them so that when they were turned on, instead of yielding a smooth flow of power they would explode. And four men of the earth ship's crew remained always in spacesuits with closed helmets, to fight the ship should it be punctured in many compartments by an unwarned attack.

Such an attack, however, would not be treacherous. The alien skipper had spoken frankly. His manner was that of one who wryly admits the uselessness of lies. The skipper and the *Llanvabon*, in turn, heavily admitted the virtue of frankness. Each insisted—perhaps truthfully—that he wished for friendship between the two races. But neither could trust the other not to make every conceivable effort to find out the one thing he needed most desperately to conceal—the location of his home planet. And neither dared believe that the other was unable to trail him and find out. Because each felt it his own duty to accomplish that unbearable—to the other—act, neither could risk the possible existence of his race by trusting the other. They must fight because they could not do anything else.

They could raise the stakes of the battle by an exchange of information beforehand. But there was a limit to the stake either would put up. No information on weapons, population, or resources would be given by either. Not even the distance of their home bases from the Crab Nebula would be told. They exchanged information, to be sure, but they knew a battle to the death must follow, and each strove to represent his own civilization as powerful enough to give pause to the other's ideas of possible conquest—and thereby increased its appearance of menace to the other, and made battle more unavoidable.

It was curious how completely such alien brains could mesh, however. Tommy Dort, sweating over the coding and decoding machines, found a personal equation emerging from the at first stilted arrays of word-cards which arranged themselves. He had seen the aliens only in the vision screen, and then only in light at least one octave removed from the light they saw by. They, in turn, saw him very strangely, by transposed illumination from what to them would be the far ultraviolet. But their brains worked alike. Amazingly alike. Tommy Dort felt actual sympathy and even something close to friendship for the gill-breathing, bald, and dryly ironic creatures of the black space vessel.

Because of that mental kinship he set up—though hopelessly—a sort of table of the aspects of the problem before them. He did not believe that the aliens had any instinctive desire to destroy man. In fact, the study of communications from the aliens had produced on the *Llanvabon* a feeling of tolerance not unlike that between enemy soldiers during a truce on Earth. The men felt no enmity, and probably neither did the aliens. But they had to kill or be killed for strictly logical reasons.

Tommy's table was specific. He made a list of objectives the men must try to achieve, in the order of their importance. The first was the carrying back of news of the existence of the alien culture. The second was the location of that alien culture in the galaxy. The third was the carrying back of as much information as possible about that culture. The third was being worked on, but the second was probably impossible. The first—and all—would depend on the result of the fight which must take place.

The aliens' objectives would be exactly similar, so that the men must prevent, first, news of the existence of Earth's culture from being taken back by the aliens, second, alien discovery of the location of Earth, and third, the acquiring by the aliens of information which would help them or encourage them to attack humanity. And again the third was in train, and the second was probably taken care of, and the first must await the battle.

There was no possible way to avoid the grim necessity of the destruction of the black ship. The aliens would see no solution to their problems but the destruction of the *Llanvabon*. But Tommy Dort, regarding his tabulation ruefully, realized that even complete victory would not be a perfect solution. The ideal would be for the *Llanvabon* to take back the alien ship for study. Nothing less would be a complete attainment of the third objective. But Tommy realized that he hated the idea of so complete a victory, even if it could be accomplished. He would hate the idea of killing even nonhuman creatures who understood a human joke. And beyond that, he would hate the idea of Earth fitting out a fleet of fighting ships to destroy an alien culture because its existence was dangerous. The pure accident of this encounter, between peoples who could like each other, had created a situation which could only result in wholesale destruction.

Tommy Dort soured on his own brain which could find no answer which would work. But there had to be an answer! The gamble was too big! It was too absurd that two spaceships should fight—neither one primarily designed for fighting—so that the survivor could carry back news which would set one case to frenzied preparation for war against the unwarned other.

If both races could be warned, though, and each knew that the other did not want to fight, and if they could communicate with each other but not locate each other until some grounds for mutual trust could be reached—

It was impossible. It was chimerical. It was a daydream. It was nonsense. But it was such luring nonsense that Tommy Dort ruefully put it into the coder to his gill-breathing friend Buck, then some hundred thousand miles off in the misty brightness of the nebula.

"Sure," said Buck, in the decoder's word-cards flicking into place in the message frame. "That is a good dream. But I like you and still won't believe you. If I said that first, you would like me but not believe me either. I tell you the truth more than you believe, and maybe you tell me the truth more than I believe. But there is no way to know. I am sorry."

Tommy Dort stared gloomily at the message. He felt a very horrible sense of responsibility. Everyone did, on the *Llanvabon*. If they failed in this encounter, the human race would run a very good chance of being exterminated in time to come. If they succeeded, the race of the aliens would be the one to face destruction, most likely. Millions or billions of lives hung upon the actions of a few men.

Then Tommy Dort saw the answer.

It would be amazingly simple, if it worked. At worst it might give a partial victory to humanity and the *Llanvabon*. He sat quite still, not daring to move lest he break the chain of thought that followed the first tenuous idea. He went over and over it, excitedly finding objections here and meeting them, and overcoming impossibilities there. It was the answer! He felt sure of it.

He felt almost dizzy with relief when he found his way to the captain's room and asked leave to speak.

It is the function of a skipper, among others, to find things to worry about. But the *Llanvabon's* skipper did not have to look. In the three weeks and four days since the first contact with the alien black ship, the skipper's face had grown lined and old. He had not only the *Llanvabon* to worry about. He had all of humanity.

"Sir," said Tommy Dort, his mouth rather dry because of his enormous earnestness, "may I offer a method of attack on the black ship? I'll undertake it myself, sir, and if it doesn't work our ship won't be weakened."

The skipper looked at him unseeingly.

"The tactics are all worked out, Mr. Dort," he said heavily. "They're being cut on tape now, for the ship's handling. It's a terrible gamble, but it has to be done."

"I think," said Tommy carefully, "I've worked out a way to take the gamble out. Suppose, sir, we send a message to the other ship, offering—"

His voice went on in the utterly quiet captain's room, with the visiplates showing only a vast mistiness outside and the two fiercely burning stars in the nebula's heart.

IV

The skipper himself went through the air lock with Tommy. For one reason, the action Tommy had suggested would need his authority behind it. For another, the skipper had worried more intensively than anybody else on the *Llanvabon*, and he was tired of it. If he went with Tommy, he would do the thing himself, and if he failed he would be the first one killed—and the tape for the Earth ship's maneuvering was already fed into the control board and correlated with the master-timer. If Tommy and the skipper were killed, a single control pushed home would throw the *Llanvabon* into the most furious possible all-out attack, which would end in the complete destruction of one ship or the other—or both. So the skipper was not deserting his post.

The outer air lock door swung wide. It opened upon that shining emptiness which was the nebula. Twenty miles away, the little round robot hung in space, drifting in an incredible orbit about the twin central suns, and floating ever nearer and nearer. It would never reach either of them, of course. The white star alone was so much hotter than Earth's sun that its heat-effect would produce Earth's temperature on an object five times as far from it as Neptune is from Sol. Even removed to the distance of Pluto, the little robot would be raised to cherry-red heat by the blazing white dwarf. And it could not possibly approach to the ninety-odd million miles which is the Earth's distance from the sun. So near, its metal would melt and boil away as vapor. But, half a light-year out, the bulbous object bobbed in emptiness.

The two spacesuited figures soared away from the *Llanvabon*. The small atomic drives which made them minute spaceships on their own had been subtly altered, but the change did not interfere with their functioning. They headed for the communication robot. The skipper, out in space, said gruffly:

"Mr. Dort, all my life I have longed for adventure. This is the first time I could ever justify it to myself."

His voice came through Tommy's space-phone receivers. Tommy wetted his lips and said:

"It doesn't seem like adventure to me, sir. I want terribly for the plan to go through. I thought adventure was when you didn't care."

"Oh, no," said the skipper. "Adventure is when you toss your life on the scales of chance and wait for the pointer to stop."

They reached the round object. They clung to its short, scanner-tipped horns.

"Intelligent, those creatures," said the skipper heavily. "They must want desperately to see more of our ship than the communications room, to agree to this exchange of visits before the fight."

"Yes, sir," said Tommy. But privately, he suspected that Buck—his gill-breathing friend—would like to see him in the flesh before one or both of them died. And it seemed to him that between the two ships had grown up an odd tradition of courtesy, like that between two ancient knights before a tourney, when they admired each other wholeheartedly before hacking at each other with all the contents of their respective armories.

They waited.

Then, out of the mist, came two other figures. The alien spacesuits were also power-driven. The aliens themselves were shorter than men, and their helmet openings were coated with a filtering material to cut off visible and ultraviolet rays which to them would be lethal. It was not possible to see more than the outline of the heads within.

Tommy's helmet phone said, from the communications room on the *Llanvabon*:

"They say that their ship is waiting for you, sir. The airlock door will be open."

The skipper's voice said heavily:

"Mr. Dort, have you seen their spacesuits before? If so, are you sure they're not carrying anything extra, such as bombs?"

"Yes, sir," said Tommy. "We've showed each other our space equipment. They've nothing but regular stuff in view, sir."

The skipper made a gesture to the two aliens. He and Tommy Dort plunged on for the black vessel. They could not make out the ship very clearly with the naked eye, but directions for change of course came from the communication room.

The black ship loomed up. It was huge; as long as the *Llanvabon* and vastly thicker. The air lock did stand open. The two spacesuited men moved in and anchored themselves with magnetic-soled boots. The outer door closed. There was a rush of air and simultaneously the sharp quick tug of artificial gravity. Then the inner door opened.

All was darkness. Tommy switched on his helmet light at the same instant as the skipper. Since the aliens saw by infrared, a white light would have been intolerable to them. The men's helmet lights were, therefore, of the deep-red tint used to illuminate instrument panels so there will be no dazzling of eyes that must be able to detect the minutest specks of white light on a navigating vision plate. There were aliens waiting to receive them. They blinked at the brightness of the helmet lights. The space-phone receivers said in Tommy's ear:

"They say, sir, their skipper is waiting for you."

Tommy and the skipper were in a long corridor with a soft flooring underfoot. Their lights showed details of which every one was exotic.

"I think I'll crack my helmet, sir," said Tommy.

He did. The air was good. By analysis it was thirty percent oxygen instead of twenty for normal air on Earth, but the pressure was less. It felt just right. The artificial gravity, too, was less than that maintained on the *Llanvabon*. The home planet of the aliens would be smaller than Earth, and—by the infrared data—circling close to a nearly dead, dull-red sun. The air had smells in it. They were utterly strange, but not unpleasant.

An arched opening. A ramp with the same soft stuff underfoot. Lights which actually shed a dim, dull-red glow about. The aliens had stepped up some of their illu-minating equipment as an act of courtesy. The light might hurt their eyes, but it was a gesture of consideration which made Tommy even more anxious for his plan to go through.

The alien skipper faced them with what seemed to Tommy a gesture of wryly humorous deprecation. The helmet phones said:

"He says, sir, that he greets you with pleasure, but he has been able to think of only one way in which the problem created by the meeting of these two ships can be solved."

"He means a fight," said the skipper. "Tell him I'm here to offer another choice."

The *Llanvabon's* skipper and the skipper of the alien ship were face to face, but their communication was weirdly indirect. The aliens used no sound in communi-cation. Their talk, in fact, took place on microwaves and approximated telepathy. But they could not hear, in any ordinary sense of the word, so the skipper's and Tommy's speech approached telepathy, too, as far as they were concerned. When the skipper spoke, his space phone sent his words back to the *Llanvabon*, where the words were fed into the coder and short-wave equivalents sent back to the black ship. The alien skipper's reply went to the *Llanvabon* and through the decoder, and was re-transmitted by space phone in words read from the message frame. It was awkward, but it worked.

The short and stocky alien skipper paused. The helmet phones relayed his translated, soundless reply.

"He is anxious to hear, sir."

The skipper took off his helmet. He put his hands at his belt in a belligerent pose.

"Look here!" he said truculently to the bald, strange creature in the unearthly red glow before him. "It looks like we have to fight and one batch of us get killed. We're ready to do it if we have to. But if you win, we've got it fixed so you'll never find out where Earth is, and there's a good chance we'll get you anyhow! If we win, we'll be in the same fix. And if we win and go back home, our government will fit out a fleet and start hunting your planet. And if we find it we'll be ready to blast it to hell! If you win, the same thing will happen to us! And it's all foolishness! We've stayed here a month, and we've swapped information, and we don't hate each other. There's no reason for us to fight except for the rest of our respective races!"

The skipper stopped for breath, scowling. Tommy Dort inconspicuously put his own hands on the belt of his spacesuit. He waited, hoping desperately that the trick would work.

"He says, sir," reported the helmet phones, "that all you say is true. But that his race has to be protected, just as you feel that yours must be."

"Naturally!" said the skipper angrily, "but the sensible thing to do is to figure out how to protect it! Putting its future up as a gamble in a fight is not sensible. Our races have to be warned of each other's existence. That's true. But each should have proof that the other doesn't want to fight, but wants to be friendly. And we shouldn't be able to find each other, but we should be able to communicate with each other to work out grounds for a common trust. If our governments want to be fools, let them! But we should give them the chance to make friends, instead of starting a space war out of mutual funk!"

Briefly, the space phone said:

"He says that the difficulty is that of trusting each other now. With the possible existence of his race at stake, he cannot take any chance, and neither can you, of yielding an advantage."

"But my race," boomed the skipper, glaring at the alien captain, "my race has an advantage now. We came here to your ship in atompowered spacesuits! Before we left, we altered the drives! We can set off ten pounds of sensitized fuel apiece, right here in this ship, or it can be set off by remote control from our ship! It will be rather remarkable if your fuel store doesn't blow up with us! In other words, if you don't accept my proposal for a commonsense approach to this predicament, Dort and I blow up in an atomic explosion, and your ship will be wrecked if not destroyed— and the *Llanvabon* will be attacking with everything it's got within two seconds after the blast goes off!"

The captain's room of the alien ship was a strange scene, with its dull-red illumination and the strange, bald, gill-breathing aliens watching the skipper and waiting for the inaudible translation of the harangue they could not hear. But a sudden tensity appeared in the air. A sharp, savage feeling of strain. The alien skipper made a gesture. The helmet phones hummed.

"He says, sir, what is your proposal?"

"Swap ships!" roared the skipper. "Swap ships and go on home! We can fix our instruments so they'll do no trailing, he can do the same with his. We'll each remove our star maps and records. We'll each dismantle our weapons. The air will serve, and we'll take their ship and they'll take ours, and neither one can harm or trail the other, and each will carry home more information than can be taken otherwise! We can agree on this same Crab

Nebula as a rendezvous when the double-star has made another circuit, and if our people want to meet them they can do it, and if they are scared they can duck it! That's my proposal! And he'll take it, or Dort and I blow up their ship and the *Llanvabon* blasts what's left!''

He glared about him while he waited for the translation to reach the tense small stocky figures about him. He could tell when it came because the tenseness changed. The figures stirred. They made gestures. One of them made convulsive movements. It lay down on the soft floor and kicked. Others leaned against its walls and shook.

The voice in Tommy Dort's helmet phones had been strictly crisp and professional, before, but now it sounded blankly amazed.

''He says, sir, that it is a good joke. Because the two crew members he sent to our ship, and that you passed on the way, have their spacesuits stuffed with atomic explosive too, sir, and he intended to make the very same offer and threat! Of course he accepts, sir. Your ship is worth more to him than his own, and his is worth more to you than the *Llanvabon*. It appears, sir, to be a deal.''

Then Tommy Dort realized what the convulsive movements of the aliens were. They were laughter.

It wasn't quite as simple as the skipper had outlined it. The actual working-out of the proposal was complicated. For three days the crews of the two ships were intermingled, the aliens learning the workings of the *Llanvabon's* engines, and the men learning the controls of the black spaceship. It was a good joke—but it wasn't all a joke. There were men on the black ship, and aliens on the *Llanvabon*, ready at an instant's notice to blow up the vessels in question. And they would have done it in case of need, for which reason the need did not appear. But it was, actually, a better arrangement to have two expeditions return to two civilizations, under the current arrangement, than for either to return alone.

There were differences, though. There was some dispute about the removal of records. In most cases the dispute was settled by the destruction of the records. There was more trouble caused by the *Llanvabon's* books, and the alien equivalent of a ship's library, containing works which approximated the novels of Earth. But those items were valuable to possible friendship, because they would show the two cultures, each to the other, from the viewpoint of normal citizens and without propaganda.

But nerves were tense during those three days. Aliens unloaded and inspected the foodstuffs intended for the men on the black ship. Men transshipped the foodstuffs the aliens would need to return to their home. There were endless details, from the exchange of lighting equipment to suit the eyesight of the exchanging crews, to a final check-up of apparatus. A joint inspection party of both races verified that all detector devices had been smashed but not removed, so that they could not be used for trailing and had not been smuggled away. And of course, the aliens were anxious not to leave any useful weapon on the black ship, nor the men upon the *Llanvabon*. It was a curious fact that each crew was best qualified to take exactly the measures which made an evasion of the agreement impossible.

There was a final conference before the two ships parted, back in the communication room of the *Llanvabon*.

"Tell the little runt," rumbled the *Llanvabon's* former skipper, "that he's got a good ship and he'd better treat her right."

The message frame flicked wordcards into position.

"I believe," it said on the alien skipper's behalf, "that your ship is just as good. I will hope to meet you here when the double star has turned one turn."

The last man left the *Llanvabon*. It moved away into the misty nebula before they had returned to the black ship. The vision plates in that vessel had been altered for human eyes, and human crewmen watched jealously for any trace of their former ship as their new craft took a crazy, evading course to a remote part of the nebula. It came to a crevasse of nothingness, leading to the stars. It rose swiftly to clear space. There was the instant of breathlessness which the overdrive field produces as it goes on, and then the black ship whipped away into the void at many times the speed of light.

Many days later, the skipper saw Tommy Dort poring over one of the strange objects which were the equivalent of books. It was fascinating to puzzle over. The skipper was pleased with himself. The technicians of the *Llanvabon's* former crew were finding out desirable things about the ship almost momently. Doubtless the aliens were as pleased with their discoveries in the *Llanvabon*. But the black ship would be enormously worth while— and the solution that had been found was by any standard much superior even to a combat in which the Earthmen had been overwhelmingly victorious.

"Hm-m-m. Mr. Dort," said the skipper profoundly. "You've no equipment to make another photographic record on the way back. It was left on the *Llanvabon*. But fortunately, we have your record taken on the way out, and I shall report most favorably on your suggestion and your assistance in carrying it out. I think very well of you, sir."

"Thank you, sir," said Tommy Dort.

He waited. The skipper cleared his throat.

"You ... ah ... first realized the close similarity of mental processes between the aliens and ourselves," he observed. "What do you think of the prospects of a friendly arrangement if we keep a rendezvous with them at the nebula as agreed?"

"Oh, we'll get along all right, sir," said Tommy. "We've got a good start toward friendship. After all, since they see by infrared, the planets they'd want to make use of wouldn't suit us. There's no reason why we shouldn't get along. We're almost alike in psychology."

"Hm-m-m. Now just what do you mean by that?" demanded the skipper.

"Why, they're just like us, sir!" said Tommy. "Of course they breathe through gills and they see by heat waves, and their blood has a copper base instead of iron and a few little details like that. But otherwise we're just alike! There were only men in their crew, sir, but they have two sexes as we have and they have families, and ... er ... their sense of humor— In fact—"

Tommy hesitated.

"Go on, sir," said the skipper.

"Well— There was the one I called Buck, sir, because he hasn't any name that goes into sound waves," said Tommy. "We got along very well. I'd really call him my friend, sir. And we were together for a couple of hours just before the two ships separated and we'd nothing in particular to do. So I became convinced that humans and aliens are bound to be good friends if they have only half a chance. You see, sir, we spent those two hours telling dirty jokes."

NOT FINAL!

by Isaac Asimov

Nicholas Orloff inserted a monocle in his left eye with all the incorruptible Briticism of a Russian educated at Oxford, and said reproachfully, "But, my dear Mr. Secretary! Half a billion dollars!"

Leo Birnam shrugged his shoulders wearily and allowed his lank body to cramp up still farther in the chair. "The appropriation must go through, Commissioner. The Dominion government here at Ganymede is becoming desperate. So far I've been holding them off, but as secretary of scientific affairs, my powers are small."

"I know, but—" and Orloff spread his hands helplessly.

"I suppose so," agreed Birnam. "The Empire government finds it easier to look the other way. They've done it consistently up to now. I've tried for a year now to have them understand the nature of the danger that hangs over the entire System, but it seems that it can't be done. But I'm appealing to you, Mr. Commissioner. You're new in your post and can approach this Jovian affair with an unjaundiced eye."

Orloff coughed and eyed the tips of his boots. In the three months since he had succeeded Gridley as colonial commissioner he had tabled unread everything relating to "those damned Jovian D.T.'s." That had been according to the established cabinet policy which had labeled the Jovian affair as "deadwood" long before he had entered office.

But now that Ganymede was becoming nasty, he found himself sent out to Jovopolis with instructions to hold the "blasted provincials" down. It was a nasty spot.

Birnam was speaking. "The Dominion government has reached the point where it needs the money so badly, in fact, that if they don't get it, they're going to publicize everything."

Orloff's phlegm broke completely, and he snatched at the monocle as it dropped. "My dear fellow!"

"I know what it would mean. I've advised against it, but they're justified. Once the inside of the Jovian affair is out, once the people know about it, the Empire government won't stay in power a week. And when the Technocrats come in, they'll give us whatever we ask. Public opinion will see to that."

"But you'll also create a panic and hysteria—"

"Surely! That is why we hesitate. But you might call this an ultimatum. We want secrecy, we *need* secrecy; but we need money more."

"I see." Orloff was thinking rapidly, and the conclusions he came to were not pleasant. "In that case, it would be advisable to investigate the case further. If you have the papers concerning the communications with the planet Jupiter—"

"I have them," replied Birnam dryly, "and so has the Empire government at Washington. That won't do, Commissioner. It's the same cud that's been chewed by Earth officials for the last year, and it's gotten us nowhere. I want you to come to Ether Station with me."

The Ganymedan had risen from his chair, and he glowered down upon Orloff from his six and a half feet of height.

Orloff flushed. "Are you ordering me?"

"In a way, yes. I tell you there is no time. If you intend acting, you must act quickly or not at all." Birnam paused, then added, "You don't mind walking, I hope. Power vehicles aren't allowed to approach Ether Station ordinarily, and I can use the walk to explain a few of the facts. It's only two miles off."

"I'll walk," was the brusque reply.

The trip upward to subground level was made in silence, which was broken by Orloff when they stepped into the dimly lit anteroom.

"It's chilly here."

"I know. It's difficult to keep the temperature up to norm this near the surface. But it will be colder outside. Here!"

Birnam had kicked open a closet door and was indicating the garments suspended from the ceiling. "Put them on. You'll need them."

Orloff fingered them doubtfully. "Are they heavy enough?"

Birnam was pouring into his own costume as he spoke. "They're electrically heated. You'll find them plenty warm. That's it! Tuck the trouser legs inside the boots and lace them tight."

He turned then and, with a grunt, brought out a double compressed-gas cylinder from its rack in one corner of the closet. He glanced at the dial reading and then turned the stopcock. There was a thin wheeze of escaping gas, at which Birnam sniffed with satisfaction.

"Do you know how to work one of these?" he asked, as he screwed onto the jet a flexible tube of metal mesh, at the other end of which was a curiously curved object of thick, clear glass.

"What is it?"

"Oxygen nosepiece! What there is of Ganymede's atmosphere is argon and nitrogen, just about half and half. It isn't particularly breathable." He heaved the double cylinder into position and tightened it in its harness on Orloff's back.

Orloff staggered, "It's heavy. I can't walk two miles with this."

"It won't be heavy out there." Birnam nodded carelessly upward and lowered the glass nosepiece over Orloff's head. "Just remember to breathe in through the nose and out through the mouth, and you won't have any trouble. By the way, did you eat recently?"

"I lunched before I came to your place."

Birnam sniffed dubiously. "Well, that's a little awkward." He drew a small metal container from one of his pockets and tossed it to the commissioner. "Put one of those pills in your mouth and keep sucking on it."

Orloff worked clumsily with gloved fingers and

finally managed to get a brown spheroid out of the tin and into his mouth. He followed Birnam up a gently sloped ramp. The blind-alley ending of the corridor slid aside smoothly when they reached it, and there was a faint soughing as air slipped out into the thinner atmosphere of Ganymede.

Birnam caught the other's elbow and fairly dragged him out.

"I've turned your air tank on full," he shouted. "Breathe deeply and keep sucking at that pill."

Gravity had flicked to Ganymedan normality as they crossed the threshold, and Orloff, after one horrible moment of apparent levitation, felt his stomach turn a somersault and explode.

He gagged, and fumbled the pill with his tongue in a desperate attempt at self-control. The oxygen-rich mixture from the air cylinders burned his throat, and gradually Ganymede steadied. His stomach shuddered back into place. He tried walking.

"Take it easy, now," came Birnam's soothing voice. "It gets you that way the first few times you change gravity fields quickly. Walk slowly and get the rhythm, or you'll take a tumble. That's right, you're getting it."

The ground seemed resilient. Orloff could feel the pressure of the other's arm holding him down at each step to keep him from springing too high. Steps were longer now—and flatter, as he got the rhythm. Birnam continued speaking, a voice a little muffled from behind the leather flap drawn loosely across mouth and chin.

"Each to his own world," he grinned. "I visited Earth a few years back, with my wife, and had a hell of a time. I couldn't get myself to learn to walk on a planet's surface without a nosepiece. I kept choking—I really did. The sunlight was too bright and the sky was too blue and the grass was too green. And the buildings were right out on the surface. I'll never forget the time they tried to get me to sleep in a room twenty stories up in the air, with the window wide open and the moon shining in.

"I went back on the first spaceship going my way and don't ever intend returning. How are you feeling now?"

"Fine! Splendid!" Now that the first discomfort had gone, Orloff found the low gravity exhilarating. He looked about him. The broken, hilly ground, bathed in a drenching yellow light, was covered with ground-hugging broad-leaved shrubs that showed the orderly arrangement of careful cultivation.

Birnam answered the unspoken question. "There's enough carbon dioxide in the air to keep the plants alive, and they all have the power to fix atmospheric nitrogen. That's what makes agriculture Ganymede's greatest industry. Those plants are worth their weight in gold as fertilizers back on Earth and worth double or triple that as sources for half a hundred alkaloids that can't be gotten anywhere else in the System. And, of course, everyone knows that Ganymedan green-leaf has Terrestrial tobacco beat hollow."

There was the drone of a strato-rocket overhead, shrill in the thin atmosphere, and Orloff looked up.

He stopped—stopped dead—and forgot to breathe!

It was his first glimpse of Jupiter in the sky.

It is one thing to see Jupiter, coldly harsh, against the ebon backdrop of space. At six hundred thousand miles, it is majestic enough. But on Ganymede, barely topping the hills, its outlines softened and ever so faintly hazed by the thin atmosphere, shining mellowly from a purple sky in which only a few fugitive stars dare compete with the Jovian giant—it can be described by no conceivable combination of words.

At first, Orloff absorbed the gibbous disk insilence. It was gigantic, thirty-two times the apparent diameter of the Sun as seen from Earth. Its stripes stood out in faint washes of color against the yellowness beneath, and the Great Red Spot was an oval splotch of orange near the western rim.

And finally Orloff murmured weakly, "It's beautiful!"

Leo Birnam stared, too, but there was no awe in his eyes. There was the mechanical weariness of viewing a sight often seen, and besides that, an expression of sick revulsion. The chinflap hid his twitching smile, but his grasp upon Orloff's arm left bruises through the tough fabric of the surface suit.

He said slowly, "It's the most horrible sight in the System."

Orloff turned reluctant attention to his companion. "Eh?" Then, disagreeably, "Oh, yes, those mysterious Jovians."

At that, the Ganymedan turned away angrily and broke into swinging, fifteen-foot strides. Orloff followed clumsily after, keeping his balance with difficulty.

"Here, now," he gasped.

But Birnam wasn't listening. He was speaking coldly, bitterly. "You on Earth can afford to ignore Jupiter. You know nothing of it. It's a little pinprick in your sky, a little flyspeck. You don't live here on Ganymede, watching that damned colossus gloating over you. Up and over fifteen hours—hiding God knows what on its surface. Hiding something that's waiting and waiting and *trying to get out*. Like a giant bomb just waiting to explode!"

"Nonsense!" Orloff managed to jerk out. "*Will* you slow down. I can't keep up."

Birnam cut his strides in half and said tensely, "Everyone knows that Jupiter is inhabited, but practically no one ever stops to realize what that means. I tell you that those Jovians, whatever they are, are born to the purple. *They are the natural rulers of the Solar System.*"

"Pure hysteria," murmured Orloff. "The Empire government has been hearing nothing else from your Dominion for a year."

"And you've shrugged it off. Well, listen! Jupiter, discounting the thickness of its colossal atmosphere, is eighty thousand miles in diameter. That means it possesses a surface one hundred times that of Earth, and more than fifty times that of the entire Terrestrial Empire. Its population, its resources, its war potential are in proportion."

"Mere numbers—"

"I know what you mean," Birnam drove on passion

ately. "Wars are not fought with numbers but with science and with organization. The Jovians have both. In the quarter of a century during which we have communicated with them, we've learned a bit. They have atomic power and they have radio. And in a world of ammonia under great pressure—a world, in other words, in which almost none of the metals can exist *as* metals for any length of time because of the tendency to form soluble ammonia complexes—they have managed to build up a complicated civilization. That means they have had to work through plastics, glasses, silicates, and synthetic building materials of one sort or another. *That* means a chemistry developed just as far as ours is, and I'd put odds on its having developed further."

Orloff waited long before answering. And then, "But how certain are you people about the Jovians' last message? We on Earth are inclined to doubt that the Jovians can possibly be as unreasonably belligerent as they have been described."

The Ganymedan laughed shortly. "They broke off all communication after that last message, didn't they? That doesn't sound friendly on their part, does it? I assure you that we've all but stood on our ears trying to contact them.

"Here, now, don't talk. Let me explain something to you. For twenty-five years here on Ganymede a little group of men have worked their hearts out trying to make sense out of a static-ridden, gravity-distorted set of variable clicks in our radio apparatus, for those clicks were our only connection with living intelligence upon Jupiter. It was a job for a world of scientists, but we never had more than two dozen at the Station at any one time. I was one of them from the very beginning and, as a philologist, did my part in helping construct and interpret the code that developed between ourselves and the Jovians, so that you can see I am speaking from the real inside.

"It was a devil of a heartbreaking job. It was five years before we got past the elementary clicks of arithmetic: three and four are seven; the square root of twenty-five is five; factorial six is seven hundred and twenty. After that, months sometimes passed before we could work out and check by further communication a single new fragment of thought.

"*But*—and this is the point—by the time the Jovians broke off relations, we understood them *thoroughly*. There was no more chance of a mistake in comprehension than there was of Ganymede's suddenly cutting loose from Jupiter. And their last message was a threat and a promise of destruction. Oh, there's no doubt—there's no doubt!"

They were walking through a shallow pass in which the yellow Jupiter light gave way to a clammy darkness.

Orloff was disturbed. He had never had the case presented to him in this fashion before. He said, "But the reason, man. What reason did we give them—"

"No reason! It was simply this: the Jovians had finally discovered from our messages—just where and how I don't know—that *we* were *not* Jovians."

"Well, of course."

"It wasn't 'of course' to them. In their experiences they had never come across intelligences that were not Jovian. Why should they make an exception in favor of those from outer space?"

"You say they were scientists." Orloff's voice had assumed a wary frigidity. "Wouldn't they realize that alien environments would breed alien life? *We* knew it. We never thought the Jovians were Earthmen, though we had never met intelligences other than those of Earth."

They were back in the drenching wash of Jupiter light again, and a spreading region of ice glimmered amberly in a depression to the right.

Birnam answered, "I said they were chemists and physicists—but I never said they were astronomers. Jupiter, my dear Commissioner, has an atmosphere three thousand miles or more thick, and those miles of gas block off everything but the Sun and the four largest of Jupiter's moons. The Jovians know nothing of alien environments."

Orloff considered. "And so they decided we were aliens. What next?"

"If we weren't Jovians, then, in their eyes, we weren't people. It turned out that a non-Jovian was 'vermin' by definition."

Orloff's automatic protest was cut off sharply by Birnam. "In their eyes, I said, vermin we were; and vermin we are. Moreover, we were vermin with the peculiar audacity of having dared to attempt to treat with Jovians—with *human beings*. Their last message was this, word for word—'Jovians are the masters. There is no room for vermin. We will destroy you immediately.' I doubt if there was any animosity in that message—simply a cold statement of fact. But they mean it."

"But why?"

"Why did man exterminate the housefly?"

"Come sir. You're not seriously presenting an analogy of that nature."

"Why not, since it is certain that the Jovian considers us a sort of housefly—an insufferable type of housefly that dares aspire to intelligence."

Orloff made a last attempt. "But truly, Mr. Secretary, it seems impossible for intelligent life to adopt such an attitude."

"Do you possess much of an acquaintance with any other type of intelligent life than our own?" came with immediate sarcasm. "Do you feel competent to pass on Jovian psychology? Do you know just *how* alien Jovians must be physically? Just think of their world, with its gravity at two and one-half Earth normal; with its ammonia oceans—oceans that you might throw all Earth into without raising a respectable splash; with its three-thousand-mile atmosphere, dragged down by the colossal gravity into densities and pressures in its surface layers that make the sea bottoms of Earth resemble a medium-thick vacuum. I tell you, we've tried to figure out what sort of life could exist under those conditions and we've given up. It's thoroughly incomprehensible. Do you expect their mentality, then, to be any more understandable? Never! Accept it as it is. They intend destroying us. That's all we know and all we need to know."

He lifted a gloved hand as he finished, and one finger pointed. "There's Ether Station just ahead."

Orloff's head swiveled. "Underground?"

"Certainly! All except the Observatory. That's that steel-and-quartz dome to the right—the small one."

They had stopped before two large boulders that flanked an earthy embankment, and from behind either one a nosepieced, suited soldier in Ganymedan orange, with blasters ready, advanced upon the two.

Birnam lifted his face into Jupiter's light, and the soldiers saluted and stepped aside. A short word was barked into the wrist mike of one of them, and the camouflaged opening between the boulders fell into two and Orloff followed the secretary into the yawning airlock.

The Earthman caught one last glimpse of sprawling Jupiter before the closing door cut off the surface altogether.

It was no longer quite so beautiful.

Orloff did not feel quite normal again until he had seated himself in the overstuffed chair in Dr. Edward Prosser's private office. With a sigh of utter relaxation he propped his monocle under his eyebrow.

"Would Dr. Prosser mind if I smoked in here while we're waiting?" he asked.

"Go ahead," replied Birnam carelessly. "My own idea would be to drag Prosser away from whatever he's fooling with just now, but he's a queer chap. We'll get more out of him if we wait until he's ready for us." He withdrew a gnarled stick of greenish tobacco from its case and bit off the edge viciously.

Orloff smiled through the smoke of his own cigarette. "I don't mind waiting. I still have something to say. You see, for the moment, Mr. Secretary, you gave me the jitters, but, after all, granted that the Jovians intend mischief once they get at us, it remains a fact," and here he spaced his words emphatically, "that they can't get at us."

"A bomb without a fuse, hey?"

"Exactly! It's simplicity itself, and not really worth discussing. You will admit, I suppose that under no circumstances can the Jovians get away from Jupiter."

"Under *no* circumstances?" There was a quizzical tinge to Birnam's slow reply. "Shall we analyze that?"

He stared hard at the purple flame of his cigar. "It's an old trite saying that the Jovians can't leave Jupiter. The fact has been highly publicized by the sensation mongers of Earth and Ganymede, and a great deal of sentiment has been driveled about the unfortunate intelligences who are irrevocably surface-bound and must forever stare into the Universe without, watching, wondering, and never attaining.

"But, after all, what holds the Jovians to their planet? Two factors! That's all! The first is the immense gravity field of the planet. Two and a half Earth normal."

Orloff nodded. "Pretty bad!" he agreed.

"And Jupiter's gravitational potential is even worse, for, because of its greater diameter, the intensity of its gravitational field decreases with distance only one-tenth as rapidly as Earth's field does. It's a terrible problem—*but it's been solved.*"

"Hey?" Orloff straightened.

"They've got atomic power. Gravity—even Jupiter's—means nothing once you've put unstable atomic nuclei to work for you."

Orloff crushed his cigarette to extinction with a nervous gesture. "But their atmosphere—"

"Yes, that's what's stopping them. They're living at the bottom of a three-thousand-mile-deep ocean of it, where the hydrogen of which it is composed is collapsed by sheer pressure to something approaching the density of *solid* hydrogen. It stays a gas because the temperature of Jupiter is above the critical point of hydrogen, but you just try to figure out the pressure that can make hydrogen *gas* half as heavy as water. You'll be surprised at the number of zeros you'll have to put down.

"No spaceship of metal or of any kind of matter can stand that pressure. No Terrestrial spaceship can land on Jupiter without smashing like an eggshell, and no Jovian spaceship can leave Jupiter without exploding like a soap bubble. That problem has not yet been solved, but it will be some day. Maybe tomorrow, maybe not for a hundred years, or a thousand. We don't know, but when it is solved, the Jovians will be on top of us. And it can be solved in a specific way."

"I don't see how—"

"Force fields! We've got them now, you know."

"Force fields!" Orloff seemed genuinely astonished, and he chewed the word over and over to himself for a few moments. "They're used as meteor shields for ships in the asteroid zone—but I don't see the application to the Jovian problem."

"The ordinary force field," explained Birnam, "is a feeble rarefied zone of energy extending over a hundred miles or more outside the ship. It'll stop meteors, but it's just so much empty ether to an object like a gas molecule. *But* what if you took that same zone of energy and compressed it to a thickness of a tenth of an inch. Molecules would bounce off it like this—*ping-g-g-g!* And if you used stronger generators, and compressed the field to a hundredth of an inch, molecules would bounce off even when driven by the unthinkable pressure of Jupiter's atmosphere—and then if you build a ship inside—" He left the sentence dangling.

Orloff was pale. "You're not saying it can be done?"

"I'll bet you anything you like that the Jovians are *trying* to do it. And *we're* trying to do it right here at Ether Station."

The colonial commissioner jerked his chair closer to Birnam and grabbed the Ganymedan's wrist. "Why can't we bombard Jupiter with atomic bombs? Give it a thorough going over, I mean! With her gravity and her surface area, we can't miss."

Birnam smiled faintly. "We've thought of that. But atomite bombs would merely tear holes in the atmosphere. And even if you could penetrate, just divide the surface of Jupiter by the area of damage of a single bomb and find how many years we must bombard Jupiter at the rate of a bomb a minute before we begin to do significant damage. Jupiter's *big!* Don't ever forget that!''

His cigar had gone out, but he did not pause to relight. He continued in a low, tense voice. ''No, we can't attack the Jovians as long as they're on Jupiter. We must wait for them to come out—and once they do, they're going to have the edge on us in numbers. A terrific, heartbreaking edge—so we'll just have to have the edge on them in science.''

''But,'' Orloff broke in, and there was a note of fascinated horror in his voice, ''how can we tell in advance what they'll have?''

''We can't. We've got to scrape up everything we can lay our hands on and hope for the best. But there's one thing we *do* know they have, and that's force fields. They can't get out without them. And if they have them, we must, too, and that's the problem we're trying to solve here. They will not insure us victory, but without them we will suffer certain defeat. And now you know why we need money—and more than that. We want Earth itself to get to work. It's got to start a drive for scientific armaments and subordinate everything to that. You see?''

Orloff was on his feet. ''Birnam, I'm with you—a hundred per cent with you. You can count on me back in Washington.''

There was no mistaking his sincerity. Birnam gripped the hand outstretched toward him and wrung it—and at the moment the door flew open and a little pixie of a man hurtled in.

The newcomer spoke in rapid jerks, and exclusively to Birnam. ''Where'd you come from? Been trying to get in touch with you. Secretary said you weren't in. Then five minutes later you show up on your own. Can't understand it.'' He busied himself furiously at his desk.

Birnam grinned. ''If you'll take time out, doc, you might say hello to Colonial Commissioner Orloff.''

Dr. Edward Prosser turned on his toe like a ballet dancer and looked the Earthman up and down twice. ''The new un, hey? We getting any money? We ought to. Been working on a shoestring ever since. At that we might not be needing any. It depends." He was back at the desk.

Orloff seemed a trifle disconcerted, but Birnam winked impressively, and he contented himself with a glassy stare through the monocle.

Prosser pounced upon a black leather booklet in the recesses of a pigeonhole, threw himself into his swivel chair, and wheeled about.

"Glad you came, Birnam," he said, leafing through the booklet. "Got something to show you. Commissioner Orloff, too."

"What were you keeping us waiting for?" demanded Birnam. "Where were you?"

"Busy! Busy as a pig! No sleep for three nights." He looked up and his small puckered face fairly flushed with delight. "Everything fell into place of a sudden. Like a jigsaw puzzle. Never saw anything like it. Kept us hopping, I tell you."

"You've gotten the dense force fields you're after?" asked Orloff in sudden excitement.

Prosser seemed annoyed. "No, not that. Something else. Come on." He glared at his watch and jumped out of his seat. "We've got half an hour. Let's go."

An electric-motored flivver waited outside, and Prosser spoke excitedly as he sped the purring vehicle down the ramps into the depths of the Station.

"Theory!" he said. "Theory! Damned important, that. You set a technician on a problem. He'll fool around. Waste lifetimes. Get nowhere. Just putter about at random. A true scientist works with theory. Lets math solve his problems." He overflowed with self-satisfaction.

The flivver stopped on a dime before a huge double door, and Prosser tumbled out, followed by the other two at a more leisurely pace.

"Through here! Through here!" he said. He shoved the door open and led them down the corridor and up a narrow flight of stairs onto a wall-hugging passageway that circled a huge three-level room. Orloff recognized the gleaming quartz-and-steel pipe-sprouting ellipsoid two levels below as an atomic generator.

He adjusted his monocle and watched the scurrying activity below. An earphoned man on a high stool before a control board studded with dials looked up and waved. Prosser waved back and grinned.

Orloff said, "You create your force fields here?"

"That's right! Ever see one?"

"No." The commissioner smiled ruefully. "I don't even know what one *is*, except that it can be used as a meteor shield."

Prosser said, "It's very simple. Elementary matter. All matter is composed of atoms. Atoms are held together by interatomic forces. Take away atoms. Leave interatomic forces behind. *That's* a force field."

Orloff looked blank, and Birnam chuckled deep in his throat and scratched the back of his ear.

"That explanation reminds me of our Ganymedan method of suspending an egg a mile high in the air. It goes like this. You find a mountain just a mile high and put the egg on top. Then, keeping the egg where it is, you take the mountain away. That's all."

The colonial commissioner threw his head back to laugh, and the irascible Dr. Prosser puckered his lips into a pursed symbol of disapproval.

"Come, come. No joke, you know. Force field most important. Got to be ready for the Jovians when they come."

A sudden rasping burr from below sent Prosser back from the railing.

"Get behind screen here," he babbled. "The twenty-millimeter field is going up. Bad radiation."

The burr muted almost into silence, and the three walked out onto the passageway again. There was no apparent change, but Prosser shoved his hand out over the railing and said, "Feel!"

Orloff extended a cautious finger, gasped, and slapped out with the palm of his hand. It was like pushing against very soft sponge rubber or super-resilient steel springs.

Birnam tried, too. "That's better than anything we've done yet, isn't it?" He explained to Orloff, "A twenty-millimeter screen is one that can hold an atmosphere of a pressure of twenty millimeters of mercury against a vacuum without appreciable leakage.''

The commissioner nodded. ''I see! You'd need a seven-hundred-sixty-millimeter screen to hold Earth's atmosphere, then.''

''Yes! That would be a unit atmosphere screen. Well, Prosser, is this what got you excited?''

''This twenty-millimeter screen. Of course not. I can go up to two hundred fifty millimeters using the activated vanadium pentasulphide in the praseodymium breakdown. But it's not necessary. Technician would do it and blow up the place. Scientist checks on theory and goes slow.''. He winked. ''We're hardening the field now. Watch!''

''Shall we get behind the screen?''

''Not necessary now. Radiation bad only at beginning.''

The burring waxed again, but not as loudly as before. Prosser shouted to the man at the control board, and a spreading wave of the hand was the only reply.

Then the control man waved a clenched fist and Prosser cried, ''We've passed fifty millimeters! Feel the field!''

Orloff extended his hand and poked it curiously. The sponge rubber had hardened! He tried to pinch it between finger and thumb, so perfect was the illusion, but here the ''rubber'' faded to unresisting air.

Prosser *tch-tched* impatiently. ''No resistance at right angles to force. Elementary mechanics that is.''

The control man was gesturing again. ''Past seventy,'' explained Prosser. ''We're slowing down now. Critical point is 83.42.''

He hung over the railing and kicked out with his feet at the other two. ''Stay away! Dangerous!''

And then he yelled, ''Careful! The generator's bucking!''

The burr had risen to a hoarse maximum and the control man worked frantically at his switches. From within the quartz heart of the central atomic generator the sullen red glow of the busting atoms had brightened dangerously.

There was a break in the burr, a reverberant roar, and a blast of air that threw Orloff hard against the wall.

Prosser dashed up. There was a cut over his eye. "Hurt? No? Good, good! I was expecting something of the sort. Should have warned you. Let's go down. Where's Birnam?"

The tall Ganymedan picked himself up off the floor and bushed at his clothes. "Here I am. What blew up?"

"Nothing blew up. Something buckled. Come on, down we go." He dabbed at his forehead with a handkerchief and led the way downward.

The control man removed his earphones as he approached, and got off his stool. He looked tired, and his dirt-smeared face was greasy with perspiration.

"The damn thing started going at 82.8, boss. It almost caught me."

"It did, did it?" growled Prosser. "Within limits of error, isn't it? How's the generator? Hey, Stoddard!"

The technician addressed replied from his station at the generator, "Tube Five died. It'll take two days to replace."

Prosser turned in satisfaction and said, "It worked. Went exactly as presumed. Problem solved, gentlemen. Trouble over. Let's get back to my office. I want to eat. And then I want to sleep."

He did not refer to the subject again until once more behind the desk in his office, and then he spoke between huge bites of a liver-and-onion sandwich.

He addressed Birnam. "Remember the work on space strain last June? It flopped, but we kept at it. Finch got a lead last week and I developed it. Everything fell into place. Slick as goose grease. Never saw anything like it."

"Go ahead," said Birnam calmly. He knew Prosser sufficiently well to avoid showing impatience.

"You saw what happened. When a field tops 83.42 millimeters, it becomes unstable. Space won't stand the strain. It buckles and the field blows. *Boom!*"

Birnam's mouth dropped open, and the arms of Orloff's chair creaked under sudden pressure. Silence for a while, and then Birnam said unsteadily. "You mean force fields stronger than that are impossible."

"They're possible. You can create them. But the denser they are, the more unstable they are. If I had turned on the two-hundred-and-fifty-millimeter field, it would have lasted one-tenth of a second. Then, blooie! would have blown up the Station! *And* myself! Technician would have done it. Scientist is warned by theory. Works carefully, the way I did. No harm done."

Orloff tucked his monocle into his vest pocket and said tremulously, "But if a force field is the same thing as interatomic forces, why is it that steel has such a strong interatomic binding force without bucking space? There's a flaw there."

Prosser eyed him in annoyance. "No flaw. Critical strength depends on number of generators. In steel, each atom is a force-field generator. That means about three hundred billion trillion generators for every ounce of matter. If we could use that many—As it is, one hundred generators would be the practical limit. That only raises the critical point to ninety-seven or thereabouts."

He got to his feet and continued with sudden fervor, "No. Problem's over, I tell you. Absolutely impossible to create a force field capable of holding Earth's atmosphere for more than a hundredth of a second. Jovian atmosphere entirely out of question. Cold figures say that; backed by experiment. *Space won't stand it!*

"Let the Jovians do their damnedest. They can't get out! That's final! That's final! *That's final!*"

Orloff said, "Mr. Secretary, can I send a spacegram anywhere in the Station? I want to tell Earth that I'm returning by the next ship and that the Jovian problem is liquidated—entirely and for good."

Birnam said nothing, but the relief on his face as he shook hands with the colonial commissioner transfigured its gaunt homeliness unbelievably.

And Dr. Prosser repeated, with a birdlike jerk of his head, "That's *final!*"

Hal Tuttle looked up as Captain Everett, of the spaceship

Transparent, newest ship of the Comet Space Lines, entered his private observation room in the nose of the ship.

The captain said, "A spacegram has just reached me from the home offices at Tucson. We're to pick up Colonial Commissioner Orloff at Jovopolis, Ganymede, and take him back to Earth."

"Good. We haven't sighted any ships?"

"No, no! We're way off the regular space lanes. The first the System will know of us will be the landing of the *Transparent* on Ganymede. It will be the greatest thing in space travel since the first trip to the Moon." His voice softened suddenly. "What's wrong, Hal? This is *your* triumph, after all."

Hal Tuttle looked up and out into the blackness of space. "I suppose it is. Ten years of work, Sam. I lost an arm and an eye in that first explosion, but I don't regret them. It's the reaction that's got me. The problem is solved; my lifework is finished."

"So is every steel-hulled ship in the System."

Tuttle smiled. "Yes. It's hard to realize, isn't it?" He gestured outward. "You see the stars? Part of the time there's nothing between them and us. It gives us a queasy feeling." His voice brooded, "Nine years I worked for nothing. I wasn't a theoretician, and never really knew where I was headed—just tried everything. I tried a little too hard, and space wouldn't stand it. I paid an arm and an eye and started fresh."

Captain Everett balled his fist and pounded the hull—the hull through which the stars shone unobstructed. There was the muffled thud of flies striking an unyielding surface—but no response whatever from the invisible wall.

Tuttle nodded. "It's solid enough, now—though it flicks on and off eight hundred thousand times a second. I got the idea from the stroboscopic lamp. You know them—they flash on and off so rapidly that it gives all the impression of steady illumination.

"And so it is with the hull. It's not on long enough to buckle space. It's not off long enough to allow appreciable leakage of the atmosphere. And the net effect is a strength better than steel."

He paused and added slowly, "And there's no telling how far we can go. Speed up the intermission effect. Have the field flick off and on millions of times per second—billions of times. You can get fields strong enough to hold an atomic explosion. My lifework!"

Captain Everett pounded the other's shoulder. "Snap out of it, man. Think of the landing on Ganymede. The devil! It will be great publicity. Think of Orloff's face, for instance, when he finds he is to be the first passenger in history ever to travel in a spaceship with a forcefield hull. How do you suppose he'll feel?"

Hal Tuttle shrugged. "I imagine he'll be rather pleased."

ANGEL'S EGG

by Edgar Pangborn

LETTER OF RECORD, BLAINE TO MC CARRAN, DATED AUGUST 10, 1951.

Mr. Cleveland McCarran
Federal Bureau of Investigation
Washington, D.C.

Dear Sir:

In compliance with your request I enclose herewith a transcript of the pertinent sections of the journal of Dr. David Bannerman, deceased. The original document is being held at this office until proper disposition can be determined.

Our investigation has shown no connection between Dr. Bannerman and any organization, subversive or otherwise. So far as we can learn, he was exactly what he seemed, an inoffensive summer resident, retired, with a small independent income—a recluse to some extent, but well spoken of by local tradesmen and other neighbors. A connection between Dr. Bannerman and the type of activity that concerns your department would seem most unlikely.

The following information is summarized from the earlier parts of Dr. Bannerman's journal, and tallies with the results of our own limited inquiry. He was born in 1898 at Springfield, Massachusetts, attended public school there, and was graduated from Harvard College in 1922, his studies having been interrupted by two years' military service. He was wounded in action in Argonne, receiving a spinal injury. He earned a doctorate in biology in 1926. Delayed aftereffects of his war injury necessitated hospitalization, 1927-28. From 1929 to 1948 he taught elementary sciences in a private school in Boston. He published two textboks in introductory biology, 1927 and 1937. In 1948 he retired from teaching: a pension and a modest income from textbook royalties evidently made this possibe. Aside from the spinal deformity, which caused him to walk with a stoop, his health is said to have been fair. Autopsy findings suggested that the spinal condition must have given him considerable pain; he is not known to have mentioned this to anyone, not even to his physician, Dr. Lester Morse. There is no evidence whatever of drug addiction or alcoholism.

At one point early in his journal Dr. Bannerman describes himself as "a naturalist of the puttering type—I would rather sit on a log than write monographs: it pays off better." Dr. Morse, and others who knew Dr. Bannerman personally, tell me that this conveys a hint of his personality.

I am not qualified to comment on the material of this journal, except to say I have no evidence to support (or to contradict) Dr. Bannerman's statements. The journal has been studied only by my immediate superiors, by Dr. Morse, and by myself. I take it for granted you will hold the matter in strictest confidence.

With the journal I am also enclosing a statement by Dr. Morse, written at my request for our records and for your information. You will note that he says, with some qualifications, that "death was not inconsistent with an embolism." He has signed a death certificate on that basis. You will recall from my letter of August 5 that it was Dr. Morse who discovered Dr. Bannerman's body. Because he was a close personal friend of the deceased, Dr. Morse did not feel able to perform the autopsy himself. It was done by a Dr. Stephen Clyde of this city, and was virtually negative as regards cause of death, neither comfirming nor contradicting Dr. Morse's original tentative diagnosis. If you wish to read the autopsy report in full I shall be glad to forward a copy.

Dr. Morse tells me that so far as he knows Dr. Bannerman had no near relatives. He never married. For the last twelve summers he occupied a small cottage on a back road about twenty-five miles from this city, and had few visitors. The neighbor, Steele, mentioned in the journal is a farmer, age 68, of good character, who tells me he "never got really acquainted with Dr. Bannerman."

At this office we feel that unless new information comes to light, further active investigation is hardly justified.

> Respectfully yours,
> Garrison Blaine
> Capt., State Police
> Augusta, Me.

Encl: Extract from Journal of David Bannerman,
     dec'd.
     Statement by Lester Morse, M.D.

LIBRARIAN'S NOTE: The following document, originally attached as an unofficial "rider" to the foregoing letter, was donated to this institution in 1994 through the courtesy of Mrs. Helen McCarran, widow of the martyred first President of the World Federation. Other personal and state papers of President McCarran, many of them dating from the early period when he was employed by the FBI, are accessible to public view at the Institute of World History, Copenhagen.

PERSONAL NOTE, BLAINE TO MC CARRAN, DATED AUGUST 10, 1951

Dear Cleve:

Guess I didn't make it clear in my other letter that that bastard Clyde was responsible for my having to drag you into this. He is something to handle with tongs. Happened thusly—When he came in to heave the autopsy report at me, he was already having pups just because it was so completely negative (he does have certain types of honesty), and he caught sight of a page or two of the journal on my desk. Doc Morse was with me at the time. I fear we both got up-stage with him. (Clyde has that effect, and we were both in a State of Mind anyway), so right away the old drip thinks he smells something subversive. Belongs to the atomize-'em-NOW-WOW-WOW school of thought—nuf sed? He went into a grand whuff-whuff about referring to Higher Authority, and I knew that meant your hive, so I wanted to get ahead of the letter I knew he'd write. I suppose his literary effort couldn't be just sort of quietly transferred to File 13, otherwise known as the Appropriate Receptacle?

He can say what he likes about my character, if any, but even I never supposed he'd take a sideswipe at his professional colleague. Doc Morse is the best of the best and would not dream of suppressing any evidence important to us, as you say Clyde's letter hints. What Doc did do was to tell Clyde, pleasantly, in the privacy of my office, to go take a flying this-and-that at the moon. I only wish I'd thought of the expression myself. So Clyde rushes off to tell teacher. See what I mean about the tongs? However (knock on wood) I don't think Clyde saw enough of the journal to get any notion of what it's all about.

As for that journal, damn it, Cleve, I don't know. If you have any ideas I want them, of course. I'm afraid I believe in angels, myself. But when I think of the effect on local opinion if the story ever gets out—brother! Here was this old Bannerman living alone with a female angel and they wuzn't even common-law married. Aw, gee ... And the flood of phone calls from other crackpots anxious to explain it all to me. Experts in the care and feeding of angels. Methods of angel-proofing. Angels right outside the window a minute ago. Make Angels a Profitable Enterprise in Your Spare Time!!!

When do I see you? You said you might have a week clear in October. If we could get together maybe we could make sense where there is none. I hear the cider promises to be good this year. Try and make it. My best to Ginny and the other young fry, and Helen of course.

                              Respeckfully yourn,
                              Garry

P.S. If you do see any angels down your way, and they aren't willing to wait for a Republican Administration, by all means have them investigated by the Senate—then we'll *know* we're all nuts.

G.

EXTRACT FROM JOURNAL OF DAVID BANNERMAN, JUNE 1-JULY 29, 1951

June 1

It must have been at least three weeks ago when we had that flying saucer flurry. Observers the other side of Katahdin saw it come down this side; observers this side saw it come down the other. Size anywhere from six inches to sixty feet in diameter (or was it cigar-shaped?) and speed whatever you please. Seem to recall that witnesses agreed on a rosy-pink light. There was the inevitable gobbledegookery of official explanation designed to leave everyone impressed, soothed, and disappointed. I paid scant attention to the excitement and less to the explanations—naturally, I thought it was just a flying saucer. But now Camilla has hatched out an angel.

It would have to be Camilla. Perhaps I haven't mentioned my hens enough. In the last day or two it has dawned on me that this journal may be of importance to other eyes than mine, not merely a lonely man's plaything to blunt the edge of mortality: an angel in the house makes a difference. I had better show consideration for possible readers.

I have eight hens, all yearlings except Camilla: this is her third spring. I boarded her two winters at my neighbor Steel's farm when I closed this shack and shuffled my chilly bones off to Florida, because even as a pullet she had a manner which overbore me. I could never have eaten Camilla: if she had looked at the ax with that same expression of rancid disapproval (and she would), I should have felt I was beheading a favorite aunt. Her only concession to sentiment is the annual rush of maternity to the brain—normal, for a case-hardened White Plymouth Rock.

This year she stole a nest successfuly in a tangle of blackberry. By the time I located it, I estimated I was about two weeks too late. I had to outwit her by watching from a window—she is far too acute to be openly trailed from feeding ground to nest. When I had bled and pruned my way to her hideout she was sitting on nine eggs and hating my guts. They could not be fertile, since I keep no rooster, and I was about to rob her when I saw the ninth egg was nothing of hers. It was a deep blue and transparent, with flecks of inner light that made me think of the first stars in a clear evening. It was the same size as Camilla's own. There was an embryo, but I could make nothing of it. I returned the egg to Camilla's bare and fevered breastbone and went back to the house for a long, cool drink.

That was ten days ago. I know I ought to have kept a record; I examined the blue egg every day, watching how some nameless life grew within it. The angel has been out of the shell three days now. This is the first time I have felt equal to facing pen and ink.

I have been experiencing a sort of mental lassitude unfamiliar to me. Wrong word: not so much lassitude as a preoccupation, with no sure clue to what it is that preoccupies me. By reputation I am a scientist of sorts. Right now I have no impulse to look for data; I want to sit quiet and let truth come to a relaxed mind if it will. Could be merely a part of growing older, but I doubt that. The broken pieces of the wonderful blue shell are on my desk. I have been peering at them—into them—for the last ten minutes or more. Can't call it study: my thought wanders into their blue, learning nothing I can retain in words. It does not convey much to say I have gone into a vision of open sky—and of peace, if such a thing there be.

The angel chipped the shell deftly in two parts. This was evidently done with the aid of small horny outgrowths on her elbows; these growths were sloughed off on the second day. I wish I had seen her break the shell, but when I visited the blackberry tangle three days ago she was already out. She poked her exquisite head through Camilla's neck feathers, smiled sleepily, and snuggled back into darkness to finish drying off. So what could I do, more than save the broken shell and wriggle my clumsy self out of there? I had removed Camilla's own eggs the day before—Camilla was only moderately annoyed. I was nervous about disposing of them, even though they were obviously Camilla's, but no harm was done. I cracked each one to be sure. Very frankly rotten eggs and nothing more.

In the evening of that day I thought of rats and weasles as I should have done earlier. I prepared a box in the kitchen and brought the two in, the angel quiet in my closed hand. They are there now. I think they are comfortable.

Three days after hatching, the angel is the length of my forefinger, say three inches tall, with about the relative proportions of a six-year old girl. Except for head, hands, and probably the soles of her feet, she is clothed in down the color of ivory; what can be seen of her skin is a glowing pink—I do mean a glowing, like the inside of certain sea shells. Just above the small of her back are two stubs which I take to be infantile wings. They do not suggest an extra pair of specialized forelimbs. I think they are wholly differentiated organs; perhaps they will be like the wings on an insect. Somehow, I never thought of angels buzzing. Maybe she won't. I know very little about angels. At present the stubs are covered with some dull tissue, no doubt a protective sheath to be discarded when the membranes (if they are membranes) are ready to grow. Between the stubs is a not very prominent ridge—special musculature, I suppose. Otherwise her shape is quite human, even to a pair of minuscule mammalian buttons just visible under the down; how that can make sense in an egg-laying organism is beyond my comprehension. (Just for the record, so is a Corot landscape; so is Schubert's *Unfinished*; so is the flight of a hummingbird, or the other-world of frost on a window pane.) The down on her head has grown visibly in three days and is of different quality from the body down —later it may resemble human hair, as a diamond resembles a chunk of granite . . .

A curious thing has happened. I went to Camilla's box after writing that. Judy* was already lying in front of it,

---

*Dr. Bannerman's dog, mentioned often earlier in the journal. A nine-year old English setter. According to an entry of May 15, 1951, she was then beginning to go blind. — BLAINE.

unexcited. The angel's head was out from under the feathers, and I thought—with more verbal distinctness than such thoughts commonly take, "So here I am, a naturalist of middle years and cold sober, observing a three-inch oviparous mammal with down and wings." The thing is—she giggled. Now it might have been only amusement at my appearance, which to her must be enormously gross and comic. But another thought formed unspoken: "I am no longer lonely." And her face (hardly bigger than a dime) immediately changed from laughter to a brooding and friendly thoughtfulness.

Judy and Camilla are old friends. Judy seems untroubled by the angel. I have no wories about leaving them alone together. I must sleep.

June 3

I made no entry last night. The angel was talking to me, and when that was finished I drowsed off immediately on a cot that I have moved into the kitchen so as to be near them.

I have never been strongly impressed by the evidence for extrasensory perception. It is fortunate my mind was able to accept the novelty, since to the angel it is clearly a matter of course. Her tiny mouth is most expressive but moves only for that reason and for eating—not for speech. Probably she could speak to her own kind if she wished, but I dare say the sound would be outside the range of my hearing as well as my understanding.

Last night after I brought the cot in and was about to finish my puttering bachelor supper, she climbed to the edge of the box and pointed, first at herself and then at the top of the kitchen table. Afraid to let my cast hand take hold of her, I held it out flat and she sat in my palm. Camilla was inclined to fuss, but the angel looked over her shoulder and Camilla subsided, watchful but no longer alarmed.

The table top is porcelain, and the angel shivered. I folded a towel and spread a silk handkerchief on top of that; the angel sat on this arrangement with apparent comfort, near my face. I was not even bewildered. Possibly she had already instructed me to blank out my mind. At any rate, I did so, without conscious effort to that end.

She reached me first with visual imagery. How can I make it plain that this had nothing in common with my sleeping dreams? There was no weight of symbolism from my littered past; no discoverable connection with any of yesterday's commonplace; indeed, no actual involvement of my personality at all. I saw. I was moving vision, though without eyes or other flesh. And while my mind saw, it also knew where my flesh was, slumped at the kitchen table. If anyone had entered the kitchen, if there had been a noise of alarm out in the henhouse, I should have known it.

There was a valley such as I have not seen (and never will) on Earth. I have seen many beautiful places on this planet—some of them were even tranquil. Once I took a slow steamer to New Zealand and had the Pacific as a plaything for many days. I can hardly say how I knew this was not Earth. The grass of the valley was an earthly green; a river below me was a blue-and-silver thread under familiar-seeming sunlight; there were trees much like pine and maple, and maybe that is what they were. But it was not Earth. I was aware of mountains heaped to strange heights on either side of the valley—snow, rose, amber gold. Perhaps the amber tint was unlike any mountain color I have noticed in this world at midday.

Or I may have known it was not Earth simply because her mind—dwelling within some unimaginable brain smaller than the tip of my little finger—told me so.

I watched two inhabitants of that world come flying, to rest in the field of sunny grass where my bodiless vision had brought me. Adult forms, such as my angel would surely be when she had her growth, except that both of these were male and one of them was dark-skinned. The latter was also old, with a thousand-wrinkled face, knowing and full of tranquility; the other was flushed and lively with youth; both were beautiful. The down on the brown-skinned old one was reddish-tawny; the other's was ivory with hints of orange. Their wings were true membranes, with more variety of subtle iridescence than I have seen even in the wings of a dragonfly; I could not say that any color was dominant, for each motion brought a ripple of change. These two sat at their ease on the grass. I realized that they were talking to each other, though their lips did not move in speech more than once or twice. They would nod, smile, now and then illustrate something with twinkling hands.

A huge rabbit lolloped past them. I knew (thanks to my own angel's efforts, I suppose) that this animal was of the same size of our common wild ones. Later, a blue-green snake three times the size of the angels came flowing through the grass; the old one reached out to stroke its head carelessly, and I think he did it without interrupting whatever he was saying.

Another creature came, in leisured leaps. He was monstrous, yet I felt no alarm in the angels or in myself. Imagine a being built somewhat like a kangaroo up to the head, about eight feet tall, and katydid-green. Really, the thick balancing tail and enormous legs were the only kangaroo-like features about him: the body above the massive thighs was not dwarfed but thick and square; the arms and hands were quite humanoid: the head was round, manlike except for its face—there was only a single nostril and his mouth was set in the vertical; the eyes were large and mild. I received an impression of high intelligence and natural gentleness. In one of his manlike hands two tools so familiar and ordinary that I knew my body by the kitchen table had laughed in startled recognition. But, after all, a garden spade and rake are basic. Once invented—I expect we did it ourselves in the Neolithic Age—there is little reason why they should change much down the millennia.

This farmer halted by the angels, and the three conversed a while. The big head nodded agreeably. I believe the young angel made a joke; certainly the convulsions in the huge green face made me think of laughter. Then this amiable monster turned up the grass in a patch a few yards square, broke the sod and raked the surface smooth, just as any competent gardener might do—except that he moved with the relaxed smoothness of a being whose strength far exceeds the requirements of his task . . .

I was back in my kitchen with everyday eyes. My angel was exploring the table. I had a loaf of bread there and a dish of strawberries and cream. She was trying a bread crumb, seemed to like it fairly well. I offered the strawberries; she broke off one of the seeds and nibbled it but didn't care so much for the pulp. I held up the great spoon with sugary cream; she steadied it with both hands to try some. I think she liked it. It had been most stupid of me not to realize that she would be hungry. I brought wine from the cupboard; she watched inquiringly, so I put a couple of drops on the handle of a spoon. This really pleased her: she chuckled and patted her tiny stomach, though I'm afraid it wasn't awfully good sherry. I brought some crumbs of cake, but she indicated that she was full, came close to my face, and motioned me to lower my head.

She reached towards me until she could press both hands against my forehead—I felt it only enough to know her hands were there—she stood so a long time, trying to tell me something.

It was difficult. Pictures come through with relative ease, but now she was transmitting an abstraction of a complex kind: my clumsy brain really suffered in the effort to receive. Something did come across. I have only the crudest way of passing it on. Imagine an equilateral triangle; place the following words one at each corner—"recruiting," "collecting," "saving." The meaning she wanted to convey ought to be near the center of the triangle.

I had also the sense that her message provided a partial explanation of her errand in this lovable and damnable world.

She looked weary when she stood away from me. I put out my palm and she climbed into it, to be carried back to the nest.

She did not talk to me tonight, nor eat, but she gave a reason, coming out from Camilla's feathers long enough to turn her back and show me the wing stubs. The protective sheaths have dropped off; the wings are rapidly growing. They are probably damp and weak. She was quite tired and went back into the warm darkness almost at once.

Camilla must be exhausted, too. I don't think she has been off the nest more than twice since I brought them into the house.

June 4

Today she can fly.

I learned it in the afternoon, when I was fiddling about in the garden and Judy was loafing in the sunshine she loves. Something apart from sight and sound called me to hurry back to the house. I saw my angel through the screen door before I opened it. One of her feet had caught in a hideous loop of loose wire at a break in the mesh. Her first tug of alarm must have tightened the loop so that her hands were not strong enough to force it open.

Fortunately I was able to cut the wire with a pair of shears before I lost my head; then she could free her foot without injury. Camilla had been frantic, rushing around fluffed up, but—here's an odd thing—perfectly silent. None of the recognized chicken noises of dismay: if an ordinary chick had been in trouble she would have raised the roof.

The angel flew to me and hovered, pressing her hands on my forehead. The message was clear at once: "No harm done." She flew down to tell Camilla the same thing.

Yes, in the same way. I saw Camilla standing near my feet with her neck out and head low, and the angel put a hand on either side of her scraggy comb. Camilla relaxed, clucked in the normal way, and spread her wings for a shelter. The angel went under it, but only to oblige Camilla, I think—at least, she stuck her head through the wing feathers and winked.

She must have seen something else, then, for she came out and flew back to me and touched a finger to my cheek, looked at the finger, saw it was wet, put it in her mouth, made a face and laughed at me.

We went outdoors into the sun (Camilla, too), and the angel gave me an exhibition of what flying ought to be. Not even Schubert can speak of joy as her first free flying did. At one moment she would be hanging in front of my eyes, radiant and delighted; the next instant she would be a dot of color against a cloud. Try to imagine something that would make a hummingbird seem a bit dull and sluggish.

They do hum. Softer than a hummingbird, louder than a dragonfly.

Something like the sound of hawk-moths—*Heinmaris thisbe*, for instance: the one I used to call Hummingbird Moth when I was a child.

I was frightened, naturally. Frightened first at what might happen to her, but that was unnecessary; I don't think she would be in danger from any savage animal except possibly Man. I saw a Cooper's hawk slant down the visible ray toward the swirl of color where she was dancing by herself; presently she was drawing iridescent rings around him; then, while he soared in smaller circles, I could not see her, but (maybe she felt my fright) she was again in front of me, pressing my forehead in the now familiar way. I knew she was amused and caught the idea that the hawk was a "lazy character." Not quite the way I'd describe *Accipiter Cooperi*, but it's all in the point of view. I believe she had been riding his back, no doubt with her speaking hands on his terrible head.

And later I was frightened by the thought that she might not want to return to me. Can I compete with sunlight and open sky? The passage of that terror through me brought her back swiftly, and her hands said with great clarity: "Don't ever be afraid of anything—it isn't necessary for you."

Once this afternoon I was saddened by the realization that old Judy can take little part in what goes on now. I can well remember Judy running like the wind. The angel must have heard this thought in me, for she stood a long time beside Judy's drowsy head, while Judy's tail thumped cheerfully on the warm grass . . .

In the evening the angel made a heavy meal on two or three cake crumbs and another drop of sherry, and we had what was almost a sustained conversation. I will write it in that form this time, rather than grope for anything more exact. I asked her, "How far away is your home?"

"My home is here."

"Thank God!—but I meant, the place your people came from."

"Ten light-years."

"The images you showed me—that quiet valley—that is ten light-years away?"

"Yes. But that was my father talking to you, through me. He was grown when the journey began. He is two hundred and forty years old—our years, thirty-two days longer than yours."

Mainly I was conscious of a flood of relief: I had feared on the basis of terrestrial biology, that her explosively rapid growth after hatching must foretell a brief life. But it's all right—she can outlive me, and by a few hundred years, at that. "Your father is here now, on this planet—shall I see him?"

She took her hands away—listening, I believe. The answer was: "No. He is sorry. He is ill and cannot live long. I am to see him for a few days, when I fly a little better. He taught me for twenty years after I was born."

"I don't understand. I thought—"

"Later, friend. My father is grateful for your kindness to me."

I don't know what I thought about that. I felt no faintest trace of condescension in the message. "And he was showing me things he had seen with his own eyes, ten light-years away?"

"Yes." Then she wanted me to rest a while; I am sure she knows what a huge effort it is for my primitive brain to function in this way. But before she ended the conversation by humming down to her nest she gave me this, and I received it with such clarity that I cannot be mistaken: "He says that only fifty million years ago it was a jungle there, just as Terra is now."

June 8

When I woke four days ago the angel was having breakfast, and little Camilla was dead. The angel watched me rub sleep out of my eyes, watched me discover Camilla, and then flew to me. I received this: "Does it make you unhappy?"

"I don't know exactly." You can get fond of a hen, especially a cantankerous and homely old one whose personality has a lot in common with your own.

"She was old. She wanted a flock of chicks, and I couldn't stay with her. So I—" Something obscure here: probably my mind was trying too hard to grasp it—" . . . so I saved her life." I could make nothing else out of it. She said "saved."

Camilla's death looked natural, except that I should have expected the death contractions to muss the straw, and that hadn't happened. Maybe the angel had arranged the old lady's body for decorum, though I don't see how her muscular strength would have been equal to it— Camilla weighed at least seven pounds.

As I was burying her at the edge of the garden and the angel was humming over my head, I recalled a thing which, when it happened, I had dismissed as a dream. Merely a moonlight image of the angel standing in the nest box with her hands on Camilla's head, then pressing her mouth gently on Camilla's throat, just before the hen's head sank down out of my line of vision. Probably I actually waked and saw it happen. I am somehow unconcerned—even, as I think more about it, pleased. . .

After the burial the angel's hands said, "Sit on the grass and we'll talk . . . Question me. I'll tell you what I can. My father asks you to write it down."

So that is what we have been doing for the last four days, I have been going to school, a slow but willing pupil. Rather than enter anything in this journal (for in the evenings I was exhausted), I made notes as best I could. The angel has gone now to see her father and will not return until morning. I shall try to make a readable version of my notes.

Since she had invited questions, I began with something which had been bothering me, as a would-be naturalist, exceedingly. I couldn't see how creatures no larger than the adults I had observed could lay eggs as large as Camilla's. Nor could I undersand why, if they were hatched in an almost adult condition and able to eat a varied diet, she had any use for that ridiculous, lovely, and apparently functional pair of breasts. When the angel grasped my difficulty she exploded with laughter —her kind, which buzzed her all over the garden and caused her to fluff my hair on the wing and pinch my ear lobe. She lit on a rhubarb leaf and gave a delectably naughty representation of herself as a hen laying an egg, including the cackle. She got me to bumbling helplessly —my kind of laughter—and it was some time before we could quiet down. Then she did her best to explain.

They are true mammals, and the young—not more than two or at most three in a lifetime averaging two hundred and fifty years—are delivered in very much the human way. The baby is nursed—human fashion—until his brain begins to respond a little to their unspoken language; that takes three to four weeks. Then he is placed in an altogether different medium. She could not describe that clearly, because there was very little in my educational storehouse to help me grasp it. It is some gaseous medium that arrests bodily growth for an almost indefinite period, while mental growth continues. It took them, she says, about seven thousand years to perfect this technique after they first hit on the idea: they are never in a hurry. The infant remains under this delicate and precise control for anywhere from fifteen to thirty years, the period depending not only on his mental vigor but also on the type of lifework he tentatively elects as soon as his brain is knowing enough to make a choice. During this period his mind is guided with unwavering patience by teachers who—

It seems those teachers know their business. This was peculiarly difficult for me to assimilate, although the fact came through clearly enough. In their world, the profession of teacher is more highly honored than any other— can such a thing be possible?—and so difficult to enter that only the strongest minds dare attempt it. (I had to rest a while after absorbing that.) An aspirant must spend fifty years (not including the period of infantile education) in merely getting ready to begin, and the acquisition of factual knowledge, while not under-stressed, takes only a small portion of those fifty years. Then—if he's good enough—he can take a small part in the elementary instruction of a few babies, and if he does well on that basis for another thirty or forty years, he is considered a fair beginner . . . Once upon a time I lurched around stuffy classrooms trying to insert a few predigested

facts (I wonder how many of them *were* facts?) into the
minds of bored and preoccupied adolescents, some of
whom may have liked me moderately well. I was even able
to shake hands and be nice while their terribly well-
meaning parents explained to me how they ought to be
educated. So much of our human effort goes down the
drain of futility, I sometimes wonder how we ever got as
far as the Bronze Age. Somehow we did, though, and a
short way beyond.

After that preliminary stage of an angel's education is
finished, the baby is transferred to more ordinary
surroundings, and his bodily growth completes itself in a
very short time. Wings grow abruptly (as I have seen),
and he reaches a maximum height of six inches (our
measure). Only then does he enter on that lifetime of two
hundred and fifty years for not until then does his body
begin to age. My angel has been a living personality for
many years but will not celebrate her first birthday for
almost a year. I like to think of that.

At about the same time that they learned the principles
of interplanetary travel (approximately twelve million
years ago) these people also learned how, by the use of a
slightly different method, growth could be arrested at any
point short of full maturity. At first the knowledge served
no purpose except in the control of illnesses which still
occasionally struck them at that time. But when the long
periods of time required for space travel were considered,
the advantages became obvious.

So it happens that my angel was born ten-light years
away. She was trained by her father and many others in
the wisdom of seventy million years (that, she tells me, is
the approximate sum of their *record* history), and then
she was safely sealed and cherished in what my super-
amoebic brain regarded as a blue egg. Education did not
proceed at that time; her mind went to sleep with the rest
of her. When Camilla's temperature made her wake and
grow again, she remembered what to do with the little
horny bumps provided for her elbows. And came out—
into this planet, God help her.

I wondered why her father should have chosen any
combination so unreliable as an old hen and a human

being. Surely he must have had plenty of excellent ways to bring the shell to the right temperature. Her answer should have satisfied me immensely, but I am still compelled to wonder about it. "Camilla was a nice hen, and my father studied your mind while you were asleep. It was a bad landing, and much was broken—no such landing was ever made before after so long a journey: forty years. Only four other grown-ups could come with my father. Three of them died en route and he is very ill. And there were nine other children to care for."

Yes I knew she'd said that an angel thought I was good enough to be trusted with his daughter. If it upsets me, all I need to do is look at her and then in the mirror. As for the explanation, I can only conclude there must be more that I am not ready to understand. I was worried about those nine others, but she assured me they were all well, and I sensed that I ought not to ask more about them at present . . .

Their planet, she says, is closely similar to this. A trifle larger, moving in a somewhat longer orbit around a sun like ours. Two gleaming moons, smaller than ours—their orbits are such that two-moon nights come rarely. They are magic, and she will ask her father to show me one, if he can. Their year is thirty-two days longer than ours; because of a slower rotation, their day has twenty-six of our hours. Their atmosphere is mainly nitrogen and oxygen in the proportions familiar to us; slightly richer in some of the rare gases. The climate is now what we should call tropical and subtropical, but they have known glacial rigors like those in our world's past. There are only two great continental land masses, and many thousands of large islands.

Their total population is only five billion . . .

Most of the forms of life we know have parallels there—some quite exact parallels: rabbits, deer, mice, cats. The cats have been bred to an even higher intelligence than they possess on our Earth; it is possible, she says to have a good deal of intellectual intercourse with their cats, who learned several million years ago that when they kill, it must be done with lightning precision and without torture. The cats had some difficulty grasping the possibility of pain in other organisms, but once that educational hurdle was passed, development was easy. Nowadays many of the cats are popular story-tellers; about forty million years ago they were still occasionally needed as a special police force, and served the angels with real heroism.

It seems my angel wants to become a student of animal life here on Earth. I, a teacher!—but bless her heart for the notion, anyhow. We sat and traded animals for a couple of hours last night. I found it restful, after the mental struggle to grasp more difficult matters. Judy was something new to her. They have several luscious monsters on that planet but, in her view, so have we. She told me of a blue sea snake fifty feet long (relatively harmless) that bellows cow-like and comes into the tidal marshes to lay black eggs; so I gave her a whale. She offered a bat-winged, day-flying ball of mammalian fluff as big as my head and weighing under an ounce; I matched her with a marmoset. She tried me with a small-sized pink brontosaur (very rare), but I was ready with the duck-billed platypus, and that caused us to exchange some pretty smart remarks about mammalian eggs; she bounced. All trivial in a way; also, the happiest evening in my fifty-three tangled years of life.

She was a trifle hesitant to explain these kangaroo-like people, until she was sure I really wanted to know. It seems they are about the nearest parallel to human life on that planet; not a near parallel, of course, as she was careful to explain. Agreeable and always friendly souls (though they weren't always so, I'm sure) and of a some-what more alert intelligence than we possess. Manual workers, mainly, because they prefer it nowadays, but some of them are excellent mathematicians. The first practical spaceship was invented by a group of them, with some assistance . . .

Names offer difficulties. Because of the nature of the angelic language, they have scant use for them except for the purpose of written record, and writing naturally plays little part in their daily lives—no occasion to write a letter when a thousand miles is no obstacle to the speech of your mind. An angel's formal name is about as important to him as, say, my Social Security number is to me. She has not told me hers, because the phonetics on which their written language is based have no parallel in my mind. As we would speak a friend's name, an angel will project the friend's image to his friend's receiving mind. More pleasant and more intimate, I think—although it was a shock to me at first to glimpse my own ugly mug in my mind's eye. Stories are occasionally written, if there is something in them that should be preserved precisely as it was in the first telling; but in their world the true story-teller has a more important place than the printer—he offers one of the best of their quieter pleasures: a good one can hold his audience for a week and never tire them.

"What is this 'angel' in your mind when you think of me?"

"A being men have imagined for centuries, when they thought of themselves as they might like to be and not as they are."

I did not try too painfully hard to learn much about the principles of space travel. The most my brain could take in of her explanation was something like: "Rocket—then phototropism." Now, that makes scant sense. So far as I know, phototropism—movement toward light—is an organic phenomenon. One thinks of it as a response of protoplasm, in some plants and animal organisms (most of them simple), to the stimulus of light; certainly not as a force capable of moving inorganic matter. I think that whatever may be the principle she was describing, this word "phototropism" was merely the nearest thing to it in my reservoir of language. Not even the angels can create understanding out of blank ignorance. At least I have learned not to set neat limits to the possible.

(There was a time when I did, though. I can see myself, not so many years back, like a homunculus squatting at the foot of Mt. McKinley, throwing together two handfuls of mud and shouting, "Look at the big mountain *I* made!")

And if I did know the physical principles which brought them here, and could write them in terms accessible to technicians resembling myself, I would not do it.

Here is a thing I am afraid no reader of this journal will

believe: these people, as I have written, learned their method of space travel some twelve million years ago. But this is the first time they have ever used it to convey them to another planet. The heavens are rich in worlds, she tells me; on many of them there is life, often on very primitive levels. No external force prevented her people from going forth, colonizing, conquering, as far as they pleased. They could have populated a Galaxy. They did not, and for this reason: they believed they were not ready. More precisely: *not good enough.*

Only some fifty million years ago, by her account, did they learn (as we may learn eventually) that intelligence without goodness is worse than high explosive in the hands of a baboon. For beings advanced beyond the level of Pithecanthropus, intelligence is a cheap commodity —not too hard to develop, hellishly easy to use for unconsidered ends. Whereas goodness is not to be achieved without unending effort of the hardest kind, within the self, whether the self be man or angel.

It is clear even to me that the conquest of evil is only one step, not the most important. For goodness, so she tried to tell me, is an altogether positive quality; the part of living nature that swarms with such monstrosities as cruelty, meanness, bitterness, greed, is not to be filled by a vacuum when these horrors are eliminated. When you clear away a poisonous gas, you try to fill the whole room with clean air. Kindness, for only one example: one who can define kindness only as the absence of cruelty has surely not begun to understand the nature of either.

They do not aim at perfection, these angels: only at the attainable ... That time fifty million years ago was evidently one of great suffering and confusion. War and all its attendant plagues. They passed through many centuries while advances in technology merely worsened their condition and increased the peril of self-annihilation. They came through that, in time. War was at length so far outgrown that its recurrence was impossible, and the development of wholly rational beings could begin. Then they were ready to start growing up, through millennia of self-searching, self-discipline, seeking to derive the simple from the complex, discovering how to use knowledge and not be used by it. Even then, of course, they slipped back often enough. There were what she refers to as "eras of fatigue." In their dimmer past, they had had many dark ages, lost civilizations, hopeful beginnings ending in dust. Earlier still, they had come out of the slime, as we did.

But their period of deepest uncertainty and sternest self-appraisal did not come until twelve million years ago, when they knew a Universe could be theirs for the taking and knew they were not yet good enough.

They are in no more hurry than the stars. She tried to convey something tentatively, at this point, which was really beyond both of us. It had to do with time (not as I understand time) being perhaps the most essential attribute of God (not as I was ever able to understand that word). Seeing my mental exhaustion, she gave up the effort and later told me that the conception was extremely difficult for her, too—not only, I gathered, because of her youth and relative ignorance. There was also a hint that her father might not have wished her to bring my brain up to a hurdle like that one ...

Of course, they explored. Their little spaceships were roaming the ether before there was anything like Man on this earth—roaming and listening, observing, recording; never entering nor taking part in the life of any home but their own. For five million years they even forbade themselves to go beyond their own Solar Sysem, though it would have been easy to do so. And in the following seven million years, although they traveled to incredible distances, the same stern restraint was in force. It was altogether unrelated to what we should call fear—that, I think, is as extinct in them as hate. There was so much to do at home!—I wish I could imagine it. They mapped the heavens and played in their own sunlight.

Naturally, I cannot tell you what goodness is. I know only, moderately well, what it seems to mean to us human beings. It appears that the best of us can, with enormous difficulty, achieve a manner of life in which goodness is reasonably dominant, by a not too precarious balance, for the greater part of the time. Often, wise men have indicated they hope for nothing better than that in our present condition. We are, in other words, a fraction alive; the rest is in the dark. Dante was a bitter masochist, Beethoven a frantic and miserable snob, Shakespeare wrote potboilers. And Christ said, "My Father, if it be possible, let this cup pass from me."

But give us fifty million years—I am no pessimist. After all, I've watched one-celled organisms on the slide and listened to Brahms' Fourth. Night before last I said to the angel, "In spite of everything, you and I are kindred."

She granted me agreement.

June 9

She was lying on my pillow this morning so that I could see her when I waked.

Her father has died, and she was with him when it happened. There was again that thought-impression that I could interpret only to mean that his life had been "saved." I was still sleep-bound when my mind asked, "What will you do?"

"Stay with you, if you wish it, for the rest of your life." Now, the last part of the message was clouded, but I am familiar with that—it seems to mean there is some further element that eludes me. I could not be mistaken about the part I did receive. It gives me amazing speculations. After all, I am only fifty-three; I might live for another thirty or forty years . . .

She was preoccupied this morning, but whatever she felt about her father's death that might be paralleled by sadness in a human being was hidden from me. She did say her father was sorry he had not been able to show me a two-moon night.

One adult, then, remains in this world. Except to say that he is two hundred years old and full of knowledge, and that he endured the long journey without serious ill effects, she has told me little about him. And there are ten children, including herself.

Something was sparkling at her throat. When she was aware of my interest in it she took it off, and I fetched a magnifying glass. A necklace; under the glass, much like our finest human workmanship, if your imagination can reduce it to the proper scale. The stones appeared similar to the jewels we know: diamonds, sapphires, rubies, emeralds, the diamonds snapping out every color under heaven; but there were two or three very dark-purple stones unlike anything I know—not amethysts, I am sure. The necklace was strung on something more slender than cobweb, and the design of the joining clasp was too delicate for my glass to help me. The necklace had been her mother's, she told me; as she put it back around her throat I thought I saw the same shy pride that any human girl might feel in displaying a new pretty.

She wanted to show me other things she had brought, and flew to the table where she had left a sort of satchel an inch and a half long—quite a load for her to fly with, but the translucent substance is so light that when she rested the satchel on my finger I scarcely felt it. She arranged a few articles happily for my inspection, and I put the glass to work again. One was a jeweled comb; she ran it through the down on her chest and legs to show me its use. There was a set of tools too small for the glass to interpret; I learned later they were a sewing kit. A book, and some writing instrument much like a metal pencil: imagine a book and pencil that could be used comfortably by hands hardly bigger than the paws of a mouse— that is the best I can do. The book, I understand, is a blank record for her use as needed.

And finally, when I was fully awake and dressed and we had finished breakfast, she reached in the bottom of the satchel for a parcel (heavy for her) and made me understand it was a gift for me. "My father made it for you, but I put in the stone myself, last night." She unwrapped it. A ring, precisely the size for my little finger.

I broke down, rather. She understood that, and sat on my shoulder petting my ear lobe till I had command of myself.

I have no idea what the jewel is. It shifts with the light from purple to jade-green to amber. The metal resembles platinum in appearance except for a tinge of rose at certain angles of light ... When I stare into the stone, I think I see—never mind that now. I am not ready to write it down, and perhaps never will be; anyway, I must be sure.

We improved our housekeeping later in the morning. I showed her over the house. It isn't much—Cape Codder, two rooms up and two down. Every corner interested her, and when she found a shoe box in the bedroom closet, she asked for it. At her direction, I have arranged it on a chest near my bed and near the window, which will always be open; she says the mosquitoes will not bother me, and I don't doubt her. I unearthed a white silk scarf for the bottom of the box; after asking my permission (as if I could want to refuse her anything!) she got her sewing kit and snipped off a piece of the scarf several inches square, folded it on itself several times, and sewed it into a narrow pillow an inch long. So now she had a proper bed and a room of her own. I wish I had something less coarse than silk, but she insists it's nice.

We have not talked very much today. In the afternoon she flew out for an hour's play in the cloud country; when she returned she let me know that she needed a long sleep. She is still sleeping, I think; I am writing this downstairs, fearing the light might disturb her.

Is it possible I can have thirty or forty years in her company? I wonder how teachable my mind still is. I seem to be able to assimilate new facts as well as I ever could; this ungainly carcass should be durable, with reasonable care. Of course, facts without a synthetic imagination are no better than scattered bricks; but perhaps my imagination—

I don't know.

Judy wants out. I shall turn in when she comes back. I wonder if poor Judy's life could be—the word is certainly "saved." I must ask.

Last night when I stopped writing I did go to bed but I was restless, refusing sleep. At some time in the small hours—there was light from a single room—she flew over to me. The tensions dissolved like an illness, and my mind was able to respond with a certain calm.

I made plain (what I am sure she already knew) that I would never willingly part company with her, and then she gave me to understand that there are two alternatives for the remainder of my life. The choice, she says, is altogether mine, and I must take time to be sure of my decision.

I can live out my natural span, whatever it proves to be, and she will not leave me for long at any time. She will be there to counsel, teach, help me in anything good I care to undertake. She says she would enjoy this; for some reason she is, as we'd say in our language, fond of me. We'd have fun.

Lord, the books I could write! I fumble for words now, in the usual human way: whatever I put on the paper is a miserable fraction of the potential; the words themselves are rarely the right ones. But under her guidance—

I could take a fair part in shaking the world. With words alone. I could preach to my own people. Before long, I would be heard.

I could study and explore. What small nibblings we have made at the sum of available knowledge! Suppose I brought in one leaf from outdoors, or one common little bug—in a few hours of studying it with her I'd know more of my own specialty than a flood of the best textbooks could tell me.

She has also let me know that when she and those who came with her have learned a little more about the human picture, it should be possible to improve my health greatly, and probably my life expectancy. I don't imagine my back could ever straighten, but she thinks the pain might be cleared away, possibly without drugs. I could have a clearer mind, in a body that would neither fail nor torment me.

Then there is the other alternative.

It seems they have developed a technique by means of which any unresisting living subject whose brain is capable of memory at all can experience a total recall. It is a by-product, I understand, of their silent speech, and a very recent one. They have practiced it for only a few thousand years, and since their own understanding of the phenomenon is very incomplete, they classify it among their experimental techniques. In a general way, it may somewhat resemble that reliving of the past that psychoanalysis can sometimes bring about in a limited way for therapeutic purposes; but you must imagine that sort of thing tremendously magnified and clarified, capable of including every detail that has ever registered on the

subject's brain; and the end result is very different. The
purpose is not therapeutic, as we would understand it:
quite the opposite. The end result is death. Whatever is
recalled by this process is transmitted to the receiving
mind, which can retain it and record any or all of it if such
a record is desired; but to the subject who recalls it, it is a
flowing away, without return. Thus it is not a true
"remembering" but a giving. The mind is swept clear,
naked of all its past, and, along with memory, life
withdraws also: Very quietly. At the end, I suppose it
must be like standing without resistance in the engulf-
ment of a flood time, until finally the waters close over.

That, it seems, is how Camilla's life was "saved."
Now, when I finally grasped that, I laughed, and the
angel of course caught my joke. I was thinking about my
neighbor Steele, who boarded the old lady for me in his
henhouse for a couple of winters. Somewhat safe in the
angelic records there must be a hen's-eye image of the
patch in the seat of Steele's pants. Well—good. And,
naturally, Camilla's view of me, too: not too unkind, I
hope—she couldn't help the expression on her rigid little
face, and I don't believe it ever meant anything.

At the other end of the scale is the saved life of my
angel's father. Recall can be a long process, she says,
depending on the intricacy and richness of the mind
recalling; and in all but the last stages it can be halted at
will. Her father's recall was begun when they were still far
out in space and he knew that he could not long survive
the journey. When that journey ended, the recall had progressed so far that very little actual memory remained to
him of his life on that other planet. He had what must be
called a "deductive memory"; from the material of the
years not yet given away, he could reconstruct what must
have been; and I assume the other adult who survived the
passage must have been able to shelter him from errors
that loss of memory might involve. This, I infer, is why he
could not show me a two-moon night. I forgot to ask her
whether the images he did send me were from actual or
deductive memory. Deductive, I think, for there was a
certain dimness about them not present when my angel
gives me a picture of something seen with her own eyes.

Jade-green eyes, by the way—were you wondering?

In the same fashion, my own life could be saved. Every aspect of existence that I ever touched, that ever touched me, could be transmitted to some perfect record. The nature of the written record is beyond me, but I have no doubt of its relative perfection. Nothing important, good or bad, would be lost. And they need a knowledge of humanity, if they are to carry out whatever it is they have in mind.

It would be difficult, she tells me, and sometimes painful. Most of the effort would be hers, but some of it would have to be mine. In her period of infantile education, she elected what we should call zoology as her lifework; for that reason she was given intensive theoretical training in this technique. Right now, I guess she knows more than anyone else on this planet not only about what makes a hen tick but about how it feels to be a hen. Though a beginner, she is in all essentials already an expert. She can help me, she thinks (if I choose this alternative)—at any rate, ease me over the toughest spots, soothe away resistance, keep my courage from too much flagging.

For it seems that this process of recall is painful to an advanced intellect (she, without condescension, calls us very advanced) because, while all pretense and self-delusion are stripped away, there remains conscience, still functioning by whatever standards of good and bad the individual has developed in his lifetime. Our present knowledge of our own motives is such a pathetically small beginning!—hardly stronger than an infant's first effort to focus his eyes. I am merely wondering how much of my life (if I choose this way) will seem to me altogether hideous. Certainly plenty of the "good deeds" that I still cherish in memory like so many well-behaved cherubs will turn up with the leering aspect of greed or petty vanity or worse.

Not that I am a bad man, in any reasonable sense of the term; not a bit of it. I respect myself; no occasion to grovel and beat my chest; I'm not ashamed to stand comparison with any other fair sample of the species. But there you are: I *am* human, and under the aspect of eternity so far, plus this afternoon's newspaper, that is a rather serious thing.

Without real knowledge, I think of this total recall as something like a passage down a corridor of myriad images—now dark, now brilliant; now pleasant, now horrible—guided by no certainty except an awareness of the open blind door at the end of it. It could have its pleasing moments and its consolations. I don't see how it could ever approximate the delight and satisfaction of living a few more years in this world with the angel lighting on my shoulder when she wishes, and talking to me.

I had to ask her of how great value such a record would be to them. Very great. Obvious enough—they can be of little use to us, by their standards, until they understand us; and they came here to be of use to us as well as to themselves. And understanding us, to them, means knowing us inside out with a completeness such as our most dedicated and laborious scholars could never imagine. I remember those twelve million years: they will not touch us until they are certain no harm will come of it. On our tortured planet, however, there is a time factor. They know that well enough, of course . . . Recall cannot begin unless the subject is willing or unresisting; to them, that has to mean willing, for any being with intellect enough to make a considered choice. Now, I wonder how many they could find who would be honestly willing to make that uneasy journey into death, for no reward except an assurance that they were serving their own kind and the angels?

More to the point, I wonder if I would be able to achieve such willingness myself, even with her help?

When this had been explained to me, she urged me again to make no hasty decision. And she pointed out to me what my thoughts were already groping at—why not both alternatives, within a reasonable limit of time? Why couldn't I have ten or fifteen years or more with her and then undertake the total recall—perhaps not until my physical powers had started toward senility? I thought that over.

This morning I had almost decided to choose that most

welcome and comforting solution. Then the mailman brought my daily paper. Not that I needed any such reminder.

In the afternoon I asked her if she knew whether, in the present state of human technology, it would be possible for our folly to actually destroy this planet. She did not know, for certain. Three of the other children have gone away to different parts of the world, to learn what they can about that. But she had to tell me that such a thing has happened before, elsewhere in the heavens. I guess I won't write a letter to the papers advancing an explanation for the occasional appearance of a nova among the stars. Doubtless others have hit on the same hypothesis without the aid of angels.

And that is not all I must consider. I could die by accident or sudden disease before I had begun to give my life.

Only now, at this very late moment, rubbing my sweaty forehead and gazing into the lights of that wonderful ring, have I been able to put together some obvious facts in the required synthesis.

I don't know, of course, what forms their assistance to us will take. I suspect human beings won't see or hear much of the angels for a long time to come. Now and then disastrous decisions may be altered, and those who believe themselves wholly responsible won't quite know why their minds worked that way. Here and there, maybe an influential mind will be rather strangely nudged into a better course. Something like that. There may be sudden new discoveries and inventions of kinds that will tend to neutralize the menace of our nastiest playthings. But whatever the angels decide to do, the record and analysis of my not too atypical life will be an aid: it could even be the small weight deciding the balance between triumph and failure. That fact is one.

Two: my angel and her brothers and sisters, for all their amazing level of advancement, are of perishable protoplasm, even as I am. Therefore, if this ball of earth becomes a ball of flame, they also will be destroyed. Even if they have the means to use their spaceship again or to build another, it might easily happen that they would not learn their danger in time to escape. And for all I know, this could be tomorrow. Or tonight.

So there can no longer be any doubt as to my choice, and I will tell her when she wakes.

July 9

Tonight* there is no recall—I am to rest a while. I see it is almost a month since I last wrote in this journal. My total recall began three weeks ago, and I have already been able to give away the first twenty-eight years of my life.

Since I no longer require normal sleep, the recall begins at night, as soon as the lights begin to go out over there in the village and there is little danger of interruption. Daytimes, I putter about in my usual fashion. I have sold Steele my hens and Judy's life was saved a week ago; that practically winds up my affairs, except that I want to write a codicil to my will. I might as well do that now, right here in this journal, instead of bothering my lawyer. It should be legal.

TO WHOM IT MAY CONCERN: I hereby bequeath to my friend Lester Morse, M.D., of Augusta, Maine, the ring which will be found at my death on the fifth finger of my left hand; and I would urge Dr. Morse to retain this ring in his private possession at all times, and to make provision for its disposal, in the event of his own death, to some person in whose character he places the utmost faith.
                                   (Signed) David Bannerman†

Tonight she has gone away for a while, and I am to rest and do as I please until she returns. I shall spend the time filling in some blanks in this record, but I am afraid it will be a spotty job, unsatisfactory to any readers who are subject to the blessed old itch for facts. Mainly because

---

*At this point Dr. Bannerman's handwriting alters curiously. From here on he used a soft pencil instead of a pen, and the script shows signs of haste. In spite of this, however, it is actually much clearer, steadier, and easier to read than the earlier entries in his normal hand. — BLAINE.
†In spite of superficial changes in the handwriting, this signature has been certified genuine by an expert graphologist — BLAINE.

there is so much I no longer care about. It is troublesome to try to decide what things would be considered important by interested strangers.

Except for the lack of any desire for sleep, and a bodily weariness that is not at all unpleasant, I notice no physical effects thus far. I have no faintest recollection of anything that happened earlier than my twenty-eighth birthday. My deductive memory seems rather efficient, and I am sure I could reconstruct most of the story if it were worth the bother: this afternoon I grubbed around among some old letters of that period, but they weren't very interesting. My knowledge of English is unaffected; I can still read scientific German and some French, because I had occasion to use those languages fairly often after I was twenty-eight. The scraps of Latin dating from high school are quite gone. So are algebra and all but the simplest propositions of high-school geometry: I never needed 'em. I can remember thinking of my mother after twenty-eight, but do not know whether the image this provides really resembles her; my father died when I was thirty-one, so I remember him as a sick old man. I believe I had a younger brother, but he must have died in childhood.*

Judy's passing was tranquil—pleasant for her, I think. It took the better part of a day. We went out to an abandoned field I know, and she lay in the sunshine with the angel sitting by her, while I dug a grave and then rambled off after wild raspberries. Toward evening the angel came and told me it was finished. And most interesting, she said. I don't see how there can have been anything distresssing about it for Judy; after all, what hurts us worst is to have our favorite self-deceptions stripped away.

As the angel has explained it to me, her people, their cats, those kangaroo-folk, Man, and just possibly the cats on our planet (she hasn't met them yet) are the only animals she knows who are introspective enough to develop self-delusion and related pretenses. I suggested

---

*Dr. Bannerman's mother died in 1918 of influenza. His brother (three years older, not younger) died of pneumonia, 1906. — BLAINE.

she might find something of the sort, at least in rudimentary form, among some of the other primates. She was immensely interested and wanted to learn everything I could tell her about monkeys and apes. It seems that long ago on the other planet there used to be clumsy, winged creatures resembling the angels to about the degree that the large anthropoids resemble us. They became extinct some forty million years ago, in spite of enlightened efforts to keep their kind alive. Their birth rate became insufficient for replacement, as if some necessary spark had simply flickered out; almost as if nature, or whatever name you prefer for the unknown, had with gentle finality written them off . . .

I have not found the recall painful, at least, not in retrospect. There must have been sharp moments, mercifully forgotten, along with their causes, as if the process had gone on under anesthesia. Certainly there were plenty of incidents in my first twenty-eight years that I should not care to offer to the understanding of any but the angels. Quite often I must have been mean, selfish, base in any number of ways, if only to judge by the record since twenty-eight. Those old letters touch on a few of these things. To me, they now matter only as material for a record which is safely out of my hands.

However, to any persons I may have harmed, I wish to say this: you were hurt by aspects of my humanity which may not, in a few million years, be quite so common among us all. Against these darker elements I struggled, in my human fashion, as you do yourselves. The effort is not wasted.

It was a week after I told the angel my decision before she was prepared to start the recall. During that week she searched my present mind more closely than I should have imagined was possible: she had to be sure. During that week of hard questions I dare say she learned more about my kind than has ever gone on record even in a physician's office; I hope she did. To any psychiatrist who might question that, I offer a naturalist's suggestion: it is easy to imagine, after some laborious time, that we have noticed everything a given patch of ground can show us; but alter the viewpoint only a little—dig down a foot with a spade, say, or climb a tree branch and look downward—it's a whole new world.

When the angel was not exploring me in this fashion, she took pains to make me glimpse the satisfactions and million rewarding experiences I might have if I chose the other way. I see how necessary that was; at the time it seemed almost cruel. She had to do it, for my own sake, and I am glad that I was somehow able to stand fast to my original choice. So was she, in the end; she has even said she loves me for it. What that troubling word means to her is not within my mind: I am satisfied to take it in the human sense.

Some evening during that week—I think it was June 12—Lester dropped around for sherry and chess. Hadn't seen him in quite a while, and haven't since. There is a moderate polio scare this summer, and it keeps him on the jump. The angel retired behind some books on an upper shelf—I'm afraid it was dusty—and had fun with our chess. She had a fair view of your bald spot, Lester: later she remarked that she liked your looks, and can't you do something about that weight? She suggested an odd expedient, which I believe has occurred to your medical self from time to time—eating less.

Maybe she shouldn't have done what she did with those chess games. Nothing more than my usual blundering happened until after my first ten moves; by that time I suppose she had absorbed the principles and she took over, slightly. I was not fully aware of it until I saw Lester looking like a boiled duck: I had imagined my astonishing moves were the result of my own damn cleverness.

Seriously, Lester, think back to that evening. You've played in stiff amateur tournaments; you know your own abilities and you know mine. Ask yourself whether I could have done anything like that without help. I tell you again, I didn't study the game in the interval when you weren't there, I've never had a chess book in the library, and if I had, no amount of study would take me into your class. Haven't that sort of mentality—just your humble sparring partner, and I've enjoyed it on that basis, as you might enjoy watching a prima-donna surgeon pull off some miracle you wouldn't dream of attempting

yourself. Even if your game had been way below par that
evening (I don't think it was), I could never have pinned
your ears back three times running, without help. That
evening you were a long way out of *your* class, that's all.

I couldn't tell you anything about it at the time—she
was clear on that point—so I could only bumble and
preen myself and leave you mystified. But she wants me
to write anything I choose in this journal, and somehow,
Lester, I think you may find the next few decades pretty
interesting. You're still young—some ten years younger
than I. I think you'll see many things that I do wish I
myself might see come to pass—or I would so wish if I
were not convinced that my choice was the right one.

Most of those new events will not be spectacular, I'd
guess. Many of the turns to a better way will hardly be
recognized at the time for what they are, by you or anyone
else. Obviously, our nature being what it is, we shall not
jump into heaven overnight. To hope for that would be as
absurd as it is to imagine that any formula, idealogy,
theory of social pattern, can bring us into Utopia. As I see
it, Lester—I think your consulting room would have told
you the same even if your own intuition were not
enough—there is only one battle of importance:
Armageddon. And Armageddon field is within each self,
world without end.

At the moment I believe I am the happiest man who
ever lived.

July 20

All but the last ten years now given away. The physical
fatigue (still pleasant) is quite overwhelming. I am not
troubled by the weeds in my garden patch—merely a
different sort of flowers where I had planned something
else. An hour ago she brought me the seed of a blown
dandelion, to show me how lovely it was—I don't
suppose I had ever noticed. I hope whoever takes over this
place will bring it back to farming: they say the ten acres
below the house used to be good potato land—nice early
ground.

It is delightful to sit in the sun, as if I were old.

After thumbling over earlier entries in this journal, I

see I have often felt quite bitter toward my own kind. I deduce that I must have been a lonely man—much of the loneliness self-imposed. A great part of my bitterness must have been no more than one ugly by-product of a life spent too much apart. Some of it doubtless came from objective causes, yet I don't believe I ever had more cause than any moderately intelligent man who would like to see his world a pleasanter place than it ever has been. My angel tells me that the pain in my back is due to an injury received in some early stage of the world war that still goes on. That could have soured me, perhaps. It's all right—it's all in the record.

She is racing with a hummingbird—holding back, I think, to give the ball of green fluff a break.

Another note for you, Lester. I have already indicated that my ring is to be yours. I don't want to tell you what I have discovered of its properties, for fear it might not give you the same pleasure and interest that it has given me. Of course, like any spot of shifting light and color, it is an aid to self-hypnosis. It is much, much more than that, but—find out for yourself, at some time when you are a little protected from everyday distractions. I know it can't harm you, because I know its source.

By the way, I wish you would convey to my publishers my request that they either discontinue manufacture of my *Introductory Biology* or else bring out a new edition revised in accordance with some notes you will find in the top left drawer of my library desk. I glanced through that book after my angel assured me that I wrote it, and I was amazed. However, I'm afraid my notes are messy (I call them mine by a poetic license), and they may be too advanced for the present day—though the revision is mainly a matter of leaving out certain generalities that ain't so. Use your best judgement: it's a very minor text-book, and the thing isn't too important. A last wriggle of my personal vanity.

July 27

I have seen a two-moon night.

It was given to me by that other grownup, at the end of a wonderful visit, when he and six of those nine other

Hadwell selected a pen with a finer point, and wrote, "There's a girl named Mele who—" He crossed out the line and wrote, "A black-haired girl named Mele, beautiful beyond compare, came close to me and gazed deep into my eyes—" He crossed that out, too.

Frowning deeply, he tried several possible lines:

"Her limpid brown eyes gave promise of joys beyond—"

"Her small red mouth quivered ever so slightly when I—"

"Though her small hand rested on my arm for but a moment—"

He crumpled the page. Five months of enforced celibacy in space was having its effect, he decided. He had better return to the main issue and leave Mele for later.

He wrote:

There are many ways in which a sympathetic observer could help these people. But the temptation is strong to do *absolutely nothing*, for fear of disrupting their culture.

Closing his notebook, Hadwell looked out a port at the distant village, now lighted by torches. Then he opened the notebook again.

However their culture appears to be strong and flexible. Certain kinds of aid can do nothing but profit them. And these I will freely give.

He closed the notebook with a snap and put away his pens.

The following day, Hadwell began his good works. He found many Igathians suffering from mosquito-transmitted diseases. By judicious selection of antibiotics, he was able to arrest all except the most advanced cases. Then he directed work teams to drain the pools of stagnant water where the mosquitoes bred.

As he went on his healing rounds, Mele accompanied him. The beautiful Igathian girl quickly learned the rudiments of nursing, and Hadwell found her assistance invaluable.

Soon, all significant disease was cleared up in the village. Hadwell then began to spend his days in a sunny grove not far from Igathi, where he rested and worked on his book.

A town meeting was called at once by Lag, to discuss the import of this.

"Friends," said the old priest, "our friend, Hadwell, has done wonderful things for the village. He has cured our sick, so they too may live to partake of Thangookari's gift. Now Hadwell is tired and rests in the sun. Now Hadwell expects the reward he came here for."

"It is fitting," said the merchant, Vassi, "that the emissary receive his reward. I suggest that the priest take his mace and go forth—"

"Why so stingy?" asked Juele, a priest in training. "Is Thangookari's messenger deserving of no finer death? Hadwell deserves more than the mace! Much more!"

"You are right," Vassi admitted slowly. "In that case, I suggest that we drive poisonous legenberry quills under his fingernails."

"Maybe that's good enough for a merchant," said Tgara, the stonecutter, "but not for Hadwell. He deserves a chief's death! I move that we tie him down and kindle a small fire beneath his toes, gradually—"

"Wait," said Lag. "The emissary has earned the Death of an Adept. Therefore, let him be taken, tenderly and firmly, to the nearest giant anthill, and there buried to his neck."

There were shouts of approval. Tgara said, "And as long as he screams, the ancient ceremonial drums will pound."

"And there will be dances for him," said Vassi.

"And a glorious drunk," said Kataga.

Everyone agreed that it would be a beautiful death.

So the final details were decided, and a time was set. The village throbbed with religious ecstacy. All the huts were decorated with flowers, except the Shrine of the Instrument, which had to remain bare. The women laughed and sang as they prepared the death feast. Only Mele, for some unaccountable reason, was forlorn. With lowered head she walked through the village and climbed slowly to the hills beyond, to Hadwell.

Hadwell was stripped to the waist and basking under the two suns. "Hi, Mele," he said. "I heard the drums. Is something up?"

"There will be a celebration," Mele said, sitting down beside him.

"That's nice. OK if I attend?"

Mele stared at him, nodding slowly. Her heart melted at the sight of such courage. The emissary was showing a true observance of the ancient punctilio, by which a man pretended that his own death feast was something that really didn't concern him. Men in this day and age were not able to maintain the necessary aplomb. But of course, an emissary of Thangookari would follow the rules better than anyone.

"How soon does it start?"

"In an hour," Mele said. Formerly she had been straightforward and free with him. Now her heart was heavy, oppressed. She didn't know why. Shyly she glanced at his bright alien garments, his red hair.

"Oughta be nice," Hadwell said. "Yessir, it oughta be nice ..." His voice trailed away. From under lowered eyelids he looked at the comely Igathian girl, observed the pure line of neck and shoulder, her straight dark hair, and sensed rather than smelt her faint sachet. Nervously he plucked a blade of grass.

"Mele," he said, "I ..."

The words died on his lips. Suddenly, startlingly, she was in his arms.

"Oh, Mele!"

"Hadwell!" she cried, and strained close to him. Abruptly she pulled free, looking at him with worried eyes.

"What's the matter, honey?" Hadwell asked.

"Hadwell, is there anything more you could do for the village? Anything? My people would appreciate it so."

"Sure there is," Hadwell said, "But I thought I'd rest up first, take it easy."

"No! Please!" she begged. "Those irrigation ditches you spoke of. Could you start them now?"

"If you want me to," Hadwell said. "But—"

"Oh darling!" She sprang to her feet. Hadwell reached for her, but she stepped back.

"There is no time! I must hurry back and tell the village!"

She ran from him. And Hadwell was left to ponder the strange ways of aliens and particularly of alien women.

Mele ran back to the village and found the priest in the temple, praying for wisdom and guidance. Quickly she told him about the emissary's new plans for aiding the village.

The old priest nodded slowly. "Then the ceremony shall be deferred. But tell me, daughter. Why are *you* involved in this?"

Mele blushed and could not answer.

The old priest smiled. But then his face became stern. "I understand. But listen to me, girl. Do not allow love to sway you from the proper worship of Thangookari and from the observances of the ancient ways of our village."

"Of course not!" Mele said. "I simply felt that an Adept's death was not good enough for Hadwell. He deserves more! He deserves—the Ultimate!"

"No man has been worthy of the Ultimate for six hundred years," Lag said, "Not since the hero and demigod, V'Ktat, saved the Igathian race from the dread Huelva Beasts."

"But Hadwell has the stuff of heroes in him," Mele cried. "Give him time, let him strive! He will prove worthy!"

"Perhaps so," the priest mused. "It would be a great thing for the village . . . But consider, Mele! It might take a lifetime for Hadwell to prove himself."

"Wouldn't it be worth waiting for?" she asked.

The old priest fingered his mace, and his forehead wrinkled in thought. "You may be right," he said slowly, "yes, you may be right." Suddenly he straightened and glanced sharply at her.

"But tell me the truth, Mele. Are you really trying to preserve him for the Ultimate Death? Or do you merely want to keep him for yourself?"

"He must have the death he deserves," Mele said serenely. But she was unable to meet the priest's eye.

"I wonder," the old man said. "I wonder what lies in

your heart. I think you tread dangerously close to heresy, Mele. You, who were among the most orthodox."

Mele was about to answer when the merchant, Vassi, rushed into the temple.

"Come quickly!" he cried. "It is the farmer, Iglai! *He has evaded the taboo!*"

The fat, jolly farmer had died a terrible death. He had been walking his usual route from his hut to the village center, past an old thorn tree. Without warning, the tree toppled on him. Thorns had impaled him through and through. Eyewitnesses said the farmer had writhed and moaned for over an hour before expiring.

But he had died with a smile on his face.

The priest looked at the crowd surrounding Iglai's body. Several of the villagers were hiding grins behind their hands. Lag walked over to the thorn tree and examined it. There were faint marks of a saw blade, which had been roughened over and concealed with clay. The priest turned to the crowd.

"Was Iglai near this tree often?" he asked.

"He sure was," another farmer said. "Always ate his lunch under this tree."

The crowd was grinning openly now, proud of Iglai's achievement. Remarks began to fly back and forth.

"I *wondered* why he always ate here."

"Never wanted company. Said he liked to eat alone."

"Hah!"

"He must have been sawing all the time."

"For months, probably. That's tough wood."

"Very clever of Iglai."

"I'll say! He was only a farmer, and no one would call him religious. But he got himself a damned fine death."

"Listen, good people!" cried Lag. "Iglai did a sacrilegious thing! Only a priest can grant a violent death!"

"What the priests don't see can't hurt them," someone muttered.

"So it was sacrilege," another man said. "Iglai got himself a beautiful death. *That's* the important thing."

The old priest turned sadly away. There was nothing he could do. If he had caught Iglai in time, he would have applied strict sanctions. Iglai would never have dared arrange another death and would probably have died quietly and forlornly in bed, at a ripe old age. But now it was too late. The farmer had achieved his death and on the wings of it had already gone to Rookechangi. Asking the god to punish Iglai in the afterlife was useless, for the farmer was right there on the spot to plead his own case.

Lag asked, "Didn't any of you see him sawing that tree?"

If anyone had, he wouldn't admit it. They stuck together, Lag knew. In spite of the religious training he had instilled in them from earliest childhood, they persisted in trying to outwit the priests.

When would they realize that an unauthorized death could never be so satisfying as a death one worked for, deserved, and had performed with all ceremonial observations?

He sighed. Life was sometimes a burden.

A week later, Hadwell wrote in his diary:

There has never been a race like these Igathians. I have lived among them now, eaten and drunk with them, and observed their ceremonies. I know and understand them. And the truth about them is startling, to say the least.

The fact is, *the Igathians do not know the meaning of war*! Consider that, Civilized Man! Never in all their recorded and oral history have they had one. They simply cannot conceive of it. I give the following illustration.

I tried to explain war to Kataga, father of the incomparable Mele. The man scratched his head, and asked, "You say that many kill many? That is war?"

"That's part of it," I said. "Thousands, killing thousands."

"In that case," Kataga said, "many are dead at the same time, in the same way?"

"Correct," said I.

He pondered this for a long time, then turned to me

and said, "It is not good for many to die at the same time in the same way. Not satisfactory. Every man should die his own individual death."

Consider, Civilized Man, the incredible naïveté of that reply. And yet, think of the considerable truth which resides beneath the naïveté; a truth which all might do well to learn.

Moreover, these people do not engage in quarrels among themselves, have no blood feuds, no crimes of passion, no murder.

The conclusion I come to is this: Violent death is *unknown* among these people—except, of course, for accidents.

It is a shame that accidents occur so often here and are so often fatal. But this I ascribe to the wildness of the surroundings and to the lighthearted, devil-may-care nature of the people. And as a matter of fact, even accidents do not go unnoticed and unchecked. The priest, with whom I have formed a considerable friendship, deplores the high accident rate, and is constantly proclaiming against it. Always he urges the people to take more caution.

He is a good man.

And now I write the final, most wonderful news of all. (Hadwell smiled sheepishly, hesitated for a moment, then returned to his notebook.)

Mele has consented to become my wife! As soon as I complete this, the ceremony begins. Already the festivities have started, the feast prepared. I consider myself the most fortunate of men, for Mele is a beautiful woman. And a most unusual woman, as well.

She has great social consciousness. A little *too* much, perhaps. She has been urging me constantly to do work for the village. And I have done much. I have completed an irrigation system for them, introduced several fast-growing food crops, started the profession of metal-working, and other things too numerous to mention. And she wants me to do more, much more.

But here I have put my foot down. I have a right to rest. I want a long, languorous honeymoon, and then a year or so of basking in the sun and finishing my book.

Mele finds this difficult to understand. She keeps on trying to tell me that I *must* continue working. And she speaks of some ceremony involving the "Ultimate" (if my translation is correct).

But I have done enough work. I refused to do more, for a year or two, at least.

This "Ultimate" ceremony is to take place directly after our wedding. I suppose it will be some high honor or other that these simple people wish to bestow on me. I have signified my willingness to accept it.

It should be interesting.

For the wedding the entire village, led by the old priest, marched to the Pinnacle, where all Igathian marriages were performed. The men wore ceremonial feathers, and the women were decked in shell jewelry and iridescent stones. Four husky villagers in the middle of the procession bore a strange-looking apparatus. Hadwell caught only a glimpse of it, but he knew it had been taken, with solemn ceremony, from a plain black-thatched hut which seemed to be a shrine of some sort.

In single file they proceeded over the shaky bridge of vines. Kataga, bringing up the rear, grinned to himself as he secretively slashed again at the worn spot.

The Pinnacle was a narrow spur of black rock thrust out over the sea. Hadwell and Mele stood on the end of it, faced by the priest. The people fell silent as Lag raised his arms.

"Oh great Thangookari!" the priest cried. "Cherish this man Hadwell, your emissary, who has come to us from out of the sky in a shining vehicle, and who has done service for the Igathi such as no man has ever done. And cherish your daughter, Mele. Teach her to love the memory of her husband—*and to remain strong in her tribal beliefs.*"

The priest stared hard at Mele as he said that. And Mele, her head held high, gave him look for look.

"I now pronounce you," said the priest, "man and wife!"

Hadwell clasped his wife in his arms and kissed her. The people cheered. Kataga grinned his sly grin.

"And now," said the priest in his warmest voice, "I have good news for you, Hadwell. Great news!"

"Oh?" Hadwell said, reluctantly releasing his bride.

"We have judged you," said Lag, "and we have found you worthy—of the Ultimate!"

"Why, thanks," Hadwell said.

The priest motioned. Four men came up lugging the strange apparatus which Hadwell had glimpsed earlier. Now he saw that it was a platform the size of a large bed, made of some ancient-looking black wood. Lashed to the frame were various barbs, hooks, sharpened shells and needle-shaped thorns. There were cups, which contained no liquid as yet. And there were other things, strange in shape, whose purpose Hadwell could not guess.

"Not for six hundred years," said Lag, "has this instrument been removed from the Shrine of the Instrument. Not since the days of V'ktat, the hero-god who single-handed saved the Igathian people from destruction. But it has been removed for you, Hadwell!"

"Really, I'm not worthy," Hadwell said.

A murmur rose from the crowd at such modesty.

"Believe me," Lag said earnestly, "you *are* worthy. Do you accept the Ultimate, Hadwell?"

Hadwell looked at Mele. He could not read the expression on her beautiful face. He looked at the priest. Lag's face was impassive. The crowd was deathly still. Hadwell looked at the Instrument. He didn't like its appearance. A doubt began to creep into his mind.

Had he misjudged these people? That Instrument must have been used for torture at some ancient time. Those barbs and hooks . . . But what were the other things for? Thinking hard, Hadwell conceived some of their possible usages, and shuddered. The crowd was closely packed in front of him. Behind him was the narrow point of rock and a sheer thousand-foot drop below it. Hadwell looked again at Mele.

The love and devotion in her face was unmistakable.

Glancing at the villagers, he saw their concern for him. What was he worried about? They would never do anything to harm him, not after all he had done for the village.

The Instrument undoubtedly had some symbolic use.

"I accept the Ultimate," Hadwell said to the priest.

The villagers shouted, a deep-throated roar that echoed from the mountains. They formed closely around him, smiling, shaking his hands.

"The ceremony will take place at once," said the priest. "In the village in front of the statue of Thangookari."

Immediately they started back, the priest leading. Hadwell and his bride were in the center now. Mele still had not spoken since the ceremony.

Silently they crossed the swaying bridge of vines. Once across, the villagers pressed more closely around Hadwell than before, giving him a slightly claustrophobic feeling. If he had not been convinced of their essential goodness, he told himself, he might have felt apprehensive.

Ahead lay the village and the altar of Thangookari. The priest hurried toward it.

Suddenly there was a shriek. Everyone turned and rushed back to the bridge.

At the brink of the river, Hadwell saw what had happened. Kataga, Mele's father, had brought up the rear of the procession. As he had reached the midpoint, the central supporting vine had inexplicably snapped. Kataga had managed to clutch a secondary vine, but only for a moment. As the villagers watched, his hold weakened, released, and he dropped into the river.

Hadwell watched, frozen into shock. With dreamlike clarity he saw it all: Kataga falling, a smile of magnificent courage on his face, the raging white water, the jagged rocks below.

It was a certain terrible death.

"Can he swim?" Hadwell asked Mele.

"No," the girl said. "He refused to learn ... Oh, Father! How could you?"

The raging white water frightened Hadwell more than anything he had ever seen, more than the emptiness of space. But the father of his wife was in danger. A man had to act.

He plunged headlong into the icy water.

Kataga was almost unconscious when Hadwell reached him, which was fortunate, for the Igathian did not struggle when Hadwell seized him by the hair and started to swim vigorously for the nearest shore. But he couldn't make it. Currents swept the men along, pulling them under and throwing them to the surface again. By a strenuous effort, Hadwell was able to avoid the first rocks. But more loomed ahead.

The villagers ran along the bank, shouting at him.

With his strength ebbing rapidly, Hadwell fought again for the shore. A submerged rock scraped his side and his grip on Kataga's hair began to weaken. The Igathian was starting to recover and struggle.

"Don't give up, old man," Hadwell gasped. The bank sped past. Hadwell came within ten feet of it, then the current began to carry him out again.

With his last surge of strength, he managed to grab an overhead branch and to hold on while the current wrenched and tore at his body. Moments later, guided by the priest, the villagers pulled the two men in to the safety of the shore.

They were carried to the village. When Hadwell was able to breathe normally again, he turned and grinned feebly at Kataga.

"Close call, old man," he said.

"Meddler!" Kataga said. He spat at Hadwell and stalked off.

Hadwell stared after him, scratching his head. "Must have affected his brain," he said. "Well, shall we get on with the Ultimate?"

The villagers drew close to him, their faces menacing.

"Hah! The Ultimate he wants!"

"A man like that."

"After dragging poor Kataga out of the river, he has the nerve. . . "

"His own father-in-law and he saves his life!"

"A man like that doesn't even deserve the Ultimate!"

"A man like that," Vassie, the merchant, summed up, "damned well doesn't deserve to die!"

Hadwell wondered if they had all gone temporarily insane. He stood up, a bit shakily, and appealed to the priest.

"What *is* all this?" Hadwell asked.

Lag, with mournful eyes and pale, set lips, stared at him and did not answer.

"Can't I have the Ultimate ceremony?" Hadwell asked, a plaintive note in his voice.

"You *do* deserve it," the priest said. "If any man has ever deserved the Ultimate, you do, Hadwell. I feel you should have it, as a matter of abstract justice. But there is more involved here than abstract justice. There are principles of mercy and human pity which are dear to Thangookari. By these principles, Hadwell, you did a terrible and inhuman thing when you rescued poor Kataga from the river. I am afraid the action is unforgivable."

Hadwell didn't know what to say. Apparently there was some taboo against rescuing men who had fallen into the river. But how could they expect him to know about it? How could they let this one little thing outweigh all he had done for them?

"Isn't there *some* ceremony you can give me?" he begged. "I like you people. I want to live here. Surely there's something you can do."

The old priest's eyes misted with compassion. He gripped his mace, started to lift it.

He was stopped by an ominous roar from the crowd.

"There is nothing I can do," he said. "Leave us, false emissary. Leave us, oh Hadwell—who does not deserve to die!"

"All right!" Hadwell shouted, his temper suddenly snapping. "To hell with you bunch of dirty savages. I wouldn't stay here if you begged me. I'm going. Are you with me, Mele?"

The girl blinked convulsively, looked at Hadwell, then at the priest. There was a long moment of silence. Then the priest murmured, "Remember your father, Mele. Remember the beliefs of your people."

Mele's proud little chin came up. "I know where my duty lies," she said. "Let's go, Richard dear."

"Right," said Hadwell. He stalked off to his spaceship, followed by Mele.

In despair, the old priest watched. He cried, "Mele!"

once, in a heartbroken voice. But Mele did not turn back. He saw her enter the ship, and the port slide shut.

Within minutes, red and blue flames bathed the silver sphere. The sphere lifted, gained speed, dwindled to a speck, and vanished.

Tears rolled down the old priest's cheeks as he watched it go.

Hours later, Hadwell said, "Darling, I'm taking you to Earth, the planet I come from. You'll like it there."

"I know I will," Mele murmured, staring out a porthole at the brilliant spear points of the stars.

Somewhere among them was her home, lost to her forever. She was homesick already. But there had been no other choice. Not for her. A woman goes with the man she loves. And a woman who loves truly and well never loses faith in her man.

Mele hadn't lost faith in Hadwell.

She fingered a tiny sheathed dagger concealed in her clothing. The dagger was tipped with a peculiarly painful and slow-acting poison. It was a family heirloom, to be used when there was no priest around, and only on those one loved most dearly.

"I'm through wasting my time," Hadwell said. "With your help I'm going to do great things. You'll be proud of me, sweetheart."

Mele knew he meant it. Someday, she thought, Hadwell would atone for the sin against her father. He would do something, some fine deed, perhaps today, perhaps tomorrow, perhaps next year. And then she would give him the most precious thing a woman can give to a man.

A painful death.

INVASION OF PRIVACY

by Bob Shaw

"I saw Granny Cummins again today," Sammy said through a mouthful of turnip and potato.

May's fork clattered into her plate. She turned her head away, and I could see there were tears in her eyes. In my opinion she had always been much too deeply attached to her mother, but this time I could sympathize with her—there was something about the way the kid had said it.

"Listen to me, Sammy." I leaned across the table and gripped his shoulder. "The next time you make a dumb remark like that I'll paddle your backside good and hard. It wasn't funny."

He gazed at me with all the bland defiance a seven-year-old can muster. "I wasn't trying to be funny. I saw her."

"Your Granny's been dead for two weeks," I snapped, exasperated both at him and at May, who was letting the incident get too far under her skin. Her lips had begun to tremble.

"Two weeks," Sammy repeated, savoring the words. He had just discovered sarcasm and I could tell by his eyes he was about to try some on. "If she'd only been dead two days it woulda been all right, I suppose. But not two weeks, eh?" He rammed a huge blob of creamed potato into his mouth with a flourish.

"George!" May's brown eyes were spilling as she looked at me and the copper strands of her hair quivered with anger. "Do something to that *child*! Make him drop dead."

"I can't smack him for that, hon," I said reasonably. "The kid was only being logical. Remember in *Decline and Fall* where a saint got her head chopped off, then was supposed to get up and walk a mile or so to the burial ground, and religious writers made a great fuss about the distance she'd covered, and Gibbon said in a case like that the distance wasn't the big thing—it was the taking of the first step? Well—" I broke off as May fled from the table and ran upstairs. The red sunlight of an October evening glowed on her empty chair, and Sammy continued eating.

"See what you've done?" I rapped his blonde head with my knuckles, but not sharply enough to hurt. "I'm letting you off this time—for the *last* time—but I can't let you go on upsetting your mother with a stupid joke. Now cut it out."

Sammy addressed the remains of his dinner. "I wasn't joking. I . . . saw . . . Granny . . . Cummins."

"She's been dead and buried for—" I almost said two weeks again, but stopped as an expectant look appeared on his face. He was quite capable of reproducing the same sarcasm word for word. "How do you explain that?"

"Me?" A studied look of surprise. "I can't explain it. I'm just telling you what I seen."

"All right—where did you see her?"

"In the old Guthrie place, of course."

Of course, I thought with a thrill of something like nostalgia. Where else? Every town, every district in every city, has its equivalent of the old Guthrie place. To find it, you simply stop any small boy and ask him if he knows of a haunted house where grisly murders are committed on a weekly schedule and vampires issue forth at night. I sometimes think that if no suitable building existed already the community of children would create one to answer a dark longing in their collective mind. But the building is always there—a big, empty, ramshackle place, usually screened by near-black evergreens, never put up for sale, never pulled down, always possessing a magical immunity to property developers. And in the small town where I live the old Guthrie house was the one which filled the bill. I hadn't really thought about it since childhood, but it looked just the same as ever—dark, shabby and forbidding—and I should have known it would have the same associations for another generation of kids. At the mention of the house Sammy had become solemn and I almost laughed aloud as I saw myself, a quarter of a century younger, in his face.

"How could you have seen anything in there?" I decided to play along a little further as long as May was out of earshot. "It's too far from the road."

"I climbed through the fence."

"Who was with you?"

"Nobody."

"You went in alone?"

"Course I did." Sammy tilted his head proudly and I recalled that as a seven-year-old nothing in the world would have induced me to approach that house, even in company. I looked at my son with a new respect, and the first illogical stirrings of alarm.

"I don't want you hanging around that old place, Sammy—it could be dangerous."

"It isn't dangerous." He was scornful. "They just sit there in big chairs, and never move."

"I meant you could fall or . . . *what*?"

"The old people just sit there." Sammy pushed his empty plate away. "They'd never catch me in a hundred years even if they seen me, but I don't let them see me, cause I just take one quick look through the back window and get out of there."

"You mean there are people living in the Guthrie place?"

"Old people. Lots of them. They just sit there in big chairs."

I hadn't heard anything about the house being occupied, but I began to guess what had been going on. It was big enough for conversion to a private home for old people—and to a child one silver-haired old lady could look very much like another. Perhaps Sammy preferred to believe his grandmother had moved away rather than accept the idea that she was dead and buried beneath the ground in a box.

"Then you were trespassing as well as risking—" I lowered my voice to a whisper as May's footsteps sounded on the stairs again. "You didn't see your Granny Cummins, you're not to go near the old Guthrie place again, and you're not to upset your mother. Got that?"

Sammy nodded, but his lips were moving silently and I knew he was repeating his original statement over and over to himself. Any anger I felt was lost in a tide of affection—my entire life had been one of compromise and equivocation, and it was with gratitude I had discovered that my son had been born with enough will and sheer character for the two of us.

May came back into the room and sat down, her face wearing a slightly shamefaced expression behind the gold sequins of its freckles. "I took a tranquilizer."

"Oh? I thought you were out of them."

"I was, but Doctor Pitman stopped by this afternoon and he let me have some more."

"Did you call him?"

"No—he was in the neighborhood and he looked in just to see how I was. He's been very good since ... since—"

"Since your mother died—you've got to get used to the idea, May."

She nodded silently and began to gather up the dinner plates. Her own food had scarcely been touched.

"Mom?" Sammy tugged her sleeve. I tensed, waiting for him to start it all over again, but he had other things on his mind. His normally ruddy cheeks were pale as tallow and his forehead was beaded with perspiration. I darted from my chair barely in time to catch him as he fell sideways to the floor.

Bob Pitman had been a white-haired, apple-cheeked old gentleman when he was steering me through boyhood illnesses, and he appeared not to have aged any further in the interim. He lived alone in an unfashionably large house, still wore a conservative dark suit with a watch chain's gold parabola spanning the vest, played chess as much as possible and drank specially imported non-blended Scotch. The sight of his square hands, with their ridged and slablike fingernails, moving over Sammy's sleeping figure comforted me even before he stood up and folded the stethoscope.

"The boy has eaten something he shouldn't," he said drawing the covers up to Sammy's chin.

"But he'll be all right?" May and I spoke simultaneously.

"Right as rain."

"Thank God," May said and sat down very suddenly. I knew she had been thinking about her mother and wondering if we were going to lose Sammy with as little warning.

"You'd better get some rest," Dr. Pitman looked at her with kindly severity. "Young Sammy here will sleep all night, and you should follow his example. Take another of those caps I gave you this morning."

I'd forgotten about his earlier visit. "We seem to be monopolizing your time today, doctor."

"Just think of it as providing me with a little employment—everybody's far too healthy these days." He shepherded us out of Sammy's room. "I'll call again in the morning."

May wasn't quite satisfied; she was scrupulously hygienic in the kitchen and the idea that our boy had food poisoning was particularly unacceptable to her. "But what could Sammy have eaten, Doctor? We've had everything he's had and we're all right."

"It's hard to say. When he brought up his dinner did you notice anything else there? Berries? Exotic candies?"

"No. Nothing like that," I said, "but they wouldn't always be obvious, would they?" I put my arm around May's shoulders and tried to force her to relax. She was rigid with tension and it came to me that if Sammy ever were to contract a fatal illness or be killed in an accident it would destroy her. We of the twentieth century have abandoned the practice of holding something in reserve when we love our children, assuming—as our ancestors would never have dared to do—that they will reach adulthood as a matter of course.

The doctor, nodding and smiling and wheezing, exuded reassurance for a couple more minutes before he left. When I took May to bed she huddled in the crook of my left arm, lonely in spite of our intimacy, and it was a long time before I was able to soothe her to sleep.

In spite of her difficulty in getting to sleep, or perhaps because of it, May failed to waken when I slipped out of bed early next morning. I went into Sammy's room, and knew immediately that something was wrong. His breathing was noisy and rapid as that of a pup which has been running. I went to the bed. He was unconscious, mouth wide open in the ghastly breathing, and his forehead hotter than I would have believed it possible for a human's to be.

Fear spurted coldly in my guts as I turned and ran for the phone. I dialed Dr. Pitman's number. While it was ringing I debated shouting upstairs to waken May, but far from being able to help Sammy she would probably have become hysterical. I decided to let her sleep as long as possible. After a seemingly interminable wait the phone clicked.

"Dr. Pitman speaking." The voice was sleepy.

"This is George Ferguson. Sammy's very ill. Could you get over here right away?" I babbled a description of the symptoms.

"I'll be right there." The sleepiness had left his voice. I hung up, opened the front door wide so that the doctor could come straight in, then went back upstairs and waited beside the bed. Sammy's hair was plastered to his forehead and his every breath was accompanied by harsh metalic clicks in his throat. My mind became an anvil for the hammer blows of the passing seconds. Bleak eons went by before I heard Dr. Pitman's footsteps on the stairs.

He came into the room, looking uncharacteristically disheveled, took one look at Sammy and lifted him in his arms in a cocoon of bedding.

"Pneumonia," he said tersely. "The boy will have to be hospitalized immediately."

Somehow I managed to speak. "Pneumonia! But you said he'd eaten something."

"There's no connection between this and what was wrong yesterday. There's a lightning pneumonia on the move across the country."

"Oh. Shall I ring for an ambulance?"

"No. I'll drive him to the clinic myself. The streets are clear at this hour of the morning and we'll make better time." He carried Sammy towards the door with surprising ease.

"Wait. I'm coming with you."

"You could help more by phoning the clinic and alerting them, George. Where's your wife?"

"Still asleep—she doesn't know." I had almost forgotten about May.

He raised his eyebrows, pausing briefly on the landing. "Ring the clinic first, tell them I'm coming, then waken your wife. Don't let her get too worried, and don't get too tensed up yourself—I've an emergency oxygen kit in the car, and Sammy should be all right once we get him into an intensive care unit."

I nodded gratefully, watching my son's blindly lolling face as he was carried down the stairs, then went to the phone and called the clinic. The people I spoke to sounded both efficient and sympathetic, and it was only a matter of seconds before I was sprinting upstairs to waken May. She was sitting on the edge of the bed as I entered the room.

"George?" Her voice was cautious. "What's happening?"

"Sammy has pneumonia. Dr. Pitman's driving him to the clinic now, and he's going to be well taken care of." I was getting dressed as I spoke, praying she would be able to take the news with some semblance of calm. She stood up quietly and began to put on clothes, moving with mechanical exactitude, and when I glimpsed her eyes I suddenly realized it would have been better had she screamed or thrown a fit. We went down to the car, shivering in the thick gray air of the October morning, and drove towards the clinic. At the end of the street I remembered I had left the front door of the house open, but didn't turn back. I think I'd done it deliberately, hoping—with a quasireligious irrationality—that we might be robbed and thus appease the Fates, diverting their attention from Sammy. There was little traffic on the roads but I drove at moderate speed, aware that I had virtually no powers of concentration for anything extraneous to the domestic tragedy. May sat beside me and gazed out the windows with the air of a child reluctantly returning from a long vacation.

It was with a sense of surprise that, on turning into the

clinic grounds, I saw Dr. Pitman's blue Buick sliding to a halt under the canopy of the main entrance. In my estimation he should have been a good ten minutes ahead of us. May's fingers clawed into my thigh as she saw the white bundle being lifted out and carried into the building by a male nurse. I parked close to the entrance, heedless of painted notices telling me the space was for doctors only, and we ran into the dimness of the reception hall. There was no sign of Sammy, but Dr. Pitman was waiting for us.

"You just got here," I accused. "What held you up?"

"Be calm, George. Getting into a panic won't help things in the least." He urged us towards a row of empty chairs. "Nothing held me back—I was driving with one hand and feeding your boy oxygen with the other."

"I'm sorry, it's just . . . how is he?"

"Still breathing, and that's the main thing. Pneumonia's never to be taken lightly—especially this twelve-hour variety we've been getting lately—but there's every reason for confidence."

May stirred slightly at that—I think she had been expecting to hear the worst—but I had a conviction Dr. Pitman was merely trying to let us down as gently as he could. He had always had an uncompromisingly level stare, but now his gaze kept sliding away from mine. We waited a long time for the news of Sammy's condition, and on the few occasions when I caught Dr. Pitman looking directly at me his eyes were strangely like those of a man in torment.

I thought, too, that he was relieved when one of the doctors on the staff of the clinic used all his authority to persuade May it would be much better for everybody if she waited at home.

The house was lonely that evening. May had refused sedation and was sitting with the telephone, nursing it in her lap, as though it might at any minute speak with Sammy's own voice. I made sandwiches and coffee but she wouldn't eat, and this somehow made it impossible for me to eat anything. Tiny particles of darkness came drifting at dusk, gathering in all the corners and passageways of the house, and I finally realized I would have to get out under the sky. May nodded abstractedly when I told her I was going for a short walk. I switched on all the lights in the lounge before leaving, but when I looked back from the sidewalk she had turned them off again.

Go ahead, I raged. *Sit in the darkness—a lot of good that will do him*.

My anger subsided when I remembered that May was at least clinging to hope; whereas I had resigned myself, betraying my own son but not daring to believe he would recover in case I'd be hurt once more. I walked quickly but aimlessly, trying to think practical thoughts about how long I'd be absent from the drafting office where I worked and wondering if the contract I was partway through could be taken over by another man. But instead I kept seeing my boy's face, and at times I sobbed aloud to the uncomprehending quietness of suburban avenues.

I don't know what took me in the direction of the old Guthrie place—perhaps some association between it and dark forces threatening Sammy—but there it was, looming up at the end of a short cul-de-sac, looking exactly as it had when I was at school. The stray fingers of light reaching it from the road showed boarded-up windows, sagging gutters and unpainted boards which were silver-gray from exposure. I examined the building, soberly, feeling echoes of the childhood dread it had once inspired. My theory about it having been renovated and put to use had been wrong, I realized—I'd been a victim of Sammy's hyperactive imagination and mischieviousness.

I was turning away when I noticed fresh car tracks in the gravel of the leaf-stewn drive leading up to the house. Nothing very odd about that, I thought. Curiosity could lead anybody to drive up to the old pile for a closer look, and yet . . .

Suddenly I could see apples in a tree at the rear of the house.

The fruit appeared as blobs of yellowish luminescence in the tree's black silhouette, and I stared at them for several seconds wondering why the sight should fill me with unease. Then the answer came. At that distance from the streetlights the apples should have been invisible, but they were glowing like dim fairy lanterns—

which meant they were being illuminated from another, nearer source. This simple application of the inverse square law led me to the astonishing conclusion that there was a lighted window at the back of the Guthrie house.

On the instant, I was a small boy again. I wanted to run away, but in my adult world there was no longer any place to which I could flee—and I was curious about what was going on in the old house. There was enough corroboration of Sammy's story to make it clear that he had seen something. But old people sitting in big chairs? I went slowly and self-consciously through the drifts of moist leaves, inhaling the toadstool smell of decay, and moved along the side of the house towards crawling blackness. It seemed impossible that there could be anybody within those flaking walls; the light must have been left burning, perhaps weeks earlier, by a careless real estate man.

I skirted a heap of rubbish and reached the back of the house. A board had been loosened on one of the downstairs windows, creating a small triangular aperture through which streamed a wan lemon radiance. I approached it quietly and looked in. The room beyond was lit by a naked bulb and contained perhaps eight armchairs, each of which was occupied by an old man or an old woman. Most were reading magazines, but one woman was knitting. My eyes took in the entire scene in a single sweep, then fastened on the awful, familiar face of the woman in the chair nearest the window.

Sammy had been right—it was the face of his dead grandmother.

That was when the nightmare really began. The frightened child within me and the adult George Ferguson both agreed they had stumbled on something monstrous, and that adrenaline-boosted flight was called for, yet—as in a nightmare—I was unable to do anything but move closer to the focus of horror. I stared at the old woman in dread. Her rawboned face, the lump beneath one ear, the very way she held her magazine—all these told me I was looking at May's mother, Mrs. Martha Cummins, who had died suddenly of a brain hemorrhage more than two weeks earlier, and who was buried in the family plot.

Of its own accord, my right hand went snaking into the triangular opening and tapped the dusty glass. It was a timid gesture and none of the people within responded to the faint sound, but a second later one of the men raised his head briefly as he turned a page, and I recognized him: Joe Bryant, the caretaker at Sammy's school. He had died a year ago of a heart attack.

Explanation? I couldn't conceive one, but I had to speak to the woman who appeared to be May's mother.

I turned away from the window and went to the back rectangle of the house's rear door. It was locked in the normal way and further secured by a bolted-on padlock. A slick moisture on its working parts told me the padlock was in good condition. I moved further along and tried another smaller window in what could have been the kitchen. It too was boarded up, but when I pulled experimentally at the short planks the whole frame moved slightly with a pulpy sound. A more determined tug brought the entire metal window frame clear of its surround of rotting wood, creating a dark opening. The operation was noisier than I had expected, but the house still remained still and I set the window down against the wall.

Part of my mind was screaming its dismay, but I used the window frame as a ladder and climbed through onto a greasy complicated surface which proved to be the top of an old-fashioned gas cooker. My cigarette lighter shed silver sparks as I flicked it on. Its transparent blue shoot of flame cast virtually no light, so I tore pages from my notebook and lit them. The kitchen was a shambles and obviously not in use—in fact which, had I thought about it, would have increased my sense of alarm. A short corridor led from it in the general direction of the lighted room. Burning more pages, I went towards the room, freezing each time a bare floorboard groaned or a loose strip of wallpaper brushed my shoulder, and soon was able to discern a gleam of light coming from below a door. I gripped the handle firmly and, afraid to hesitate, flung open the door. The old people in the big armchairs turned their pink, lined faces toward mine. Mrs. Cummins stared at me, face lengthening with what could have been recognition or shock.

"It's George," I heard myself say in the distance. "What's happening here?"

She stood up and her lips moved. "Nigi olon prittle o czanig *sovisess!*" On the final word the others jumped to their feet with strangely lithe movements.

"Mrs. Cummins?" I said. "Mr. Bryant?"

The old people set their magazines down and came towards the door, and I saw that their feet were bare. I backed out into the corridor, shaking my head apologetically, then turned to run. Could I get out through the small kitchen window quickly enough? A hand clawed down my back. I beat it off and ran in the direction opposite to the kitchen, guided by the light spilling from the room behind me. A door loomed up on my left. I burst through into pitch darkness, slammed it, miraculously found a key in the lock and twisted it. The door quivered as something heavy thudded against the wood from the other side, and a woman's voice began an unnerving wail—thin, high, anxious.

I groped for the light switch and turned it on, but nothing happened. Afraid to take a step forward, I stared into the blackness that pressed against my face, gradually becoming aware of a faint soupy odor and a feeling of warmth. I guessed I was in a room at the front of the house and might be able to break out if only I could find a window. The wallpaper beside the switch had felt loose. I gripped a free edge, pulled off a huge swathe and rolled it into the shape of a torch while the hammering of the door grew more frantic. The blue cone of flame from my cigarette lighter ignited the dry paper immediately. I held the torch high and got a flickering view of a large square room, a bank of electronic equipment along one wall, and a waist-high tank which occupied most of the floor space. The sweet soupy smell appeared to be coming from the dark liquid in the tank. I looked into it and saw a half-submerged *thing* floating face upwards. It was about the size of a seven-year-old boy and the dissolving, jellied features had a resemblance to . . .

No!

I screamed and threw the flaming torch from me, seeking my former state of blindness. The torch landed

close to a wall and trailing streamers of wallpaper caught
alight. I ran around the tank to a window, wadded its
moldering drapes and smashed the glass outwards against
the boards. The planking resisted the onslaught of my
feet and fists for what seemed an eternity, then I was out
in the cool fresh air and running, barely feeling the
ground below my feet, swept along by the dark winds of
night.

When I finally looked back, blocks away, the sky
above the old Guthrie place was already stained red, and
clouds of angry sparks wheeled and wavered in the
ascending smoke.

How does one assimilate an experience like that? There
were some aspects of the nightmare which my mind was
completely unable to handle as I walked homewards,
accompanied by the sound of distant fire sirens. There
was, for example, the hard fact that I had started a fire in
which at that very instant a group of old people could be
perishing—but somehow, I felt no guilt. In its place was a
conviction that if the blaze hadn't begun by accident I
would have been entitled, *obliged*, to start one to rid the
world of something which hadn't any right to exist. There
was no element of the religious in my thinking, because
the final horror in the house's front room had dispelled
the aura of the supernatural surrounding the previous
events.

I had seen an array of electronic equipment—unfamiliar in type, but unmistakable—and I had seen a
thing floating in a tank of heated organic-smelling fluid,
a thing which resembled . . .

No! Madness lay along that avenue of thought. Insup-
portable pain.

What else had I stumbled across? Granny Cummins
was dead—but she had been sitting in the back room of an
unused house and had spoken in a tongue unlike any
language I'd ever heard. Joe Bryant was dead, for a year,
yet he too had been sitting under that naked bulb. My son
was seriously ill in hospital, and yet . . .

No!

Retreating from monstrosities as yet unguessed, my

mind produced an image of Dr. Pitman. He had attended
Granny Cummins. He had, I was almost certain, been the
Bryant's family doctor. He had attended Sammy that
morning. He had been in my home the previous day—
perhaps when Sammy had come in and spoke of seeing
people in the old Guthrie place. My mind then threw up
another image—that of the long-barreled .22 target pistol
lying in a drawer in my den. I began to walk more quickly.

On reaching home the first impression was that May
had gone out, but when I went in she was sitting in exactly
the same place in the darkness of the lounge. I glanced at
my watch and discovered that, incredibly, only forty
minutes had passed since I had gone out. That was all the
time it had taken for reality to rot and dissolve.

"May?" I spoke from the doorway. "Did the clinic
call?"

A long pause. "No."

"Don't you want the light on?"

Another pause. "No."

This time I didn't mind, because the darkness
concealed the fact that my clothes were smeared with dirt
and blood from my damaged hands. I went upstairs, past
the aching emptiness of Sammy's room, washed in cold
water, taped my knuckles and put on fresh clothes. In my
den I discovered that the saw-handled target pistol was
never meant for concealment, but I was able to tuck it
into my belt on the left side and cover it fairly well with
my jacket. Coming downstairs, I hesitated at the door of
the lounge before telling May I was going out again. She
nodded without speaking, without caring what I might
do. If Sammy died she would die too—not physically, not
clinically, but just as surely—which meant that two
important lives depended on my actions of the next hour.

I went out and found the atmosphere of the night had
changed to one of feverish excitement. The streets were
alive with cars, pedestrians, running children, all con-
verging on the gigantic bonfire which had appeared,
gratuitously, to turn a dull evening into an event. Two
blocks away to the south the old Guthrie house was an
inferno which streaked the windows of the entire neighborhood with amber and gold. Its timbers exploding in

ragged volleys, were fireworks contributing to the Fourth of July atmosphere. A group of small boys scampering past me whooped with glee, and one part of my mind acknowledged that I had made a major contribution to the childish lore of the district. Legends would be born tonight, to be passed in endless succession from the mouths of ten-year-olds to the ears of five-year-olds. *The night the old Guthrie place burned down* . . .

Dr. Pitman lived only a mile from me, and I decided it would be almost as quick and a lot less conspicuous to go on foot. I walked automatically, trying to balance the elements of reality, nightmare and carnival, and reached the doctor's home in a little over ten minutes. His Buick was sitting in the driveway and lights were showing in the upper windows of the house. I looked around carefully —the fire was further away now and neighbors were less likely to be distracted by it—before stepping into the shadowed drive and approaching the front door. It burst open just as I was reaching the steps and Dr. Pitman came running out, still shrugging on his coat. I reached for the pistol but there was no need to bring it into view, for he stopped as soon as he saw me.

"George!" His face creased with concern. "What brings you here? Is it your boy?"

"You've guessed it." I put my hand on his chest and pushed him back into the orange-lit hall.

"What is this?" He surged against my hand with surprising strength and I had to fight to contain him. "You're acting a little strangely, George."

"You made Sammy sick," I told him. "And if you don't make him well again I'll kill you."

"Hold on, George—I told you not to get over-wrought."

"I'm not overwrought."

"It's the strain—"

"*That's enough*!" I shouted at him, almost losing control. "I know you're making Sammy ill, and I'm going to make you stop."

"But why should I . . . ?"

"Because he was in back of the old Guthrie place and saw too much—that's why." I pushed harder on his chest and he took a step backwards into the hall.

"The Guthrie house! No, George, *no!*"

Until that moment I had been half-prepared to back down, to accept the idea that I'd gone off the rails with worry, but his face became a slack gray mask. The strength seemed to leave his body, making him smaller and older.

"Yes, the old Guthrie place." I closed the door behind him. "What do you do there, doctor?"

"Listen, George, I can't talk to you now—I've just heard there's a fire in the district and I've got to go to it. My help will be needed." Dr. Pitman drew himself up into a semblance of the authoritative figure I had once known, and tried to push past me.

"You're too late," I said, blocking his way. "The place went up like a torch. Your equipment's all gone." I paused and stared into his eyes. "*They're* all gone."

"I . . . I don't know what you mean."

"The things you make. The things which look like people, but which aren't because the original people are dead. Those are all gone, doctor—burnt up." I was shooting wildly in the dark, but I could tell some of my words were finding a mark and I pressed on. "I was there, and I've seen it, and I'll tell the whole world—so Sammy isn't alone now. His death won't cover up anything. Do you hear me, doctor?"

He shook his head, then walked away from me and went up the broad carpeted stairs. I reached for the pistol, changed my mind and ran after him, catching him just as he reached the landing. He brushed my hands away. Using all my strength, I bundled him against the wall with my forearm pressed across his throat, determined to force the truth out of him—no matter what it might be. He twisted away, I grappled again, and we overbalanced and went on a jarring rollercoaster ride down the stairs, bouncing and flailing, caroming off wall and bannisters. Twice on the way down I felt, and heard, bones breaking; and I had been lying on the hall floor for a good ten seconds before being certain they weren't mine.

I raised myself on one arm and looked down into Dr. Pitman's face. His teeth were smeared with blood and for a moment I felt the beginnings of doubt. He was an old man, and supposing he genuinely hadn't understood a word I had been saying. . . .

"You've done it now, George," he whispered. "You've finished us."

"What do you mean?"

"There's one thing I want you to believe . . . we never harmed anybody . . . we've seen too much pain for that—" He coughed and a transparent crimson film spanned his lips.

"What are you saying?"

"It was to be a very quiet, very gradual invasion . . . invasion's the wrong word . . . no conquest or displacement intended . . . physical journey from our world virtually impossible . . . we observed incurably ill humans, terminal cases . . . built duplicates and substituted them . . . that way we too could live normally, almost normally, for a while . . . until death returned—"

"Dr. Pitman," I said desperately, "you're not making sense."

"I'm not real Dr. Pitman . . . he died many years ago . . . first subject in this town—a doctor is in best position for our . . . I was *skorded*—you have no word for it—transmitted into a duplicate of his body—"

The hall floor seemed to rock beneath me. "You're saying you're from another planet!"

"That's right, George."

"But, for God's sake, *why*? Why would anybody—"

"Just be thankful you can't imagine the circumstances which made such a project . . . desirable." His body convulsed with sudden pain.

"I still don't understand," I pleaded. "Why should you duplicate the bodies of dying people if it means being locked in an old house for the rest of your life?"

"Usually it doesn't mean that . . . we substitute and integrate . . . the dying person appears to recover . . . but the duplication process takes time, and sometimes the subject dies suddenly, at home, providing us with no chance to take his place . . . and there can be no going back—"

I froze as a brilliant golden light flooded through the

hall. It was followed by the sound of wheels on gravel and I realized a car had pulled into the driveway of the house. The man I knew as Dr. Pitman closed his eyes and sighed deeply, with an awful finality.

"But what about Sammy?" I shook the inert figure. "You've told me nothing about my son."

The eyes blinked open, slowly, and in spite of the pain there I saw—kindness. "It was all a mistake, George." His voice was distant as he attempted more of the broken sentences. "I had no idea he had been around the old house . . . aren't like you—we're bad organizers . . . *nald denbo sovisegg* . . . sorry . . . I had nothing to do with his illness—"

A car door slammed outside. I wanted to run, but there was one more question which had to be asked. "I was in the old house. I saw the tank and . . . something . . . which looked like a boy. Does that mean Sammy's dying? That you were going to replace him?"

"Sammy's going to be all right, George . . . though at first I wasn't hopeful . . . I haven't known you and May as long as Dr. Pitman did, but I'm very fond of . . . I knew May couldn't take the loss, so I arranged a substitution . . . tentatively, you understand, *kleyl nurr* . . . not needed now . . . Sammy will be fine—" He tried to smile at me and blood welled up between his lips just as the doorbell rang with callous stridency.

I stared down at the tired, broken old man with—in spite of everything—a curious sense of regret. What kind of hell had he been born into originally? What conditions would prompt anybody to make the journey he had made for such meager rewards? The bell rang again and I opened the door.

"Call for an ambulance," I said to the stranger on the steps. "Dr. Pitman seems to have fallen down the stairs—I think he's dying."

It was quite late when the police cruiser finally dropped me outside my home, but the house was ablaze with light. I thanked the sergeant who had driven me from the mortuary where they had taken the body of Dr. Pitman (I couldn't think of him by any other name) and hurried along the white concrete of the path to the door. The lights seemed to signal a change in May's mood but I was afraid to begin hoping, in case . . .

"George!" May met me at the door, dressed to go out, face pale but jubilant. "Where've you been? I tried everywhere. The clinic called me half an hour ago. You've been out for hours. Sammy's feeling better and he's asking to see us. I brought the car out for you. Should I drive? We're allowed to see him, and I—"

"Slow down, May. Slow down." I put my arms around her, feeling the taut gratification in her slim body, and made her go over the story again. She spilled it out eagerly.

Sammy's response to drug treatment had been dramatic and now he was fully conscious and asking for his parents. The senior doctor had decided to bend regulations a little and let us in to talk with the boy for a few minutes. A starshell of happiness burst behind my eyes as May spoke, and a minute later we were on our way to the clinic. A big moon, the exact color of a candle flame, was rising behind the rooftops, trees were stirring gently in their sleep, and the red glow from the direction of the Guthrie house had vanished. May was at the wheel, driving with zestful competence, and for the first time in hours the pressure was off me.

I relaxed into the seat and discovered I had forgotten to rid myself of the pistol which had nudged my ribs constantly the whole time I was talking to the police. It was on the side next to May so there was little chance of slipping it into the glove compartment unnoticed. Shame at having carried the weapon, plus a desire not to alarm May in any way after what she had been through, made me decide to keep it out of sight a little longer. Suddenly very tired, I closed my eyes and allowed the mental backwash of the night's events to carry me away.

The disjointed fragments from Dr. Pitman made an unbelievable story when pieced together, yet I had seen the ghastly proof. There was something macabre about the idea of the group of alien beings, duplicates of dead people, cooped up in a dingy room in an unused house, patiently waiting to die. The memory of seeing Granny

Cummins' face again, two weeks after her funeral, was going to take a long time to fade. She, the duplicate, had recognized me, which meant that the copying technique used by the aliens was incredibly detailed, extending right down to the arrangement of the brain cells. Presumably, the only physical changes they would introduce would be improvements—if a person was dying of cancer the duplicate would be cancer-free. Aging muscles might be strengthened—Dr. Pitman and those who had been in the house all moved with exceptional ease. But would they have been able to escape the fire? Perhaps some code of their own would not allow them to leave the house, even under peril of death, unless a place had been prepared to enable them to enter our society without raising any alarms . . .

The aliens may have a code of ethics, I thought, *but could I permit them to come among us unhindered*? For that matter, had I any idea how far their infiltration had proceeded? I'd been told that Dr Pitman was the first subject *in this town*—did that mean the invasion covered the entire state? The country? The world? There was also a question of its intensity. The dying man had said the substitution technique failed when a person's death occurred suddenly *at home*, which implied the clinic was well infiltrated—but how thoroughly? Would there come a day when every old person in the world, and a proportion of younger people as well, would be substitutes?

Street lights flickering past the car pulsed redly through my closed eyelids, and fresh questions pounded in my mind to the same rhythm. Could I believe anything "Dr. Pitman" had said about the aliens' objectives? True, he had appeared kind, genuinely concerned about Sammy and May—but how did one interpret facial expressions controlled by a being who may once have possessed an entirely different form? Another question came looming —and something in my subconscious cowered away from it—why, if secrecy were so vital to the aliens' scheme, had "Dr. Pitman" told me the whole fantastic story? Had he been manipulating me in some way I had not yet begun to understand? Once again I saw my son's face blindly lolling as he was carried down the stairs, and a fear greater than any I had known before began to unfold its black petals.

I jerked my eyes open, unwilling to think any further.

"Poor thing—you're tired," May said. "You keep everything bottled up, and it takes far more out of you that way."

I nodded. *She's mothering me*, I thought. *She's happy, serene, confident again—and it's because our boy is getting better. Sammy's life is her life.*

May slowed the car down. "Here we are. We mustn't stay too long—it's very good of Dr. Milligan even to let us in at this time."

I remembered Dr. Milligan—tall, stooped and *old*. Another Dr. Pitman? It came to me suddenly that I had told May nothing at all about the events of the evening, but before I could work out a suitably edited version we were getting out of the car. I decided to leave it till later. In contrast to the boisterous leaf-scented air outside the atmosphere in the clinic seemed inert, dead. The reception office was empty but a blonde young doctor with an in-twisted foot limped up to us, then beckoned to a staff nurse when we gave our names. The nurse, a tall woman with mottled red forearms, ushered us into the elevator and pressed the button for the third floor.

"Samuel is making exceptional progress," she said to May. "He's a very strong little boy."

"Thank you." May nodded gratefully. "Thank you."

I wanted to change the subject, because Sammy had never appeared particularly strong to my eyes, and the loathsome blossom of fear was fleshing its leaves within me. "How's business been tonight?"

"Quiet, for once. Very quiet."

"Oh. I heard there was a fire."

"It hasn't affected us."

"That's fine," I said vaguely. If the aliens were constructed with precisely the same biological building blocks as humans their remains would appear like those of normal fire victims. *There'll be hell to pay*, I told myself and desperately tried to adhere to that line of thought, but the black flower was getting bigger now, unmanageable, reaching out to swallow me. Biological building blocks—where did they come from? The dark soupy liquid in the tank—was it of synthetic or natural origin? The thing I'd seen floating in there—was it a body being constructed?

Or was it being dissolved and fed into a stockpile of organic matter?

Had I seen my son's corpse?

Other thoughts came yammering and cavorting like demons. "Dr. Pitman" had taken Sammy to the clinic in his own car, but he had been strangely delayed in arriving. Obviously he had taken the boy to the Guthrie place. Why? Because, according to his own dying statement he had despaired of Sammy's life, wanted to spare May the shock of losing her son and had arranged for a substitution—just in case. Altruistic. Unbelievably altruistic. How gullible did "Dr. Pitman" think I was going to be? If Sammy had died naturally, or had been killed, and replaced by a being from beyond the stars I was going to make trouble for the aliens. I was going to shout and burn and kill . . .

With an effort I controlled the sudden trembling in my limbs as the nurse opened the door to a small private room. The shaded light within showed Sammy sleeping peacefully in a single bed. My heart ached with the recognition of the flesh of my flesh.

"You may go in for a minute, but *just* a minute," the nurse said. Her eyes lingered for a moment on May's face and something she saw there prompted her to remain in the corridor while we went into the room. Sammy was pale but breathing easily. The skin of his forehead shone with gold borrowed from last summer's sun. May held my arm with both hands as we stood beside the bed.

"He's all right," she breathed. "Oh, George—I would have died."

At the sound of her voice Sammy's eyelids seemed to flicker slightly, but he remained still. May began to sob, silently and effortlessly, adjusting emotional potentials.

"Take it easy, hon," I said. "He's all right, remember."

"I know, but I felt it was all my fault."

"Your fault?"

"Yes. Yesterday at dinner he made me so angry by talking that way about my mother . . . I said I wanted him to drop dead."

"That's being silly."

"I know, but I *said* it, and you should never say anything like that in case—"

"Fate isn't so easily tempted," I said with a calm reasonableness I had no right to assume. "Besides you didn't mean it. Every parent knows that when a kid starts wearing you down you can say anything."

Sammy's eyes opened wide. "Mom?"

May dropped to her knees. "I'm here, Sammy. I'm here."

"I'm sorry I made you mad." His voice was small and drowsy.

"You didn't make me mad, darling." She took his hand and pressed her lips to it.

"I did. I shouldn't have talked that way about seeing Gran." He shifted his gaze to my face. "It was all a stupid joke like dad said. I never saw Granny Cummins anywhere." His eyes were bright and deliberate, holding mine.

I took a step back from the bed and the black flower which had been poised and waiting, closed its hungry petals around me. Sammy, *my* Sammy, had seen the duplicate of Granny Cummins in the old Guthrie place—and no amount of punishment or bribery would have got him to back down on that point. Unlike me, my son had never compromised in his whole life.

Of its own accord, my right hand slid under my jacket and settled on the butt of the target pistol. My boy was dead and this—right here and now—was the time to begin avenging him.

But I looked down on May's bowed, gently shaking shoulders; and all at once I understood why "Dr. Pitman" had told me the whole story. Had the macabre scenes in the Guthrie place remained a mystery to me, had I not understood their purpose, I could never have remained silent. Eventually I would have had to go to the police, start investigation, cause trouble . . .

Now I knew that the very first casualty of any such

action would be May—she would be destroyed, on learning the truth, as surely as if I had put a bullet through her head. My hand moved away from the butt of the pistol.

Sammy's life, I thought, *is her life*.

In a way it isn't a bad thing to be the compromising type—it makes life easier not only for yourself but for those around you. May smiles a lot now and she is very happy over the way Sammy has grown up to be a handsome, quick-minded fourteen-year-old. The discovery of a number of "human" remains in the ashes of the Guthrie house was a nine-day wonder in our little town, but I doubt if May remembers it now. As I said, she smiles a lot.

I still think about my son, of course, and occasionally it occurs to me that if May were to die, say in an accident, all restraints would be removed from me. But the years are slipping by and there's no sign of the human race coming to harm as a result of the quiet invasion. For all I know it never amounted to anything more than a local phenomenon, an experiment which didn't quite work out.

And when I look at Sammy growing up tall and straight—looking so much like his mother—it is easy to convince myself that I could have made a mistake. After all, I'm only human.

SHADOWS

Darkest fantasies by masters of the macabre including STEPHEN KING

EDITED BY CHARLES L GRANT

Imagine a collection of nightmarish tales as dark as a
freshly opened grave.
So terrifying that they scatter dreams like leaves before
a midnight wind.
So macabre that they freeze the blood. So horrific that
Evil itself turns away.
Imagine. Now open and read.

FICTION   0-7472-3002-1   £2.50

More SF/Fantasy from Headline:

Bradley Denton

WRACK
AND ROLL

Murdered megastar Bitch Alice's last request: destroy
the American space programme. Her Wracker
followers did just that and changed the course of
history.

Now her daughter, The Bastard Child, is out for
vengeance. With the Music, the Power and her band,
Blunt Instrument, she will start a concert tour to rock
the world and push it over the brink – to sanity . . . or
apocalyspe . . .

SCIENCE FICTION   0-7472-3009-9   £3.50

SIMON HAWKE

THE IVANHOE GAMBIT

FIRST IN THE EXCITING NEW TIME TRAVEL ADVENTURE SERIES

TIME WARS BOOK ONE

Lucas Priest is a Sergeant Major in the US Army Temporal Corps. But fighting the Time Wars isn't an easy way to make a living – not when you have to sail with Lord Nelson, battle Custer at Little Big Horn and spend a year pillaging with Attila and his infamous Huns.

Now a demented scheme to impersonate the King of England in the twelfth century is threatening to change the course of history. Two army teams have already failed to intercept the madman.

So Lucas and his band of men clock back to try and prevent an irreversible split in time. They are the last hope for the future of the world. . .

0 7472 3059 5   £2.50

Headline books are available at your bookshop or newsagent, or can be ordered from the following address:

Headline Book Publishing PLC
Cash Sales Department
PO Box 11
Falmouth
Cornwall
TR10 9EN
England

UK customers please send cheque or postal order (no currency), allowing 60p for postage and packing for the first book, plus 25p for the second book and 15p for each additional book ordered up to a maximum charge of £1.90 in UK.

BFPO customers please allow 60p for postage and packing for the first book, plus 25p for the second book and 15p per copy for the next seven books, thereafter 9p per book.

Overseas and Eire customers please allow £1.25 for postage and packing for the first book, plus 75p for the second book and 28p for each subsequent book.